P9-DEA-870

Liberty Street

ALSO BY DIANNE WARREN

Juliet in August (published in Canada as *Cool Water*)
A Reckless Moon
Bad Luck Dog
The Wednesday Flower Man

Liberty Street

Dianne Warren

A MARIAN WOOD BOOK
Published by G. P. Putnam's Sons
an imprint of Penguin Random House
New York

A MARIAN WOOD BOOK
Published by G. P. Putnam's Sons
Publishers Since 1838
An imprint of Penguin Random House LLC
375 Hudson Street
New York, New York 10014

Copyright © 2015 by Dianne Warren
Originally published in Canada by HarperCollins in 2015
First U.S. edition published by G. P. Putnam's Sons in 2016
Penguin supports copyright. Copyright fuels creativity, encourages diverse voices,
promotes free speech, and creates a vibrant culture. Thank you for buying an authorized
edition of this book and for complying with copyright laws by not reproducing, scanning,
or distributing any part of it in any form without permission. You are supporting
writers and allowing Penguin to continue to publish books for every reader.

ISBN 978-0-399-15801-8

Printed in the United States of America
1   3   5   7   9   10   8   6   4   2

This is a work of fiction. Names, characters, places, and incidents either are the product of
the author's imagination or are used fictitiously, and any resemblance to actual persons,
living or dead, businesses, companies, events, or locales is entirely coincidental.

For Cody, Travis, and Bruce

1. My Cold, Cold Heart

WE WERE FIRMLY LODGED in a traffic jam in a small Irish town. Gridlock. No way for our rental car to move forward or back. Several tour buses—which we encountered wherever we went, even though it was May and not yet high season—made matters worse. It was hard to imagine how the roads could handle any more of them. A policeman was maneuvering on foot through the mess, trying to direct cars to an opening here and there, but it was impossible. Any opening inevitably led to another jam. A bicycle would have been hard-pressed to get through. People began to step out of their vehicles and walk away—surrendering, it seemed, to a hopeless situation.

I could see that we were stopped in front of a churchyard, and that many of the people leaving their cars were heading for the church. It began to make some sort of sense. A hearse was parked in front of the church, the coffin still inside. Attendants in dark suits were staring at the traffic snarl-up.

"It's a funeral," I said. "That's what has caused this."

Ian rolled down his driver's-side window and motioned to the policeman, who was now standing close to our car, no longer attempting to untangle the mess. He was staring, like us, at the churchyard.

"What's going on?" Ian asked him.

"It's the funeral," the policeman said.

"What I mean is, how long do you think we'll have to sit here?"

"A young girl and her tiny baby," the policeman said, ignoring his question. "Just nineteen years, and the baby a few months. They're in the coffin together. Terrible tragedy. The whole county's come."

"That's so sad," I said, still looking at the hearse, imagining the mother and baby.

"It is, yes." The policeman looked at his watch. "If you walk a quarter mile back the way you came, you'll find a pub or two or three. Have a Guinness and wait it out."

Then he left us and headed toward the church, and was soon lost among the others arriving from all directions.

"A girl and her baby," I said. "I wonder what happened, but at the same time, I don't want to know."

"Can you believe it?" Ian said. "The only policeman in sight just gave up and went to the funeral."

"Yes, and I like him for it. Never mind if we're late. It can't be helped."

I couldn't take my eyes off the scene unfolding in the churchyard. *Just nineteen*, I thought, *and a baby too*. The pallbearers were lifting the coffin from the hearse. There were so many flowers on top they spilled onto the ground and left a trail as the coffin was carried toward the church steps. I thought, *I lost a baby when I was nineteen*. I was surprised by how easily the memory had slipped into my consciousness. It was something I had not thought about for years.

"I lost a baby when I was nineteen," I said. "And by lost, I don't mean misplaced. The baby died."

I watched as the men carried the coffin up the steps and into the church, carefully, so as not to disturb its precious cargo, and the mourners began to follow, and I realized what I had done—spoken the words aloud.

"It was a long time ago. Until now, I've never told a soul who wasn't there. Even my mother and I barely spoke of it."

"Let me understand," Ian said. "You had a child? A baby?"

"Yes, and it died," I said. "Before that, I was married. But not to the father of the baby. That's a different story. I was married before the baby's father, to someone else."

He said nothing in response to this, stunned into silence, as anyone would be who'd lived with a person for over twenty years and had not been told such a thing.

An old man with a carved walking stick passed by, laying his free hand briefly on the hood of our car. He reminded me of a man we'd met in a pub in Dublin who had told us he'd once been an actor. He'd used the term "player," and said that he'd been onstage many times at the famous Abbey Theatre, a claim Ian hadn't believed. The man with the walking stick turned into the churchyard and fell into line with the people there while we sat without speaking, marooned in the car, the jumbled disorder of vehicles all around us, until a dog began to bark in a yard nearby. When another answered, and then another, and the barking grew into a frenzy, Ian opened his door and said, "I can't stand this. We might as well find a pub. I don't see what else we can do."

We started back toward the town center about the time three buses emptied out, the tour directors having come to the same conclusion we had—that there was no point in waiting. Over a hundred people were now walking along with us, many of them elderly. Good sports, I thought, with their arthritic knees and hearing aids. We were soon ahead of most of them, which turned out to be an advantage, since there were only three or four tiny pubs in the town.

We chose one and found ourselves a table in a corner. It was an old pub with mud walls and wooden beams and a fireplace burning peat. There were several signed photos of famous pop stars above the bar, and one of them was Sinéad O'Connor. The photo was hanging crookedly, as though no one had paid attention to it for years. The fact that it was hanging there at all meant something, I thought, since Sinéad's famous tirade against the pope had been on television the night Ian and I first met.

I pointed at the photograph and said, "Remember when Sinéad ripped up the photo of the pope? It's a wonder they've kept her picture here. She's always offending Catholics. She was in the news again recently."

Ian didn't reply.

Which could have meant a number of things.

Several noisy Englishmen were sitting at a table near us, they too having been stranded by the funeral. Two of them looked to be about my age, nearer sixty than fifty, and the others were younger. They all wore hiking boots, and I imagined that they were on a hill-walking expedition of some sort. A hill walk had been on my holiday wish list, but we'd soon figured out how easy it would be to get lost, especially here in the west, where the cliffs dropped to the sea and you never knew when the fog would descend. A few days earlier, we had tried to walk to a hillside that looked to be within easy reach, but in no time we'd found ourselves ankle-deep in a peat bog and had given up.

A waiter came to the table and asked us what we'd like.

I ordered a Guinness, said to cure everything from gout to migraine headaches—at least by people my age. Ian ordered something else. I wasn't paying attention.

"So tell me," he said once the drinks had been placed on the table in front of us. The label on his read Oyster, which I thought was an odd name for a beer. "Were you still married when you met me?"

Well. There it was, *the* question, and it was my own fault that it was now being put to me.

I could have said no. It would have been easier, and maybe we would have been better off if I had. But it would not have been the truth, and although there was a part of my life I had never told Ian about, I was not in the habit of lying to him.

"I'm still married now," I said. "Unless my husband has died, in which case I guess I'd be a widow. That's highly probable. He was twenty-three years older than me."

And then there I was, with my head between my knees because the room had begun to spin. It was the word "husband" that did it—the fact I had spoken the word out loud. It was perhaps the first time I had ever referred to Joe Fletcher as my husband. When the room stilled, I lifted myself to upright, and I saw that Ian was looking at me with little sympathy for my vertiginous state.

He said, "You're still married to the first one, or to the baby's father?"

I picked up my glass of Guinness, drank from it, swallowed, and set it down on the table again.

Then I said, to finish what I'd started, "The baby's father was just a boy and we were never married. The husband was a man old enough to be my father. The baby was born too early and died, which I've already told you. There, now you know everything. These are things I swore I would never tell anyone. I became a different person afterward. But I've told you now, haven't I? And I hope I'm not that other person again. I don't want to be."

The waiter returned then and asked if we wanted anything to eat. I ordered a plate of chips, even though I wasn't hungry. When he brought them to me a few minutes later, I pointed once again at the off-kilter photograph above the bar and said to him, "I think Sinéad went into a tailspin after that business with the pope."

"Ah, Sinéad," the waiter said. "Tempest in a teapot. Vinegar? Red sauce?"

I shook my head. "Neither. Just salt."

We sat in the pub for another hour, not talking, picking at the chips, and waiting for enough time to pass that we could return to the car. I was beginning to feel ill, wondering what tempest I myself had unleashed, and whether it would fit into a teapot. I'd spoken of things that I could not explain because I had no explanation. They'd happened. I regretted that they had. I knew no more than that. My life had started over afterward, and then it had started over again when I met Ian. I began to fear that Joe Fletcher and all that followed might once again be the cause of sorrow.

When we finally got back to the car, we found that the traffic had cleared out. The churchyard was deserted and there were no signs of the funeral save for the flowers that had fallen when the coffin was removed from the hearse. It was now possible to maneuver around the few remaining cars and tour buses, and we left, several hours behind schedule, concerned about the promise we'd made to a bed-and-breakfast owner named Mr. Burke, who'd asked us if we could manage an early arrival because his day was going to be complicated.

"Maybe we should have phoned from the pub," I said.

"He's got no reason to give our room away," Ian said. "It's paid for."

"Still, just to be courteous."

"We have a long drive ahead of us. Plenty of time for you to tell me quite a lot more than what you've told me so far."

The highway, when we found it, was narrow and winding. Ian drove as though he were trying to make up time. I asked him to slow down, and when he did, I said, "You're the one who gets annoyed when people expound on things they don't know much about. Politics. The stock market. Genetically modified food. This is a bit the same. I can't explain what happened a lifetime ago. I was barely out of high school."

"What I'd really like to know," he said, "is why you told me at all after twenty years."

"I don't know," I said, "but I did."

When we arrived at Mr. Burke's West Country Inn, our host seemed to have forgotten all about his request that we come early. We still had a room for the night. All was well, at least in that regard.

By chance, the English climbers we'd seen in the pub—seven of them—were also staying that night at Mr. Burke's. When the climbers acknowledged us in the parking lot, after Ian and I had returned from a painfully quiet dinner in a village up the road, it seemed right to speak, and we shared stories about the traffic bottleneck. Before we all retired to our rooms, the climbers asked us if we'd like to accompany them on a hill walk the next day—a relatively easy walk, safe for beginners. I said yes and Ian said no at the same time. The man who appeared to be the group leader said, "Just meet us in the breakfast room at six o'clock if you decide to come. Bring a daypack. We'll bring lunch. Wear layers and walking shoes. That's it. Nothing else."

Once we were alone in our room, Ian said, "I'm not going. You do what you like."

I set the alarm and opened a bottle of wine and poured myself a glass, which I drank sitting by the window and listening to the ocean below while Ian had a shower. Then we went to bed.

We were lying in the darkness when he said to me, "Stop it. Whatever you're doing, stop it."

It took me a minute to realize he was referring to my fingers, which were tapping madly on the cotton duvet, an old habit. I rolled onto my side and shoved both hands under my pillow, the way I used to when I was a child.

When I fell asleep, I dreamed I *was* a child, wearing a dental retainer. I was with my mother in the grocery store in my old hometown, and when her back was turned, I removed the retainer and hid it under a head of lettuce in the produce section, thinking that if it were lost, I would never have to wear it again. But the store clerk, who had been watching me, retrieved it and held it out to me as though she were holding a dead cat, and I woke up with a start.

It was not a dream. It was a memory, because it had really happened, and this was unsettling—to be dreaming about memories. I remembered my embarrassment that the clerk had seen me put the retainer under the lettuce, and my mother saying, "It serves you right, Frances. That was disgusting."

When I went back to sleep I dreamed that Mr. Burke's inn was falling over the cliff into the sea below, and on the way down I was shouting over the sound of the waves, "Are we good now? Ian? We're good?"

The alarm buzzed.

I quickly turned it off and slipped out of bed and got myself ready for the hill walk. Before I left the room, I sat down on the edge of the bed beside Ian and wondered if I should wake him and ask if he'd changed his mind. I didn't suppose he had, but I bent and kissed his bare arm anyway. He twitched as though he were flicking away a bug, and he opened his eyes. I could see their color, green, in the morning light.

"I'm going now," I said. "On the hill walk. I don't think they said what time we'd be back. Are you sure you don't want to come?"

When he didn't answer I assumed he meant no and I stood to leave, but he reached out and grabbed my hand.

"I'm going back to Dublin today," he said.

"Dublin? Why?" I didn't understand. I thought he was telling me that he was going for the day. We were scheduled to fly home from Dublin in four days' time. Driving there for the day made no sense.

"I'm going to see if I can get an early ticket home. You can come if you want. If not, I'll take the car and you can catch the train."

I pulled my hand away.

"You're going home?" I said. "That's crazy."

"Are you coming with me or not?" he asked.

I tried to think. He wasn't serious; he was just lashing out with a childish threat, although that was not like him.

"No," I said. "Of course I'm not."

He rolled away from me and dragged a pillow over his head.

I took a last look at him lying there, completely covered by the duvet and the pillow, and then I left and went hill walking, quite certain he would still be at the inn when I returned.

A HIRED DRIVER with a van took us to the trailhead, and the climber in charge—Philip, a man about my own age—recorded the route of our walk in a notebook and then tore the page out and handed it to the driver. "In case we don't show up when you come to collect us," he said, and I wondered how often that happened. I noted the ropes and carabiners that were being secured to belts and backpacks—equipment I hadn't thought would be needed for hill walking. When Philip saw me looking, he said that the equipment was precautionary, and that he was an experienced climbing instructor and had taken countless beginners on treks a lot more challenging than this one. We were standing beside the van in a gravel lot and I looked down at his feet. His boots were solid, and at the same time they were worn. He had no doubt owned them for years.

"Your boots look like veterans," I said. "That's reassuring."

He laughed. "Don't worry, you'll have a good day."

I did. The hill walk was exhilarating, and one of those things that just happens unexpectedly and was, therefore, a gift. Although most of the men were younger than me—a few of them young enough to be my sons—I didn't give the age difference more than a thought. Nor did I think about the fact that I was the only woman in the group. There were times when we climbed single file and there wasn't much talking, all of us keeping our eyes on the footing. At other times, when we crossed a more level, open area, there was friendly chatter, and I discovered that what the Englishmen had in common, besides a love of hill walking, was Christianity. Normally, faith was a concept not remotely interesting to me—I required proof to believe in something—but these men charmed me with their easy ways, and I wondered whether I'd be joining a cult by the end of the day.

We stopped for a quick lunch—quick, Philip told me, so we would retain our body heat, even though it was a warm day and I didn't feel as though I was losing any. As we ate our bologna sandwiches and orange slices, I noticed that two of the men appeared to be together, a couple, and then I began to wonder whether, in addition to being Christians, all the men were gay, and I believed they might be. I had never been with a group of exclusively gay men before. I found myself wondering what religion they belonged to that was so accepting of their sexuality, and why they had accepted me so willingly into their fold, if only for a day.

Not long after lunch, we reached the height of the hill walk—a peak with a spectacular view of the sea far below—and prepared for the trip back. I had assumed we would return the way we'd come, but no, we were to begin the descent by traversing the backside of the sea cliff, a steep face of loose black shale. I felt close to panic when I looked down and saw what was expected of me, disbelieving that we could possibly descend this way. But when Philip told me it was my turn to go, I went, running back and forth, following the directions he shouted at me, not stopping once I was moving, because to stop would be to slip and send myself and a cascade of loose rocks straight down to the bottom. I did what I was told, my heart pounding, two of the younger men already at the bottom and cheering me on, and I saw myself the way they saw me—a middle-aged woman doing something she'd never imagined herself doing—and I didn't care, and my worry was forgotten. For a moment, I was fearless, the way my mother and I had once been, or thought we were, until we found out—first one and then the other—that we were not.

The rest of the day was spent walking, often single file, on a narrow, winding trail. Fog settled and there wasn't much to see other than the few sheep that appeared out of the mist from time to time with splashes of red or blue on their coats to identify their owners. Somewhere along the trail I joined up with Philip and we chatted, exchanging pleasantries about where we lived and what we did. He said he was a secondary school teacher, which didn't surprise me. I told him I was a microbiologist in the water department of a mid-sized city in western Canada. He thought that was impressive, but I assured him it really wasn't, since my job was now mostly administrative and I barely understood modern water treatment systems. I said I'd come to realize I was slouching my way to retirement. I told him also that my parents had emigrated from England, and he asked me if I'd ever been there, and I said no, there were no family ties. I wasn't even sure where in England they'd come from. The north, I thought, although they'd worked in London during the war. Philip thought it was unusual that I expressed no interest in knowing more. I agreed. "But they're both gone now," I said. "I wouldn't know where to begin."

My hamstrings turned to jelly from hours of walking

downhill, and I was never so glad as when I saw the van waiting for us at the pickup point. The men congratulated me on
my stamina—they actually applauded as I climbed into the
van—and they confessed that there *had* been an easier way
down, which they would have taken had they not believed I
could handle the shale slope. I was flattered and, now that I
was safely in the van, elated. I was ceremoniously given the
slip of paper with our route on it as a souvenir, and I folded
it and put it in my pocket. I almost fell asleep on the winding
drive to Mr. Burke's inn. I didn't wonder whether Ian would
be there when we got back. In fact, I'd completely forgotten
about Dublin and an early flight home.

When we arrived, the driver dropped us in the parking lot
and two of the younger men transferred their gear from the
van to the trunks of their cars. I found myself walking with
Philip across the lot to the inn, and it wasn't until then that
I noticed our rental car—mine and Ian's—was not where it
should have been. I stopped walking. Philip stopped beside
me. I stood staring, as though a crack had opened in the parking lot and swallowed our car.

"What is it?" Philip asked.

"I've made a mistake," I said.

"Sorry?"

I felt myself somewhere between tears and anger, but I
managed to hold both at bay.

"I think Ian is gone," I said. "It's my fault. I haven't been
honest with him. I'm not a good partner. In fact, I'm not even
a very good person."

Philip looked at me as though he was thinking, and then
he said, "I don't know you well enough. I'm sorry."

Of course he was right. What had I expected him to

say? Did I think he would be comforting because he was a Christian, or a man who liked a good confidence because he was gay? We walked on then, as if I had not spoken, and I tried to cover my embarrassment by babbling about how tired I was, and who would have thought walking downhill would be as tiring as walking up? We parted in the foyer of the inn and I returned to our room, where I found that Ian had indeed left.

I could have thought, Why would he do that? But instead I sat by the open window wrapped in a blanket, shivering, thinking about how I deserved to be left behind. I was the same person I'd always been, the silly girl who ignored every bit of advice and every warning she'd been given by people who cared about her. I'd revealed my true history to Ian when it was too late for him to make his own choice about things as important as marriage and children. He'd been duped by a charlatan in a black dress on the night we'd met, when he was still a handsome twenty-six-year-old, recently jilted and far too good for my cold heart—or at least that's the way I saw it at that moment.

I went to bed without eating, my body tired and aching. I didn't know whether it was self-pity that kept me awake or euphoria from the hill-walking adventure. The two vied for my attention, and I managed to snatch only a few minutes of sleep here and there.

MY ENCOUNTER with the Englishmen was not quite over. At breakfast the next morning they greeted me as though I were an old friend and told me they were all going to church, an Irish Sunday mass. I hadn't been to church since the last wedding I'd attended, but I agreed to go—not because I wanted to go to mass, but because I wanted to be with them. I noticed Philip looking at the spot in the parking lot where our car should have been, but he didn't mention Ian. We walked to the church in a group and sat in a long pew and the locals stared at us, especially the children. Some of the climbers knelt and genuflected during the mass, and they all prayed and sang joyously. One of the younger men had a beautiful voice, and I wondered if he might even be a professional singer.

We exchanged fellowship greetings at the end of the service with the large family in the pew in front of us. Afterward, we went back to the bed-and-breakfast and collected our bags, but still we didn't go our separate ways, because when I told them I would be taking the train to Dublin to arrange an early flight home, they said they were going there too. They'd traveled in two rental cars, and they made room for me in one. They even drove me to the airport. No one asked about Ian or why I was traveling alone now, so I assumed Philip had told them what I'd said to him. My eyes filled with tears as we said our goodbyes. They hugged me one by one, and I didn't hold back but fell into them, each one, like a person desperate for comfort. Philip told me I was special and I didn't know what to say, but I felt, briefly, that it might be true.

Afterward, when they were gone and I was inside the Dublin airport, I remembered that the business of believing anyone could be special was what had made me, like my mother before me, suspicious of Christians, or at least the ones who insisted on telling you they were Christians. As though anything at all—goodness, intelligence, least of all faith—made you special. I was glad to have that straight again, even though I appreciated the kindness of the men and believed it had been genuine.

Because the flight to Toronto was full, I had to wait to find out if there would be a seat for me, but eventually I heard my name on the intercom—*Frances Moon, please report to the Air Canada counter*—and I was told that, yes, I could change my ticket, and I was given a boarding pass. I wondered if Ian would be on the same flight, but I didn't see him anywhere and assumed he had flown home the previous day.

As I got in the boarding lineup, I noticed an enormously obese man in front of me. I followed him onto the plane, and he made his way through business class and past the plus-size seats, which were all taken, to an ordinary aisle seat in row 23, where he sat after lifting the armrest between it and the next seat.

Row 23. I glanced at my own boarding pass, and sure enough, row 23, right next to the man. I slipped out of the line of passengers, ducking my head beneath the overhead bins, and tried to decide what to do. I could see that there was only half a seat remaining next to him. I wasn't a big person, but I would be in for an uncomfortable flight home if that was the only spot available to me. Could I ask a flight attendant to find me another? Could I do so without making a scene or humiliating the man? It seemed like some kind of ethical dilemma.

I felt a hand on my shoulder.

"Ms. Moon?" a voice said. I turned around to see a flight attendant, who asked for my boarding pass. Then she quietly told me they were upgrading me to business class because there were no other free seats in economy. She was speaking almost in a whisper. No mention was made of the reason for the move. I followed her back through the line of people and their carry-on luggage, dodging the traffic by popping in and out of the rows until we arrived at the front of the plane, where I was directed to my own little pod. I wondered briefly whether I should have offered the upgrade to the obese man, who was bound to be uncomfortable even in two economy seats, but instead I accepted my own good fortune and settled in to take full advantage of it. I ordered a Scotch.

"Or make that a double," I said. "Save you a trip."

I could see the flight attendant wondering if she'd made a mistake in rescuing me, but she brought me my drinks.

Once we were in the air, my thoughts settled and I began to consider the rental property I owned in the small town of Elliot, Saskatchewan, left to me by my mother. It made sense for me to think of the house now, since it was the full repository of what remained of my family's history. In other words, my former life was in its basement.

The house had been built by my uncle Vince, although he never lived in it. When he died, it went to my parents. My mother claimed it as her backup plan, and she had in fact lived in it for a time after she sold our dairy farm. She probably should have moved instead to a place that appealed to her, although at that point in her life, I don't know where that place would have been. After she died in the care home in Yellowhead, I moved her possessions to the basement of the house and stored them there, alongside the furniture and old clothing and boxes of knickknacks and dishes from the farm—all the remnants of my childhood. I found long-term renters for the house, a responsible retired couple who didn't mind doing caretaking duty for the remains of the Moon household, and they lived there for fifteen years, never missing a rent payment. They did all the necessary home repairs, except for a new roof, which I happily paid for. I'd not had to worry about a thing until one of them—I couldn't remember which—developed a need for dialysis twice a week and they moved to Yellowhead. I would have sold the house then, but a real estate agent named Mavis had appeared on the scene with a young couple looking for a place to rent. Mavis had offered to manage the rental herself, and once again the arrangements became easy and had remained so for several years.

Now, under the weight of my confession to Ian, I saw the house and its possessions as an unresolved burden. They would have to go. There were no renters at the moment, although a pair of first-year teachers had arranged to move in later in the summer. Maybe Mavis could convince them to buy the house instead. I could direct her to take whatever she could get for it—practically give it away, just to be rid of it. I could tell her to hire someone to haul everything in the basement to the dump—every box, every bag of clothing—something I should have done years ago.

Immediately, I saw a problem. I knew Elliot well enough to know that anyone Mavis hired would be appalled at the idea of throwing good things in the dump, and I'd have some Tom, Dick, or Harry in the basement with his girlfriend or his mother or perhaps his whole family, salvaging my family's things. And could I even trust Mavis, whom I had never actually met, to do as I asked? Maybe she herself would be rifling through my possessions. She'd already asked me if she could bring some of the furniture upstairs, since the young teachers had requested a furnished house—"We could do a vintage look," she'd said; "there's that cute fifties dinette"—and I had agreed.

Our flight attendant was on her way up the aisle again, this time with boxed meals. Instead of a meal, I asked for another double Scotch, because I was now considering a return to Elliot to take care of the family archive myself. A man across the aisle was clearly assessing whether I was on my way to causing trouble. The attendant rummaged through her trolley and handed me two little bottles with a look that said they were the last. I tried to seem good-natured. I wondered whether the easiest solution to the house and its contents was to ask Mavis to start a fire in the kitchen and burn it down.

After the meals were cleared away, I attempted to sleep under a blanket. I dozed fitfully, and then, what seemed like minutes later, the attendants were serving coffee and handing us Canadian newspapers as though they had just arrived, hot off the press. I tucked a paper in my carry-on bag for later and tried to dilute the Scotch in my system. When the plane was almost ready to land in Toronto, I fell asleep in earnest, and then woke up again to an attendant trying to check my seat belt, and for a brief moment I thought she was my mother.

Once we'd landed, I collected my carry-on and stumbled from the plane. I swayed on my feet while I went through customs, fell asleep while I was waiting for my connecting flight west, almost missing it, and finally ended up on a small and noisy turboprop, with an excruciating headache and a fear of what was waiting for me. The husband and baby finding their way to the surface of my consciousness meant something. Ian leaving me in Ireland meant something. The house in Elliot was plaguing me for a reason. They were all part of the same quagmire, and I had no idea how to keep myself from sinking.

The plane hummed like it might fall apart. I pulled the newspaper from my bag and read through the headlines. One on the second page caught my eye: *Saskatchewan Homeless Man Dies After Waiting Full Day in Hospital ER for Treatment.* I read the article. The incident had happened in my local hospital, in my home city. The man died of a catastrophic head injury that could have been treated had he not been ignored—*allegedly* ignored, as they are always careful to say—because he was known by the staff and was unpredictable, according to an unnamed hospital source. I wanted to weep because someone had died for being unpredictable. I folded the newspaper and stuck it in the seatback pocket in front of me. By the time we began our descent it was midnight and I watched the city lights rise toward me from the surrounding blackness.

We landed. I retrieved my bag and caught a cab.

THE CENTERPIECE of our living room was a poppy-red couch with lime-green piping. Ian and I had chosen it together. In months of searching, it was the only one we'd looked at that we both loved. We'd sat on it side by side in the store, nodding our heads in agreement that this was the one. Now we sat at opposite ends, eating the fried-egg sandwiches I'd made and watching the evening news, my suitcase still by the door where I'd left it the night before. Ian had worked that day, Monday, even though he wasn't scheduled to return until later in the week.

The story of the homeless man was on every network. The family was threatening to sue. A hospital spokesperson was trying his best to prevent this by being apologetic without admitting liability, or really anything at all. He described the incident as unfortunate. The camera cut to a memorial that was growing in the hospital parking lot: flowers, cards, messages, prayer flags, stuffed animals. The homeless man's sister spoke on behalf of the family. A reporter asked her if she was angry. She didn't answer his question.

"He didn't deserve to die," she said.

After we'd eaten, Ian did the dishes, as usual. We both read for a while, or pretended to, and then went to bed. We slept in the same bed, an invisible line drawn up the middle, my confession in the room with us like a smothering fog. In the morning, Ian got ready for work again. As he went out the door, he told me he was flying to Vancouver the next day for meetings. He'd be home the day after.

All morning I sat on the couch and thought about Elliot, the place I'd grown up, a place that had not been my home for a long time. Then I thought about how little I really knew of the city I did call home, and where I'd lived most of my adult life. I knew the neighborhood I lived in with Ian, which was not the kind of neighborhood where people held block parties and community picnics. I had known the neighborhood where I'd lived as a student, but I did not know it now. I knew the pathway I walked between home and work each day—unless it was too cold, in which case I took the bus, my small contribution to environmental responsibility. I knew the malls where I shopped and banked and went to a movie once in a while. But there were many areas of the city that I didn't know at all, neighborhoods I had never visited, streets I had never been down.

I chose a part of the city that was unfamiliar to me, and I drove there and parked and walked along the street. It was as if I were in a different city. It was mid-afternoon and the street was busy with a stream of women with baby strollers and preschool children, many of them aboriginal, many of them new immigrants from African countries or the Philippines. I saw one woman wearing a niqab. Besides the mothers and children, there were a number of teenage boys wearing baggy jeans and walking, I thought, with that rolling gait of gang kids, although they didn't look especially dangerous and none of them paid any attention to me. In fact, I felt invisible.

I saw an old-style Safeway sign up ahead, and as I got closer I heard hip-hop music coming from an outdoor sound system, and I saw that there was a massive garage sale going on in the parking lot. I recalled a time when my mother and I had come to the city, and we'd been robbed and carjacked and forced to drive to a Safeway store. I wondered whether this was the store, but I had no idea. Even at the time we hadn't known where we were and had been unable to tell the police anything of use. A few years later, when I was refusing to go to university for the good education my mother so badly wanted for me, she asked me if I was afraid to go. I knew what she was getting at. I lied and said no. I didn't want to admit to being afraid of anything. "You were the one who was a complete coward," I'd said. "Like a mouse in the corner." It was mean and I knew it. As though my own mother was the cause of the damage done, instead of a blond-haired woman in cowboy boots and her silent partner.

As I joined the festivities in the Safeway parking lot, I saw a vendor selling hot dogs from a cart for a dollar, so I stopped and bought one. I stood eating my hot dog, listening to the music, and watching people wander from stall to stall looking through the used clothing and furniture. Then I went into the store and felt immediately as though I didn't belong

among the strangers loading their carts with diapers and groceries and kitty litter, so I left. On my way out, I heard one
woman call to another, "Sister, it's good to see you. I heard
you've been sick." I wondered how you could not know that
about your sister, and then I realized they weren't really sisters, and I was envious of a neighborhood where you could
run into someone who might call you sister.

I got back in my car, but my one foray into an unknown
part of the city didn't seem to be enough. I drove south on
the expressway until I came to the new Walmart, then I
parked in the lot and walked around in a brand-new subdivision, one with monster houses with double or even triple
garages and bare dirt waiting for landscaping. Sometimes I
had to walk on the newly paved road because there was
not yet a sidewalk. House after house I saw, with people
obviously living in them but no signs of life on the streets. I
came across one child, a boy who was simply inert in front
of a house, sitting on his bicycle in a Spider-Man suit, going
nowhere. I had no idea how to speak to children, but I gave
it a try anyway.

"Hello there," I said, but he looked away from me and
at his house, as though checking to see if his mother—or a
nanny, perhaps—was watching. An orange cat wandered
down the dirt driveway toward the boy.

"Is this your cat?" I asked. "He looks like his name should
be Marmalade."

No answer. His parents had wisely taught him not to
speak to people he didn't know.

The cat meowed at me and brushed up against my legs.
The front door of the house opened and a woman poked her
head out.

"So long, then, Spider-Man," I said, and walked on. The boy followed me for a ways on his bicycle, and I heard the woman calling for him to come back.

I made my way to the Walmart, where I'd left my car, and I went inside and bought a houseplant, which I placed in the kitchen window when I got home. I listened to the phone messages and learned that Ian was not coming home for dinner. I didn't bother cooking anything. I didn't feel hungry.

At dusk, I got in my car once more and drove up the block where I'd lived with a Greek family when I first came to university, and then several blocks over to the street where I had lived with a boy named Rudy. The house was gone, torn down and replaced. The owners had tried to make the new one fit into the neighborhood, but it stood out with its faux brick facing and its ostentatious columns on either side of the front door. The house across the street, where an evolving stream of art students had lived, was still there, but it was run-down, and I supposed that in no time the whole block would be developed with infill houses. Student housing in these neighborhoods was no longer needed. The university now had many residence buildings on campus.

As the city settled into darkness, I found myself on a street near the hospital where the homeless man had died. I pulled into the parking lot by the emergency entrance and there it was, the makeshift memorial, up against a fence. A bored-looking security guard stood nearby with his hands in his pockets. A few candles in glass containers had been placed in front of a framed picture of the dead man. Perhaps the security guard was there to prevent a fire. There seemed to be no other reason for his presence, since there were no mourners or spectators that I could see.

As I stopped my car to look, he came to my window and motioned for me to lower it.

"Have a look and move along," he said. "This is still the emergency entrance."

"It's touching," I said to him. "The memorial."

"They're tearing it down tomorrow. Have a look and move along."

And so I did. I drove slowly by the fence and saw the dead man's face flickering in the candlelight. He had a pleasant face, at least in that photo.

I left the parking lot and joined a line of traffic that took me through downtown and to an area known as the warehouse district, where the clubs were. I had never been in one, and I had no desire to go in now because I could hear the pounding techno dance music even as I passed by in the car.

I came upon a junkyard, well lit to prevent theft, although I wasn't sure who would want to break into a junkyard. I could see the outline of rusty piles of scrap metal through the chain-link fence. Another pile of nothing but bathtubs. Two German shepherd dogs on patrol sniffed the periphery of the fence, bored by the lack of action. What was the real business of a junkyard with dogs? I wondered. A front for drugs, one of my colleagues at work would always say whenever a questionable license application came to the attention of city hall. I did a U-turn so I was on the same side of the street as the dogs, and I pulled up to the curb and rolled down my window. The dogs stopped and looked at me, alert now, and went back to sniffing their way along the fence line only when I put the car in gear and moved off down the street.

As I turned back toward the city center, I checked the

time. It was almost midnight. I'd had nothing to eat since the hot dog in the Safeway parking lot, and I was now hungry. I wondered if Ian would be home yet. I could see the lights of city hall up ahead, and I drove there and parked the car in front of the building, and I imagined a cocktail party taking place beyond the floor-to-ceiling windows of the main floor, the genteel tinkle of champagne flutes, myself in a black dress, snow blowing into impossible drifts in the courtyard.

My office was on the tenth floor. I looked up and saw the lights on in the office below mine, as though someone was working late, which would not be unusual. *I* often worked late, one spreadsheet or another on the computer screen in front of me. I could leave the car right now if I chose, use my access fob to open the front door and enter the elevator, step onto the tenth floor, and turn the light on in my office and go to work. On the other hand, I could just quit. It seemed like such a good idea, I wondered why I hadn't thought of it before. I started the car and drove to a Tim Hortons and picked up a sandwich and a coffee, and then I went home.

The bedroom door was closed and I assumed Ian was behind it, asleep, so I lay down on the couch rather than disturb him. Half an hour later, I heard a key in the front door and he came in, drunk and stumbling, disheveled in a way that I had never before seen him.

"Go to hell, Frances," he said when he saw me on the couch, and then he went to the bedroom. But half an hour later, he came back and sat down on the couch by my feet and stared out into the dark room. He said, in a drunken voice, "Do you remember that I once asked you to marry me?

No, that's not right. I didn't quite ask, because I was hedging my bets. I *suggested* we get married, and you did just what I thought you would—you blew it off like dust, as though it wasn't worth discussing."

Before I could speak, he got up, stumbled back to the bedroom, and closed the door.

I knew the time he was talking about. People he worked with had been getting married, having babies. People his age. He was right that I hadn't taken his suggestion seriously. I was over forty. And I was already married, which he now knew, but he hadn't then.

I heard sounds coming from the bedroom and realized that Ian was crying. I had never seen him cry. I was five years old the only other time I'd known a man to cry, when my mother briefly left my father and me, and I heard my father crying in the night. I'd woken up alone in my parents' bed and heard a strange, muffled noise coming from the living room, and when I figured out it was my father crying, I thought my mother must have died. In the morning I'd fished for information by saying, "I wonder what Mom is having for breakfast," and my father had said, "I suppose she's having Cheerios, as usual," and then everything seemed to be okay again, even though my mother was still not home.

I heard another sob coming from Ian in the bedroom, and then it was quiet.

If he hadn't told me to go to hell—if he hadn't left me on the couch the way he had—I might have gone to him, but I did not believe he wanted me to.

I lay down again. All night, pictures of the city kept coming back to me—not familiar places where Ian and I had been together, but mysterious places and dark streets filled with strangers I would never know, or never remember if we did meet in a brief exchange. I felt as if my entire adult life here had been a series of brief exchanges. Even the people I worked with every day would remember me for only a short while if I left. "Remember Frances?" someone might say six months later. "She was difficult, aloof, not much interested in the rest of us." I was surprised the thought had come to me so easily, that I would be remembered for being difficult, and so, I reasoned, it must be true. I could only hope that someone might jump in and say, in my defense, that I was smart, or right, or at least cared about public health and safe drinking water.

In the morning, early, I got up and e-mailed Mavis to let her know I was on my way to Elliot and I wanted to sell the house. Then I wrote a letter of resignation, and sealed it in an envelope along with my access fob. A short time later I heard the shower running, and then Ian came from the bedroom with his carry-on, wearing a crisp and fashionable suit. I asked him if he wanted a ride to the airport and he said no, he would drive himself and leave his car there. I found it hard to believe that he had been such a mess the night before.

He picked up my empty takeout coffee cup from the floor where I'd left it, and threw it in the paper recycle bin. When he was on his way out the door, he turned and said, or rather asked, "You know that you are a person who resists happiness, right?"

"That's not true," I said.

"It is true. You don't trust it."

Then he closed the door and left.

I didn't want to think about what he'd said. I did not

believe it. I retrieved my suitcase from the front hall, and emptied out the dirty clothes and packed clean ones. I took only what I thought I would need for a brief stay at a time of year that could be either hot or cold: jeans, shorts, T-shirts, walking shoes, sandals. A rain jacket. A book and my laptop. Toiletries. I put the dirty clothes in the laundry, collected my suitcase, and left the house. On my way out of town, I stopped at city hall and dropped off the envelope containing my letter of resignation.

I hit only green lights as I drove out of the city. Once the lights were behind me, I called our home voicemail and left a message saying that I was on my way to Elliot to take care of some business regarding the rental house, and I would call again when I'd arrived. As I dropped the phone on the seat beside me, I realized that it should have been included in the package I'd left at city hall, and that it would be disabled when my account was canceled, and then I'd be without one.

As I looked at the city skyline in the rearview mirror, I began to wish that I hadn't left Ian the message I had. There was an assumption built into it—that is, that he would be relieved to know where I had gone. Perhaps it wasn't true. Perhaps I was a stranger to him now. I thought back to the moment when the marriage and the baby had slipped from their hiding places. I was like one of those women who commits a bank robbery and then goes into hiding as someone else, marries a doctor, becomes a soccer mom, and does volunteer work with the Girl Guides or the Humane Society, until it all comes tumbling apart when she is recognized from an old newspaper photograph by a neighbor in the suburbs.

Only I hadn't been recognized by anyone. I had done this to myself.

When a number of semitrailers passed me in the left-hand lane, I realized I was driving too slow. I stepped on the gas and turned my attention to the road ahead, to where I was going, or rather from where I had come.

2. We Two Girls

It's November, a cold day. Five-year-old Frances Mary Moon, wearing new blue mitts and a matching toque her mother knit for her, sits on an old tractor tire filled with sand and surveys the yard around her: the white house that used to be just a log house but now has a modern addition on the back; the red barn with its hayloft on top and Kaw-Liga, the wooden Indian, standing guard by the side door, the one you can use to avoid walking through the cow muck; the bins and sheds and machinery, all lined up neatly along the fence; the caragana hedges and poplars that surround the yard and line the approach from the road. Everything is in its proper place, ready for winter. The sky is gray, as though today is the day winter might come, and even Kaw-Liga looks cold. The cows out in the pasture are all standing in one direction, facing away from the wind. Frances doesn't like cows. She's allergic to milk (which her father says is tragic for a dairy farmer's daughter), plus she doesn't trust them not to kick in that sneaky way they have, out to the side. She doesn't like her mother's chickens either, because of the time the rooster escaped and came at her, talons bared and wings flapping, and her mother materialized out of nowhere and grabbed it and strangled it right there, and then later made soup. Ha. So much for that rooster, but Frances hadn't known which was more fierce: the rooster or her mother. She decides it's a good thing to have a mother who can win a fight with, say, a nasty rooster or an ornery cow.

Frances shifts herself around on the tractor tire so she can better see any cars or trucks that might come up the road, besides the milk truck, which has already been. She examines her new mitts and wishes they were pink, but her mother says blue looks better with red hair. Frances loves pink, and she's decided red is a terrible hair color to have if it doesn't go with pink. Besides having terrible hair, she has no front teeth—none at all—because the orthodontist in Yellowhead pulled them. Frances had thought he was going to give her new ones, but her mother has since explained that she has to wait for them to grow in, and when they do she will have to wear a retainer to make sure they grow straight and not crooked like the old ones. It's been months since they went to Yellowhead and stayed with her mother's friend Doreen (who is called a war bride), and still no new teeth. Doreen isn't there anymore. She and her son, Joey—the one her mother thought was such a nice boy; the one who tried to put his hand in Frances's underpants, but she ran away and her mother didn't believe her when Frances told her later—moved back to England, without Joey's dad. Frances didn't know a mother could do that. She hopes *her* mother is planning to come back from wherever she's gone, which is probably not England but might be almost as far away—a place called Nashville, where people go when they want to be famous singers. She also hopes that she will have new teeth by Christmas. Her father has assured her she will, but her mother says she won't and her teeth will arrive in their own good time. This is not unusual, for the two of them to have different opinions. Her mother always says, "What kind of world would it be if everyone agreed? Pretty boring." Her father says, "Well, maybe just once in a while."

Here are some other things Frances Mary Moon knows about her parents, gathered in equal measure from stories they've told her and from conversations not meant for little pitchers and their ears. Her father is Basie, short for Basil, and her mother's name is Alice. Her mother comes from a family of tossers in England, which is not a good kind of family, and she might be the only mother in Elliot—and who knows, maybe all of Canada now that Doreen is gone—who speaks the way she does, that is, with an accent. She used to work in a cheese-and-curio shop in London, but it was bombed to smithereens one night during the war, which meant she didn't have a job anymore. The nice people who owned the shop gave her a gift of expensive cheese and an antique mahogany tea caddy, so it wasn't all for naught. She met Frances's father—who also has an accent, but people say he's easier to understand—in London. He couldn't be a soldier because of his poor eyesight, but he served the war effort by working in a government office. After they were married, they made a plan to move to Canada so that any children they had would not be in danger of turning out like Alice's family (this fully admitted to by her), and also because Basie had grown up reading Hopalong Cassidy books and secretly longed for a frontier life (not admitted to by him).

In 1955—a year Frances does not remember because she hadn't yet been born—they bought a farm in western Canada with some money they got when Basie's father died, and they crossed the ocean on a boat with their two steamer trunks, two suitcases, and some taped-up cardboard boxes. Once they got to Montreal, Basie bought them each a cowboy hat for the train trip west, assuming that everyone beyond the Ontario border wore a Stetson (this also not admitted to by him, but reported to Doreen anyway). There's a picture taken by a colored train conductor (*What does "colored" mean?*) of the two of them standing on a platform with their belongings, wearing their new hats. Alice told Doreen that she took hers off as soon as the picture was snapped because she was already certain there would be no cowboys or hitching posts on the high street in Elliot. She had done her reading. Even after they were settled on their new farm (dairy, not beef) and Basie had traded his own hat for a cap like the ones the other men wore, he went to an auction sale and purchased a sofa-and-chair set with wagon-wheel arms, two table lamps with western scenes on the shades, and an old cigar store Indian that he thought Alice would welcome into the house, but she did not. The sofa set and lamps stayed, but the wooden Indian ended up outside by the barn door. He got named poor old Kaw-Liga after Hank Williams's famous song on the radio. While Frances waits to see which of her parents will come home first, she studies Kaw-Liga across the yard and wonders if he can feel the cold. She wonders if Hank Williams can feel the cold now that he's dead. He fell asleep in the back of a car and didn't wake up. (*What? Can that happen?*)

Snow begins to fall. Frances looks at her hands and sees that it is clinging to her mitts. She can feel it on her eyelashes. She looks up at the falling flakes—growing bigger and bigger as they drift down toward her—and sticks out her tongue. She wonders how far her mother has got on her way to being a singer, and whether she is singing right now, driving south, as the crow flies. Her mother sings when she thinks no one is listening: along with the radio, when she's in the bathtub with the door locked, when she's cooking, or sterilizing, or doing barn chores. Skeeter Davis is her favorite singer, and in fact, Frances is named after her. Mary Frances Skeeter Davis. Frances Mary Moon. (Her father hadn't liked the Skeeter part.) Frances believes her mother could be a famous singer like Skeeter Davis or maybe Kitty Wells, who both live in Nashville, which is where you go if you want to be on the radio.

"Where's Nashville?" Frances once asked.

"Straight south, as the crow flies."

Which is why Frances is sitting on the tire by herself, wondering whether her mother will get famous and end up on TV, or change her mind about the Grand Ole Opry and come back. She's thinking that she can't feel her fingers in her mittens. She's hoping her mother is driving carefully now, because she'd spun gravel from the whitewalls of her pride-and-joy Ford when she left.

She hears a car coming up the road, but she can't see it yet. Not a car, a truck. Her father's truck turns onto the approach and appears through the bare branches of the trees. He parks down by the barn as he always does and walks back toward Frances.

"I think your sandbox is done for until spring," he says to her. Then he notices that Alice's car isn't in its usual spot by the house and he says, "Where's your mother?"

Frances shrugs. "Nashville, I guess." She gets up and slaps her mitts together to get the snow off.

"You come up with the darnedest things," her father says as she follows him into the house. He takes off his coat and looks around for a note. "Are you sure you don't know where she's gone?" he says. "That's not like her to leave you alone."

"We're not supposed to worry," Frances says.

"Nashville, eh?" he says. "Well, no reason to worry about that." Then he washes up and turns on the television, and waits for Alice to come home and put his tea on the table.

When six o'clock rolls around and her mother still hasn't returned, Frances goes to the fridge and gets out a plate of sliced ham and the butter dish and a jar of mustard, and puts them on the table along with a loaf of bread and two plates out of the cupboard. The old mahogany tea caddy from England is on the table next to the salt and pepper. It used to have a lock, because at one time tea was precious. ("Imagine," her mother said. "So precious people used to lock it up as though it were gold.") Frances thinks about making tea for her father, but she's not allowed to use the gas stove, so she gets a pitcher of Tang from the fridge instead.

"What's this, then?" Frances's father asks when she calls him to the table and tells him she's going to make him a sandwich.

"Our tea," she says.

"Oh, I think your mother will be home soon to fix us something better than ham sandwiches."

Clearly, he hadn't believed Frances about Nashville, but then he hadn't heard her mother that time in the car on the way to Yellowhead, singing about honky-tonk angels and saying to Frances, after the song was over, "I could be on the radio, don't you think?" Then later, in the orthodontist's office, when Frances had asked about the woman with sunglasses and blond hair on a magazine cover, her mother told her it was Marilyn Monroe. "People hound Marilyn for autographs everywhere she goes," she'd said. "Of course, that's partly because she's a sexpot, and don't ask me what that means."

"So would you want to be a movie star?" Frances asked.

"If I had my druthers, I'd rather be a famous singer. But neither milks cows or shovels manure, that's for sure."

"How do you get to be a singing star?"

"You go to Nashville," her mother said. "If you want to be a movie star, you go to Hollywood, but singers go to Nashville."

So that was it. When she left the house with her white overnight case, saying, "No, you can't come with me," and "Oh, don't look at me like that, and tell your father not to worry," Frances knew where she was headed.

She pours two glasses of Tang from the pitcher and then pulls out one of the chrome chairs—carefully, because they're tippy—and says, "I'm too hungry to wait."

"Frances," her father says, getting up from his chair in the living room, "is there something you're not telling me?"

So then she has to tell him again, and she adds the fact that her mother took her overnight case, the one from the Eaton's catalogue.

He looks concerned. He scratches his chin. "You're sure?" he asks. "She took her little suitcase? The white one?"

Frances nods. "But we're not supposed to worry," she says again, although she *is* beginning to worry. She's thinking about the way her mother drove out of the yard without stopping to look. A truck could have T-boned her and that would have been that. How was she supposed to not worry? She gets a bad feeling in her stomach.

Then her father sits at the table and makes himself a sandwich, and Frances takes that as a sign that *he* isn't worried, that everything is all right, but he eats only half of it. He throws the remaining half in the slop bucket, and then he puts the ham and mustard and Tang back in the fridge.

Frances is still sitting at the table. He turns her chair toward him and kneels in front of her and says, "Now, Frances, I want you to remember everything. What exactly did your mother say? Don't tell me anything that she didn't say right out loud. Nothing that might have been just in your head. I want to know only what she said."

"Don't look at me like that," Frances says.

"I'm not," he says.

"That's what she said. Don't look at me like that. And don't worry."

"That's it?"

Frances nods.

"And all she took was the overnight case?"

"Yes, that's all. And her sunglasses. Are they a clue?"

"They're a clue that the sun was shining," her father says, even though it hadn't been. "All right, then. Your mother has gone to Yellowhead for a holiday. The overnight case is just that, for overnight. She'll be back tomorrow."

Then he sends Frances to bed, but he forgets to run the bath for her, so she doesn't have one. In the middle of the night she leaves her own bed and crawls in with him, and he doesn't send her back to her room. She knows he's awake. He's lying on his back and staring at the ceiling. There's enough light in the room that she can see that.

When Frances wakes up in the morning, she can hear her father on the phone. She knows what he's doing. Calling people. When he gets off the phone, he sits and twirls his cap on his index finger the way he does when he's thinking, then he puts on his coat and tells Frances not to get into any trouble while he's in the barn.

Frances says, "I don't think anyone else knows about Nashville."

Her father stops and looks at her and says, "Why do you keep going on about Nashville?"

"She's gone to be a singer," Frances says. "Like Skeeter Davis and Kitty Wells."

"Oh," he says. "Well, that's ridiculous, Frances. Your mother has the singing voice of a frog." Then he puts his cap on his head. "Judas Priest," he says on his way out the door to finish his chores.

The voice of a frog? What?

It warms up that day, and the skiff of snow that fell the day before melts. The new barn kittens are now big enough to take away from the mother cat, so Frances goes to the hay shed and gets her favorite. She takes the kitten to the bare caragana hedge where she has a tree house (which is really a platform on the ground) and names it Marilyn, and she pretends that she and Marilyn have all kinds of fans wanting autographs. That night she sleeps in her parents' bed again, and she wakes up in the darkness and her father isn't there. She hears a sound coming from the living room and realizes it's her father crying. She puts a pillow over her head and wraps herself up in a blanket like a mummy. Later, she hears him come back to bed, and he unwinds her so he can get under the covers.

In the morning, they have scrambled eggs. When Frances asks what her mother is having for breakfast, her father says that she's eating Cheerios somewhere, as usual. Later that afternoon, she comes back. Frances is in the hedge again with Marilyn when she sees her mother's car come through the trees. She's about to run to the car, but then she feels suddenly shy, and she hides in the hedge and watches as her mother stops at the house and gets out. Her father is at the barn and Frances waits for him to come, but he doesn't. Maybe he hasn't heard the car. She decides someone has to welcome her mother home, so she steps from the hedge, and as she does her mother turns toward her, still wearing her sunglasses and what must be a new blue scarf. She holds out her arms—"Franny, Franny, come here," she's saying—and it's as if she's been gone for a month, maybe two, and Frances does run to her. Her mother is carrying the white overnight case and also a shopping bag (which Frances later finds out has new clothes in it), so Frances can't fall into her the way she wants to, and she stops herself and is shy again and doesn't know what to do, so she blurts out, "How was the drive?" the way her father might.

Her mother laughs. "How was the drive? Is that all you have to say? Not, I'm glad you're back and I'm so happy to see you?"

Frances doesn't like being laughed at. She starts to cry. Her mother puts her bags on the ground and says, "Oh, for heaven's sake, stop your wailing. I've only been gone a few days. Come here and give us a proper hug."

Instead, Frances runs back to the caragana hedge, where she discovers that Marilyn has gone missing. She crawls around on her hands and knees in the muddy hedge until she finds her, and then she takes her back to the hay shed. The mother gives Marilyn a couple of licks on the head, but then she wanders off, which Frances thinks is mean, but she knows cats do that when the kittens get big.

When Frances finally goes to the house, her jeans are so muddy she has to take them off at the door. Her father is watching the news and something is cooking on the stove, and it's as though her mother had never left. Frances pulls out one of the chrome chairs to sit at the table, but it tips over and makes a loud bang as it hits the floor, and her mother says, "Those darn tippy chairs." Frances can feel the dark building inside her—a storm, a big angry tornado. She hates the chrome chairs, hates the way you always have to think about how you move them away from the table, always have to be careful. Other people's chairs don't tip over, even when you're sitting on them and not being careful, and she gives the chair a good kick, and then another, and before she knows it she's shouting about how she hates these stupid chairs and why can't her mother once and for all buy some new ones so they don't all break their necks.

Her mother stands staring at her, the stew ladle frozen in her hand.

"Hey, hey, hey," her father says, getting up from his chair.

Her mother puts the ladle in the pot. "Okay," she says. "You're mad."

Frances stops kicking and says, "You can bet that Kitty Wells doesn't have chairs like these."

"Kitty Wells?" her mother says. "What does Kitty Wells have to do with this?"

"Pick up the chair, Frances," her father says. "There's no point taking it out on a chair. They may be stupid, but they're the only ones we have."

Frances picks up her chair and sits on it, still in her socks and underwear because she's taken off her muddy jeans.

"Aren't you cold?" her mother asks.

"No," Frances says. "I'm boiling."

After that, her mother puts the meal on the table and they all eat in silence. At bedtime, Frances wants to sleep in her parents' bed, but they make her go back to her own. Her mother reads aloud a chapter from *The Wonderful Wizard of Oz*, which means it's not an ordinary night, and then she closes the book and says, "Nashville? Honestly, Frances, don't you think if I were going somewhere that far away, I'd just go back to England?" She must have seen the look on Frances's face, because she adds, "Oh, don't you dare start worrying about that. I'm home now and I'm not going anywhere. Do you understand? Tell me you do so we can all sleep tonight."

Frances nods, but that's not good enough and her mother makes her say it out loud.

"No one is going to Nashville or back to England," Frances says.

"Right," says her mother. "No one is going anywhere." And that's that. Out goes the light.

But oh, Frances would love to hear what her parents are talking about. She climbs out of bed and opens her door just a crack—just enough to hear—and there's her mother, standing in the hallway with her hands on her hips, looking right at Frances's door.

"Get back in bed right now and go to sleep," she says, so Frances gives up.

THE NEXT DAY, her mother shows her the new clothes she bought in Yellowhead—a skirt and bolero jacket ("All the rage, according to the lady in the shop"), a sweater set, and a new pair of high-heeled shoes. ("Pumps, they're called. Who knows where I'll wear them.") She has a present for Frances: a package of underwear, seven pairs, each a different color and each with the day of the week embroidered near the waistband. Today is Thursday, the day Frances was born, but she puts on Monday because Monday is pink, and also Monday's child is fair of face. Thursday's child has far to go, whatever that means. Who would ever want to be born on Thursday?

After supper that evening, while her mother is having a bath and Frances is alone with her father, he tells her that Alice hadn't really been missing, that she'd just gone on a little shopping trip, and she'd meant to leave a note but had forgotten, and Frances is not to worry anymore, or talk to anyone about it, especially not about Nashville.

"Do you understand me, Frances?" he asks.

Frances nods.

"Tell me you understand," her father says. "Out loud."

"No one is going anywhere and I'm to forget about it and not talk."

"You can talk," her father says. "Just not about . . . well, you know."

Then her mother comes out of the bathroom and sits down beside her on the wagon-wheel couch, and when Basie goes to the kitchen for a glass of water, Alice says to Frances, "Stop looking at me like that. It's not like I did something wrong, is it?"

Frances isn't sure.

When her father comes back, they watch *Country Hoedown*, which is set inside a barn. Frances wants to know if the barn is in Nashville, and her mother says no, it's a fake barn set up in a TV studio in Canada.

Maybe there is no real Nashville, Frances thinks. Maybe

it's just a place on television or the radio. When the Singin' Swingin' Eight come on TV, her mother grabs her and they do-si-do around the living room. She didn't realize her mother knew about square dancing, but it's fun.

The shopping trip is not mentioned again. It disappears just like the cowboy hats, the ones Frances has never been able to find. Too bad. They would have come in handy for the do-si-do.

FRANCES'S FATHER has a brother in England. His name is Vince, and there's lots of excitement when Vince says he's coming to Canada for Christmas. When they pick him up at the train station in Yellowhead, he tells Basie he sounds like a proper Canadian now and then he turns to Frances and says, "Give us a speech, luv, so I can hear what you sound like." But she's too shy to say anything. On the way home, Uncle Vince keeps whistling his admiration of Frances's mother's blue-and-white Fairlane—"You don't see cars like this in England"—and also they learn that he is not just staying for Christmas, he's moving here. To help with the farm, he says, until he can buy his own place nearby. Frances's father says, "Well, that's just great news, Vince," but her mother does not look entirely happy (although she looks happy enough later, when Vince unpacks and gets out a box of canned fish and pies from Marks & Spencer, and for Frances there's a rag doll that he calls a golliwog). They have steak-and-kidney pie for supper, and when it's bedtime, Uncle Vince sleeps on the top bunk in Frances's bedroom. He groans in his sleep. Frances tells her mother he sounds like a bear.

After New Year's, when Vince has been there for two

weeks, Frances overhears her mother say to her father that the house isn't big enough for three adults (especially when one of them is in his cups as much as Uncle Vince is—which means, she tells Frances when she asks, that he drinks too much coffee). Uncle Vince has his own money, so he should get looking for a place to live if he's serious about staying.

Then Uncle Vince comes in the door with a letter in a blue airmail envelope from a woman named Bertie, and he says he's asked Bertie to marry him.

Frances can tell that her mother is surprised, but she manages to hide it and says, "Well, then, you've got a reply there, I imagine. Has she said yes?"

Uncle Vince's glasses are all steamed up. He hangs his new winter coat on a hook by the door and says, "She's thinking about it." Then he takes off his glasses and cleans them on his shirt. "Did I say her name is Bertie? You'll like her. She's more fun than monkeys in a coconut tree."

Monkeys in a coconut tree do sound like fun to Frances, but not, apparently, to her mother. She says four adults can't possibly all live under the same roof. Frances thinks she's being rude, but Uncle Vince says, "No, no, right you are. I'll get on that. Bertie will want her own place and all."

A week later, another letter comes from Bertie.

"Still thinking about it," Vince reports.

The problem is that Bertie is afraid to live out in the country due to wild Red Indians, even though Vince has assured her that they've been tamed. She wants to live in a town. In fact, she will say yes to his proposal only if he promises her a place in town.

Frances's mother has an idea. She remembers something

about a veterans' subdivision in Elliot. Vince is an English veteran, not a Canadian one, but maybe that won't matter. She's heard the lots are inexpensive. Vince could work with them on the farm—God knows, they need the help—but he and Bertie could live in the veterans' subdivision.

Vince says, "Brilliant."

He looks into the veterans' lots and learns that what Alice heard is true. Years ago, Elliot had somehow acquired a strip of land along the rail line, but it wasn't much use because it was separated from the town by the tracks, so after the war the council had come up with the idea of honoring its young returning veterans by offering them cheap, tax-free lots on the vacant land. The town built a road, surveyed, ran the power line, and erected a lamppost and a street sign that said Liberty Street. From a clerk in the town office, Vince learns that in the years since the war they hadn't sold a single lot— because the veterans were all farm boys and didn't want to live in town—but the tax-free offer is still in place. The clerk is beside herself with excitement when Vince tells her he's interested. It might be the start of something, she says, who knows, one purchase leads to another and, yes, absolutely, he can buy a lot even though he was in the British army, not a problem, it's the Commonwealth, after all, and all the boys were fighting the same enemy, weren't they.

When Vince takes Frances and her parents to look at his lot, they have to walk up Liberty Street in the snow because it hasn't been plowed. There is a line of bush between the tracks and the lots, and the trees are bent to the ground with snow blown about by the passing trains. The lots themselves are empty. Basie says he hopes they don't flood when the snow melts.

Alice, a bit bewildered by the desolation, even though the town is just across the tracks, asks, "Which lot is yours?"

Vince says he doesn't know, and he doesn't suppose it matters—one is as good as another—but he and Basie check the paperwork so they'll be sure to put the foundation on the right lot in the spring. As they're studying the map Vince was given at the town office, a train goes by and they have to stop talking. Frances watches the blankets of snow that fly up all around the train as it passes.

"Bertie is going to love this," her mother says under her breath.

Frances hears her and wants to know, What is it that Bertie will love?

"Oh, the fresh Canadian air," her mother says.

Because the survey stakes are covered by snow, Basie and Vince have to guess at the location of the lot he's bought. Once they've decided, Vince wants to put stakes at the corners, even though they'll fall away when the snow melts. They cut some willow shoots with Vince's pocketknife and stand them in the snow, and by the time they're done, their feet are all frozen. Vince stands with his shoulders hunched up and his hands in his pockets looking at his lot, and announces that he's going to build his bride-to-be an English country cottage so she'll feel right at home.

"With shutters and window boxes and all," he says. "She likes flowers. She's a hundred pounds soaking wet. She'd get lost in a big house."

As they tramp back to the car through the snow, Vince says, "This country is colder than a witch's tit," and Frances's mother says, "Vince, please."

Frances's nose drips from the cold and she wipes it on

her mitts. She sits between her parents and takes off her boots and puts her stockinged feet right on the heater.

When they get home, Vince sits down at the kitchen table and draws a picture of the house he has in mind. Frances's mother says it looks like a dollhouse. Frances thinks it looks like a house for Peter Rabbit or Mrs. Tittlemouse. Her feet hurt from being so cold, but her mother says that will go away by bedtime.

"Best not mention that to Bertie when she gets here," Uncle Vince says. "Frostbite and all."

WHEN SPRING COMES, Uncle Vince begins work on what he calls Bertie's cottage. Frances's father helps with the construction when he can, which leaves her mother with all the barn chores and the evening milking, but she is so worried Bertie will arrive and have to move into her house that she doesn't complain. Frances argues her way to town with the two men most days. She's there the day a load of lumber is delivered by a man from the lumberyard, and she overhears Uncle Vince ask her father under his breath whether the man is a genuine Red Indian, and if so, what he's doing off the reservation, aren't they all on reservations now? Frances's dad says no, he supposes not, if they have jobs like everyone else. They unload the lumber and stack it in a big pile by the foundation while Frances watches, and then the man from the lumberyard drives away. As he passes Frances with his window down, he winks and tips his cap.

Under orders from her mother, Frances stays away from the railway tracks, but she watches the cars flash by every time there's a train. When the men stop work for lunch one day, Uncle Vince shows her how to put a penny on the track so the train will flatten it, and then as an afterthought he tells her she is never to do that on her own because she might lose an arm, and he suggests that she not tell her mother about that particular trick. The next day Frances tries to leave the house with a pocketful of coins from her piggy bank, and her mother finds out about Vince showing her the trick and decides she shouldn't be allowed to go to town anymore. Frances decides she doesn't care. She was getting bored in town.

Uncle Vince says, "Well, you're a big girl now. It's time you stayed home to milk the cows anyway. No more skiving off."

"I don't like cows," Frances says.

"I don't like work," says Uncle Vince, "but someone has to do it."

Later that morning, it warms up so much that Frances goes outside without even a sweater. When her mother has finished cleaning up after the milking, she suggests that Frances help her wash her car, the car that no one but her gets to drive because it was she who had the premonition about winning it. She'd lined up at the fair in Yellowhead and paid her two dollars while Basie waited impatiently, thinking they might as well give the two dollars to a beggar man, better use for it, and then that evening at the grandstand, right after a man in a tuxedo did an act with spinning plates, what if they didn't draw her ticket out of the barrel they'd wheeled onto the stage? When they read her name—Mrs. Alice Moon—she almost fell off the bleachers. She had her picture taken with the car for the Yellowhead paper—she was wearing a checked cotton maternity smock because she was expecting a baby (who turned out to be Frances)—and then she got to drive it home because it was the last day of the fair. She didn't even have a driver's license, but she declared that it would be a frosty Friday before she'd let anyone else drive her new car, which had only seventeen miles showing on the odometer. Basie followed her home in the truck, holding his breath the whole way.

Frances walks the length of the car and runs her hand along the shiny chrome molding, picturing her mother as she waved to the crowd at the fair. She's all ready for scrubbing in her rubber boots (wellies, her mother calls them) and rubber gloves (which come up to her elbows), while her mother is in the house gathering her buckets and cleaning supplies. The car radio is on and the front windows are partway down so they can hear it. Ray Price is singing "Heartaches by the Number." Her mother likes this song. When she comes from the house with two buckets full of warm, soapy water, she's singing along.

"Do you think you sing like a frog?" Frances asks her.

"Did your father tell you that?"

"Maybe."

"Well, what does he know about singing?"

Frances's job is to wash all the whitewall tires. She squeezes her sponge onto a front tire and tries to make the water run around the circle of white. She sticks her hands so far in the bucket that her gloves fill up with water, and when she lifts them it runs up her arms and her shirt gets wet. Her mother tells her to quit playing and get busy. Frances squeezes the sponge so water fills her rubber boots.

"It's called work, Frances," her mother says. "Vince was right—you could be doing something to help out. We'll all have to work harder around here if your father's eyesight goes."

"Goes where?" Frances asks.

"I don't know. Down the road, I suppose."

Ha ha. Her father is usually the joker, but that's funny—his eyesight heading down the road without him.

"Will he be blind then?" she asks.

"No. Forget I said that."

Frances gets a better idea than washing the car. She decides to wash the spring mud from Kaw-Liga, and she struggles off toward the barn with her bucket and sponge and her boots full of water.

"Frances!" her mother calls, but Frances ignores her. The bucket is slopping water all over her pant legs. Halfway to the barn, she gives up and sits down in the dirt. She pictures a train flattening a dime and a nickel. She changes her mind about town being boring and wishes she were there. She leaves the bucket in the middle of the yard and asks her mother if they can do something else. Her mother says, "Get that bucket back here and finish what you started."

Frances pouts, but she does what she's told. It takes hours for her mother to finish washing and waxing the car. Frances wants to know why it has to be so sparkling clean.

"This car was a windfall," her mother says. "Let this be a lesson."

Frances doesn't know what the lesson is, or a windfall either.

IT'S JULY NOW, and it's really hot almost every day. Uncle Vince says he had no idea Canada could get so hot. "Hardly fit for an Englishman," he complains at breakfast. Bertie has still not arrived from England. She's waiting for her house to be done.

It's washday and Alice is hanging the sheets on the

clothesline while Frances hands her the pegs. It's so hot and breezy that the first sheet is dry by the time her mother gets the last one up. She starts to take the dry ones down but then pegs them back up again and says, "Oh bother, let's we two girls go to the lake."

Frances can't believe it. She hadn't even asked.

She puts on her bathing suit while her mother packs a lunch and their beach bag. She says they can stay for only an hour—"so don't pester me to stay longer"—and they get in the car and go. Her mother has changed into clean shorts and a sleeveless blouse, and she has her sunglasses on. Frances sits on the seat beside her in her yellow cotton bathing suit, wishing she had some sunglasses too.

It takes half an hour to get there. There are no other people at the spot they like because it's a weekday, but there are several cars in the parking lot and a few families down the beach where the picnic tables are. Frances immediately goes to the shore and begs her mother to go in the water with her and hold her for the dead man's float, which Alice does, but not for long because, she says, their white English skin burns too easily. She makes Frances put on a hat and convinces her to sit on the blanket in the shade and play crazy eights.

When her mother says she has to go to the toilet ("Badly, Frances—I can't wait"), Frances doesn't want to go with her. She hates the pee smell of the outhouses and tells her mother that she will throw up if she has to go near them. Her mother says she can wait outside, but even then Frances digs her heels into the sand and has to be dragged along until they reach a path through the trees, and then she gives in and follows.

"You wait right here," her mother says when they come

to the outhouses, one for men and one for ladies. There's another path through the trees, which is the one Frances thinks leads to the playground. Her mother sees her looking at it and makes her promise she will stay right where she is. Frances promises, then her mother lifts the latch on the ladies' toilet and goes in.

Frances can smell the toilets, even outside. She starts to walk backwards away from the smell, but it follows her, so she turns and runs through the trees and down to the beach, even though she knows her mother will be mad. She's just about to sit on the blanket when she sees an old Styrofoam rescue ring lapping at the water's edge, so she walks down to the shore to check it out. She looks up and down the beach. In one direction, there are some teenagers throwing each other around in the water and a man tossing a stick as far as he can into the lake for a dog to fetch. In the other direction, there's a little point of land with shrubby trees on it but no people. There doesn't seem to be anyone watching Frances.

She'll be quick, she thinks. Try out the ring and then be back on the blanket before her mother returns. (*Is that her mother calling now?*) She knows she should wait—she's not allowed to go in the water on her own—but instead she grabs the ring and runs along the beach until she's out of sight around the point. She steps into the ring, pulls it up to her middle, and wades into the water until she feels her feet lift off the sandy bottom (magic!), and all of a sudden she's bobbing like a frog on a lily pad.

She forgets about her mother and the blanket. All she thinks about is how perfect it is to be floating on the warm surface of the water as if she's in a magic water world. When she looks down, she can see rocks on the bottom of the lake and big brown fish nestled there with their fins rippling and minnows everywhere—hundreds of them—and she thinks she's living in a fish world, and they don't seem to mind. A brown duck comes close with six ducklings peeping and darting around like water bugs, and they don't seem to mind her being there either. Her legs dangle down into the clear water, and when she wriggles her toes or kicks her feet, the fish move lazily along the bottom right underneath her, their bodies curving one way and then the other, and they give not one sign that they think Frances shouldn't be there, or that they are afraid of her.

Then a man and woman in a canoe come along and ruin everything. They get excited when they see her, and the man wants her to come with them in the canoe, but she says no thank you, even though she is beginning to shiver, and the closer the man and woman come in the canoe, the more Frances wishes she were back onshore because now the chills are going right down to her toes dangling in the water. The woman suggests they tow her back to shore and Frances thinks about that and then nods. She lets the man wrap a rope around the ring, and the woman holds the end of it while the man paddles. They paddle back to the beach, staying close to the shore, while Frances hangs on to the ring. She points to the blanket where she'd been sitting with her mother, who still isn't there. The woman watches Frances the whole time, as though they might lose her. Just before they get to shore, she takes out a camera and snaps Frances's picture. "Smile," she says.

The man beaches the canoe and the woman hands him the rope, and he hauls Frances to the water's edge. Once she's on land, she drops the ring in the sand and heads for the blanket, shivering so badly she can hardly hold herself up. She wonders why her mother isn't back yet.

The couple follow her to the blanket, where they both stand looking confused until the man asks, "Where are your parents, little girl?"

"My mother is here somewhere," Frances says.

"Heavens, your lips are blue," the woman says.

They still look like they don't know what to do. Frances wants them to go away. She sits down and wraps herself up in the blanket, playing cards and all. "My mother's car is just up there," she says. "The blue-and-white one. She won it at the fair. You don't have to wait. She'll be right back."

The couple finally leave her alone after making her promise she won't go in the water again (not a chance, she's too cold), and they get in their canoe and paddle away, taking the ring with them. Frances is glad when the canoe is around the point and she can't see it anymore.

Then her mother steps out of the trees with another woman and two teenage girls, and she sees Frances wrapped up on the beach. "Thank God," the other woman says. Then she says, "We'll tell the others," and she and the teenagers leave and walk back toward the picnic tables. Through the trees, Frances hears her call, "We found her."

After Frances's mother gets over being relieved, it becomes clear just how mad she is, and also how embarrassed, because she had to ask people to help her look.

"Where were you?" she asks. "You weren't at the playground. We checked the water. I thought you'd got lost in the bush."

Frances says she went for a ride with a man in a canoe.

She doesn't mention the woman. Since it's a lie anyway, it doesn't seem necessary to say there'd been two people.

"What man?" her mother asks, looking up and down the shore. "Where is he? I don't see a man with a canoe."

"He left," Frances says. "That way." She points, and the blanket falls away and her mother sees her wet bathing suit.

"You went in the water, didn't you?" she says. "After I told you not to. You snuck in someplace where I wouldn't see you."

Frances sees no reason to deny it.

They pack up the blanket and the playing cards, and all the way home her mother says things like "A six-year-old girl is old enough to listen to her mother."

Frances is not quite six—she is *almost* six—but she doesn't argue. She worries that her mother won't ever take her to the lake again. She wishes the people in the canoe hadn't taken the Styrofoam ring with them.

And then, a week later, the Yellowhead paper comes in the mail, and there's a grainy black-and-white picture on page 3 of a girl in a floating water-rescue device. The headline says *Lost Little Mermaid*. Frances's mother reads the story to her. It's about a couple who found a little girl floating in the lake and didn't know where her parents were, but the girl had shown them her mother's car and said her mother won it at the fair, and she'd convinced them that the mother was there somewhere, although perhaps they shouldn't have left her alone on the beach.

Frances's mother puts the paper down and looks at her. "Is that girl in the story you?" she asks.

Frances says no. Her mother gets out a magnifying glass and looks at the photo again, and then says, "Oh, that is certainly not you. Of course it isn't. How could I even ask?"

Good, Frances thinks. She's survived her lie.

That evening, her mother looks at her from across the room and says, "You're getting sneaky, and I don't like it." Then she says, "I hope the girl in the paper—who could have drowned, by the way—I just hope she learned her lesson."

The way her mother looks at her, Frances realizes that she has not, in fact, survived her lie.

At breakfast the next morning, Uncle Vince slaps his leg and says, "Lost little mermaid. That's a corker."

BERTIE'S NEW HOUSE is ready—at least ready enough to live in—by the middle of August. They have a painting bee and Frances's mother paints inside (eggshell everywhere, Bertie can change it if she likes), while Vince and her father paint the outside glossy white with green shutters and window boxes. Bertie is ready too, all set to come to Canada and get married. She has her things packed and is waiting on the Canadian government to say she can come. Any day now, Vince says. Bertie reports in a letter (to Frances's mother) that her sisters had a bridal shower for her, and that she has her wedding dress purchased and will be bringing it with her. She even drew a little picture of the dress.

Then one day Uncle Vince goes to town for the mail and doesn't come back. Instead, he falls over and dies. Dead. Gone forever. Frances's parents phone England long-distance to tell Bertie. After they get off the phone, Frances's mother says that Bertie sounded kind of relieved.

"Not that she doesn't have to marry Vince," she says. "I didn't mean that. But that she doesn't have to come to Canada."

Frances wants to know what Bertie will do with her dress.

"Hang on to it until she marries someone else, I suppose," Frances's mother says.

Since Vince didn't know anyone in Canada, there is no funeral. He gets buried in the graveyard in town. Her parents aren't sure what to do about the house: Does it belong to Bertie now? they wonder. But a lawyer says not. The house goes to the next of kin—Basie—and after everything is settled Basie wants to sell it, but Alice says it might come in handy if they have to move to town someday. It's just too bad, she says, that Vince didn't build a more practical house—a one-story bungalow, say, like the other new houses in Elliot.

Basie says, "Talk all you want, woman, but the day I move to town is a day you'll never see with your twenty-twenty vision. After I'm gone, you can do as you like. If I go first, you're more than welcome to move into Vince's toy house."

"We'll see."

"Apparently I won't."

Frances wants to know what they're talking about.

"Your mother thinks I'm going blind," her father says, and then he puts on his cap and goes outside.

What? Really?

"You said he wasn't," Frances says.

"I never said for sure. Anyway, don't mind him. He's upset about Uncle Vince."

Worrying about her father going blind is one thing, but now the phrase "after I'm gone" keeps repeating itself in Frances's head. What did her father mean by that? She worries that he's planning to leave the way her mother did that time, the way Doreen did when she went back to England.

Then she understands that he means "leave" in the way Uncle Vince left.

Which is much, much worse.

. . .

IN SEPTEMBER, school begins. Not kindergarten, which Frances didn't attend because her birthday is late in the year, but real all-day first grade, which her mother made a case for because Frances knows her colors, and what else do they learn in kindergarten? The bus stops at the approach every day to pick up Frances and take her to the Elliot elementary school, an old two-story brick building. The bus drops the younger students off first and then drives around the block to the high school, which is a newer building across the schoolyard. She's the only grade one on the bus. She sits at the front and the bigger kids sit at the back, unless the bus driver hauls one of them up closer for being rowdy. Frances looks down most of the time she's on the bus. If someone talks to her, she pretends she doesn't hear. She does the same thing at school, except with the teacher. Her mother tells her she has to pay attention to the teacher.

Six weeks into school now and Frances has begun tapping her fingers as if she's playing the piano, although her parents have no piano and she doesn't know the first thing about white and black keys or holding your hands as if they have oranges under them. One, two, three . . . she counts in her head as she taps one finger at a time. When she runs out of fingers, she makes up patterns—one, three, five, two, four—or she counts backwards or practices tapping finger four by itself because it won't behave like the others do. She wonders why this is.

She tap, tap, taps for a reason, although she's afraid to explain it to anyone in case it stops working. The teacher at school is always telling them to count to ten before they decide whether they have to cry (girls) or hit someone (boys). Frances rarely wants to cry or hit anyone, but sometimes a storm brews up inside of her and makes her think of Dorothy and Toto being tossed around in the cyclone, and when she tries counting—one, two, three . . . tap, tap, tap—bingo, it works, and the storm settles back to stillness. Tapping becomes a habit that feels good, like laying your cheek on the coolness of the kitchen countertop or running your fingers along the satin edge of a blanket.

At home, it annoys her mother. She says, "I don't know why you do that. It's not normal."

One day at school, Jimmy Gulka sees her tapping on her knees under her desk and says, "Look what Loony-Moony is doing." He gets in trouble for calling her a name, but after that, Frances tries so hard to keep her fingers from tapping that she forgets to listen to the teacher.

Frances is just in the door after school one day when the phone rings. She can see her mother turning away from her, the phone cord wrapped around her shoulder, for what she calls a private conversation, which is still not very private.

"Oh, for Pete's sake," Frances hears her mother say. "I hardly think 'slow learner' is the right term. What are the teacher's qualifications for making an assessment like that? (A pause, listening.) Well, yes, we do know that . . . she's an only child, remember? And yes, I know she has trouble paying attention. (Another pause.) A psychologist? Really? I hardly think that's necessary. (Long pause.) Well, at least he sounds more qualified than your teacher—or you, for that matter. I will agree, yes, but for no other reason than to prove you wrong."

"Who was that?" Frances asks as she hangs her coat by the door, even though she's guessed it was the principal calling.

"Just some divvy," her mother says. "Never mind."

Ha ha. Frances knows what a divvy is. An idiot. Her mother has just called the principal an idiot.

On the day of her appointment with an educational psychologist who is making his rounds of the rural schools, Frances wears new brown corduroy pants and a blue sweater with buttons. She likes the blue sweater and agrees now with her mother that blue looks good with her red hair. It would look better still, she thinks, if she had her new front teeth. She worries every day that they won't grow back, and that she will have no teeth all her life. No other kids in her class have had to have all their teeth pulled. Why her?

Once she gets to school, she doesn't have to wait long before the teacher takes her to the principal's office and introduces her to Doctor Somebody-or-other. Not a medical doctor, he explains to Frances—not someone you go to with measles or chicken pox—but a different kind of doctor. He sits with her at a child-size table looking funny because his knees are almost up to his chin. He has a briefcase with papers and pencils in it, and he tells Frances that she's lucky because she has been chosen to play a few special games with him. He gets out some activity papers that require her to match shapes and do things with numbers, which she is happy to do—very happy, because now she's in a quiet room, just her and this doctor.

After she's done, he says, "Now, Frances, your teacher tells me that you are reluctant to talk in class. I'm going to ask you some questions about school, and I hope you will try to answer them. Is that all right?" She nods. He begins to ask his questions and she practically explodes with talking: the teacher is nice, the other students aren't very, she doesn't like being called Loony-Moony, she likes swimming and knows how to do the dead man's float, she'd like to know how it feels to be a fish, she wishes her teeth would grow in, her mother sings with the radio even though she sounds like a frog, her father might go blind someday.

"Thank you, Frances," the doctor says when she seems to be done. "Do you have any questions you would like to ask me?"

She tells him about Uncle Vince dropping dead in front of the post office and asks him if he knew that could happen—*bango*—dead as a doornail and lying on top of a letter from his girlfriend in England.

"And I wonder," she says, "does Uncle Vince, even though he's dead, know that Bertie's going to marry someone else? And is Uncle Vince still wishing, even though he's dead, that he'd waited to keel over until after he'd opened the letter so he could see what was in it? Or once you're dead, can you read right through the envelope? Is that possible? Even though you're in the ground?"

"What do *you* think was in the letter?" the doctor asks.

"I don't know for sure," Frances says. "But here's something else I wonder: Do people write their letters with accents? The way they speak. Do they write that way?"

The doctor studies her and Frances wants to drop her eyes, but she doesn't. She looks right back at him. He places a hand over hers to stop the tapping (she didn't realize she'd been tapping), and then he says that he does know a person can die unexpectedly, and it's hard for those left behind. The doctor tells her he will think about her other questions, about the letter and writing with accents, and get back to her. (Which he never does.)

A few days later he calls Frances's mother and says he's had a look at Frances's tests and thought about their little chat, and he thinks he's gotten to the bottom of things.

"She's a bit of a worrier, isn't she?" he says. "And a girl with, shall we say, an active imagination."

Frances's mother gets right to the point. "But is she a slow learner?" she asks, trying to erase from her mind the picture of an uneducated grown-up Frances aging into a dim-witted spinster.

"Quite the opposite," the doctor says, and he explains that Frances is "very bright" and probably needs more mental stimulation. He asks Frances's mother if they have an encyclopedia in the home, and perhaps a globe of the world, and whether she reads aloud to Frances. He says he believes she will open up in the classroom once her teeth have grown back. Other grade one students are losing their front teeth too, he says, but not all at once, the way Frances has. And the death of her uncle . . . it's normal for children, especially bright children, to worry about death.

Alice can't wait to get off the phone. She thanks the doctor for calling, and once the telephone receiver is back in place and she has exhaled with relief, she immediately inhales with indignation that a teacher could be so foolish as to believe that Frances is anything but bright—especially a teacher who looks like a high school student. She calls the school and asks to speak with the teacher.

"Might you be giving my daughter some extra attention for being the smartest student in the class?" she asks her, making no attempt to hide the sarcasm.

The teacher, making no attempt to hide her condescension, says, "Well, Mrs. Moon, I don't think the psychologist said she was the smartest student. And Frances certainly needs to make more of an effort. She seems to be a bit lazy."

Frances's mother is stunned by this response. She tracks down Frances and reports the news—that she's smart but lazy—waving a finger at her and saying, "You'd better prove that teacher wrong, Frances, that's all I can say."

Frances feels as though she's done something wrong. She's been caught in a lie again or caught hiding something from her mother, or maybe the teacher. When her father comes in from the barn and is told what the psychologist thinks, he says, "Huh. Wonder how much money he was paid to come up with something I already knew." When he hears what the teacher dared to say, he is unfazed. "I imagine we should just turn a blind eye to that."

Ha ha. Her father is *so* good at jokes, especially blind jokes. Frances is relieved that he at least isn't blaming her for anything.

Her mother calms down and makes supper, and then they all play cribbage. Soon after, they get the *World Book Encyclopedia*, and Frances and her mother start going to the library in town for new books. Her mother begins reading to her every night before bed and not just on the weekend or rainy days. She gets up on the bed with her and stretches her legs out, puts on her glasses, and reads from *Little Women* and *Anne of Green Gables*, which Frances loves because Anne has red hair. She gets her mother to read the good parts over twice.

One night, Frances asks her mother if someone used to read stories aloud to her.

Her mother says, "I told you. They were tossers." Then she asks Frances what she thinks of the other kids at school. Does she like anyone in particular? Would she like to invite one of the other girls to the farm to play with her someday—a Saturday, perhaps? Like Anne's friend Diana, she says. Maybe there's a girl like Diana in her class.

Frances thinks for a minute and then says no, not really.

"Not one?"

"No," says Frances. "Not even one."

It snows and snows. All winter, as though it's never going to quit. Frances thinks about the snow piling up on Uncle Vince, and she sees how it builds, layer upon layer, on Kaw-Liga's head, the points of his feather headdress sticking up out of it. She tries playing outside after school, but there's so much snow she's restricted to the parts of the yard that have been plowed by the blade on the tractor, and there's no fun to be had there.

"What do you think about ice-skating?" her mother asks her one day. She doesn't know how to ice-skate herself, but she saw *Rhapsody on Ice* at Covent Garden before the war. She tells Frances there's a flyer in the post office about figure-skating lessons beginning in the new year for ages five to seven, Tuesdays and Thursdays after school, and she suggests that perhaps Frances would like to be signed up. Frances barely knows what figure skating is. Dancing on ice, with costumes, her mother says. Frances gets talked into it because she likes the idea of costumes.

For Christmas, Frances's dad gives Alice a new record player console and her first LP, Patsy Cline. Along with a spinning globe of the world—inflatable, like a beach ball— Frances gets new white skates from the catalogue. She tries them on and walks around the house in them, but she has to stop because the blades make marks on the floor.

On the first day of lessons, Frances gets picked up after

school by her mother and driven to the new indoor rink. She puts on her skates and her mother does them up tight, and she stumbles out onto the ice with the other kids, some of whom (like Frances) fall all over the place because they've never had skates on before. Their coach, a girl named Melody who comes twice a week from Yellowhead, divides them into two groups—the ones who can stand up and the ones who can't—and she asks the parents of Frances's group to come onto the ice and hold their children up until they get their balance. Frances's mother tells the other mothers about seeing *Rhapsody on Ice* in London just before the war, and Frances thinks she hears one of them saying, "I don't know who she thinks she is."

Once they can all stand without falling, Melody sends the mothers off the ice and tells the kids she is going to teach them forward, stop, turn. Then she does a demonstration, first skating backwards and then doing a jump and a spin, and she tells the beginners they too will be able to do this before long if they keep trying. "Try, try, try, and don't give up," she says. "That's how you learn." A girl from school— Caroline Smith, whose new front teeth are already growing in—says, "Like this, teacher?" and she skates backwards in a circle. The teacher divides them into two groups again, the ones who can skate backwards and the ones who can't. Frances hates Caroline.

After several lessons, Frances is able to make it all the way around the rink without falling, as long as no one bumps into her and knocks her over, which the boys sometimes do on purpose. (She hates them too.) Sometimes there are older girls skating—teenagers, girls who already know how to skate—and Frances watches them and has to tap, tap, tap her fingers inside her mitts because she so, so, so badly wants to skate like the big girls. She can just see herself. It's boring going around the ice, forward, stop, turn.

The two beginner groups eventually get joined into one again, and they begin to gear up for the spring recital. The beginners are to wear animal costumes—squirrels and rabbits and raccoons—and get pretend-chased around the ice by one of the older boys in a wolf costume, to *Peter and the Wolf* music. Then the more experienced skaters will do their routines. Frances can't believe it when the coach selects her and Jimmy Gulka to do a duet. Jimmy Gulka immediately launches a protest, as does Caroline—"Teacher, teacher," with her hand in the air—but Melody says, "Shhhh, you don't argue with your coach, and Frances is right for the part. You'll see why."

"But her teeth," Jimmy Gulka says.

"Jimmy," Melody says sharply. "That's rude."

They are called a pair. The routine Frances and Jimmy Gulka are to do is really the opening part of a routine an older boy and girl are doing. Frances has been selected for her hair, which is like the older girl's hair, red and curly, and Jimmy has been selected because he is the right height for Frances. The routine begins with a simple waltz, and Frances and Jimmy are to skate once around the rink to the music, holding arms in a crisscrossed, old-fashioned way, and then they leave the ice and the bigger girl and boy come on in the exact same costumes as Frances and Jimmy and do more fancy skating.

"You two will be so adorable," the coach says. Frances believes they will be. She decides she has a crush on Jimmy Gulka. The two of them get to practice their routine at the rink with the older pair, without the other beginners there.

Once they know what they're supposed to do, they begin to practice with the music. They learn to listen for their cue and step onto the ice when they hear it. After they've done their waltz around the rink, the two older skaters take over. Frances watches closely from the boards as they skate in circles, together and apart and together again, and the red-haired girl spins like a ballerina and skates backwards with one leg lifted behind her while the boy holds her arms. Frances can see herself in a few years' time.

Then she sees herself right now. She can just *see* herself doing this, with Jimmy Gulka holding her arms so she doesn't fall. At home in the living room (without her skates because her mother won't let her wear them in the house), she holds the wagon-wheel arm of the couch for balance and practices lifting her leg the way the older girl does. She practices until she can do it perfectly. On the day of the recital, once they're in their makeup and costumes and waiting to go onto the ice, she whispers to Jimmy what she's going to do and what he's supposed to do (just hold her arms for balance), and says they will impress everyone.

Jimmy doesn't want to. He says no, they'll get in trouble with the coach. Frances tells him she's going to do it, and he should hold her arms when she says or they'll both fall. He looks around for someone to tell, but the coach is talking to the older pair, giving them last-minute instructions.

"Are you two ready?" Melody says to Frances and Jimmy, and Frances can see that he is about to tell, but then their music starts and they hear their cue, and they have to step out onto the ice.

Jimmy Gulka looks terrified. When they're most of the way around the ice, Frances says, "Now," and he says, "No," and holds on tight to her arms, and she tries to turn around and face him so she can lift her leg and go backwards, and of course she falls and pulls Jimmy over on top of her, and his skate gets caught in her fancy sequinned skirt (painstakingly sewn by her mother) and rips it. Melody comes running on the outside of the boards to where they lie in a heap and hisses, "What the hell was that? Get up. Finish your circle." Frances and Jimmy get to their feet and Frances thinks they should waltz the rest of the way around, but Jimmy skates for the boards and the gate without her, so she follows him. By this time everyone is laughing—they think it's so cute, and maybe even part of the routine. The older boy and girl step onto the ice, both of them trying not to laugh, and Frances heads for her parents instead of following Jimmy to the dressing rooms, because now she knows he's mad at her. When Frances does find her parents she starts to cry, but she doesn't tell them she was responsible for the fiasco and just says, "I fell."

Jimmy Gulka's parents hear what really happened, though, and they complain to the coach. Melody searches out Frances, and she takes her aside and tells her she can't just do things like that on her own, especially when she's a beginner and can barely skate a circle around the rink. "I trusted you, Frances," she says, "even though Caroline is a better skater."

What? Now she hates Caroline even more.

"It's Jimmy Gulka's fault," she says. If he'd held her arms like he was supposed to, they wouldn't have fallen. She says this even though she knows it isn't true.

"You can't blame your mistakes on someone else, Frances," the coach says.

After the recital, figure-skating lessons are over. Frances

says she's never taking skating lessons again. She says she's never going back to school either, but her mother says she has to. She expects Jimmy Gulka to call her stupid Loony-Moony at school on Monday, but he does something worse: he ignores her completely. He hates her so much that he won't even look at her. Frances taps her fingers under her desk so fast she can't keep track of the patterns.

That weekend, Frances's father clears the snow off the shallow slough just behind the barn. The slough is still frozen over. He puts a bench on the edge of the ice, and he hauls Kaw-Liga down the hill and props him in the snow so she'll have company. She can practice by herself, her father says, whenever she wants.

"By next year, you'll take the biscuit at skating," he says.

She practices her circles, but that's all she knows how to do. Every time she tries a fancy move, even a little turn, she falls, so she quits going down to the slough. Her father says if she isn't going to use the ice, he isn't going to waste his time clearing it off for her, and not long after that, the snow gets soft and freezes into slushy ridges. Her father forgets to move Kaw-Liga and the bench back to the barn, and when spring finally comes and the ice melts, they both fall into the slough. Frances's dad fishes the bench out, but he leaves Kaw-Liga there because he's falling apart anyway.

"Poor old Kaw-Liga," Frances says at the supper table that night.

"Kaw-Liga nothing," her mother says. "Poor Patsy Cline." She says this because Patsy Cline died in a plane crash a month ago.

"Are you still going on about that?" says her father.

Alice puts her Patsy Cline album on the record player that evening, and plays it over and over.

One good thing: not long after that, Frances's new teeth start to come in.

JIMMY GULKA and Caroline Smith and the other kids at school are ignoring Frances. She experiments to see if she can get anyone to pay attention to her. She turns around in her seat and asks the boy behind her if she can borrow his eraser. He quickly tucks it into his desk. "Why can't I borrow it?" she says to him, and the teacher tells her to turn back around and quit talking. She waits five minutes and taps the shoulder of the girl in front of her—a girl she doesn't even like named Daphne Rose—but she shrugs Frances's hand away and whispers, "Can't you see I'm busy?" When Frances does it again, Daphne puts up her hand and tells the teacher that Frances is bothering her, and the teacher tells Frances to stop annoying the other students and do her work. Frances looks down at her math workbook, but she can't concentrate. She wishes she really were invisible. She waits another five minutes and puts up her hand to ask if she can go to the bathroom. The teacher looks as though she is about to say no, but then she nods and Frances leaves the classroom and walks slowly down the hall toward the door that says *Girls* in tarnished brass letters.

Inside the bathroom, there's a window wide open. Frances goes to the window and looks down at the empty playground. The snow is gone now, and the grass is starting to turn green. She imagines her invisible self on a swing, pumping with her legs and going higher and higher, the swing going back and forth, all on its own to anyone watching. Then Frances hears a sound above her, and when she looks up she sees a boy's legs hanging out of a window. He must be sitting in the open window, she thinks, a big boy, grade eight, because that's the class right above the bathroom. He's wearing jeans and black canvas running shoes, but that's all she can see. Then all of a sudden he's coming right at her, out the window and falling, and as he passes her on his way down, she sees that it's Dooley Sullivan, a boy whose name she knows—everyone knows—because he's older than the other grade eights and always doing funny things and getting hauled out of assemblies by the ear. Their eyes meet as he goes by the window, his face just a few feet from hers, and he looks surprised to see her there. She instinctively holds her hand out to him, but he's gone—he's passed her—and then he hits the ground right beneath her. He tries to roll when he lands, but mostly he lands on his ankle. He makes an attempt at getting up to run but he can't, and she hears a yelp and he flops down on the ground again, and then he puts on a clown's pantomime of *ow, ow, ow, I'm dying.* He looks up and grins. At first she thinks he's looking at her, but then she hears cheering above her, and she cranes her neck and sees that all the second-story windows are full of students, who begin to yell things like "He did it! Hey, Dooley. Ha ha, crazy Dooley, did you see what he did?" That's when Frances realizes he didn't fall—he jumped, on purpose. Then teachers' faces begin popping out of the windows to see what's going on, and bang, bang, bang comes the sound of windows closing.

Now that it's quiet, Frances can hear Dooley moaning below her for real, and she's glad when someone comes running out to help him. It's the principal, who says, "Dooley Sullivan, what have you done now?" A few minutes later, the town's ambulance arrives, and the one attendant and the principal help Dooley onto a stretcher. Then it's as if Dooley remembers Frances in the window, and he looks up and sees that she's still there, and he waves. She waves back. Then she quickly ducks down so the principal won't see her. By the time she peeks over the window ledge again, they're putting Dooley in the ambulance. When she returns to the grade one classroom, her teacher says, "Frances, I was just about to go looking for you," and Frances doesn't say anything about Dooley and what she's seen, because she doesn't want to share it with the other students, the ones who are ignoring her. She doesn't tell anyone she saw the whole thing, even when the story circulates on the school bus.

That night she dreams about Dooley Sullivan falling past the window. He stops falling when he reaches the place where she's standing in the window, and he floats there, hovering, grinning at her. She says, "Come inside now, Dooley Sullivan," the way a teacher might, and she reaches out and offers him her hand, but he doesn't take it, and then he starts to fall again and disappears in blackness below her. When she wakes up she wonders what would have happened in the dream if he had taken her hand, whether she would have tumbled out the window and fallen with him.

When Frances's mother hears about what happened, she says, "What in the world was that boy trying to do? Kill himself?"

"He did it for a laugh," Frances says.

"How do you know that?"

"He's the funniest boy in the school," she says. "He does everything for a laugh."

She knows there is more to it than that, although she's not sure what. She keeps thinking about the look on his face as he fell past her—or was it in the dream? She isn't sure, because the two memories have become one. He'd looked puzzled, as if he wasn't sure how he ended up in the air, or perhaps was trying to decide whether he liked falling through space.

"I hope you won't do anything that stupid when you get to be a teenager," her mother says.

Frances would never do that—jump out a window.

"I don't even like tobogganing," she says.

A few days later, Dooley is back at school with crutches and a cast on his foot. In the hallway, Frances overhears the grade eight teacher telling him he'd better pull up his socks, and Dooley says he can't, he isn't wearing any under his cast.

The teacher says, "Dooley, Dooley, Dooley."

FRANCES AND HER PARENTS are going to a wedding anniversary party in the town hall, where there will be dancing and a live orchestra, although Frances's mother says on the way there, holding two homemade apple pies on her lap, that "orchestra" is hardly the word for it, since it's just Alvin Brown with his accordion and two of his neighbors. "Oh, listen to you, then," Basie says, "sounding like a proper English toff," which makes Frances laugh.

Several of the kids from her class at school are there. Frances's parents think she is playing with them somewhere, but she's not. Instead, she's hiding from them under a table, peeking out from under the white cloth, watching everyone's legs—all the people dancing—and she's also watching Dooley Sullivan, who still has the cast on his foot. From her vantage point under the banquet table, Frances can easily follow Dooley's legs around the big hall because of the cast and crutches. Girls' legs have been following his all night. She can see girls' legs following Dooley's now—four legs, two girls. One girl is wearing flat white shoes with bows on the toes, and she has a swishy yellow dress. The other girl is wearing pumps. They're white too, and this girl's dress is turquoise, the same color as the one Frances is wearing, only Frances's has checks. Both girls have bare legs. Frances is wearing white socks that come halfway up her calves. She takes off her shoes and her socks, and then puts her shoes back on so she has bare legs like the older girls who are following Dooley. She watches as the girls flank him, one on each side, but then he makes a break for it and his cast disappears among the dancing legs.

Several ladies' legs appear then, and Frances can hear the sound of dishes being placed on the table above her. People gather and disperse and gather again—she can hear the clatter of forks on china—and the ladies come back with more of whatever is up there. When the legs around the table seem to be gone, temporarily at least, she sneaks out from her hiding place to have a look. Pie. Slice after slice of pie on little white plates, each with a fork. People keep arriving to study the choices—lemon, apple, rhubarb, some kind of red berry—and then they pick up a plate and leave a hole to be filled by the ladies with trays. Frances waits until the coast is clear, and then she grabs a plate of lemon pie and slips back under the table with it.

She sees Dooley's cast coming again, no girls following him this time, and she thinks he's come for pie. Then he's shoving his crutches under the table and his face appears, and then the rest of him, and he's under the table with her.

"Howdy," he says.

It's dark under the table. She wouldn't know this was Dooley if it weren't for the cast. She doesn't say anything. Dooley is a big boy. What do you say to big boys?

"Don't worry," he says. "I won't tell anyone you're under here."

She can't really see him, but he looks too tall for under the table. He's hunched forward with his arms wrapped around his knees. The crutches are sticking out and some-one trips on one, so Dooley grabs it and pulls it under. She remembers Joey, Doreen's son—the boy who wanted to put his hand in her underpants—and how she knew she should run away from him, knew she should be afraid of him. She's not afraid of Dooley. She puts her plate of pie on the floor next to her and waits to see what will happen. She knows why *she's* under the table, but Dooley can't be there for the same reason. Then Frances sees the white shoes coming toward them, and Dooley says, "Shhhh," and she realizes he *is* there for the same reason, more or less. The reason is called hiding.

One of the girls—the one in the yellow dress—lifts the tablecloth and says, "You can't escape from us, Dooley."

"I guess not," Dooley says. He turns to Frances in the dark. "What's your name?" he asks.

"You know my name, silly," says the girl. Her hair doesn't move around her face even though she's bent over. Frances wants to reach out and touch it, to see what it feels like.

"Frances Mary Moon," says Frances.

"Who's under there with you?" asks the girl.

Dooley says, "Why, Frances Mary Moon, who else?" Out go the crutches and then Dooley, and Frances waits for the tablecloth to drop back down, but it doesn't.

"Are you coming?" Dooley asks her once he's on his feet, peering back at her under the table.

Frances crawls out, dragging one toe through the slice of lemon pie.

"Let's dance," Dooley says to her.

Frances doesn't know how to dance, and Dooley can't really dance with his cast, but he hands one crutch to the yellow-dress girl and takes Frances's hand with his free hand, and there she is, dancing with Dooley Sullivan—if dancing is what it can be called.

"What in the world are you doing?" says the yellow-dress girl as Dooley leads Frances all around the dance floor. People clear out of their way because of Dooley's crutch. Frances can hear herself laughing, it's so much fun. As Dooley spins her around, she can see Caroline from school watching—Caroline, who is not dancing with anyone, ha ha, and especially not a big boy like Dooley.

Then Frances's father is there and he says, "Mind if I cut in?" and Dooley hands Frances over and hobbles back to retrieve his other crutch. Frances's father dances her around the floor to where her mother is standing with two other women, and he says, "I think it's time we got on home, don't you, Alice? It's getting late for a dairy farmer." Her mother goes to the kitchen to retrieve her pie plates and then disappears for half an hour.

When they finally leave it's dark outside, but the hall's parking lot is well lit thanks to a pair of yard lights. They pass a sprawling group of young people—girls in dresses, and boys in jeans and light-colored shirts with collars. Dooley is there, the girl in the yellow dress hanging on to his arm. Frances thinks the kids he's with must go to the high school, or maybe they're from other towns, because she doesn't recognize them. They stop talking when Frances and her parents pass them, but then Dooley says, "Don't let the bedbugs bite, Frances Mary Moon."

Frances looks back at him, and all the kids he's with

laugh. The yellow-dress girl says, "Don't you think she's too young for you, Dooley?"

Frances's mother grabs her hand and pulls her to the car. When they're inside and the doors are closed, her mother says, "That boy was Dooley Sullivan. How does he know your name?"

"From school," Frances says.

"Well, don't you talk to him," her mother says. "Trouble is that one's middle name. They say he failed grade seven twice and barely made it through the third time."

Frances knows better than to say that when she's old enough to have a boyfriend, she wants him to be Dooley Sullivan. She wonders if Dooley and the yellow-dress girl will kiss later.

"I think those young people were probably drinking," her mother says. "Even the girls."

When they get home, her mother realizes that Frances is not wearing her socks, and that there's a big blob of lemon pie hardening on the toe of her shoe.

"What am I going to do with you?" she says.

"Nothing," says Frances.

That night she dreams about Dooley falling again, this time from the roof of her father's barn, and he lands in the hay and doesn't break anything. The yellow-dress girl is looking for him, but she's going the wrong way, out to the pasture with the cows. Dooley lies in the hay laughing. Frances laughs along with him, until he stops and puts his finger to his lips and says, "Shush," because he doesn't want the girl in the cow pasture to hear them. When Frances puts her finger to her own lips to shush him back, she realizes that she has all her teeth, and they're perfectly straight.

When she wakes up, she thinks that was the best dream she's ever had.

FRANCES'S MOTHER DECIDES that they should rent out Uncle Vince's house, which was tied up in what her parents called probate for a long time, and now belongs to them. It's had a For Sale sign in front of it for months, but no one wants to buy it, perhaps because it's still the only house on the street—a poor advertisement for a subdivision. Their first renter is the new bank manager, but he doesn't like the noise from the freight trains passing in the middle of the night and moves out almost as soon as he's moved in. After that, there's a year of single male renters who work in the bush or the lumber mill. They pay their rent, but they have a tendency to leave cigarette burns on the windowsills and holes in the plaster when they move out. Frances's mother gets good at patching holes with plaster and doing spot paint touch-ups.

One Saturday afternoon in August, Frances and her father leave her mother at the house fixing holes for the next renter, and they drive across the tracks to the post office for the mail. On their way back, Frances's father goes through the town's one and only stop sign and runs smack into a red truck, and who should get out, hopping mad, but Dooley Sullivan. No one is hurt, but Dooley's truck got the worst of it, and they have to call the RCMP to come and take their statements for the insurance. Frances's father pulls his truck over to the curb to wait. He says, "I feel badly about this, Frances. I hear Dooley fixed that old truck up himself." Then he adds, "He shouldn't have been driving so fast."

Frances hasn't seen Dooley since he finished grade eight and moved across the schoolyard to the high school, and she watches him as he paces around the street, his red truck stalled in the middle of the intersection. He stops pacing periodically to glower at his hanging front bumper and the truck's hood, which is popped up and buckled. He's wearing a white T-shirt with the sleeves rolled up and has a cigarette pack stuck in the roll. He has some kind of oil in his dark hair to keep it slicked back. He doesn't look like the same boy who jumped out the window.

It's hot inside Frances's father's truck. The two of them get out and Frances waits on the bench in front of the bank while her father inspects the relatively minor damage to his vehicle. Frances watches Dooley. The memory of him falling through the air outside the bathroom window is vague now. Maybe she'd just imagined that he was close enough she could have touched him.

Several people have gathered on the sidewalk in front of the bank to watch the action, to stare at Dooley and his truck. One man says, "You could see that coming," and Frances's dad says, "Apparently I didn't." They laugh, and Dooley strides toward them, saying, "You think this is funny, do you?"

Frances's father says, "No, Dooley, of course not."

When her father sits beside her on the bench, she takes his hand. She wonders whether Dooley remembers her, the girl in the window, the girl under the table. He says to her father, "That's a new paint job. Candy-apple red. You stupid farmers. Don't you know what a stop sign is?"

Dooley's cigarette pack is threatening to fall out of his rolled-up sleeve, and Frances doesn't know whether to point this out.

"Candy-apple red," he says again, and then—*plop*—the cigarette pack lands on the sidewalk, right at Frances's feet.

She picks it up and holds it out to Dooley, but when he goes to snatch it from her, his hand hesitates for just a second and she thinks, *He does remember*. Then he takes the pack without saying thank you. He lights a cigarette and strides off again to pace another circle around his truck. He throws back at Frances's father, "Where the hell did you learn to drive anyway?"

Where did the old Dooley go? she wonders. The funny one who could make the whole school laugh. Is this what happens when boys go to high school?

Finally, an RCMP officer comes and takes statements, and after that Frances and her father can leave, but Dooley has to stay and wait for a tow truck. As they get in their truck, Frances hears Dooley say, "You're going to let him drive away? Don't you know he's blind as a bat? Everyone knows that. And he's got that little girl with him."

The policeman says, "You haven't been drinking, have you, Dooley?"

Once they're across the tracks and on their way up Liberty Street, Frances's father says, "I don't know what all that candy-apple red was about. I suppose he should have painted the truck powder blue and then it wouldn't have been such a tragedy. Let that be a lesson to him."

Frances wonders if Dooley was right—if her father's bad eyes caused the accident.

"No need to tell your mother about this," he says.

They pick up Frances's mother at the rental house and she doesn't notice the damage. When they get back to the farm, Frances's father right away takes the truck to the shop to bang the dent out of it, but someone phones and tells Alice about the accident, and then she's the one who's mad.

"Anyone can go through a stop sign, Alice," Frances's father says.

When Frances wakes up in the middle of the night, she discovers that she can't turn her head without it hurting. In the morning, her mother notices and asks her if she has a stiff neck and she says no, but it's clear she does and her mother gives her a piece of an aspirin tablet.

FRANCES STANDS in the kitchen of Uncle Vince's house with her father, leaning up against his pant leg, one arm wrapped around him. A man has rented the house, the Indian man who works at the lumberyard—the one who delivered the lumber to Uncle Vince and winked at Frances when he was leaving. There are several coat hooks by the door and his green plaid cap has fallen from one of them to the floor. She stares at the cap, too shy to look at its owner, wondering what it is about Indians that made her mother not want to rent the house to him until Basie convinced her that he was a hard-working man with a steady job.

Her father says, "Frances, this is Mr. Chance," and Silas nods to her. He hands her father a white envelope containing cash for the rent. He has a checkerboard on the kitchen table, and when he sees Frances looking at it, he asks her if she knows how to play. She shakes her head and he says, "Don't they teach checkers at school anymore? I'll have to show you, then. Which color, red or black?"

"Black," she says.

"Good choice. Black goes first. You'll probably beat me."

"Next time, Frances," her father says. "We have to get home now."

Then Silas produces a nickel from behind Frances's ear and gives it to her. A nickel! After that, she's not shy anymore and she steps away from her father to pick up the green cap and hand it to Silas. He twirls the cap on his finger the same way her father does, round and round like a pinwheel, before he hangs it back on the hook.

On November 11, there's a Remembrance Day ceremony in town, at the cenotaph, where the names of the seven local men who were killed in the war are engraved on a brass plaque. Frances and her parents attend because of Uncle Vince. Frances thinks Uncle Vince's name should be on the plaque because he's not here to be remembered in person, but her mother says that's not how it works, and there are rules about these things, and besides, he was in the British army.

Frances looks through the small crowd to see if any other grade threes are here, and she spies Silas Chance, wearing his war medals.

"I didn't know Indians fought in the war," she says, not being able to put the painted movie Indians on horseback in the same war as marching soldiers in uniforms. When Silas sees her looking at him, he winks. Frances waves then, and her mother notices and grabs her hand and holds on to it.

There's a cold wind and the sky is heavy with gray November clouds. A boy from the school band plays a hymn on his trumpet after they read out the names of the men who sacrificed their lives for freedom. When the ceremony is over, everyone goes to the hall for coffee, glad to get in out of the cold. Frances stands by her father while he visits with a man she doesn't know, and when people start lining up for coffee and sweets, he says to Frances, "Be a luv and bring me a piece of cake. And no eating all the frosting on your way back." She squeezes into the line and loads a paper plate with a big piece of white cake topped with chocolate. She sticks her finger in the chocolate and licks, and then she sees Silas Chance come in the door and stand at the back of the room with his cap in his hand. Instead of taking the cake to her father, she crosses the room to Mr. Chance and holds it out to him.

He doesn't say anything. He just takes the plate and nods. Frances holds his cap for him while he eats the cake with a plastic fork. After it's gone, she thinks he might do the nickel trick again, but he doesn't. He puts his cap back on, tousles her hair, and leaves. The cold air blows in the door. Frances goes back to the lineup to get another piece of cake for her father.

A few weeks later, Silas Chance dies. Her parents say he was hit by a car when he was walking on the highway, and that's all they know. Frances listens to her mother talking on the phone about Silas—"I just can't fathom what the man was thinking, walking on the highway in the cold and dark; something's not right about that"—and then the topic changes. To Dooley Sullivan.

"His poor grandfather," her mother says. "Tobias Sullivan is not my favorite person, I'll grant you that, but still. The boy would have ended up in foster care if it weren't for him. Well, that's what happens when teenagers mix cars and alcohol. It's a good thing he did hit that bridge or everyone would be blaming Silas Chance on him. It's a good thing he has an alibi."

After her mother gets off the phone, Frances asks, "What? What about Dooley Sullivan?"

"He was driving drunk and crashed into a bridge," her mother says. "A Good Samaritan happened along and pulled him out of his truck just before it burst into flames. He's lucky to be alive. And the Samaritan too."

"Is he going to die?"

"No. Now stop thinking about him. Stop thinking about this whole ugly business."

Frances wants to know what foster care is, and her mother says never mind. She wants to know if Silas is dead for sure— maybe there's been a mistake and the man on the highway was someone else.

Her mother says, "These things happen, don't they?"

Frances can't help it; she starts to cry.

Her mother says, "What's this about? You didn't even know the man. He was the renter." She goes to put her hand on Frances's head, but Frances pulls away.

That afternoon, two RCMP officers come to the farm to ask Frances's parents some questions, because Silas Chance lived in their house. Then Frances's father goes away with them, following their police car in his truck, to open the door to the rental house so they can look inside. When her father gets home a few hours later, he says it's true what they'd heard—that Silas Chance had died as the result of a hit-and-run and the police were searching for the driver. He looks as though he might be about to say more, but then Frances's mother looks in her direction and says, "Little pitchers and their ears."

After she's had a bath that night, Frances lies in bed and listens to the murmur of her parents' voices. She knows they'll be talking about Silas, and also Dooley. She keeps picturing Silas being hit on the side of the highway, flying through the air and landing in the snow. And then she thinks about Dooley being pulled from his red truck just in time, and she can see it in flames and Dooley's clothes on fire and his bones all broken. And then she thinks of Uncle Vince,

collapsing in front of the post office and landing right on top
of his letter from Bertie, and her father saying, "If I go first."
She still remembers that. She tries counting and tapping
her fingers, but she doesn't believe in it anymore. That was
for babies, grade ones. She falls asleep, but she wakes up
screaming and her parents let her get into bed with them.

"Go to sleep, Frances," her mother says. "Nothing bad is
going to happen to anyone in this house."

She tries to go to sleep, but she can't. She pictures Dooley wrapped up in bandages in the big hospital in Yellowhead,
not the one in Elliot. She wonders who hit Silas, and whether
the police will catch him. Then she thinks about her father
and his eyes, and how he hit someone once—Dooley in his
truck.

She whispers to her mother, "Will they think Dad did it?
Because of his eyes?"

She'd thought her father was asleep, but he sits up then,
in the dark.

"This is your fault, Alice," he says, throwing back the covers and swinging his legs over the side of the bed. "Frances,
in spite of what your mother tells you about my eyesight, I
have never hit even a rabbit, so you can get that thought out
of your head." Then he adds, "Other than Dooley Sullivan's
truck that time—but he was driving too fast." Then he leaves
and goes to sleep in Frances's bed.

"Your father never drives at night, Frances," her mother
says. Then she says, "Stop thinking about all this or you'll
make yourself sick."

The next week, Silas's sister comes to the farm to get a
key to the rental house so she can clean out her brother's
things. Frances's mother is in town. Frances stands next to

her father in the yard while he talks to Silas's sister, who does not smile, not once. Her father says they're very sorry about Silas; he was a good tenant, and never caused them any trouble.

Silas's sister snaps, "Did you expect him to be trouble?"

Frances's father is taken aback and says, "No, we didn't expect anything in particular."

Then he goes into the house for the key and Frances is left alone with Silas's sister. She seems to be studying Frances. "I'm a teacher," she says. "What grade are you in? Grade three, I'd guess."

Frances nods, wary now of being in the presence of a teacher. She says, "My dad's going blind." She's not sure why she says it.

"You mean he can't see? He doesn't look blind to me."

"He never drives at night," she says, because now it's possible that Silas's sister will think her father hit Silas on the highway, and it's her fault for spilling the beans. She is about to say, "My dad didn't do it," but then Silas's sister says, "Well, that must be hard—being blind on a farm. It sounds dangerous."

"You know what the blind carpenter said?" Frances asks.

"No, what?"

"I picked up a hammer and saw."

Silas's sister doesn't laugh.

"He was going to show me checkers," Frances says.

"Silas was?"

"Yes, because we don't play checkers at school."

Frances's father comes back then with the key. Silas's sister takes it, saying she will leave it under the mat at the rental house when she's done.

When her mother gets home, Frances tells her about Silas's sister stopping by for the key.

Frances says, "She's a teacher," and her mother says, "Oh, I don't think so. Where did you get that idea?" Before Frances can answer, her mother says, "Well, it's over and done with. The man's things are out of the house, and the less I hear about it the better."

But not all of Silas's things are out of the house. The checkerboard and its pieces have been left on the table for Frances. Her mother wants to throw them out—"It's morbid"—but Frances insists on keeping them. She takes the game home in a plastic bag.

And it isn't over and done with either, as her mother had hoped, because Silas's sister speaks to a newspaper reporter in Yellowhead and says that her brother was left to die on the highway because he was an Indian. "Civil rights are not just for Negroes in the United States," she says. "It's time you people here woke up." Flyers start appearing around town, stapled to power poles and board fences, saying *Silas Chance, Someone Knows* and giving a phone number. There's one on a pole outside the school, close to where the school buses line up at four o'clock, and Frances stops to stare at it several days in a row, thinking about the meaning of "Someone knows," until a bus driver—not hers—sees her and gets out of his bus to tear down the flyer.

"They shouldn't be putting these up by the school," he says, crumpling the poster. "Anyway, it was Dooley Sullivan, that's who. They just got the time wrong."

"It wasn't Dooley," Frances says.

"Hurry up, get on your bus," the driver says. "You'll make everyone late."

She stomps her foot. "It wasn't Dooley Sullivan. You should have to take that back." She feels like she did that time she kicked over the chair in the kitchen after her mother came home from her shopping trip. If there were a chair handy, she'd kick it now.

"Don't you sass me, missy," the bus driver says, looking stern now, but not sure what to do with her. He's saved when her own bus driver calls to her. "Frances, train's leaving the station. All aboard. Them that's late get left behind."

Frances likes her driver. She gets on the bus.

A week later, the CBC sends men with cameras and microphones, and footage of Elliot appears on the national news, a reporter walking up Liberty Street until he comes to the one lonely house: Uncle Vince's house. Frances's mother doesn't like her house being on the news. People in Elliot don't like being on the news either; it makes them look bad. And what was Silas Chance doing on the highway in the dark anyway? they ask. He should have known better. Maybe he was drunk. Frances's mother claims that people in town are giving her suspicious looks, as though it's all her fault because of the house. As though the house is some kind of disgrace.

Basie says, "Judas Priest, give the damned thing away, then."

Instead, she locks it up and waits for people to forget about Silas Chance.

Frances's father teaches her to play checkers.

MARCH COMES, then Easter holidays from school. Alice decides to give the house a makeover. Frances watches as the hardware man claps the paint cans in his machine and shakes them up the way her mother shakes eggs in a jar for scrambling. When all the paint colors are mixed, Frances and her mother drive to Uncle Vince's house and unload the cans and set them on the kitchen floor. Frances looks at the empty coat hooks by the door and thinks of Silas's green cap.

The next day, Sunday, they take other supplies into town from the farm—paintbrushes, a stepladder, old sheets and rags. They drape sheets over the furniture, and after that, Frances and her mother go to town every day to paint the house. Pastel colors, a different one for each room. Pastels are all the rage, according to the magazines.

"This house is our backup plan," Frances's mother tells her. She's wearing rolled-up blue jeans and is halfway up a ladder in the kitchen with a paintbrush in her hand and a scarf on her head to protect her hair from the drips. "We can't farm if your father goes blind as a bat. Don't tell him I said that."

"I thought you said he wouldn't go blind."

"He might. You're old enough to understand that. Just don't tell him what I said about the house, the backup plan. He says wild horses won't get him into a house in town."

Frances doesn't want to live in town either.

"I'm bored," she says.

"We're not here to play old maid, if that's what you're thinking. Walk to the playground if you like. Maybe you'll see some schoolmates."

"I won't," Frances says. "Anyway, I don't like them. I've told you."

"How do you know you don't like them? You haven't tried."

Frances puts on her coat and boots and goes outside.

Across the street from the house and just beyond the unsold lots, there's a little rise, and at the top of it is a shrine to Our Lady of the Hill, who is Mary, according to Frances's mother. Mary is special to the Catholics, she says—the holy mother. The shrine consists of a fieldstone shelter with a neatly painted wooden Mary tucked into an alcove. It's there, according to Frances's mother, because a long time ago a young girl had a vision when she went to get the family's milk cow. She had the vision three evenings in a row, and then her sick mother got better. Frances's mother says the girl no doubt had been sick herself when she had the visions, and had seen Mary in a fever.

The snow starts falling again, and when Frances gets to the top of the hill, she studies Mary in her house, looking out at the snow. She wonders how the visions work, whether the wooden Mary turns into the real Mary. Whether, if Frances were Catholic, Mary would speak to her, and if so what she would say.

Frances knows about mazes from a library book, and the idea comes to her to create a maze in the snow with Mary in the middle. She pretends there are hedges where her boot tracks are and wonders if she'd be able to find her way out of her own puzzle if the hedges were really there. She makes the maze in a circle around the hill and is just about at the bottom when she sees three boys from school watching her from the road. When Frances sees them coming toward her, she knows her maze is done for.

"Hey, it's Loony-Moony," one of the boys says as they approach. He crosses himself before he joins the other two in stomping all over Frances's paths in the snow. She knows there's no point saying anything and leaves.

"I hate boys," Frances says when she gets inside the house.

"That's good," her mother says. "Keep it that way for about another twenty years, or at least until you get a good education."

Her mother is always talking about education, as if it's the answer to everything. There's a health inspector who comes to check the barn and change the certificate on the wall of the sterile room, a woman, and after she's gone Frances's mother always says, "That could be you someday, Frances. A university education will get you a good job. I wish I'd had that chance."

Frances doesn't want the job of inspecting cow barns.

There's a crow on a telephone pole outside the window. She can see his beak opening in a caw, but of course she can't hear anything. It's still too early in the spring for crows. She knows about camouflage. They should wait until after the snow is gone to come back, because a black crow on white snow is not good where nature is concerned.

"I wonder if a magpie is partly white because of winter," Frances says. She knows magpies stay year-round, at least some of them, and they don't change color like bush rabbits do.

Her mother says, "Of course, you can always marry a farmer and work your fingers to the bone three hundred and sixty-five days a year."

"I wouldn't marry a blind one," Frances says.

Her mother shakes her paintbrush at her and says, "You watch what you say about your father, young lady." Pale yellow paint specks appear on the linoleum.

She hadn't meant to criticize her father. She looks at the crow, but then she starts to feel sick.

"I might throw up," she says.

Her mother looks at her and then jumps down from the ladder. "You're white as a sheet," she says, grabbing Frances with one hand and setting down the loaded paintbrush. She runs her to the bathroom and holds Frances's head over the toilet, but nothing happens.

They return to the kitchen and her mother gets up on her ladder again. "You're sure you're not sick?" she says. "It's flu season."

There's a bag of Fig Newtons on the table and Frances takes one to prove that she's fine. Her mother's empty teacup is on the table by the cookies, along with several old copies of the Yellowhead newspaper. The top one now has a splat of yellow paint on it from when her mother shook her brush at her. She picks up her mother's cup and reads her tea leaves. "You're going to kiss a stranger," she says. It's the only thing she knows about tea leaves.

There's an article about Silas Chance on the front page of the old paper, so Frances sits down at the table to read it. It says lots of things she already knows, but there are a few new details. There were tire tracks at the scene, as though someone had stopped and then drove on again, and footprints. A person might have left his vehicle to see what he'd hit. And Silas hadn't died right away—there was evidence suggesting he'd tried to get to town for help and hadn't made it. The police are asking anyone with information to call in. Silas's sister, whose name is Darlene Cyr, is also pleading for someone to come forward. She says that her little brother was a good man and a war veteran. She says that leaving him without help is the same as murder, and she will not rest until she knows who killed him, and someone out there knows.

"What are you reading?" Frances's mother asks.

"About Silas," Frances says. "His sister's name is Darlene Cyr."

"His sister has gone a little crazy with grief," her mother says, getting down from the ladder to take the newspaper away from Frances. "She needs to put this behind her for her own good. Anger causes cancer." She puts the paper on the floor and plunks her can of paint on it and then taps down the lid, being careful not to splatter paint.

Anger causes cancer? What?

"Are we going home now?" Frances asks. "I want to go home."

"Soon," her mother says. "I have to clean up."

Frances puts on her outdoor clothes again and goes outside to wait. There's no point going up the hill to check on the maze. Instead, she walks down Liberty Street and away from town, in the direction of home. She walks in the ditch and pretends it's a path in a maze. A crow flies along the road in front of her (*is it the same one?*) and she pretends it's a magic bird that can lead her to the exit of the maze. Or maybe the crow is really Mary, and she's seeing a vision. It starts to snow harder, and it gets more difficult to see in front of her, but Frances thinks if she just follows the ditch she'll get home. Then her mother's car pulls up alongside her, and even though her mother is angry, Frances is happy to get in because her ears are cold and her feet are getting numb.

"What if this snow had turned into a whiteout, Frances? Or what if someone came along and hit you because they couldn't see you?"

"You mean like Silas?" Frances asks.

"Yes, but please, let's not talk about that anymore."

Frances thinks about Silas's sister saying, "Someone out there knows." It must be true.

"Was it snowing the night Silas died?" Frances asks.

"No," her mother says. "Well, maybe. Maybe that was it."

The land between town and the farm is a mix of bush and cultivated fields. Frances looks out the window and watches a snowy field flash by, and then a line of trees, a push-up pile from someone's recent clearing, another field, a frozen slough, another line of bush. Everything passes in a blur of falling snowflakes that look as though they're traveling sideways, parallel to the ground, and not down from the sky.

She's wondering why this is, when her mother slams on the brakes and the car fishtails and stops, and Frances almost ends up on the floor. When she looks out the front window, there's a huge bull moose not more than a few feet in front of them. Its back is white with snow, and it's in the middle of the road, staring at them. Everything is perfectly still and quiet, even the car, because it has stalled.

"Are you all right?" Frances's mother asks in an almost-whisper. Frances nods. Then her mother says, again in a whisper, "Don't move," which doesn't make a lot of sense. Where is she going to move to? Still, Frances finds herself holding her breath. When the moose turns and trots into the ditch and away across the field, she watches its long legs lifting and reaching until it disappears, floating, into the white world outside the car windows.

"Well, that was close," Frances's mother says, this time in her normal voice. "Look at my hands. They're still shaking. I have no idea where it came from. I almost hit it."

That night, Frances throws up in her bed, and it turns out she really is sick. She has a stomach flu that lasts a week, and then her mother gets it and can't finish the painting in the Liberty Street house until they're both better. By the time she's able to get back to work on the house, the temperature has dropped again and Easter break is over and Frances doesn't want to walk from school to the house, so she takes the bus home as usual. She wonders what would have happened if she and her mother had hit the moose, and whether they would be dead now, the poor moose too, and her mother's car all smashed up and sitting on the Texaco lot next to Dooley's burned-out truck. She, Frances, disappearing the way the moose had, only really gone, not just hidden in trees and snow.

She has a dream about Kaw-Liga that night, skating around on her father's slough. Frances is cleaning the snow off the ice and she keeps hitting wet patches where the ice is thin. Then Kaw-Liga hits one and falls into the slough, and he's gone.

Like Uncle Vince.

Like Silas Chance.

But not Dooley Sullivan. Word circulates a few days later that Dooley has come home to the hospital in Elliot, and without telling anyone what she is doing, Frances takes a quarter from her piggy bank and goes to the drugstore at noon and buys a get-well card.

"Who's this for?" the clerk asks, and she says no one.

She sits on the bench in front of the bank and writes, carefully, *To Dooley, I hope you feel better soon*, and signs it *Frances Mary Moon*. On the envelope, she writes Dooley's name, and then she walks to the hospital and hands the card to the nurse at the reception desk, who looks at the name and at Frances, and then takes Frances's hand and squeezes it and says, "Thanks, sweetie. I'll be sure to give this to him."

She's late getting back to school and tells the teacher she was "running an errand." It's a phrase she's heard her mother use. It works.

She gets out her speller and tries to concentrate on the new words the teacher is writing on the blackboard.

Thankful that not everyone dies.

3. Dooley's Window

FRANCES'S MOTHER is on the telephone, trying to rent Uncle Vince's house again, even though the last renter—an evangelical pastor named Billy Helper who'd lived in the house for a year—ran off in his flea-bitten fur coat before Alice got a chance to throw him out on his ear for writing her several bad checks. The Not-So-Reverend Helper had generally caused a commotion in town when he failed to heal the many unfortunates who had given him Sunday dinner and what he called "donations." He'd offered to lay his hands on Frances's father and heal his failing eyesight, but Basie had said no thanks, and then later, when Alice said she'd found the offer presumptuous, he said, "I imagine we should just turn a blind eye to it," which Frances always thought was hilarious.

What Frances hadn't liked about Billy Helper—besides the fact that he resembled a mangy hulking animal in the fur coat—was that he called her Girlene no matter how many times she said her name was Frances. She likes to think that he was the one who hit Silas Chance on the highway, even though she knows it isn't true. Billy Helper didn't own a car. After Frances's mother gets off the phone with the potential new tenant, she reports the gist of the conversation as this:

"I'm an old woman but not ancient, don't get that idea. Does the house have stairs?"

"One bedroom upstairs under the peak," Alice said. "But the main bedroom and bathroom are on the ground floor. Four steps up to the front door with a good handrail. It's a quaint house—a cottage, really."

"I'm quaint myself, so that much is a match."

Then Mrs. Esme Bigalow—"Call me Esme, I insist"—told Alice that she'd recently had her hip replaced and found herself disinclined to remain in her own home in Yellowhead, which had the bedrooms and bathroom upstairs, not to mention a roof that needed new shingles and a yard the size of Buckingham Palace. She needed a new place to live before winter set in. She liked small towns. She'd grown up on a farm and taught for years in a country school.

"You sound trustworthy," she said to Alice. "Is there any reason I shouldn't rent your house?"

"Do you drive a car? It's a bit of a walk to Main Street."

"Walk, walk, walk, the doctor tells me. He says it will keep the Grim Reaper in the hold. I don't know where he got that idea."

"The house is fully furnished," Alice said. "Wouldn't you want your furniture?"

"Sick of the lot of it."

Alice reluctantly agreed to rent her the house—reluctantly because the whole thing sounded a little fishy to her. Why would an old lady want to move to Elliot?

A few days later, a check for three months' rent arrives in the mail along with a letter from Mrs. Bigalow explaining that it will take her that long to get her house organized and her hip rehabilitated. Alice is impressed that the letter is neatly written, and that Mrs. Bigalow hasn't asked for the house to be held, rent-free, for that period of time. Maybe she was wrong to be skeptical.

But toward the end of September, a week before Mrs. Bigalow is scheduled to move into the house, another call comes
from her at suppertime. Frances and her father listen to Alice's side of the conversation with interest because they can
tell some complicated negotiating is going on. It begins with
"Oh dear, that *is* a problem" and "I'm not sure what I can do to
help you out," and somewhere in the middle Alice says, "Well,
I suppose I do have some shopping." The conversation ends
with her scribbling directions on a piece of paper and saying,
"All right, then. I'll be there on Saturday, early in the afternoon," and then the receiver goes back on its cradle.

The look on her face means she's agreed to do something
she doesn't want to—that is, provide transportation for the
new tenant and her possessions.

On Saturday, Frances and her mother drive to Yellowhead
to collect the Widow Bigalow, which is what Basie has been
calling her. They shop first at the bulk grocery store so Alice
can stock up on baking supplies, and then they go to the A&W
drive-in and order a Mama Burger and a Teen Burger, even
though Frances is only ten and not close to being a teenager
(*so stop pretending that you are*). A girl brings their order on a
tray and hangs it on Alice's driver's-side window, and after the
girl is gone, Alice says, "That's what university education is
for—to keep you from jobs like this."

After the A&W, they follow Mrs. Bigalow's directions and
find her sitting on a wooden rocking chair in her empty living
room with her cane across her lap, her suitcases and belongings around her, and an orange cat in a wire carry case.

She introduces herself and tells Frances to call her Esme.

"You call her Mrs. Bigalow," her mother says.

There's a pickup truck loaded with furniture out front,

and for a moment Alice worries it might be Mrs. Bigalow's furniture and she's decided to take it with her, but it belongs to the new owners. Mrs. Bigalow won't let them move it in until she's gone. She says that even though she's glad to be leaving, she doesn't want to see anyone else's possessions in her house. They load her boxes and suitcases into the car, and when only the rocking chair is left, Mrs. Bigalow says she'd like to take it along, it's the chair she rocked her babies in, and how can Alice say no to that. The driver of the pickup sees her struggling with the chair and comes to help, and they decide the only place it will fit is the front if they slide the bench seat all the way back, so that's where it goes and Frances gets in the back between Mrs. Bigalow and the cat. The neighbor's dog barks at them the whole time they're packing the car, and as they pull away from the house Mrs. Bigalow says, "I won't miss that dog, that's one thing."

"I bet the cat won't either," Frances says, poking her fingers into the cage. The cat spits at her.

Alice says that she feels a bit ridiculous with only the rocking chair for company in the front seat. Then she asks Mrs. Bigalow about her family, and the new tenant tells them that she had two sons who'd both passed away. "The younger one signed up and was killed in the war," she says. "My husband never got over that, and I don't suppose the other boy did either. He developed a problem with the drink, and his liver killed him."

"That's terrible," Alice says. "I'm sorry to hear it."

"Well, it was his own fault, wasn't it? Men are foolish, I find."

"We got bombed in that war, in England," Frances says. "In London."

"Not *we*, Frances," her mother says. "You weren't born yet. But yes, in the Blitz. We moved to Canada after the war."

"Why are you moving to Elliot?" Frances asks Mrs. Bigalow.

Mrs. Bigalow says, "You have to swear to keep it a secret."

"Oh, I don't encourage Frances to make promises like that," Alice says. "Not with strangers, no offense."

Mrs. Bigalow says, "Very wise, a good rule." Then she says, "Just between the three of us and the rocking chair, I was having a problem with my love life. There are a whole lot of old men out there who still think of themselves as Romeo. And old men are drawn to girls like me who can still cook. I'm a pretty good cook, if I do say so. Word gets out and they're at your door. Like hounds to bacon. My advice to you, Miss Frances, is don't learn to cook."

That's it. That's the story. Not a story worth a promise of silence.

"Do you by any chance know a man named Tobias Sullivan?" Mrs. Bigalow asks Alice. "I believe he lives in Elliot."

Tobias Sullivan. Now, *that* catches Frances's attention.

"The old school principal, you mean?" Alice says. "Yes, he's still in Elliot. Why do you ask?"

"No reason. I knew him many years ago. I doubt he'd remember me."

"Do you know Dooley?" Frances asks.

"Dooley. No, I don't believe I know any Dooley."

Frances starts to tell her about the crash—"He was driving drunk and almost died"—but her mother says, "Never mind that, it's gossip," so instead Frances asks Mrs. Bigalow, "Do you know Darlene Cyr? She lives in Yellowhead."

"I don't believe I know her either."

Alice says, "Why would she know Darlene Cyr? Honestly, Frances."

Then Mrs. Bigalow says, "Oh, I might be mad as a March hare, it's possible," and after that she falls asleep and snores with her mouth open. When they pull into a roadside station for gas a while later, she snores right through the stop.

Once they're back on the road, Frances feels herself getting sleepy and leans her head against Mrs. Bigalow to avoid the spitting cat in the carry case. She closes her eyes and wonders if anyone will tell Mrs. Bigalow that she's moving into a house that's been on the news—one whose former tenants include a dead man and a runaway crook of a preacher. She falls asleep with the cat still spitting in the cage next to her, and she dreams about Dooley Sullivan for the first time in ages. She's standing on the bank of a river and Dooley is waving at her from a bridge with his clothes on fire. She yells at him to jump, jump into the water, but he doesn't.

When she wakes up her heart is pounding, and it's two hours later and they're already in Elliot and the car is mostly unpacked. Her mother is struggling to get the rocking chair out of the front seat.

"I had a bad dream," she says to her mother, feeling cranky.

"Not now, Frances. Please be quiet unless you can see a way to get this infernal chair out of here." Her mother pounds on one of the rockers to edge it below the doorframe.

"When can we go home?"

"Soon. Go into the house and fix Mrs. Bigalow a sandwich so she doesn't starve on us tonight. I left a few groceries in the fridge."

Frances goes inside and assembles a sandwich from the bread and lettuce and sliced meat in the fridge, but Mrs. Bigalow is now sound asleep on the couch, so she leaves the sandwich on a plate in the kitchen. Her mother finally gets the rocking chair into the house, and then she makes sure everything is hooked up and working—the phone, the hot water, the heat thermostat—and she wakes Mrs. Bigalow and tells her about the sandwich, then says that they're leaving.

On the way home, she says, "I wish she had told me about the cat. I don't like surprises."

Frances says, "I told you I had a bad dream, you know."

"I know. Stop pouting. What was it about?"

"Never mind. It's too late to tell it now."

"Suit yourself," her mother says.

When they get in the house, Frances's dad says, "That was a long day. How's the Widow Bigalow?"

Alice says, "She's eighty years old if she's a day, and she might have lost her mind. She tells wild yarns. I'm going to have to go to town on Monday morning and get the woman's groceries, and what she'll do for food tomorrow, I don't know. We'll have to take her a meal."

Basie says, "You've gone soft."

"She's here for Tobias Sullivan," Alice says. "She didn't actually say it, but you just wait and see."

"I'm going to bed," Frances says. "Since no one seems to care that I had a bad dream."

When Frances is in her own bed she decides that if she dreams about Dooley on fire again, she will *make* him jump from the bridge into the water. If she has to, she'll run onto the bridge and push him off.

She doesn't dream about him, though. She has the most boring dream ever—about Mrs. Bigalow's orange cat trying to catch a moth on the step of Uncle Vince's house. It goes on and on.

Frances's mother is right about Tobias Sullivan. Not long after Mrs. Bigalow moves in, she calls the farm and asks if Frances can walk to the house at noon hour one day that week and have lunch with her. Her parents have misgivings, but they agree. After grilled cheese sandwiches, Mrs. Bigalow asks Frances to run an errand—that is, deliver a note to Mr. Sullivan's house, which is near the school.

"But don't tell anyone," she says.

Frances knocks on the side door of the house she knows is Tobias Sullivan's, and when an old man answers, she hands him the envelope.

"What's this?" he asks.

"It's from Mrs. Bigalow."

"I don't know any Mrs. Bigalow," he says, and then he insists that Frances come in while he reads the letter, which she is happy to do because this is where Dooley Sullivan used to live, before the accident. She doesn't know where he lives now. Her mother says he moved away after they let him out of the hospital.

She steps inside and stands in the kitchen while Mr. Sullivan slits open the envelope and takes out the letter. There's a bookcase full of cookbooks against the wall, and pots and pans of all different sizes hanging from a rack on the ceiling. She's never seen such a thing. She looks for photographs or other signs of Dooley, but there are none.

When Mr. Sullivan has finished reading the letter,

he turns to Frances and says, "Mrs. Bigalow, you say?" He wheezes when he breathes like he has a bad cold.

She nods, and then he says, "Well, off you go, then," and she walks back to school and gets there just in time for the bell.

She doesn't tell her parents about the letter.

Six months later, Esme Bigalow becomes Esme Sullivan. It turns out that she and Tobias knew each other as young teachers over fifty years ago, and then he broke her heart and married the fiancée she didn't know he had in his hometown of Kingston, Ontario. She thought she'd never see him again, but then a year ago she heard the name Tobias Sullivan being called at her ophthalmologist's office in Yellowhead, where she was waiting for a cataract checkup. She looked around the waiting room to see who would stand up, but he had apparently missed his appointment. Then she did a little private investigation with the help of the chatty receptionist and learned he'd been living in Elliot for many years and was now a widower. That's why she'd rented the house on Liberty Street. She'd set her sights on the prize she lost the first time around—that is, Tobias Sullivan.

Frances and her parents are invited to the small wedding in Tobias's house. One of the first things Frances wants to know when they arrive is whether Dooley is there. No, Esme says (she's Esme now, rather than Mrs. Bigalow, having insisted so many times that Alice gave up), and she shakes her head as though Dooley is a subject not spoken about in this house.

The living room is decorated with bunches of pink and white tissue flowers, and the guests sit in a semicircle of chairs for the ceremony. Besides the Moons, there are a few neighbors, one other retired teacher from the school, and the two remaining members of Tobias's gourmet cooking club, which used to be a *going concern* in Elliot, they say, but now most of the members have passed on. After Esme becomes Mrs. Sullivan, she whispers to Frances, "Remember what I told you about men preferring girls like me for their cooking? Well, look what I found: a man who can cook better than I can!"

Frances is the only child at the wedding, although she'll be eleven her next birthday, so she's not really a child. Still, Tobias Sullivan keeps looking at her as if he expects her to do something wrong. When she goes down the hall to find the bathroom, she decides she *will* do something wrong if that's what he expects, and she snoops around for signs of Dooley. Next to the bathroom there's a small bedroom that she guesses must have been his, but when she looks inside there's nothing there but a bed, a dresser, and a picture of a sunset on the wall. She looks in the dresser drawers, but they're completely empty. No clothes, no photographs, no toys a boy might have played with in his room. It's as though Tobias has erased Dooley from his life. She goes to the kitchen for a drink of water and once again sees the pots and pans hanging from the ceiling and decides the house must have mice. The orange cat could have caught them if he hadn't been moved to the Moons' farm because Tobias is allergic. Now he's learning to be a barn cat, whether he likes it or not.

After everyone has coffee and wedding cake, the guests leave so the bride and groom can rest up for their honeymoon bus trip to the Black Hills. The retired teacher who was at the wedding is still young enough to drive, and the next morning he takes them to Yellowhead to meet their tour bus. When they return ten days later, Esme invites the Moons for supper to thank them for their part in her relocation to Elliot and subsequent reunion with Tobias. Tobias makes the meal of roast pork with herbs. Although he insists he's in charge of the kitchen, Esme has to climb on a stool whenever he needs a pot or a utensil from the rack on the ceiling (which doesn't seem like a good idea for an old lady who broke her hip, Frances's mother whispers to Basie). After supper, Tobias sets up a screen and projector, and they all look at slides of Deadwood and the faces of American presidents carved into a mountain. They can hear Tobias wheezing over the whir of the slide projector, even though there is no longer a cat in the house.

On the way home, Frances's mother says, "I don't know what she was thinking. Well, she made her bed, didn't she?" Then she asks, "Why are those pots hanging from the ceiling anyway?"

"Mice," Frances says.

Uncle Vince's house goes up for rent again, but there are no takers.

JUNE. The end of grade five and the last week of school. There's not much work, just a lot of outdoor activity. They pick teams and play softball, and Frances gets hit in the head by a fly ball because she doesn't see it coming right for her. Still, her head stops the ball and a boy picks it up and throws it to second and the batter is out, so it's not as big a humiliation as it could have been. She feels kind of dizzy for a while after being hit in the head, but she doesn't tell anyone.

On the last day—the day the report cards get handed

out—Myrna Samples shows up wearing a bra. Daphne Rose, who now sits across from Frances, pokes her and asks if she's noticed. Frances thinks Daphne must be wrong, but when she looks she can see Myrna's new pointy breasts under her sweater. Myrna's bra makes Frances feel more sick than getting hit in the head with a softball. *It's grade five. Grade eight girls wear bras, not grade fives.* When Myrna gets up and waltzes to the front of the room to sharpen her pencil (*who needs to sharpen a pencil on the last day of school?*), the girls all stare and the boys whisper and make jokes until the teacher tells them to be quiet. Frances *never* wants to wear a bra (brassieres, her mother calls them). She is suddenly terrified that her breasts will begin to grow, and what will she do then?

She worries all summer, even though there's no sign of breasts sprouting on her chest. Her parents decide she's spending too much time moping, and she needs to do something useful, such as help with the chores. She hates slopping around in her rubber boots, pushing scoops of stinking muck into a channel in the barn floor and then out the door for her father to haul away with the tractor. She complains constantly about the smell, and she's so slow that her parents give up and send her back to the house.

"You'll never make a farmer's wife," her father says.

Her mother tells her she'd better start planning a future that doesn't require manual labor, since she seems to be allergic to work as well as to milk.

"I wasn't meant to clean up cow manure," Frances says, sulking.

"Then start thinking about what you *were* meant for," her mother says.

Frances goes back to worrying about the gross unfairness

of girls having to grow breasts. Myrna and her bra ruin a perfectly good summer.

Just before school starts again, Alice finds a renter for the Liberty Street house. A new United Church minister moves to town, a thirtyish single man with a Beatles haircut. Even though Alice is not a churchgoer herself, and she doesn't think much of his hair, she hopes she can't go wrong with a United Church minister. He gives her six months of post-dated rent checks and says he doesn't mind the sound of trains passing; in fact, he likes it. He also likes Bob Dylan. Do they know Bob Dylan? He sings a few lines of "The Times They Are a-Changin'."

"Isn't he the one who has that song on the radio about drugs?" Alice asks.

"I'm pretty sure the lyrics were misinterpreted," the minister says.

He turns out to be a good tenant. He pays his rent on time, and he even knows how to fix things like dripping taps. He tells Frances that in a few years' time, she can join the teen club he'll be starting at the church. Teenagers need clubs and sports, he says, to keep them on the right track. When Esme's orange cat disappears, they find out that he's made his way back to town and moved in with the minister. They let him stay there, since both the cat and the tenant seem happy with the arrangement.

Frances manages to get through most of the next year, grade six, before her chest does betray her and she starts to grow breasts. It feels like the end of the world. Her mother says, "Oh, for heaven's sake, it happens to all girls."

Which is true. By the end of grade seven, half of the girls in her class are wearing bras, including her. Frances's new constant worry is that a boy will grab her bra at the back and snap it. *What is wrong with them?* And the girls are just as bad, the way they put up with the boys snapping their bra straps and making crude gestures, and even seem to like it. She can't understand at all how everything has changed, turning the classroom into some kind of zoo. She tells her mother what's going on and Alice says it sounds as if the girls in her class are all turning boy crazy.

"You, Frances," she says, "are going to get the hell out of here, the same way I did, only you'll actually land some place other than a cow farm because you'll have a good education."

What? Get out of Elliot?

Where would she go? The unknown destination is as remote to Frances as outer space, even though she's not meant for cow farming. She imagines herself drifting toward the moon without any kind of spacesuit or breathing tubes.

That summer, a man really does walk on the moon.

They watch on TV.

THE WEEK before school starts again—grade eight, the last year before high school—Frances's mother runs into Esme in the drugstore in town and learns that she and Tobias are about to leave on another bus trip, this time through Europe. They're to catch a Greyhound to the city and then fly to Toronto, where they'll meet up with their tour at the airport.

"The stupidest thing I've ever heard of," Alice tells Frances and Basie. "You should have seen the batch of medications she was picking up for Tobias. He's no more able to make a trip to Europe than he's able to climb Mount Everest." Alice shakes her head and says thank goodness Esme Bigalow—or Sullivan, rather—is no longer their business.

Only that turns out to be not quite true. A week later, Frances and her parents are watching TV when the phone rings. It's Esme, calling from a payphone in Toronto. Tobias has picked up a cold and the tour company won't let him continue on to Europe. They're going to spend the night in a hotel before they fly west again, and Esme wonders if Alice would mind driving to the city the next day, a Saturday, to pick them up when they land at the airport. It's a big request, she knows, from someone who isn't even family, but she can't think of anyone else to call. Tobias's friends are either unavailable or too old to drive to the city, and Tobias is not able to make the trip home by bus.

Alice agrees, no questions asked, which is a bit of a surprise to Basie because she's never driven any farther than Yellowhead, and she's certainly never driven in the city.

"Frances can come along to help navigate," she says. "We can get a city map at a gas station." Then she says, as though this thought has been lodged in her head for some time, "I'd like to drive by the university, see what it looks like. It's a good school, so I hear, and less expensive than some of those bigger universities. Maybe we could arrange a tour. Well, I suppose not, on a weekend."

Frances has no interest in the university—good or cheap or otherwise—but she'd like to see what the city looks like, a bigger city than Yellowhead. She imagines pizza parlors, hippies, the Mod Squad.

They leave early and find their way from one highway to the next, west, south, and then west again, arriving at the city limits four hours later, without incident. The land is flat and the buildings of downtown rise above the industrial outskirts in which they find themselves. "It should be straightforward," Alice tells Frances, who has the newly acquired city map open on her lap. "We just keep going west and watch for the airport signs." Frances examines the map and reports that the street they're on leads almost to the airport; there's just one turn after they get through downtown.

"Downtown?" Alice says. "You mean we have to drive through downtown? That can't be right." At the first break in the traffic, she pulls into a strip mall so she can look at the map herself.

"You used to live in London," Frances says. "There must be lots of traffic there."

"No one I knew in London owned a car," Alice says, trying to find where she is on the map. "There was no petrol then. Gas, I mean."

It's warm and they both roll down their windows to catch a breeze. Frances sees a convenience store in the mall and asks if she can get them each a cold drink, and her mother says yes, go, and gives her some change from her purse. Frances returns with two bottles of Mountain Dew, opens the passenger door, and is about to slide in when she is approached by a blonde woman in white cowboy boots. At the same time, she sees a tall man with jet-black hair approach her mother's side of the car, open the door, and ask her to step out.

"Would you mind getting into the backseat?" the blonde woman says to Frances. "Please."

Frances feels her heart begin to beat a little faster and she looks to her mother to see what she should do, but her mother is getting into the backseat on the driver's side while the man holds the seatback against the steering wheel for her. Frances doesn't know what to do other than get in, trying not to spill the two open bottles of soda. For a moment, she wonders if the man and woman are undercover police officers in need of a car, like on television, but she soon realizes that that isn't the case.

Once the couple are in the front seat and the doors are closed, the woman asks Frances's mother, "Do you mind if I have a look in your purse?" but doesn't wait for an answer before she starts rifling though it.

Frances waits. Waits for her mother to speak up, to give the pair a piece of her mind, to turn into the ferocious mother who once strangled a rooster and tell these tossers to get out of her car right this minute and hand her purse back.

It doesn't happen.

"Don't hurt us," Alice says, her terrified voice sounding unfamiliar to Frances. "Please don't hurt us."

Then she goes silent and sits, frozen, staring at the back of the seat in front of her while the man plays with the radio dial and the woman empties her purse.

"No fags," the woman says to the man. "I guess she doesn't smoke."

The man puts the car in gear and drives them first to a gas station to buy cigarettes, and next to a grocery store. While the man stays in the car with the captives, smoking, the woman goes inside with Alice's wallet and returns with several bags of groceries and a box of diapers. Then they leave the parking lot, obviously on their way to someplace else.

Frances is so completely puzzled by her mother's submissive behavior that it becomes more frightening than the couple in the front seat, who are acting as though this is a day like any other. The woman talks to herself in such an ordinary way—"You know, I think I might have left a stove burner on. No, I remember now, I turned it off, I'm pretty sure"—while the man guides them through traffic as if he's out for a routine day of running errands. *Hey*, Frances wants to say, *we're back here, in case you haven't noticed*, but she's not quite brave enough, or sure enough that the two are simply stealing their money. She keeps sneaking glances at her mother, who appears to be almost catatonic, to have gone somewhere else.

"Say something to them," she finally whispers, and her mother says, "Shush." Then she reaches over and picks up Frances's hand, which she hasn't done in many years, and Frances immediately snatches it back. She knows what the gesture means—that her mother can't think of a way to get them out of this, that they're dependent on hand-holding to see them safe again. Her mother closes her eyes and seems to be praying, even though she doesn't believe in God.

They stop next at a liquor store for a case of beer, then at Zellers for a plastic toy garage and a Barbie doll, and finally for takeaway Chinese food at a little hole of a place behind a bowling alley, as though they are simply shopping for every-day things. When Alice's purse runs out of money, the woman turns to her and asks, "Do you have any more cash?" and Alice shakes her head no and says again, "Please don't hurt us."

The woman says, "Why would we do that? You've bor-rowed us your car. It's a super car, by the way. Well main-tained. Isn't that right, hon?" Then she asks Frances, "You don't have any money, do you? I don't see a purse." Frances says no, and then she finds the courage to say, "If I had one, I wouldn't give it to you."

"Frances," her mother says.

"And we didn't *borrow* you our car," Frances says. "You took it."

"Be quiet, Frances, for God's sake." Her mother's voice at such a high pitch, about to tip over into hysteria.

"Now, now," the blonde woman says. "No squabbling in the backseat." Then she turns to the driver again and says, "I guess that's it for shopping. Anyway, we're almost out of gas. We'd better get home and put the ice cream in the freezer. It's likely melting."

They drive to a sorry-looking house with an old couch in the front yard, stuffing spilling out of the cushions, and they both get out of the car, leaving the doors wide open, to unload their loot from the trunk. Then, for the first time since he got in the driver's seat, the man speaks to Frances and her mother. He sticks his head back in the car and asks them if they want to come inside, where a party is promised.

Alice shakes her head.

The man turns to Frances and says, "How about you? Leave the old lady in the car and come inside for some fun?"

"No," she says. She tries to sound defiant, but she's not as brave with the man looking at her. What if he *makes* her come inside? "I'm not old enough for parties," she says.

"Come on," the man says. "Crawl over the old lady and come inside."

And now Frances *is* scared, and she realizes that she is no match for an *actual criminal*.

"No," she says.

The man says, "Okay, suit yourself." He closes the car door and goes inside with an armload of shopping bags and beer. The woman follows him into the house with the groceries, leaving Alice and Frances in the backseat with the car running and Alice's purse on the floor in the front.

As soon as they're inside the house, Frances's mother scrambles over the seat and into the front of the car as fast as she can, as though stepping outside might draw attention and bring the couple back out with more demands. She locks the doors and then slams the car into gear and takes off without having a clue what part of the city they're in. Frances, still in the backseat, looks out the rear window to see if anyone is following, but no one is. Her mother drives straight ahead and flies through a stop sign, and when they come to a main street with traffic lights, she turns onto it and they fall into a busy line of traffic. When a gas station appears to their right, she pulls into the parking lot and stops.

She leaves the car and goes into the station, telling Frances to lock the doors after her.

She's gone for twenty minutes. Frances realizes that she's still holding the two bottles of Mountain Dew, but they're warm now. She empties one of the sodas out the window onto the pavement and drinks the other, putting the empty bottles on the floor. Then she gets out of the car and slides back into the front seat. She doesn't bother locking the doors and leaves the windows down because it's so hot. There's music blasting into the parking lot from a radio somewhere—Elvis Presley singing about the ghetto. Some kids a few years older than she is walk by the car without looking at her, city kids with long hair, even the boys, wearing cutoffs and leather sandals. They look different from anyone in Elliot. They might be hippies.

Frances picks the city map up off the floor and tries to figure out where they are by the street signs she can see on the corner. She thinks her mother must be inside calling the police. She tries to think what she will be able to tell them, what the couple looked like and other details—black hair, blond, the white boots, the couch on the lawn in front of their house. The man might have been an Indian, but then again he might just have had black hair.

When her mother finally returns to the car, she looks composed. She gets in, sees the map on Frances's lap, and says, "Did you figure out where we are?"

"The turnoff to the airport should be ahead," Frances says, pointing in the direction they'd been going. "Do we have enough gas to get home?" She already knows they don't, but maybe her mother has a secret stash of money somewhere.

"We'll see, won't we?" her mother says, starting the car and rolling up her window. "I told you to lock the doors. Do it now, please. And roll up your window."

"No one's going to jump in the window while we're driving."

"Just do it," her mother snaps. "Do what I tell you for once and don't talk back."

Frances locks the door but doesn't roll up the window. It's too hot. She's beginning to feel sick from drinking warm pop.

"What did the police say?" she asks as they pull back into traffic.

Her mother doesn't answer.

"We have no money," Frances says. "How will we get home?"

"For God's sake would you just . . . shut up. Please."

"Sure, now's a great time to get mad," Frances says. "Maybe they would have left us alone if you'd got mad before they drove us all over and stole our money. Dad wouldn't have got in the backseat just because they asked him to." Then she tells her mother to pull over because she's going to be sick, but Alice doesn't, and Frances has to stick her head out the open window and vomit Mountain Dew onto the street.

"When you're done," Alice says, "close the window. I don't care how hot it is." Then she adds, "We are not going to speak of this. Ever. Do you understand?"

Frances doesn't understand. At this moment, she feels not a drop of sympathy for her mother, no matter how frightened she had been. What kind of mother would let her daughter throw up out a car window without even stopping? She glares at her, but her mother's eyes are fixed straight ahead, both hands tight on the steering wheel as if it might spin away if she loosens her grip.

When they arrive at the airport, they find Esme and Tobias waiting for them. After they get the old couple and their luggage into the car—Tobias in the backseat with Frances—Alice tells them that she's just discovered she forgot her wallet at home and doesn't have enough money to fill the car with gas. Tobias—looking ghastly ill, but still indignant that they wouldn't let him join the tour—struggles to retrieve his wallet from his pocket and comes up with a twenty-dollar bill, and they find a gas station and then stop at an A&W so Frances can order a Teen Burger. No one else orders anything. Frances moves to the front seat between her mother and Esme so that Tobias can lie down in the back, and he's asleep before they're even out of the city. She eats only half of the burger. She can hear Tobias wheezing in his sleep. Frances's mother says, as though she's trying to find something to talk about, "I've never been on a plane. Not once."

"I suspected he wasn't able for it," Esme says. "I'm sorry to put you to this trouble."

Frances can't help it: with the half-eaten burger on her lap, she falls asleep, thinking about what she would have told the police had she had a chance to talk to them—the woman had blond hair, the man black, she wore white boots.

When she wakes up, the car has stopped moving. It's parked on the side of the road, and her mother and Esme are standing on the shoulder beside it like stunned ducks. The passenger-side door is wide open. Tobias is still sleeping in the backseat. Frances slides out of the car and asks what's going on. "Have we run out of gas?" she asks. Her mother shakes her head and looks at Tobias.

"He's passed on, Frances," says Esme.

"Died," her mother says. "Tobias has died."

Frances looks. It's true that Tobias isn't wheezing anymore. He doesn't seem to be breathing.

Her mother suddenly crumples right where she's standing, sinks down on her knees in the gravel and weeds on the side of the road and sobs, choking out words that can't be understood, wailing like a mourner at a funeral. Frances has never seen her mother behave in such a way. She and Esme look at each other, not knowing what to do, until Esme takes Alice's elbow and lifts her to her feet, saying, "There, there, dear. You've had a bit of a shock. You don't want people to hear you in the next town, do you? He had a good, long life, we have to remember that. Not such a bad way to go, is it? No suffering—it's the way he would have wanted it."

Alice regains her composure enough to find a packet of tissues in her purse and blow her nose, and then two people in a station wagon stop to see if they need help, and suggest they drive to the nearest hospital, which is half an hour up the road. That's what they do. Tobias is officially pronounced dead, and a funeral home is contacted to transport him back to Elliot.

When Frances and her mother finally get home to the farm, the story told to Frances's dad is all about Tobias's death and the subsequent arrangements they'd had to make. Frances waits for her mother to tell the other story—about the abduction—but she doesn't. When her mother says, "I'm knackered to the bone, and I'm going to bed," Frances realizes that she isn't planning to tell it.

She says, "Oh, for heaven's sake, just tell him."

"Tell me what?" Basie asks.

"We were kidnapped in the city," Frances says. "And robbed."

Now Alice has to tell Basie what happened.

"And you didn't call the police?" he says.

"I thought that's what you were doing when we stopped," Frances says.

"I was calming myself down for your sake," Alice says. "I'm going to bed now, and no one is stopping me."

After she's gone, Frances's father makes a pot of tea and pours her a cup.

"What kind of a city is that anyway?" he says.

Frances stirs sugar into her tea and says, "Hank Williams died in the backseat of a car, you know."

"Did he now?"

Frances used to wonder about that, how someone could just die in a car without anyone noticing. Now she knows. She also used to wonder if anything could really frighten her mother. She has the answer to that too. She can't get out of her head the picture of her mother wailing on the side of the road. She knows she wasn't crying for Tobias Sullivan.

"I guess Mom was really scared," she says.

She and her father finish their tea and go to bed.

The next morning, Alice insists on washing her car and scrubbing every inch of the interior with upholstery cleaner and Windex. Basie gets on the phone and calls the local RCMP, and they come immediately and take Alice's statement. Basie has to convince her to take off her rubber gloves and sit down at the table with the officers and tell them what happened. Frances is there too, and the only thing she adds is that the woman was wearing white cowboy boots. The officers say they will send their report to the city police. When they call Alice, she refuses to talk to them.

"My wife is distraught," Basie says, and that's the end of it. They don't call again.

Her mother mentions the couple just once in the days that follow. She says, "I suppose they've gotten away with it. Well, they'll end up in jail someday anyway. I doubt they need my help with that."

She begins to think of her mother as a different person. There was before. Now there's after.

Frances begins to doubt that the rooster-strangling ever really happened.

AT TOBIAS'S FUNERAL, Frances overhears two women talking about Dooley, about whether he'll come out of the woodwork to fight for his grandfather's money. Later, back at Tobias's house, Frances asks Esme if Dooley knows Tobias is dead. Esme says that no one seems to know where Dooley is. She put the word out to people he used to know in Elliot—the crowd he used to run with, she says—but she hasn't heard from him.

And then Dooley does come back to Elliot. Frances wants to know everything that her parents learn about him. They hear that he's moved into the basement of an old friend's house and has been seen around town drunk, and maybe even on drugs. In the hotel bar, when someone expresses condolences on the death of his grandfather, Dooley goes into a rage and says he's not sorry at all, why should he be sorry about the death of an old man he could never please, no matter what he did? He would have been better off in a foster home, he claims. The story spreads around town. Esme says it's not true that Tobias didn't care about Dooley. The boy was troubled, couldn't get past the fact that he'd been deserted by his mother, and then she died before he even had a chance to meet her. Terrible for a child, Esme says, but not Tobias's fault. She asks Basie to go with her to a lawyer, and he's dismayed when Esme tells the lawyer that although Tobias has left everything to her in his will, she would like to split the estate with Dooley. She doesn't want people thinking she's done Dooley out of an inheritance. The only stipulation is that she be allowed to live in the house as long as she's able.

Then Dooley gets drunk in the bar again and says more scandalous things about Tobias—calls him a selfish bastard who had no use for his own daughter, Dooley's mother, no wonder she left. Tobias was a tyrant, he says. Just ask the students he'd bullied over the years. He calls Esme a gold digger before he drinks so much that he gets himself thrown out of the bar, and the police find him passed out on the street and put him in the drunk tank for the night. When the story gets back to Esme, she changes her mind about splitting the estate with him. She decides that he doesn't deserve anything after all, that Tobias was right. It's appalling, she says, to think that he's so disrespectful and making up wicked stories, and he didn't even have the decency to come to his grandfather's funeral. It's unforgivable, whatever unfairness he believes he suffered.

In September, there's an early snowstorm. It snows all day, big wet flakes, and that evening Esme phones the farm and asks Frances's mother if she can come into town right away. It's late and the roads are slippery, but Esme sounds desperate, so Alice goes. When she gets there, Esme tells her that she'd opened the door to see if her cat had come from the minister's house for one of his visits, and there Dooley was, on the step, his hair long and unkempt, dangerous-looking, snow falling around him. They'd stared at each other, and Esme was trying to get up the nerve to ask him in for a heart-to-heart when the wandering cat appeared and ran into the house between her legs and she lost her balance and almost fell. At least she thought it was the cat. She didn't *think* Dooley had pushed her. He'd reached out his hand then, and it was dark and she couldn't tell what he was doing, and she was afraid and had slammed and locked the door. Then later, she saw three or four young men on the lawn in the darkness, flinging snowballs at the house. When they broke the kitchen window, Esme called Frances's mother and then the RCMP. The culprits had taken off by the time an officer got there. It was dark out, the policeman said. Did Mrs. Sullivan know for sure it was Dooley? Sounded like something younger kids—bored and looking for trouble—might do. The police officer was young enough to be a kid himself, Esme said afterward, but maybe he was right. She hadn't actually seen Dooley on the lawn.

Nonetheless, Frances's mother decides that Esme shouldn't stay there alone, at least not as long as Dooley is in town. Alice packs a big suitcase and moves Esme out to the farm. Esme doesn't argue with the plan. Frances takes the top bunk in her room and Esme sleeps on the bottom. That very night, Dooley breaks into Tobias's house and falls asleep drunk on Esme's bed, then lights the mattress on fire with his cigarette and barely manages to get out alive. Half of the house is burned away, gone, and with it most of Esme's belongings. When Frances walks by the house the next day at lunch hour—the snow now melting—she finds lots of people gawking at the blackened walls and broken windows and a roof partially collapsed into the bedroom where the firemen chopped holes in it. Even one of the evergreen trees in the yard is scorched. A few days later, when the house has cooled down and the firemen say Esme can go in to see if there is anything she wants to retrieve, they find that the only room that didn't receive significant fire or water damage is the kitchen. The china and cutlery and cooking pots are salvageable, although they smell like smoke. Even the cookbooks are not too badly off. But Esme doesn't want them, so they get boxed up and sent to the church rummage along with any other odds and ends that survived the fire. The rest goes to the dump in the back of Frances's father's truck before the house gets bulldozed.

What a scandal the fire is, the biggest thing to happen in town for years—perhaps since the night Silas Chance died and Dooley crashed his red truck into the bridge. Dooley is arrested for breaking and entering, although the police aren't sure the charge will stick because there was no restraining order and the house had been Dooley's childhood home. He has to stay in jail until his court appearance, and even after that no one he knows has any money to pay his bail. Frances's father goes to see him and tells him that Esme is prepared to settle the will and provide him immediately with a check if he agrees to leave town and leave her alone. Dooley accepts. The charges are dropped, the fire is called an accident, and Dooley leaves Elliot with a good-sized inheritance in the form of a bank draft. The lawyer advises Esme to write her own will, which she does. There's a fight over insurance, one headache after another. The company doesn't want to pay because Dooley lit the fire with a cigarette. Eventually, the insurance comes through and it all gets settled.

In spite of Alice's belief that Esme's troubles are the result of a marriage that was ill advised to begin with, she invites her to stay with them at the farm. They can't send her back to live in the rental because the United Church minister is not going anywhere, no matter what people think of his hair. The teenagers in town apparently like him. He holds sing-alongs in the church basement. Alice asks Frances if she minds Esme sleeping in her room. Old people are restless. Is Esme keeping her awake? Frances says no. She likes sharing her room with Esme, even though she snores and sighs in her sleep and gets up several times a night to go to the bathroom. Frances listens sometimes to make sure Esme is asleep and not dead like Tobias in the car, or not lying there thinking she should never have followed Tobias Sullivan to Elliot. She feels a bit like a mother hen.

On Remembrance Day weekend, the temperature drops and the snow begins to fall in earnest. Frances and Esme watch winter's arrival through the living room window and Frances says, "I'm the tallest girl in my class now. I wish I wasn't."

"There's nothing wrong with height," Esme says. "Fashion models are as tall as giraffes, you know."

Then she asks Frances what she would like to be when she finishes school. Frances says the first thing that pops into her head: "I don't know. A hairdresser, I guess. You can go to beauty school in Yellowhead. I heard someone say that."

"A hairdresser?" Esme says. "I must say I wasn't expecting that. I thought for sure you'd want to be a teacher, or perhaps a newspaper reporter."

"No," Frances says, suddenly convinced that hairdressing is it, what she's meant for. "I want to learn how to make curly hair straight and red hair blond. Everyone will love me for it."

Esme laughs and says, "Well, if you do go to beauty school, I'm pretty sure you'll become famous. Hairdresser to the stars, that's my prediction, although you're only thirteen and I imagine you'll change your mind. Tell you what, though. I've left you money in my will for school tuition, and you can do whatever you want. That's what girls should do. Whatever they want."

There's a freshly baked chocolate cake on the kitchen counter, made by Esme. They sit at the table and have two slices of cake each.

"For our figures," Esme says.

ESME LIVES for only another six months. She falls while carrying a load of laundry from the bedroom, breaks her other hip, and ends up first in the hospital and then in the nursing home, and then back in the hospital when it's determined she has pneumonia. A month later, she's gone. Frances visits her a few days before she dies, and Esme opens her eyes and

says, "Ah, Frances, we are all such mysteries to one another."
They are the last words she says.

Tobias's estate is hardly settled, and then it's all muddled
up with Esme's estate. Some of her money goes to Frances's
parents (for her keep, their kindness, and Frances's education, she directed in the will). The rest goes to charities. At
least she'd already settled with Dooley. Frances's father says
they'd never be able to find him now. He's disappeared. No
one has heard from him.

It takes no time at all for Frances's room to look like Esme
was never in it. Frances and her mother go through Esme's
clothes and take them to the rummage box at the church.
They run into the minister and he tells Frances she should
come to the teen club. Frances says no thanks, even though
she is now thirteen and is curious about what happens at a
teen club.

One day Alice comes home from the post office and says
she heard that Dooley Sullivan was selling drugs in the city
and died.

"You don't live that lifestyle for long without it killing
you," she says. She believes Dooley should have gone to jail
for burning down Tobias's house. He got off too easy. They
have rehabilitation programs in jail, and maybe the disci-
pline would have helped him. "I'm tempted to think good
riddance," she says, "but you can't really when someone was
so obviously troubled."

Frances is not listening, has not heard anything after the
word "died." She's thinking about the heart—her own—no
longer beating, the air around her not feeding her lungs the
way it should, the light in the room dimming, dimming as
though it might go out altogether: *Dooley can't be dead, not
Dooley Sullivan.*

But she knows he can be.

At school the next day, she sits at her desk not listening to the teacher. *Something is wrong*, she thinks, because how can a boy drive a car into a bridge and go crazy and burn down a house with a cigarette and end up dead, and no one seems to care? She remembers Dooley jumping out the window—in the very same eighth-grade classroom that is now her own—and wonders what happened between then and the day he died. She can't stop thinking about him. How did he die? Who was he with? Where is he buried?

She asks the teacher if she can change seats so she's in the row of desks next to the windows. She sometimes stares out *that* window—Dooley's window—and pictures Dooley tumbling into nothing, disappearing. She remembers him pulling her out from under the table to dance. Whose fault is it, what happened to Dooley?

The rest of the school year is sadness and grief because Dooley died, Esme died, everyone dies in the end. Mixed up with longing to be a child again, to be the girl who took off her white socks and stuck her shoe in a slice of lemon pie. Longing to be the girl discovered by Dooley Sullivan and danced around the room before her father stepped in. Before her body changed without permission and she shot up *like a weed* and grew into a girl with periods and breasts, and even still, the boys don't seem to like her. She hates them all, the girls too, the whole class.

The school year finally comes to an end.

On the last day of June, the report cards are handed out and the grade eight students find that the teacher has written something thoughtful about each of them. They hand their cards around and compare the teacher's notes about their potential, her predictions for their paths in life. Frances doesn't show anyone her report card, but she listens as the others read their fortunes aloud to one another. Caroline Smith is caring and compassionate. Her future: something to do with children. Myrna Samples: Myrna is a take-charge girl. She will be an organizer, perhaps in business or bookkeeping. (Ha ha. Frances knows that all Myrna Samples wants to do is marry some boy named Buddy Hynde from another town.) Daphne Rose: Daphne is very sociable; retail sales might be her calling. Jimmy Gulka: Jimmy is destined for great things in the science world. (Frances still hates Jimmy Gulka because of figure skating.)

Frances's report card is almost an essay compared to the others'. It says, *We all know Frances is a smart girl with plenty of potential. She knows it herself. What she does with that is up to her. She needs to get out of her own way. Her future: Frances, anything will be possible once you decide to buckle down!*

That's that, then, Frances thinks. Caroline is the golden girl. Jimmy Gulka the boy most likely. She, Frances, is the wild card, a girl *with potential*—which means the girl most likely to disappoint. She shoves her report card into a plastic bag with the other papers and scribblers she's expected to take home, and collects her jacket from the cloakroom.

Says goodbye to Dooley's window and moves on.

4. The Stardust Motel

THE ROADS that would take me to Elliot were familiar, even though I had not traveled them for many years: east on the number one highway, north to Yellowhead—the town I'd thought of as a metropolis before I saw a real city—farther north on an increasingly narrow gravel road, then east again on a truck route that would eventually lead me to my hometown. Four hours of driving to a part of the province so far off the beaten trail that most people—even those who live in Saskatchewan—will never see it.

The day was hot, unusually so for the end of May. I lowered the driver's window partway, but the air outside was hotter still and I resorted to air-conditioning. It was hard to believe such heat would morph back into arctic cold in five short months, and the first winter storm would turn the landscape into a frozen wilderness. I thought once again of the night I'd met Ian, when the snowfall had surprised everyone because it was so early in the season, and all the weather announcers on every radio and TV channel said the same thing: "If this is any indication, folks, we're in for a long winter."

We were at an invitation-only party to celebrate the opening of the brand-new city hall. Ian was there with his girlfriend (soon to be his ex-girlfriend), and I was there alone, wearing the black dress I'd been talked into by a salesclerk when she told me I had the figure for it. Not everyone did, she said, not for that dress. The dress made me feel flirtatious, a word I barely knew the meaning of.

We were introduced by a colleague—"Frances Moon, Ian Bonder"—who told Ian that I worked in the city's water treatment department, and then told me that Ian was a brilliant pension actuary who, despite his age, was already developing quite a reputation for himself as an expert in the area of ethics. I heard the words "brilliant" and "actuary" and "ethics," and compared them to my own bland job description, "works in the water treatment department." I was thinking about how that sounded—did it hold any cachet at all, or would Ian think I was a billing clerk, and if so, did that matter?—when my coworker left to follow a waiter with a tray of appetizers, and I found myself alone with the handsome young financial analyst whose girlfriend was busy flirting with someone else. I thought, *I will never again see this man who is a decade my junior*, and that, together with the dress and the wine, gave me license to behave in a way that was uncharacteristic for the woman I had turned myself into. We sat under an umbrella tree on a bench in the lobby of the new building, watching Ian's soon-to-be-ex attach herself to a city councillor. We discussed the probable cost of the twenty-foot-tall trees, which made the lobby look like a conservatory. We talked about the early snowstorm that was blowing itself into a blizzard outside, and the next day's public bonfire and wiener roast, which would have to be canceled because of the storm. Earlier in the evening, before the snow began to fly, there were people protesting the private party as the guests arrived. I'd felt guilty walking past them.

I said to Ian—I suppose because of that word "ethics"—

"I don't feel quite right about being here. The free wine and all this food. The rumors about the unreported costs of the building. I know people here who swear the rumors are true."

"Really?"

"Yes. And they've pushed back the timeline on the new water treatment plant to pay for their excess. That's not the official reason, but that's what my sources tell me when I complain about the new plant being behind schedule."

I thought he might ask me more about my work then, but instead he was amused by the idea that I had sources.

"So, Mr. Ethics," I said, "what do you think about all that? I think I should have joined the protesters outside, but then, I had this new dress."

What had gotten into me? I was showing off.

He laughed at the comment about the dress, and said he'd heard the same rumors and thought the party was an outrageous waste of public money, but since he wasn't going to be joining the protesters, that made him a hypocrite, which was not very ethical.

"Thank you for bringing that up," he said, "and making me feel unprincipled."

At that moment, we saw the councillor to whom Ian's girlfriend had been talking leave the crowded lobby and walk toward a bank of elevators. I wondered if Ian would leave the bench then and retrieve her, but he didn't. Instead he said, "This is it. She'll look around for me, and if she doesn't see me, she'll follow him."

We watched as she waited a few minutes, scanned the room, and then made her way through the crowd to the elevators. Ian seemed more curious than hurt or angry. It was as though we were observing an experiment, something in a petri dish. I was a person of science. I understood this kind of observation.

"What now?" I asked.

"I think we can guess what now, don't you? A tumble in the councillor's office. On his desk maybe, like in the movies."

"Seriously," I said. "What now for you? What will you do?"

"Take back the present I bought her. It's her birthday next week."

"Don't you feel terrible?"

He shrugged. "She's experiencing no ethical dilemma whatsoever. I'm well rid of her, don't you think?"

"Well, yes, I do think. But still."

I looked at Ian then and saw resignation, and I saw the two of us for what we were: a young man, and a woman approaching middle age who had had too much to drink and was wearing a dress she probably should not have bought.

"People shouldn't do these things to each other," I said.

"No, they shouldn't," he said. "But this is small potatoes. At least there's no wedding ring and no children. Probably why there shouldn't ever be. It's all too tenuous."

"You're too young to talk like that," I said.

"Maybe," he said. "Do you want to mingle? I don't, but you should if you want."

"I think I'll just go home."

"There's a blizzard raging."

"There always is."

"What does that mean?"

"I don't know. I've had too much to drink."

"Then we should call cabs."

I agreed. I noted his use of the plural "cabs," and I knew two cabs was the best way to end this evening.

But we left in the same taxi after all, because thanks to the storm, we'd had to wait an hour for one to arrive, an hour that I enjoyed as much as any I'd ever spent with a man I'd just met. There was a TV set mounted in the foyer, where we waited with our coats on, and we watched *Saturday Night Live* and saw Sinéad O'Connor rip up the photo of the pope. The TV was muted, so we couldn't make out what she was saying before she held up the photo and tore it into pieces. Ian said he thought he picked out the word "evil."

"Maybe it wasn't as crazy as it looked," he said.

When a taxi finally pulled up in front of city hall, we both got in, not knowing when or if another would come, and then we had to get out again and push—me in my high-heeled shoes, since I had not had the sense to wear boots—because the taxi got stuck in the snow, which was building into huge drifts. When we finally arrived at my apartment, our feet were frozen and we were both laughing. The whole night now seemed crazy, even Ian's breakup. It crossed my mind that he might be expecting me to invite him inside, but I didn't, and he didn't ask and I was relieved, because to sleep with him impulsively was something the old Frances would have done.

I woke up hungover and wondering just how embarrassed I ought to be about my behavior the night before, and feeling enormously thankful that I was waking up alone. I vowed that I would never drink too much, or wear that dress, again. I had once cut to ribbons a dress that I wanted to be rid of, and I was tempted to do the same to the black dress, but once more I thought, That's what the old Frances would do. This Frances can cover the dress with a dry cleaner's bag and hang it in the closet and look at it once in a while to be reminded of a lesson learned.

So that's what I did. Lesson learned, I thought as I hung the dress at the back of my closet (eventually I gave it to a thrift shop). Then I went back to bed and slept most of the day.

Ian called a few days later, having got my number from the colleague who'd introduced us, and asked if I wanted to go out for dinner.

I decided to be blunt and avoid future humiliation. "You're too young for me," I said.

"What's age got to do with anything?"

"You're on the rebound."

"I get the feeling you are too."

Funny, I thought, it was kind of true. I'd been on the rebound pretty much since I left Elliot.

I agreed to meet him for dinner. We began to see each other—once a week at first, and then more often, spending the night at his house or my apartment. Our compatibility was confirmed when we discovered we both liked to don bedroom slippers as soon as we walked in the door from work. Mine were crocheted, purchased at the farmer's market, and his were leather, the kind Mister Rogers might wear. He was in the habit of cooking dinner in his suit minus the jacket, wearing slippers and an apron, which he began to do for me while I sat with a glass of wine and put my blue-and-green-mottled feet on the coffee table. We talked while he cooked, the facts of our current lives, the goings-on at our places of work. I stopped thinking about the age difference.

Six months after we met, I moved into his house. He had to convince me. I was worried it was too soon. There was no talk of marriage, and by that I was relieved. The night before I moved in, while we were eating pizza in my dismantled apartment, he said to me, "I feel I should be honest about something. I don't want to have children."

I didn't have to think before I answered. "You're safe with me, then," I said. "No desire to have kids. No desire to get married. My happiness is dependent on neither."

Free and clear, I thought. There was no further mention of children or marriage.

Until five years later, when Ian asked over dinner, a pasta dish with shrimp and lemon in a cream sauce—just when I'd been about to ask him how he kept the cream from curdling—"You *could* still have a child, right? A woman over forty can still have a child?"

I set down my fork and looked at him. I had no idea that he'd changed his mind about children, although it was now dawning on me why he'd been showing such interest in the babies born to various coworkers. Within the last week, some-one named Gary had had a baby girl. I'd thought Ian was tell-ing me about his day—*no computers because of a system crash, of all days for the new intern to start . . . lunch at that new coffee shop, you know the one . . . and oh, Gary and his wife had a baby girl, they're thrilled, over the moon . . .* It had all been leading up to the baby. They'd named her Ella after a special aunt.

"A baby is not a good idea," I said. "You're the actuary. The odds increase drastically after a woman is forty. It could have Down's syndrome."

"But not necessarily. There are tests."

"You've tied yourself to an older woman, Ian."

"We haven't exactly tied ourselves to each other, have we? I wonder if we should. Maybe we should get married."

Married.

I didn't reply. I got up and left the room, abandoning my

plate of perfectly uncurdled pasta, which had suddenly lost its appeal. Upset because he'd caught me off guard, suggested the impossible, disrupted the stability I thought I'd found. I could hear the echo of another man's voice asking a similar question in a similar way: *I wonder if you might want . . .*

Ian followed me, saying, "Frances, what the hell? I just asked you to marry me."

I was thinking, *I'm already married,* but I spoke three different words: "No. Just no."

For a while after, I worried that we, or perhaps I, had ruined everything, but we managed to drift back into our comfortable lives, baby talk thankfully forgotten, or so I'd thought. The years went by. We bought a new couch for the living room. We added on to the house and built a deck in the yard and bought a good barbecue. We talked about getting a dog but decided against it because we'd begun to travel, to go on winter holidays. The day I turned fifty, we had a few friends over for a fall barbecue—Ian's friends really, but I liked them—and we toasted the future, growing old together. I joked that it would not exactly be *together,* since I would get there first, and Ian replied that I'd be able to shop for both of us and get the senior's discount.

I held up my wineglass and clinked it against his. "Here's to me, with a Sears shopping cart full of bargain toilet paper and men's socks and underwear."

Everyone laughed. We were good.

And then Ireland, when something inexplicable came over me.

And something came over Ian, and he announced that he was returning home early with or without me, an ultimatum. I had immediately known the terms: that I open the door to a locked room, giving him permission to look around, remove drop cloths, flip latches, peek into cubbyholes, turn back clocks. I didn't know if a key to that room even existed, but if it did, I was not going to use it in his presence, and I was certainly not letting him in that room without me going through its contents first.

That is what I was thinking when I made the decision to go hill walking.

It's what I was still thinking as I drove toward Elliot for the first time in many years, cold air blasting at me from the air-conditioning vents, my T-shirt sticking to the leather seatback anyway.

What would I find when I got there?

I did not know.

Nor did I know that something as commonplace as a rusty nail was about to send me down a hallway of locked doors, which would swing in every direction before I could even lay a hand on them.

Meaning there were no locked doors, not in Elliot.

Meaning also that the weirdest fucking things just happen sometimes.

AN HOUR AFTER I turned north and went through Yellowhead, I pulled into a small town with a full-service gas station, and as the young attendant—a gawky, long-legged teenage boy named Chuck, according to the badge on his shirt—filled up my car, I collected the washroom key and found the door marked Ladies around the side of the building. As I was washing my hands, I studied the face in the mirror. My hair was still red and curly, although it was now streaked with gray. Did I look like I had when I lived in Elliot? Would anyone recognize me? I didn't know the answer to either question, but I knew my preference was to appear as a stranger in town. I left the washroom, and as I was paying for my gas, I asked Chuck if he knew where I could buy hair dye.

"The drugstore, I guess," he said, and pointed toward what I thought must be the main street.

I found the drugstore, which reminded me of the drugstore in Elliot where I'd had my ears pierced with a needle and an ice cube. I mulled over the dye choices for too long while the young clerk stared at me, this one a girl with peacock-blue streaks in her dark hair, and finally I decided to go all the way and turn myself into a blonde. I knew nothing about the rules of dyeing hair, but it seemed you could do anything you wanted with color.

I selected a box from the shelf—guaranteed, it claimed, to cover gray and make your hair soft and shiny—and took it to the counter.

"Will this work on my hair?" I asked the clerk.

It must have been a slow day because she took the question much more seriously than I expected her to. She had a good look at my hair and even reached up to touch it, which surprised me and caused me to take a step back. I wondered if she was trying to find a way to tell me I was about to make a definite fashion mistake. Perhaps I was hoping she *would* tell me that, but she didn't.

She finally spoke. "Okay. You'll need to pre-lighten the color because you still have quite a bit of natural color left. I'm not really sure what the gray will do, but you can add lowlights later if you need to. I would go with a liquid cream bleach—the higher the number, the faster it will lighten—but you have to be careful not to leave it on too long or your hair will get really dry, plus it's not that dark. And you'll need to use a toner, but don't use one with ammonia or peroxide. It'll damage your hair even more. Then you need to seal in the color. You can get a spray for that, and it will make your hair soft again too, so bonus."

My head spun. Who knew dyeing your hair with a do-it-yourself box from the drugstore would involve so many steps?

To reassure me, she said, "I use box dyes myself, even for the highlights. It's not so hard." Then she told me she was hoping to become a hairstylist when she finished high school. "I get good marks in art. My teacher says I'm artistic and I need a creative sort of job."

"I used to know some art students," I said, thinking about the ones who had once lived across the street from me, and also about my own hairdressing aspirations, which had lasted just long enough to appall my mother. "You *could* study art if you wanted to, at university. Save beauty school for later."

"Maybe," she said. "But I don't really want to be an artist. I'd rather style hair. I wish they wouldn't call it beauty school, though. 'Beauty' is kind of an old-fashioned word."

"I'm happy to hear that beauty is passé," I said. "Anyway, you can start your hairstyling career right now. Can you just pick out everything I need? I'll do whatever you say. And give me the highest number. I'll watch the time."

The girl chose three products, plus a bottle of moisturizing shampoo. I got her to write steps one, two, and three on the packages, which she did with a black marker, carefully and earnestly. I thanked her for her help and told her I was sure she would make a great hairstylist, and then I drove back to the gas station and asked Chuck once again for the key to the washroom. He gave it to me, taking note of the drugstore bag I was now carrying. I went into the washroom and put on the rubber gloves that were provided, squeezed step one's creamy liquid all over my head, and pulled it through my hair. Then I looked at the time on my watch.

I figured I couldn't spend the entire wait time in the washroom, which was clean but smelled of Pine-Sol and whatever I had just put on my head, so I went outside and found a place to sit in the grass while I kept my eye on the time and wondered what chemical transformation was taking place. I noticed that Chuck was watching me, and eventually he came over and said, "Are you dyeing your hair in our washroom?"

"Yes," I answered, "that is what I am doing: dyeing my hair." I wondered what I would do if he asked me to leave.

He didn't. "Totally random," he said. "Women do that in movies. Usually after they've robbed a bank or stabbed their husband. Not that stabbing your husband is always bad. He could have been, like, abusive."

"None of the above," I said, wondering what about me had caused him to come up with the idea of spousal homicide. I asked him if my hair was turning green or orange or anything awful, and he shook his head. He took off his cap and scratched his forehead.

"Which way are you going?" he asked.

"Northeast," I said.

"Have you heard about the fires? They're saying they might close the road. So much smoke you can't see. At least that's what I heard. From a trucker."

Then he put his cap on and walked back to the pumps, where another car had pulled in.

When the time was up, I returned to the washroom and rinsed my hair in the sink and looked in the mirror, where a bleached-blonde woman looked back at me. Unfortunately, the dye job wasn't going to change my best-before date, which would have been a welcome side effect.

I applied the toner—step two—and went outside to sit in the grass again for the required amount of time. Then I washed my hair and sprayed on step three and ran a comb through my new look. I put my sunglasses back on and stepped out into the hot day once more. I wanted to laugh. I'd dyed my hair in a gas station. I waved at my new friend Chuck as I pulled away, but he didn't wave back. Maybe he really thought he'd had a psychopath on his hands.

As I drove north, I began to see the smoke in the air, which I might have thought was dust had I not heard from Chuck about the fires. The sun, I noticed, was turning that strange red color, as it does when sunlight passes through particles of smoke and ash. You see this even in the city sometimes, when there are forest fires burning in the north.

It was now late afternoon and blistering hot, and the road shimmered in front of me. I kept stealing glances at myself, blond hair and sunglasses, and thinking, *Who is that woman?* And at one point I thought, *It's my mother.* She'd never been blonde, but she had liked her sunglasses.

When I hit the main northern traffic route, I turned east again, knowing that I was now on the road leading directly to Elliot, which I was relieved to find still open, no notices of closures up ahead. I was well into a mix of boreal forest and arable land—arable only because of persistence, since the poplars grew back like weeds when the land was cleared. This was the world of my childhood, where small farmers like my father coexisted with men who worked seasonally in the bush, cutting and hauling logs. Although my father and his neighbors were reasonably prosperous, it had for many families been a life of subsistence.

The names of the towns I passed through became more and more familiar. The smoke in the air grew thick and the day grew darker, as if a storm were approaching. I began to smell the smoke, even with the car windows up. When I came to a sign announcing that the town of St. Agnes was ahead, I knew I was close, and I began to wonder if I was making a mistake. I sensed an invisible wall going up in front of me, an argument being launched against my return to Elliot. I knew there was a T-intersection with a road going south just this side of St. Agnes, a last-chance escape route, and I found myself watching for it, slowing down, driving below the speed limit. I began to feel unwell. I couldn't tell if I was hot or cold because I was sweating and shivering at the same time, but I was uncomfortable enough that I pulled over and got out of the car. I was within sight of the intersection and having, I believed, a genuine anxiety attack.

My first thought was to go for a walk to clear my head, but it was hotter outside than I'd thought possible this far north in May, and the air was now dense with smoke. I ended up standing in the grass at the side of the road, staring at the intersection, undecided, unable to make a decision, vehicles of all descriptions coming toward me, materializing out of the smoke and then disappearing again to the west. I wondered what to do. No one was making me go to Elliot, no one was expecting me, except perhaps Mavis, and it had to be an indication that your hometown was no longer your home when the only person expecting you was your real estate agent.

An elderly man drove by in a farm truck going toward St. Agnes, gawking at me as he passed, and then he stopped and parked on the shoulder. I watched as he got out of his truck and walked back through the haze toward me. I knew exactly what was coming: the friendly greeting, some chitchat about the weather, several subtle turns and segues until we arrived at the point, which would come as a statement of fact rather than a direct question: "I suppose you could use some help. Lost or broken down, I guess." I was tempted to answer yes to all three—*lost and broken down, needing help*—but instead I stepped back onto the shoulder from where I was standing in the grass, the horseflies beginning to get bothersome, and I thanked the man for stopping and assured him that I'd just wanted a break from driving in the heat.

"Smoke's getting bad, eh?" he said. "Hope they don't close the road. Not from around here, I guess."

I said, "Just passing through. Thanks for stopping."

Then the man returned to his truck and drove on.

The exchange had happened exactly as I'd anticipated, had unfolded with such fluency. Although that could have fed the argument against my return, it didn't. Instead, I had to fight the temptation to believe I somehow *belonged* here, which was an absurd thought. Still, I realized I was not quite ready to abandon my plan and turn south.

I remembered there'd been a motel in St. Agnes, a single-story fifties L called the Stardust, with a dozen rooms. It was built for the fishermen and their families who came north in the summer, the hunters who came in the fall. Perhaps it was still there, a relic now when once it had been invitingly modern. Perhaps I could stay the night in St. Agnes and drive to Elliot the next day. Or not, depending on how I felt in the morning. I started the car and drove on toward St. Agnes, the air-conditioning once again blasting.

As I approached the town, I thought it looked pretty much the way I remembered, with its main street stretched along the roadway, although it was also different. St. Agnes had always been smaller than Elliot, and had not had a high school or a hospital, even when I was a child. As I slowed to drive through town, I could see that it was now smaller still, and dilapidated. Mom's Lunch, where the truckers used to stop, was boarded up, the grain elevator was gone, and I guessed that if I were to drive along the residential streets, the full effects of the closure of the lumber mill several years ago would reveal themselves and St. Agnes would turn out to be not much more than a ghost town.

I was happy to see, though, that the Stardust Motel was still in business on the easternmost edge of town. It looked surprisingly well kept—newly painted, the half acre of lawn freshly mown, and the old-style outdoor swimming pool filled with water, ready for the season. There were only a few vehicles, all oil-rig trucks, parked in front of the row of turquoise blue doors with numbers on them. A neon sign said, unnecessarily, Vacancy.

I parked in front of the motel office and checked myself in for the night. An indifferent middle-aged woman gave me a key and said, "By the way, there's a piano in that room." They stored the family's various surplus items in the rooms, she explained; the one next door to mine had a freezer. I drove my car just a few feet to angle-park in front of room 3, and carried my suitcase into its hot and dark interior. The room was decorated in vintage orange and brown, and I immediately inspected the bathroom (as my mother would have done) and found it to be clean. Still, I wasn't about to walk on the carpet in bare feet.

There was no air-conditioning. I opened the curtains and the window to let in some light, even though I knew I was also letting in heat and smoke. I sat on the edge of the bed and looked at the old upright piano against the wall and wondered what to do with myself. I could play the piano if I knew how, but I didn't. No one in my family played any musical instrument. If Mom's Lunch weren't boarded up, I could have gone there for a sandwich. My parents had taken me there once on a special occasion—a birthday, per-haps. It was a big deal back then, to go to a restaurant, even though Mom's Lunch, with its half-dozen tables in the front room of someone's house, wasn't much of a restaurant. The cooler for soft drinks was a fridge just like the one in my parents' kitchen.

It turned out to be a good thing that I had checked into the motel when I did. An hour later, the RCMP set up a roadblock east of town and closed the highway. The smoke had grown so thick in the low spots that visibility was down to almost zero. Until the wind changed direction and blew it away, the road would remain closed. The motel began to fill up, mostly with truckers, but there were also a few businessmen, a family with several young children, and a couple with a Labrador dog. I wondered when it had last been this full.

A number of semis were parked on the shoulder across the road, and the trucks continued to stop and line up, their drivers knowing there was a roadblock ahead. It was like win-ter, when snow shuts down the highway. The smoke was heavy in the air, and its smell mixed with the smells of exhaust and diesel, as well as the distinct odor of a nearby pig farm.

I decided a dip in the pool was the only reasonable choice

for passing the time. I had no bathing suit with me, so I changed into lightweight shorts and a sleeveless T-shirt, wondering if the chlorine would turn my new hair green. No one else was in the pool area, which was enclosed by a chain-link fence. The metal gate squeaked as I opened it. There were a few flotation devices and paddleboards on the concrete, and I selected an inflatable lounge chair and launched myself from the pool's edge to drift in the middle. The water was clear and cool, and a welcome relief from the heat and the long drive, and I wished I had a drink of some kind—a cold beer or a margarita, poolside, like in Mexico. I thought about the woman in the motel office. There was no chance that anyone was going to wait on me here.

As I floated in the pool, my legs dangling in the water, I thought about the time I appeared as the "Lost Little Mermaid" in the Yellowhead paper and lied and told my mother that it wasn't me, even though the proof—the photograph— was right there in front of me. I wanted to laugh at that impudent little girl, but there was something disturbing about the way she'd stuck to her guns. Maybe I'd missed my calling, and I should have been a hard-nosed professional gambler, or a jewel thief, or an international spy. Something more audacious than a drinking-water bureaucrat.

When I saw the family with all the kids coming toward the pool, I paddled myself back to the edge and got out, refreshed. I showered and dressed, and then bought a Coke from the drink machine in front of the office. The smell of meat barbecuing came from somewhere behind the motel, and I realized I was famished.

I was sitting on the edge of the bed in my room, wondering what I could eat, when there was a knock on the door. I answered and a little girl of seven or eight handed me a hamburger on a paper plate. She was holding several other plates as well, expertly, like a waitress.

"Mom said to bring you this," the girl said. "There's no café anymore."

I barely had time to thank the girl before she turned and went on to the next room and knocked.

I ate the hamburger, which was good, although a little charred. I watched TV for a while, and then I went to bed, even though it was still just dusk.

In the middle of the night, I woke up to the sound of a diesel truck pulling into the motel lot and parking just outside my door, and soon after a party started up in the room next to mine. I tried wrapping a pillow around my head, but it was no use. The walls were like cardboard and there was nothing I could do to block out the loud male voices and the bursts of laughter. One voice kept repeating, seemingly in response to everything said, "No way, man. No freaking way." For some reason, I imagined the man whose voice it was sitting on top of the freezer.

At three o'clock in the morning I gave up on sleep, put my still-wet clothes in a plastic bag, left the room key on the bed, and said goodbye to the Stardust Motel, the decision made to carry on to Elliot and take my chances with the roadblock. As I left my room, I noticed that most of the transport trucks across the road had moved on. I backed the car out of the motel lot, planning to drive around the police barricade and make my way through the smoke, but both the roadblock and the smoke were gone.

Half an hour later, I was in Elliot, skirting the edge of town, passing a row of unfamiliar commercial buildings, a sports field of some kind, a new Super 8 motel. Everything was dead quiet. I turned toward the tracks, and up ahead I could make out the white X of the railway crossing sign. Liberty Street was just beyond it. I crossed the tracks, the *bump-bump* of the car wheels on the rails familiar in a visceral way, and I turned under the one lamppost, which cast a glow on a faded and rusty street sign. As I drove up the dirt road to where I knew the house was, the light diminished into total blackness.

I parked in front of the house and turned off the engine. In the darkness, I could just make out the gabled roof, the window shutters that were decorative rather than functional, the little covered porch with four steps up. It was a cute house, a Beatrix Potter house. Almost nothing could be called cute in this town, at least not as I remembered it.

The only thing to do at that point was go inside, so I did. I stepped through the door that led directly into the kitchen, switched on the light, and was greeted—or rather assaulted—by the old yellow-and-chrome dining set from the farm, the one Mavis had called a dinette, and to which she had applied the term "vintage." It had been in the farmhouse kitchen all the years of my upbringing, and we'd sat at that table every day, without fail, as my mother served us our three square meals. I remembered the respect with which we treated the chairs when we sat in them, because of the way they tipped over if you weren't careful.

Perhaps it was just exhaustion, but I felt a familiar kind of misery coming over me. It belied, I thought, that feeling of belonging I'd briefly sensed when I spoke with the farmer by the side of the road. It was the kind of misery that comes with knowing who you really are, and who you will always be.

I thought of what Ian had said about me resisting happiness. He was wrong. He had to be. You can't know what misery is without wanting its opposite.

I stood there in the little kitchen, my suitcase still in my hand, until finally I set it down. I put my hand on the back of one of the chairs and tipped it, and it fell over just as I knew it would, and I gave it a good kick. Then I righted the chair and ventured farther into the house and looked around. Everything was tidy, the furniture placed just so, and I sat on the brown leather couch I'd purchased for the young teachers on Mavis's recommendation (durable, easy to clean), and I could see the chrome suite from the living room, the ghosts of the house gathered around it, illuminated by the overhead kitchen light. Uncle Vince. My father with his hands wrapped around a coffee cup. My mother, shaking her paintbrush at me. Silas Chance, reaching out to pull a nickel from behind my ear. The runaway pastor who claimed he could heal by the laying on of hands. Esme, before she was Mrs. Sullivan. The long-haired United Church minister who had years ago left Elliot and moved on to a bigger parish.

I finally got up off the couch, found my purse in the kitchen, and retrieved a notepad and pen. I pulled one of the chairs from the table, carefully this time so it wouldn't tip, and sat down to write myself a list—a twelve-step plan for leaving Elliot forever, I called it—and when I was done, I attached it to the fridge door with a plastic flower magnet someone had left behind. Immediately, I changed my mind and tore it up, and got right to the point with a less complicated three-step plan that said, essentially, get to work, get the job done, and leave. Then I shooed away the ghosts and collapsed in my clothes on the double bed Mavis had readied for me, falling into a sleep that was interrupted by a parade of disjointed thoughts and unwanted night visitors—Patsy Cline botching the lyrics to "Sweet Dreams," Chuck from the gas station chaotically moving checkers around on the tabletop, the young girl from the Stardust Motel tripping and launching her burgers into space like flying saucers. Eventually, the uninvited guests went away, and I slept deeply and woke only when the sun was full in the morning sky.

I made my way to the bathroom, and when I pulled back the plastic curtains on the window, I saw an old camper trailer up on blocks a few lots to the west of me. Mavis hadn't mentioned a neighbor. Maybe I shouldn't have been surprised that someone else now lived on the street, but I was. The trailer had a screen porch built onto the front. There was a truck parked next to it. I let the curtains fall together again, resolving to ignore the fact that I wasn't alone on the street. When I looked at myself in the mirror, I was pleased with my hair. I examined it closely, checking for roots and dryness, and I decided I had done a pretty good job, considering.

In the kitchen, it struck me that I had nothing to eat. I discovered a half-full jar of instant coffee in a cupboard next to a pair of salt and pepper shakers, and I put the kettle on, prepared to make do with that because I was not yet ready to face a trip to the grocery store. As I waited for the kettle to boil, I looked out the screen door into the sunshine, and I saw that the empty lots across the road had been fenced, and there was a herd of six or seven horses grazing. I looked up and down the street, and concluded that other than the addition of the trailer and the horses, Liberty Street was the same as it had always been. I wondered why it had been such a failure as a subdivision, but when a train approached and blew by just then, I thought I had my answer.

I noticed a pink geranium on the porch with a daddy long-legs making its way up the side of the ceramic pot. I stepped outside to see if the plant needed water and found at my feet a disposable pie plate containing a half-dozen muffins covered in plastic wrap. Mavis, I thought. Very small-towny. I happily took the plate inside, letting the screen door slam after me in its familiar way, and I sat at the table for a breakfast of coffee and muffins. They were still warm, freshly baked, delicious. I ate two. A third was tempting, but I wrapped the remaining muffins up again and put them in the fridge for later. Then I called Mavis on my still-functioning cell phone to say thank you.

She said she wasn't the one who'd delivered the muffins; she wasn't due in Elliot until the day after next.

"You should come to my yoga class," she said. "Saturday at four o'clock in the United Church basement." She lived in another town a half hour away but taught yoga in several nearby communities.

I ignored the invitation to her class, and I didn't believe her about the muffins. Who else could have delivered them?

"Well, anyway," I said, "they were much appreciated, since I had nothing in the house for breakfast." Then I said, "I see I have a neighbor."

"An old hippie type," Mavis said. "Lives alone. I hear he takes medicinal marijuana. Harmless, by all accounts. Keeps to himself."

Harmless, keeps to himself—all I needed to know.

"He can smoke himself senseless," I said, "as long as he doesn't ask me to sign any petitions."

Mavis laughed. "Do you like the way I decorated?" she asked. "Those young teachers really wanted the house furnished. I suppose they're paying off student loans. Too bad we didn't know you were going to sell it, but anyway, a house looks better with furniture in it. For listing purposes, I mean."

I said I liked her decorating.

"Should I pop over before class on Saturday?" she asked. "It's up to you."

"Maybe next week," I said. "I have a lot to do. Lots of sorting. You know how it is—so many things no one but me would know what to do with."

"Just let me know," she said. "And don't forget . . . mind, body, spirit."

"Absolutely," I said, and we hung up.

I tried to picture Mavis, whom I had not yet met in person. Lululemon? A bright pink jacket and tight yoga pants? Maybe. You could order Lulu online, no reason to think it wouldn't have a presence in the United Church basement in Elliot. I set my phone down on the table and tried to imagine why she would deny leaving the muffins. I also wondered how long it would take me to sort through the boxes and furniture stored in the basement, and whether I could be as ruthless as I planned to be about photographs, ornaments, familiar dishes from my mother's kitchen—all the things that would say, *It's true. You didn't make your whole life up*.

And I wondered how long it would take my former boss to get over her anger at my sudden resignation and call me, say something like *Really, Frances? Seriously?* Maybe she wouldn't. Maybe she would just accept my resignation, cancel my cellular account, and cut me off.

From the rest of the world, although she wouldn't know that.

Mind, body, spirit, I thought, although that was not my style.

5. The Way to San Jose

SOMETHING FRANCES THOUGHT she'd never do: seek advice from a teen fashion magazine. The sixties are over, the magazine tells her, get into the swing of the new decade. Whatever that might mean in Elliot. Still, the magazine promises to guide her through high school (The Best Time of Your Life!) and help her figure out what she's doing wrong (Ten Tips for Wallflowers), and yes, any girl can become the most popular girl in the class (Losers Become Winners). An article about matching styles to your figure advises her to take off all her clothes, get naked in front of a full-length mirror, take a good long look, and be honest about (a) assets and (b) flaws. Make a list, she's told, and then circle the things on the list that she should (a) flaunt and (b) disguise. As if she would ever stand naked in front of a mirror in full daylight. Mostly, the magazine's makeover suggestions are stupid, and the fashion articles feature clothes that she'd never be able to find, even in Yellowhead. And all the models and movie stars in the pictures have long, straight hair. There's not a single picture of anyone with unruly hair like hers. The only hope she can see is for bangs. Anyone can wear bangs, according to the magazine.

The week before school starts, she convinces her mother

to make her an appointment at Brenda's Beauty Salon so she can enter the next phase of her life—that is, high school—with a new haircut. When Brenda spins her around and gives her a hand mirror so she can see her new do, she hates it. She's sure her bangs won't stay down over her eyes like that. She doesn't look a bit like, say, Goldie Hawn. Before she leaves the shop, she asks Brenda if she can work there after school, part-time, doing odd jobs.

"Goodness, no," Brenda says. "I can't afford to hire anyone. I suppose you could volunteer if you want. Sweep up hair and do laundry. That sort of thing."

Frances says she'll think about it.

She tells her mother when she gets home, and Alice says, "That's ridiculous. Of course you're not going to work for nothing for Brenda Schuman when we can't get a lick of work out of you here. Besides, do you want to end up a hairdresser, for heaven's sake?"

"I wouldn't mind," Frances says.

That look, which is becoming more and more familiar: horrified.

Her mother's contributions to Frances's launch into high school are a warning and two new firm-support bras ordered from the catalogue. As she hands Frances the bras to try on—which Frances refuses to do in front of her—she says, "Pants-chasing is a sure sign of weak character in a girl." Frances looks at the boxes the bras came in and says, "No one wears this kind anymore," and her mother says, "Well, there'll be no *braless look* in this house, so you may as well make sure they fit."

It's determined by an exchange through Frances's closed bedroom door that Alice has ordered the right size, and when Frances comes out of the bedroom, Alice says,

"Pants-chasing gets you starry-eyed blind over one boy after another until you find yourself in trouble and married to someone with a grade ten education and a wandering interest in women that isn't put to rest just because he's signed a marriage certificate—a piece of paper he can barely read."

"Whew," Frances says. "How long did you practice saying that?"

"It's true," her mother says. "Believe me. I come from the pants-chasing capital of England, maybe the Commonwealth."

"Why not go for the world?" Frances says. Then she says, "I look like Marilyn Monroe in these bras, at least from the neck down. I thought you wanted to scare boys away."

Two weeks into school, she does get a phone call from a boy. His name is Mark, and he asks her if she wants to go to the freshie dance with him. She stretches the phone cord as far as it will go and turns away from her mother, who is peeling potatoes for supper, and says, "*Who* did you say this is?"

"Mark," he says again. "Social studies. You know."

She does know. Mark from another town, not a boy she went to elementary school with.

"I guess I could," she says, in spite of herself, and Mark says, "Okay, then. You can tell me at school where you live," and he hangs up. As she places the receiver back on its cradle, she feels just a little bit pleased that she must not be a complete social loser, although now she's going to have to *go* to the dance with a boy she doesn't even know.

"Who was that?" her mother asks.

"No one," says Frances. "Just a boy."

"A boy? What did he want?"

"He wants me to go to the freshie dance with him," she says. "You don't know him. He's new this year."

"Did I hear you saying yes?" her mother asks.

"Why would I say no?" Frances says. "And before you start lecturing about pants-chasing, it's not pants-chasing when the boy phones you. Plus he's my own age, and it's a school dance. *School* dance, get it? Teachers will be there, ruining everyone's fun."

"Don't get your shirt in a knot," Alice says. "I don't have anything against school dances."

She buys Frances a new dress from the catalogue. Frances tries it on when it comes, just in time, and hopes for a big payoff—that is, that her status at school will be elevated when she shows up in the gymnasium with a date. There'd better be a big payoff, she thinks, because the closer it gets to the Friday of the dance, the more she wishes she'd said no.

The day of the dance, Mark bumps her shoulder as they pass in the hallway and says, "I'll pick you up at seven. I found out where you live, so." Then the president of the student council comes on the intercom to remind everyone about the rules—*no smoking, no drinking, no hard heels in the gym*—and Frances feels an unexpected rush of excitement when she thinks, I, Frances Moon, am going to the dance with a boy named Mark. She wonders if he'll kiss her when he takes her home afterward, and she's curious about how that happens, how the first move is made. She assumes it will all be up to him.

She also assumes one of Mark's parents will pick her up, but the driver of the truck that pulls into the yard is an older boy whom she recognizes from the hallways at school. Mark gets out of the cab so she can get in and sit in the middle; the driver doesn't say anything, and she isn't introduced. As Frances glances sideways at Mark before he pulls the door closed and the dome light goes off, she thinks he looks too polished and shiny, as though his mother had scrubbed him down. She knows she should forgive him for that, but he's wearing a red shirt, as bright as a fire engine.

Halfway to town he pulls a mickey of vodka out of the glovebox and offers her some, and then takes a swig himself when she shakes her head.

"It's okay," he says. "They can't smell vodka on your breath." He passes the bottle across her to the driver.

At the dance, in a gym decorated with streamers made from blue and yellow crepe paper—the school colors—Frances can feel (and she's sure she isn't imagining this) all eyes on her. *What is Frances Moon doing at a dance? And oh my God, look who she's with—and get a look at that shirt!* Frances follows Mark, her date, trying to be invisible, but how can that happen when you're with someone in a red shirt, wishing you'd just said no when he called, and *why did he have to wear that shirt?* The older boy, the driver, has disappeared.

The band is from Yellowhead—the Wild Things—and they're too loud. Mark keeps asking her questions—shouting in her ear—things like "What do you do for fun, anyway?" to which she has no answer. When he asks, "Do you want to dance?" she nods her head, even though she doesn't know how. She has a vague recollection of her mother offering to teach her, Frances rolling her eyes because what would her mother know about dancing? She steps her way through the song, shifting her weight from one foot to the other, trying to figure out what to do with her arms, but she feels as though everyone is watching her—*Oh my God, look at Frances Moon dancing*—and when it's over, she walks off the dance floor with Mark following.

"Don't you like dancing?" he asks, and she says, "Not really."

"What should we do, then? Do you want to go sit in the parking lot for a while, in the truck?"

She knows the mickey is in the truck, and she doesn't want him drinking any more of that. And why is he asking her what they should do? How should she know? He keeps trying to touch her, slip his arm around her shoulder, tug her toward the dance floor again, brush her hair with his hand. Why? Why is he acting like they're going steady or something? There's that other thing boys do—"feel you up," she's heard the girls at school talking. Is that what this is about? He wants to feel her up? He keeps talking about the truck, how they should go out and sit in the truck. All she can think to say in response is "I heard that's against the rules," and then more questions, and she wants to shout, "I don't know! How am I supposed to know what we should do?" but her voice closes up on her and eventually she can't manage anything, not even a polite "No, thank you" when he asks her if she wants a Coke. All she can do is shake her head.

Finally the band takes a break and Mark says, "What's the matter with you, anyway?" and he goes into a sulk, and then he leaves her alone and finds some older boys to hang out with—the driver among them—and she sits by herself on one of the chairs lined up along the gym wall. All eyes are definitely on her now. Has Frances Moon been jilted by the boy in the red shirt? She thinks about what he said—"What's the matter with you?"—and begins to get mad.

When Mark comes back, he asks her if she can call her dad and get him to pick her up so his brother (*he hadn't even told her the other boy was his brother*) doesn't have to drive all the way out to the dairy farm to take her home. Frances has been sitting by herself for half an hour, and by this time she is furious and no longer cares what people think, especially not Mark from some hick town without even its own high school. She finds her voice, and stands up and says, "Of course my dad can't pick me up. He's blind." Which isn't completely true, but he never drives to town anymore. Fucking idiot, she thinks as she heads for the pay phone in the hallway outside the gym. "Fuck" is a word she has never said, but now she knows what it's for. Myrna Samples and another girl from her grade are standing at the entrance to the gym under a drooping valance of streamers. Frances glares at them—*What the fuck are you looking at?*—and they step aside.

Naturally, Frances's mother peppers her with questions when she pulls up in front of the school and Frances gets into the car.

"At least tell me if you had a good time," Alice says.

Frances gives her the most disdainful look she can manage and says, "Do I look like I had a good time? Would I be calling for a ride home if I was having a good time?"

"Oh, dear."

"It was the worst night of my life. I hate the whole idea of a stupid dance and a student council and stupid school colors. What a bunch of idiots. I will never go to another school dance. Ever. I swear. Don't even call me to the phone if another boy gets it into his head to invite me. Not that one will. Anyway, that's that. The dating phase of my life is over, and I don't want to talk about it. Ever. Again."

Frances's mother says, "At least I won't have to worry about you running off and eloping before you get that education."

"I don't know what education you're talking about," Frances says. "And you don't have to sound so pleased, and God, I wish just for once that you'd quit harping."

At home in her room, she hangs up the new dress, which she likes. It's navy blue with a white collar, and it's short. Her mother thought it was too short. She looks at the dress on its hanger and decides to wear it—her failure—to school on Monday, just to show Mark Whatever-his-name-is that she didn't get the dress just for him, and to show everyone else that, in her opinion, school dances are nothing special.

It's sort of true, since they are regular occurrences. There's another one for Halloween, one before the Christmas holidays, and a few more before the school year is done. Valentine's Day is a big one. It seems as if the student president is always on the intercom with his "No drinking, no smoking" warning. Whenever she hears him, she thinks about Mark and his mickey of vodka. She'd like to tell a teacher what goes on in the parking lot, but she knows what the consequences of that would be.

True to her word, she doesn't even think about going to another dance.

Also true: no one asks.

WHEN FRANCES HITS grade ten, her mother insists that she make supper once a week. She tries macaroni and cheese, but it looks more like day-old porridge. (*How much flour did you use? A cup? Surely not.*) Her mother says, "Even a career woman needs to know how to cook." It sounds like the closing statement in a debate, and Frances is driven to point out the contradiction in her mother's logic, mainly to be argumentative, and says that an educated woman—the kind her mother admires so much—might not want to get married at all.

"And hypothetically," Frances says, "a career woman might earn enough money that she wouldn't have to cook. She could eat in restaurants. She could eat Kentucky Fried Chicken every day if she wanted." Kentucky Fried Chicken is now the holy grail of food to Frances. It has replaced Teen Burgers as her meal of choice when they go to Yellowhead.

"What kind of job would earn you enough money for that?" her mother asks.

Oh, her mother is so obvious, seizing on the fact that higher earnings—the ones that buy you Kentucky Fried Chicken—result from higher education. Even the word "career" coming from Frances's mouth is, to her mother, an opening.

"I'm not talking about me," Frances says. "But a lawyer, say. Some hypothetical woman lawyer."

The way the word "lawyer" creates hope in her mother's eyes.

Frances's father says, "She's got you there, Mother. No woman lawyer could cook like you do. I'd bet the farm on that."

"Oh, how would you know?" Alice snaps. "And she *could* be a lawyer, if she set her mind to it. I have dreams for you, Frances. You're not going to end up married to a few half sections of bush and cow shit if I can help it."

Even Alice looks shocked by what she's said.

"I hope that's not yourself you're talking about there," Basie says.

"And what if it is?"

Silence.

"She's got you there, Dad," says Frances, attempting levity.

Neither one of her parents laughs.

"Well, stop worrying," Frances finally says to her mother. "I have no interest in signing on as some man's domestic help." She points her fork at the macaroni-and-cheese casserole and says, "If I did, he would be disappointed."

Still no laughs.

The evening passes with nothing further said about Frances's future. Before they all go to bed, her mother says, as though apologizing, "You have to admit, Basie, farming is nothing but work."

Not long after, her mother's obsession with grandiose career choices goes into overdrive. She reminds Frances that Esme Sullivan left money for tuition, so that should not be a concern; she can afford to be picky. Frances is lucky, she says—not everyone has that kind of freedom to choose. The career suggestions come up at the supper table, in the car on the way to town, in front of the television.

"Women make good doctors. Dr. Frances Moon. I can see it on an office door. Give me one good reason why not."

"I'll give you one," Frances says. "I don't want to be a doctor. Is that good enough?"

Her mother had just learned about library science, having seen a program on the National Library of Canada. "What about that?" she asks. "You like books."

"Seriously, you want me to pay a bunch of money to learn the Dewey decimal system?"

"Biology, then. What about biology?"

"You mean a lab tech?"

"Lab tech? You need to be more ambitious than that,

Frances. You want to be *head* of the lab, not just a technician."

"All right. Here's ambition for you. I'm going to beauty school, and I'm going to be a hairdresser to the stars. Figure out how to make that happen, and I'll do it."

That look again.

Frances begins walking around the house with her transistor radio in her hand, even when her mother's talking. (The song about knowing the way to San Jose . . . Where is San Jose, anyway?)

"It's not just me, Frances," her mother says. "Your father wants you to get a good education too."

"He doesn't care," Frances says. "He'd be just as happy if I married a farmer and started having babies, one after the other."

Worse than horrified.

"That, Frances, would be a terrible mistake. I couldn't bear it."

Frances feels bad, but not bad enough. She finds herself telling her mother there's a rumor at school that Myrna Samples is pregnant and the father is Buddy Hynde, a boy from St. Agnes, and everyone is saying they might get married.

"But Myrna is in your class, isn't she? She's only fifteen."

"Sixteen," Frances corrects. "She's turned sixteen."

Her mother's face turns pale, as if she's just learned that someone died.

That night, Frances lies in bed in the dark and tries to picture herself in Myrna Samples's life, her future, Buddy and babies. Then she tries, just for the heck of it, to picture herself in the life her mother wants for her—university, an apartment in some city—but all she can see is herself in the backseat of a car with a map in her hand.

The next morning Frances wakes up cranky—the crankiest she's ever been—and it gets worse as she rummages for clothes and gets herself dressed for school. She doesn't want to go, but there's a test they've been told not to miss. She looks at herself in the bathroom mirror and *despises* what she sees. She doesn't know what she wants, maybe to go back to bed and stay there for the rest of her life. When just she and her mother are left at the breakfast table, she says, "You're the one who wanted to make something of yourself. Why don't you go to university? Become whatever it is you always wanted to be. I'll stay here and look after Dad, and we'll be fine without you."

Slap. A hand comes across the table so fast she hardly sees it.

Frances is so shocked that she just sits at the table and stares at her mother, whose face is such a mix of rage and hurt, gaskets and tear ducts about to burst like dams, that Frances has to acknowledge she went too far. Her mother has never raised a hand to her before—no one has—and Frances can't cry foul or act indignant because she knows she deserved the slap. What is the matter with her?

They are both saved when Frances's dad comes through the door smelling like the barn, and because of his failing eyesight, he can't see the looks on both their faces, although he catches the tension in the silence and knows something is going on, and he says, "Well, what hornet's nest have I walked into here?"

Frances's mother manages to say, "Frances and I were talking about her future."

Basie says, "Oh, I see. *That* hornet's nest."

Frances fights back tears, hating both her mother and herself because they are becoming more and more alike.

AT SCHOOL, all eyes and ears are on Myrna Samples. When she misses two days in a row, the know-it-all gossip girls begin to whisper things like "I wonder if it's *premature labor*." As if they know anything, Frances thinks. Then it begins to circulate that Myrna Samples isn't actually home sick but has taken off with Buddy Hynde to get married, and then stupid Daphne Rose reports that she has firsthand knowledge—has it right from Myrna—that Myrna's mother is trying to force her to give the baby up for adoption and forget about Buddy, and the two of them must have decided not to let Myrna's mother ruin their lives.

Daphne says, "I wonder where they are right now. It's so romantic. And Buddy Hynde, only the cutest boy between here and Yellowhead. Myrna is so lucky."

Frances wants to throw up at the melodrama, even though she can't stop herself from listening. There's a song she likes, about a couple moving from town to town, following a dream that never pans out, and she imagines Myrna and Buddy Hynde on the road to some unknown place, perhaps Nashville, where she once imagined her mother on a stage belting out country songs.

After lunch that day the principal comes into Frances's homeroom class and asks if anyone knows where Myrna has gone, because it is very serious to run away, and if anyone knows, he says, they should speak to him privately in his office. If they know anything at all, he says, they should come forward, because Myrna's parents are very worried about her.

Frances wonders why he doesn't mention Buddy, and whether
Daphne will say anything, since she claims to have spoken
with Myrna.

When Frances gets home from school, her mother says
she learned at the post office that Buddy Hynde abducted
Myrna from her house, took her from the breakfast table
right in front of her mother. And apparently he'd said he had
a knife. Myrna had tried to make him leave, but he wouldn't.
Then, as he was dragging her from the kitchen, she'd grabbed
her mother's arm and pulled her housecoat right off. And
Buddy had pushed Myrna into his car and they'd driven away,
and Myrna's mother is now, obviously, just beside herself.

"Do you know anything about this?" Frances's mother
asks her. "The kids must have been talking about it at school."

"The principal came to our class," Frances says. "But he
didn't tell that part of the story. He just said Myrna was gone
and her parents were worried. Someone said she and Buddy
ran off together."

"Well, they certainly didn't just run off," Alice says. "That
Hynde boy took her."

The story is on the provincial news. Two minors from
north of Yellowhead are missing, the radio says, the girl taken
against her will and presumed to be in danger. Descriptions
of Myrna, Buddy, and the car follow, along with the supposed
direction they are traveling. No names are given.

"Look at that," says Alice. "We're in the news again. What
must people think of us?" Frances knows she's referring to
Silas Chance all those years ago, his death a mystery that has
never been solved.

A couple of hours later the phone rings and it's someone Alice knows in town saying that the two have been

found. Buddy's father discovered them at his hunting cabin, the woman says. They were trying to keep warm with only a woodstove. They all went to the RCMP detachment, and now Buddy is under arrest and Myrna is home with her parents. Alice shakes her head; it's all too sordid and ignorant, the result of pants-chasing and not enough attention paid to the future.

Three days after that, Myrna is back in school telling everyone that Buddy Hynde is a loser and she hopes they lock him up forever. When Myrna and Frances end up in the washroom together, just the two of them, Myrna speaks to her like they're friends (*what?*). She gets her lipstick out of her purse and holds it up for Frances to see. "Daredevil Pink," she says. "It's new. I love it. Give me your wrist and we'll see if it suits you."

Frances doesn't give Myrna her wrist. "I don't look good in pink," she says.

For some misguided reason, Frances takes this exchange as an indication that she is in Myrna's confidence, and she thinks she has to say something sympathetic, so as Myrna purses her lips and applies Daredevil Pink, Frances says, "I guess it will be hard to give up the baby." She's looking sideways at Myrna to see if she is *showing* yet, and Myrna sees this and turns and looks at Frances like she is the most pathetic person on the face of the earth. Then she looks away without another word, drops her lipstick in her purse, and leaves the washroom as though Frances isn't even there.

Frances wants to shout after her, *Stupid bitch for getting yourself knocked up in the first place*, but she's embarrassed, and anyway, Myrna is gone now and she's in the bathroom alone. She shuts herself in a cubicle and skips the next class.

She stands on the toilet seat so no one can see her legs, but no other girls come in, and when she hears the bell she goes to her next class, social studies, and no one seems to have noticed that she's been missing. As the teacher drones on about how the Second World War started—something about the invasion of Poland and not the bombing of England—Frances thinks about Myrna and Buddy driving down the highway, and she wishes that they'd had a car accident and that Myrna had been killed, or better yet, permanently disfigured.

A week later the story of Myrna and Buddy is old news and no one seems to know for sure whether Myrna was abducted or went willingly. The RCMP let Buddy out of jail, and before you know it Myrna is *Buddy this* and *Buddy that* in the halls at school as though the whole thing never happened and she isn't pregnant and is an ordinary teenager with a boyfriend in the next town—only before long you can see that she is definitely pregnant, and Daphne begins spreading the rumor that Buddy Hynde isn't the father. There's even a fight in the parking lot at school, and Myrna grabs Daphne by the hair and bites her on the cheek before a teacher breaks it up. They're both suspended for a day, and when Daphne comes back she has a Band-Aid on her cheek and tells everyone she had to get a rabies shot.

When Frances's mother says to her one evening, "I hope this business with Myrna has taught you a lesson or two," Frances says back, "Like what? That Myrna deserves her reputation as a one-size-fits-all boot?"

Her mother says, "Well, that wasn't very nice, was it?" but she looks pleased with Frances's response.

Later that summer, Alice comes home and says that Myrna had the baby and gave it up for adoption.

"That's very sad," she says to Frances, "but for the best. I hope the rest of you girls will take a lesson from that."

Frances just shakes her head. The idea that "Don't be like Myrna" is something she needs to be told.

IN SPITE OF the constant reminders of the pitfalls of not taking school seriously, Frances finds high school easier than elementary school. She makes her mind up to aim for mediocrity, and she's able to hide in the shadows of the students who capture the teachers' attention for one reason or another, good or bad. Her lack of interest in sports or dances or other extracurricular activities goes unnoticed. Because she does well enough on her exams—somewhere between Bs and Cs—no teacher has expectations one way or the other, and she finds herself in a comfortable place in the middle. School becomes something she neither likes nor hates. One teacher suggests that she join the camera club, but when Frances politely declines, he doesn't seem to care. Her mother keeps her eye on her grades because, she says, "Someone in this house has to mind that you have good enough marks to get into university." Frances neither agrees nor argues. She can stay in the middle just by showing up, so that's what she does. She avoids thinking about graduation, still almost two years away. Something will present itself. She knows jobs for girls are few and far between in Elliot, and those that do exist get snapped up by town girls, but she has a fallback plan—that is, to stay home and be her father's eyes whenever he needs her. When she turns sixteen and gets her driver's license, she becomes his chauffeur, driving him to town and back. She often goes in with him when he has business at the bank or the lumberyard or the parts dealership. She reads for him and tells him where to sign.

Once she hits grade twelve, her mother asks, over and over again, in a panic that seems to have no effect on Frances, "What are you going to do next year? The time for university applications will be here before you know it."

Frances says, over and over again, "It's my life, not yours."

Just to get her mother off her back—to get university and doctors and lawyers out of her head—she tries once more to convince her to look into hairdressing school in Yellowhead, but her mother won't hear of it.

Her mother says, "Esme Sullivan did not leave you money to waste learning how to put curlers in people's hair."

"Esme said I should do whatever I want," Frances says. "You weren't there, but that's what she told me."

One day Frances's father tires of the arguing and says that he doesn't want to hear another word.

"Let the girl make up her own mind," he snaps at Alice. "You should know by now that she's going to anyway."

"Thank you," Frances says.

"Don't take that to mean I'm on your side," her father says. "I'm just sick of hearing about it."

The tone of his voice throws her for a loop. Up until now, she'd assumed that her father *was* on her side, or was at least ambivalent. His desertion is a bit of a blow.

The stomachaches Frances had frequently as a child come back, but she doesn't say anything. She misses a fair amount of school with what she says are headaches, and her mother accuses her of staying up too late watching TV and reading novels. "You're getting dark circles under your eyes," she tells her. Frances looks in the mirror and sees it's true. She's surprised to realize that she has apparently become as concerned with her future as her mother is. It has snuck up on her. She starts buying concealer at the drugstore in town to cover the circles. She wonders if she's dying of some rare disease. Her mother takes her to an optometrist because of the headaches and it turns out she needs glasses.

She tells herself, *Something is bound to present itself*, but she's beginning to think that perhaps nothing will.

Then it does.

IT'S A MYSTERY to Frances what exactly catches the attention of Joe Fletcher. In the spring, when she's seventeen, not quite an adult but almost, she notices him looking at her when she goes into the parts dealership with her father. She has a book with her and sits in a chair by the window to read while she waits. Her father stands at the counter as usual while Joe leafs through the parts catalogue. She can hear them talking about the weather and seeding and, eventually, the tractor part her father needs and how much it will cost and whether a used one might be available somewhere.

At first, when Frances notices Joe Fletcher looking at her, she thinks he must be trying to figure out what she's reading. Then, immediately, *How ridiculous that he would be interested in my book,* and she knows that he's looking at *her*. There he goes again, talking about something in the parts book but looking at her, because she's a girl (almost a woman) and has a girl's body and is wearing shorts with her bare legs on display. She crosses her legs in what she hopes is an attractive way and pretends she doesn't see him looking.

Later, in front of the bathroom mirror, she wonders, *What is it that Joe Fletcher sees when he looks at me? What is it that men see?*

She tries to make an honest assessment of the flaws and assets of her face, as recommended by the teen magazine years ago, and she wonders if maybe Joe Fletcher likes her hair. She's always hated her red hair, but she seems to recall reading that men like it. She regrets her choice of glasses; they're too big, and she shouldn't have let them talk her into the gray frames when she'd wanted the pink. She turns sideways and looks at her profile—her breasts are too large, and she wishes she could hide them somehow. She remembers the teen magazine telling her she should stand in front of the mirror naked and analyze her body for the purpose of "enhancing" her assets, and so she strips down and gives her body (or at least as much of it as she can see in the bathroom mirror) a good look—only she isn't thinking about what clothes to wear, she's wondering what Joe Fletcher might think if he were to see her naked. She feels her temperature rising, like she's flushed with fever, and she has the thought that someday a man will see her naked and touch her body (*everywhere!*) and she quickly steps back into her clothes.

There's a knock on the bathroom door. Her mother.

"What are you doing? You've been in there for an hour."

"I'm minding my own business," Frances says, trying not to sound guilty. She straightens her clothing and gives the bathroom to her mother.

It's perplexing for Frances to realize that she likes having caught Joe Fletcher staring at her. Is it possible that he's as old as her father? He likely has a wife somewhere, a bunch of kids. Still, a couple of times at lunch hour she walks from the school to the dealership and pretends to be looking for her father. The first time, Joe is there and she brazenly goes to the counter and asks, "Has my dad been in? Just wondering."

Joe shakes his head and then Frances isn't sure what to do or say next. She finally says, "If you do see him, tell him I'm looking for him."

Then she turns and walks back out again, enjoying the fact that she can feel Joe's eyes watching her walk. She's pleased with herself and wonders if what she's done could be called flirting.

The next time she goes in on the pretext of looking for her father, Joe isn't there. The owner's wife, Mrs. Borsa, is standing at the parts counter with the till drawer open.

Mrs. Borsa closes the drawer and says, looking at Frances over her reading glasses, "Can I help you?"

"No, that's okay," Frances says.

"You must have come in here for some reason."

Frances knows her face is turning red. Mrs. Borsa can tell she's up to something. Then Joe comes in from the warehouse out back, wiping oil off his hands, and Mrs. Borsa says, "Joe, this girl here—Basie Moon's daughter—just came into the shop for no good reason. What do you make of that?" She says it as though she suspects Frances of being up to some girl-flirting trick.

"I'm looking for my dad," Frances manages to say. "He comes here sometimes, and he needs me to read for him."

"Haven't seen him today," Joe says.

"Well," Mrs. Borsa says, "I knew there had to be a reason. High school girls don't normally come here and then blush to beat sixty when you ask them what they want."

Frances turns and leaves the shop as quickly as she can. This time she doesn't care whether Joe's eyes follow her or not. All she can think is that Mrs. Borsa is a first-class old bitch. How did she know that Frances had come in to show herself off for Joe?

But how could she know? Unless Joe himself knows— can tell what Frances is up to—and has said something, but that's not likely. Joe barely talks, that's what her father says about him, he's a man of few words, and besides, all Frances did was ask for her father. Anyway, Frances thinks, she wasn't really flirting *with Joe*, if that's what the old bag thought. She was just practicing.

She crosses the street and goes into the grocery store to buy a Coke, and when she comes out she sees that Joe is standing in front of the dealership smoking a cigarette. He gives her a nod. (*Was she just imagining that?*) She pretends not to see him and hurries back to school.

When she gets home later, Frances says to her mother, "Were you and Dad in town today?"

"No, why?"

"I thought I saw Dad in the parts shop at noon, and when I went in, Mrs. Borsa was really rude."

"She can be that way. I hope you were polite all the same. We do business there."

"Next time I see her, I won't be polite. Maybe I'll take one of those courses—bookkeeping, or whatever it's called—and come back and get *her* job. See how she likes that."

"Her husband owns the business, so I hardly think that will happen. And bookkeeping is a menial job, not much better than hairdressing."

"Oh, stop it," Frances says.

A few days later, on a Saturday, her father wants her to go to the dealership with him and she says no.

"No?" he asks. "Why not?"

"I'm sick of going in there," Frances says. "I'm never needed anyway."

"I need your driving," he says. "A blind man relies on his chauffeur."

She agrees to drive him to town, but she's not going in with him. She'll stay close, she says, in case he needs her for something.

On the way into town, Basie tells Frances that he has a new joke. "What does a turkey say when he sees a blind man with an axe?"

"Moo," Frances says. "That's as old as the hills."

She parks the truck and then goes into the drugstore while her father takes care of his business at the dealership. She sees a sign on the counter advertising an ear-piercing sale—the piercing is free if you buy the earrings—and right then and there she decides to do it, get her ears pierced. The pharmacist's wife is the piercer, and she asks Frances if she has her parents' permission and Frances lies and says she doesn't need her parents' permission because she's eighteen. The pharmacist's wife freezes Frances's earlobes with ice cubes and sticks a needle through, and then she inserts little gold sleepers and tells her to turn them several times a day and apply rubbing alcohol to prevent infection.

Because it's a slow day in the drugstore, the pharmacist's wife—who is the closest thing the town has to a cosmetologist—offers to make up Frances's eyes with liner and shadow and mascara, just for fun. Frances lets her and is pleased with the new look. Even with her glasses on, her eyes look better. She picks out some pink lipstick (pale pink, Baby Blush, because of her hair) and puts it on. She's wearing a new brown-and-green-striped T-shirt that she ordered from the Eaton's catalogue, and the whole effect is, she thinks, very stylish. She wonders if she should grow her hair long, if there's any chance she could tame the curls so she wouldn't look like a rag doll.

The ice cube freezing wears off and Frances's earlobes begin to burn. She pays for the earrings, lipstick, and eye makeup, along with a bottle of rubbing alcohol and also a Popsicle because her ears are so hot she needs something to cool herself down. The pharmacist's wife has her write her name on a piece of paper for a draw for an LP, and Frances drops it in a huge pickle jar on the counter.

When she gets outside, she doesn't want to eat the Popsicle in case it ruins her lipstick, so she puts it in the truck, which is parked in the shade. Then she waltzes into the dealership to show off her new self and collect her father, hoping that Mrs. Borsa will be there so she can ignore her. She sticks her hair behind her ears so her earrings will show up better.

Joe is inside but not her father.

"Oh," she says. "Where's my dad?" She hates the way that sounds, as if she's twelve years old instead of seventeen.

"He left," Joe says. "Didn't say where he was going." Frances is sure he's noticing the earrings and makeup. She straightens her back, showing herself off, something she would never, ever do in front of the boys at school.

"Well," she says, "if he comes back tell him I'm at—" Where, where should she go? Where would she sound more grown-up? "Tell him his limousine is leaving in fifteen minutes. I don't have all day to wait around."

And Joe laughs. "I'll tell him that," he says.

"Okay, then," she says, pleased with herself, pleased that Joe Fletcher *appreciated* her sass, and she tries to look *sassy* as she steps back outside and lets the screen door to the dealership swing closed after her.

She finds her Popsicle melted all over the seat of the truck, right where her father will have to sit, no hiding it. She looks under the seat and in the truck box for something to clean it with but comes up empty-handed. Then her father comes along and jumps into the truck before she can stop him, and he sits right in the melted Popsicle. He's all for going into the dealership to ask Joe for water and a rag, but she can just hear her father telling Joe that she'd melted her Popsicle as if she were a child. She convinces him it can wait until they get home.

"And I'm the driver," she says, "so I get to decide."

"You're getting bossy in your old age," he says, but he goes along. He throws the sticky wrapper on the floor and avoids the mess on the seat as best he can.

"Joe Fletcher's wife must talk enough for the both of them," Frances says as she starts the truck.

"I don't think he has a wife," her father says, squeezing himself up against the door.

When they get home, her mother, predictably, has a fit about the earrings and the eye makeup, but then she says, "Well, you're almost an adult, so I guess I can't stop you. Not that I ever could."

Within a week, one of Frances's earlobes is so infected she can hardly stand it. It feels as though red ants are biting. She's in the bathroom cleaning both lobes with alcohol when her mother comes in, has a look, and says, "I think you're going to have to take those out and let the holes grow over."

"Never," Frances says. Her pierced ears represent the new Frances. The one who wears makeup and knows how to get grown men like Joe Fletcher to look at her.

When she's done cleaning her ears for the umpteenth time that day, she slumps in a living room chair, miserable with the fear that her mother might be right and she'll have to let her ears grow over, and there's Patsy Cline looking at her from an album cover, and she puts the album on the record player and listens to it.

Poor Patsy Cline. Her future: nothing, because she's long dead.

Poor Frances. No future either, even though she's alive and kicking.

And then, Joe Fletcher shows up in the yard with the tractor part Frances's father ordered. A part from Borsa's has never before been delivered. Normally, Mrs. Borsa calls to say the part is in, and Frances or Alice picks it up. Frances can't help wondering why Joe Fletcher has chosen to bring the part to the farm. A tingling possibility—that he's come because of her.

"I was passing by," he says to Frances's father.

They take the part out to the tractor and Joe helps install it. He's not dressed in greasy overalls now, but rather is wearing clean jeans and a cowboy shirt. Frances sits on the step at the house and pretends to read a book, but she can't stop watching Joe Fletcher, intent on her father's tractor. Everyone is amazed that her blind father is able to maintain his own machinery, but she knows he'll be appreciating the extra set of hands—hands that belong to someone who actually knows what he's doing.

When Joe and her father are finished with the tractor and begin to walk toward the house, Frances tries to look lost in her book. She hears her father ask Joe into the house for a cup of coffee—"I owe you at least that for your trouble"—but

Joe says he has to get home, thanks all the same. Frances dares to look up, and she closes the book and stands in a way that she just knows will draw his attention. Thank goodness her father is blind. She goes in the house and doesn't look out the window until she hears Joe's truck leaving the yard.

Is it really possible that Joe Fletcher brought the tractor part because of her, and not as a service to her father? She reaches up to her ear, the one that was infected but is now almost healed, and turns the little gold hoop round and round, barely aware that she's doing it.

The next day someone from the drugstore phones to say she's won the draw for an LP, a compilation of Bobby Bare's big hits.

Who wants to listen to those old songs?

Maybe she does.

Joe Fletcher calling her baby, all night long.

GRADE TWELVE FINALS are coming up and everyone is talking about them. It annoys Frances that all the teachers assume Jimmy Gulka will graduate with the best grades, get all the scholarships, and eventually put Elliot on the map for something good, rather than crimes and accidents. She finds herself harboring a secret desire to beat Jimmy Gulka in at least one subject. She chooses math—algebra and trigonometry both—and begins to study. Her mother notices, but Frances says, "Don't get your hopes up. I just don't want to fail. Grade twelve finals are hard, you know."

When exams are finally over and the teachers begin their marking, they realize that Frances—who has been a B-minus student throughout high school—has aced almost everything. She beats Jimmy Gulka in both math courses and graduates with the second-highest average in her class. (Jimmy Gulka has the highest because of one subject, social studies, in which Frances had to settle for a B.) There's a flurry of phone calls to her house from the school about what they can do to help get Frances to university. She watches the fuss from a distance, as though it's happening to someone else.

Her mother is more disappointed than ever. If Frances was going to turn up the heat—which she obviously had—why didn't she do it sooner? And why, if she was planning to surprise everyone with this turnaround, had she not filled out the applications for scholarships and universities when the school made them available several months ago? Frances gets tired of hearing about her mother's regret, how she'd so wanted to hear it said at the graduation ceremony—and it was now clear this *could* have been said, with authority—that Frances Moon was heading for university. "Frances's future: law, commerce, teaching, architecture. The sky's the limit for Frances Moon."

Instead, on a hot night at the end of June, the principal tells one and all—students, parents, everyone in town, it seems, all dressed up for the graduation—that Frances's future is "employment" (and even that isn't a sure thing, since she doesn't have any job prospects). Jimmy Gulka's future is civil engineering. He's presented with the school's academic scholarship, plus another scholarship sponsored by an oil company. The principal also announces, perhaps prematurely, that when the provincial results are tallied, Jimmy's sure to be awarded a premier's medal for academic achievement. There's a small scholarship designated for a girl, sponsored by the local Kinette club, and it goes to Caroline Smith, who's planning to go away to take nursing and live in a nurses' residence. Her grades are not especially good, nothing like Frances's, but it's a scholarship you had to apply for, and of course Frances had not applied. Frances knows this kills her mother at the graduation, seeing Caroline Smith pick up the girls' scholarship and hearing it said that her future is medicine.

Frances does receive one award, which she is definitely not expecting. When she's asked to come to the stage as the recipient of the most improved award, she says, under her breath, "You've got to be kidding me," but then she walks up and stands under the decorated arch and accepts her plaque and a check for twenty-five dollars. When she gets back to her seat between her parents, her mother doesn't even congratulate her. It's as though most improved is a disgrace.

On the way home in the car, Alice says, "Nursing is not the same as *medicine*. You'd think that Smith girl was going in for a doctor, the way they said that. And then I had to sit there and hear it said that your future is *employment*."

"Well, at least they didn't say our girl's future is unemployment," her father says.

Frances says, "Don't take it out on Caroline. She's actually kind of nice. She'll likely make a good nurse."

Alice says, "The only positive thing I can think of to say is that you didn't end up like Myrna Samples." (Myrna was at the graduation with her giant belly on display, pregnant with more Buddy Hynde progeny. The last couple of months at school she'd been showing off her diamond engagement ring and going on and on about her *fiancé*, the same boy who had abducted her two years earlier, although there's now a lot more skepticism about that.)

"It's true," Frances says. "I didn't end up like Myrna. For one thing, you have to have a boyfriend to get pregnant."

Her mother looks at her as though she'd like to strangle her. As they pull into the yard, Alice says, "So that's that. Your education is over. You are as educated as you will ever be. A sorry state of affairs. It breaks my heart."

Frances says, "I'm not Einstein, you know. It's not like the world is going to miss out on some amazing invention, or a cure for cancer that couldn't possibly be discovered by anyone else."

When they make a trip to Yellowhead a few weeks later, Frances uses the money from her most improved prize to buy an acoustic guitar and a how-to-play book. Her parents think she's wasting it, since she's never before shown an interest in learning a musical instrument. They stop in town on the way home to pick up the mail and there it is in the paper—Jimmy Gulka has won a premier's medal. Frances's mother folds up the paper and doesn't say another word the rest of the way to the farm.

A STATEMENT OF FACT, not a question: "I've come to take you to the movie show."

It's Joe Fletcher, who has driven into the yard on a warm Saturday evening in July. Frances's father had thought he'd come on business, but Joe asked to speak to Frances.

Frances grabs a sweater off the hook by the door and says to her parents, "I'm going out for a bit." She doesn't tell them where she's going. She doesn't give them a chance to say, "You're not going anywhere with that man," which is what she knows they would say, or at least her mother would. She doesn't look back as she and Joe leave the yard and drive toward town.

The movie is a James Bond movie, with Roger Moore as

the new Bond. It's a year old because this is Elliot. While Joe buys their tickets, Frances studies the poster in the foyer and tries to guess at Roger Moore's age. Before the lights dim in the theater, she sees several people she knows from school. Daphne Rose is sitting just a few rows in front of them. On the way out of the theater after the movie, Frances stops at the washroom and Daphne follows her in and says, "Are you with Joe Fletcher—I mean *with* him?" Frances says, "He's a friend of my father's," and Daphne says, "I just wondered," and Frances knows that Daphne is going to tell everyone, it's going to be all over town that she's dating Joe Fletcher, even though she didn't say that.

She's a bit disappointed that Joe drives her straight home. She says thank you and gets out of the truck. "Bye," she says, giving him a little wave.

He nods and drives away.

Her parents are waiting up. Even her father, who normally goes to bed early, since he gets up at four-thirty every morning to feed and milk the cows.

"Well, I hope you're pleased with yourself," her mother says. "I just got a phone call telling me that you and Joe Fletcher were smooching it up in the back of the movie theater—*necking*, I believe is how it was put."

"That's a lie," Frances says. "Who told you that?"

"He is at the very least twenty years older than you, Frances. More than twice your age and definitely old enough to be your father. What does a man that age want from a young girl with no experience? I can tell you what."

"That's disgusting," Frances says. "Tell her, Dad. You know him."

Frances's father clears his throat. "I don't know him that

well," he says. "I agree with your mother, Frances. He's too old for you. We're in agreement on that."

"So you'd be happier, then, if I went out with an imbecile my own age than a nice person who's older than me," she says. "Anyway, I'm a grown-up. I can make up my own mind about who I go out with." She goes to her room. She can still hear her mother saying, "You talk to her, Basie. Maybe she'll listen to you."

The next Saturday night, Joe Fletcher pulls into the yard and they go again to the Roxy in town. He doesn't ask her if she wants to go. He just states the fact: "I've come to take you to the movie."

Maybe that's why it's easy to go with him; there are no decisions to be made—she just goes. By all rights she should be a nervous wreck at even the thought of sitting next to a man in a truck cab, but she isn't. Miraculously, she believes she knows the rules of this game. It's like when she decided to get good grades on her exams, and just like that she knew how. She begins to make an effort before Joe comes—fixes her hair, puts on lipstick and a bit of eye makeup. She believes she has a kind of power when she's with Joe Fletcher that she's never felt with boys her own age.

At the movies, they share a box of popcorn. When they accidentally make contact in the popcorn box, they both quickly pull their hands away as though some protocol has been breached. She thinks, *There's something going on here. It's not just me.* She's curious that Joe, who is obviously a shy man, has been able to drive into the yard and pick her up and take her out in public, knowing that her parents disapprove. He must know that they do, although they shouldn't. If she were out with a boy her own age, he'd no doubt be trying to kiss her or paw at her with his clumsy hands. Joe once again drops her off right after the movie without suggesting they go anywhere else, without asking for more (whatever "more" is). How long, she wonders, before you can start calling someone your boyfriend?

Her mother tries again. She tells her this is going too far. She says she's going to get Frances's father to call Joe Fletcher himself and talk to him if Frances doesn't end it. Frances says once again that she's almost eighteen years old, an adult, and her mother had better not dare get in the way of her happiness.

"You barely know the man. How can you be talking about happiness?"

"Can't you see that I'm happy?"

"I see a foolish girl about to get herself hurt or in trouble, probably both."

The next Saturday, Frances has a feeling that Joe won't come, that her parents will have warned him off. She sits in the house moping, wanting him to come right now, even though it's still early in the day. She gets out her new guitar and tries to strum the chords to the corny old songs in her book, but she can't get them and her fingers hurt. When Joe doesn't show up, she accuses her parents of interfering, but they deny that they've had anything to do with it. Her mother looks relieved.

Frances spends the evening in her bedroom. She thinks about the word "lovesick" and wonders if that's what she is. It feels the same as being allergic to milk.

The next Saturday, he's back, as usual. He doesn't miss another. Frances knows her parents are beside themselves.

. . .

FRANCES IS in the grocery store in Elliot, staring at the cash register and thinking she could figure it out pretty quickly if anyone ever quit or died and a job in the store came up, when Lana, the clerk, asks her whether she misses high school yet. Lana has worked in the store off and on, between pregnancies, for as long as Frances can remember. She's married to the guy who drives the propane truck.

"No way," Frances says. "High school is history."

"Those years will start to look like the best of your life once you've got a bunch of kids and your waistline blows up like an inner tube. And don't look at me like that. I'm right. You'll see. So what are you doing in the fall, anyway? Getting married anytime soon? There'll be a bunch of weddings in the next year, if you get my drift."

Frances doesn't. Oh. Knocked up. That's what Lana is getting at. Like Myrna Samples. Frances pays for the bag of sugar her mother sent her to town for and wonders whether Myrna got pregnant on purpose just so Buddy Hynde would marry her.

Before she drives home, she stops at the post office to pick up the mail. There's a large white envelope addressed to her, Frances Moon, and when she opens it she finds a letter, which is her acceptance letter to the college of arts and science at the university her mother had wanted to tour the day they were robbed. At first she can't figure it out—*How did this happen?*—and then she realizes that her mother must have filled out an application without her after she'd become the dark-horse A student. She drives home recklessly, furious, and storms into the house waving the envelope.

"I'm relieved," her mother says, reading the letter. "I was

worried we'd be too late. I sent in the application after the deadline had passed." Then she says, "This is the only way you'll find a good job, Frances. Girls without an education work in restaurants and walk around with gravy spills on their aprons, hoping for a ten-cent tip. That's just the way it is, and that is not what you want. Tell me now if I've got that wrong. I'm putting my foot down. I will not allow you to live here next year and sit on your backside doing nothing. I don't care what you choose to study, but university it is."

"No," Frances says. "I'm not going."

"I won't accept no for an answer. I want you to take this letter and think. I want you to stop being selfish, and I want you to grow up and act like a girl who is on the verge of becoming a woman. You're not a child anymore, or so you keep telling me."

Then her mother goes outside and leaves her alone in the kitchen with the envelope.

Frances reads the letter once more. She empties the envelope's contents on the table and looks through a brochure that tells her what to expect as a first-year student. It contains photos of smiling young men and women carrying books and looking like they're in an advertisement selling success and happiness. She rips up the letter and leaves the torn pieces next to the brochure on the table. Then she goes to her room and cries for an hour. Eventually, she falls asleep, and when she wakes up she can smell chicken frying. She expects to find her mother livid with anger, and she makes up her mind that she won't fight but will simply refuse to talk about it. But nothing more is said about the letter, which her mother no doubt found in pieces on the table. Not a word is spoken about anything, not even Joe Fletcher, as Frances and her parents sit down to chicken and mashed potatoes. They eat in silence until Frances's father wipes his plate with a slice of bread and says, "Well, I can't stand another minute of this," and he leaves the kitchen and goes back outside. Alice clears off the table and puts the dirty dishes in the sink, and Frances gets up to wash them. Her mother dries.

The silence is terrible, even to Frances, but the conversation about her education appears to be over.

IN SEPTEMBER, Frances turns eighteen without much fanfare. A cake, yes, along with eighteen candles and a set of pens in a leather box, clearly purchased some time ago and intended for the academic life that has now started without her presence. She says thank you, although what she'd really wanted was a special celebration with a boyfriend, with Joe Fletcher.

On Friday, Frances drives to town in her mother's car to return library books, or at least that's her excuse, and she walks up Main Street and past the dealership in hopes of seeing Joe, but instead she runs into Daphne Rose, who acts as though they're old school pals.

"Did you hear that Myrna had her baby?" Daphne asks. "A boy. She was in labor for *two whole days*, and they had to use forceps to pull the baby out. My God, can you imagine? I would die. Anyway, she's calling the baby Morgan after . . . oh, I can't remember. And did you know that she and Buddy broke up? They aren't getting married, but Myrna is keeping the baby anyway. Not like the other one." A commiserative look comes over Daphne's face and she says, "After all they've been through, they end up splitsville. She'll need her friends, don't you think? We should go and see her. Do you want to?"

Why? Why in the world is Daphne even talking to her, let alone suggesting they go together to see Myrna Samples? But Frances is caught off guard, and even though she wants nothing to do with Daphne, she hears herself saying, "Sure. Okay."

"You look way different since you started wearing makeup," Daphne says. "Anyway, I have to run. I'll phone you."

Frances stares after her and wonders what that was all about. She doesn't expect Daphne to call her. She hopes she doesn't.

She and her mother are making supper later—Frances is peeling potatoes and Alice is browning pork chops on the stove—when Alice asks, "What is it that you like about that man?"

Here it comes again, Frances thinks. He's too old for you.

"Joe, you mean?" she says. "His name is Joe."

"All right, then," her mother says. "Joe. What is it that you like about Joe?"

It's the first time her mother has asked a serious question about him. Maybe, Frances thinks, she is genuinely interested in the answer.

She says, "We like the same things, movies. I like the fact that he's not a stupid teenager. And he doesn't know me from school, which counts for a lot. And I don't really care about our ages, so don't start on that."

"Please don't let this go too far," Alice says. "He'll have . . . expectations. Surely you know that."

Frances sighs and digs at a potato eye. Her mother is very fussy about the eyes. She wants no black spots on her boiled potatoes. "Do you mean sex, Mother?" she asks. "Is that what you're talking about? You should just say it."

"A man that age is not going to go out with a girl for long

before he . . . well, you know what I mean. Young people are meant to go out with other young people. I'm warning you, Frances. This will not go well if you continue to see that man. Do you want to end up like Myrna Samples? Two pregnancies. Honestly."

"Joe. His name is Joe, and I have no intention of ending up like Myrna Samples. How stupid do you think I am? And by the way, Myrna had her baby, and she and Buddy broke up and she's keeping the baby anyway. That's what comes of a girl dating someone her own age. Now Myrna is saddled with a baby. Anyway, quit talking like Joe Fletcher wants to marry me." She whips at a potato with her peeler and takes a slice of skin off her knuckle. "Damn it. See what you made me do?" She grabs a Kleenex and wraps it around her knuckle.

"A man wanting to marry you is not my biggest fear," Alice says. "Quite the opposite."

"That's it," Frances says, throwing her potato peeler into the sink. "Peel your own damned potatoes."

"My potatoes, are they?" her mother says. "I suppose you aren't planning to eat them."

Frances is about to say something else, but then she sees that her mother has that look on her face again—the one that says Frances is her greatest sorrow in life—and Frances can't stand it, can't stand to be in the same room as that look, and she leaves, goes to her bedroom and wonders again what happened to the mother of her childhood, the one who would put on her sunglasses and head for the lake on a hot day, *we two girls*. This mother is whiny and dismal, and there's no pleasure to be had in fighting with her, none at all.

She resolves not to take the bait next time it's offered.

．　．　．

A FEW WEEKS after Frances's eighteenth birthday, Joe picks her up and they go to a special double feature, two Clint Eastwood movies, one of them with a little too much suspense. As they're walking out of the theater, she instinctively tucks her hand into his arm (*Clint Eastwood's arm*), and then, when she realizes what she's done, she pulls it away, embarrassed. But Joe picks it up and tucks it back in, and they leave the theater like that, with plenty of eyes watching them. Let them gawk, Frances thinks, pleased with this new step, the idea of herself on Joe's arm. Well, not just an idea. She really is *on his arm*!

When Joe drops her off, after midnight, her parents have gone to bed, but when she gets inside she can see the light under their bedroom door. Through the closed door she says, "Joe Fletcher isn't as bad as you think. If you have to know, he hasn't even tried to kiss me."

There's no answer, but the light flicks off.

The next day, Daphne phones to ask if she still wants to visit Myrna, and Frances hears herself saying yes even though she knows that she should be coming up with an excuse, knows that an overture of friendship from Daphne Rose is not to be trusted. Daphne says she'll meet her in town in front of the school and they can walk over to Myrna's house together. Frances doesn't even know where Myrna lives.

Frances gets there first, and when Daphne arrives, she says they should buy the baby a present, so they go to the drugstore—the only store open on a Sunday—and pick out a package that contains a flannelette receiving blanket, a sleeper, and a little cap that looks too small to fit anything but a doll. They buy some wrapping paper and a card and some tape, and sit on a bench on the sidewalk and wrap the gift and sign the card.

"What should we say?" Daphne asks. "How about 'All the best for the future, from your friends Daphne and Frances'?"

Phony as baloney, Frances thinks, but she says, "Sure, why not."

When they get to Myrna's house, it turns out Daphne didn't tell her they were coming. Myrna's mother answers the door and Daphne says, "Hi, Mrs. Samples. We're friends of Myrna's." Mrs. Samples looks as though she might be about to send them away. Frances wants to ditch Daphne and run, but then Mrs. Samples says, "I'm glad you've come, girls. She's feeling a little blue. The baby blues, I think." No mention of Buddy and how the blues might be because of him, and how Myrna's been left with a baby and no husband.

Myrna is lying on the couch in the living room, wearing a pink terry-cloth bathrobe and looking like she's been in a war. She looks shocked to see Frances—actually glances away before staring at her again to double-check—and she barely acknowledges Daphne. Frances thinks she's maybe made her biggest mistake ever by coming. Maybe Myrna and Daphne aren't even friends. She remembers the catfight at school. Then Myrna sits up on the couch and apologizes for the way she looks, and Daphne hands her the baby gift. Myrna opens it and looks at it and puts it on the couch beside her without saying anything, not even a thank-you. Mrs. Samples brings in three glasses of Coke on a tray and sets the tray down next to a box of tissues on the coffee table. When she sees the gift, she holds it up and says, "Oh, isn't that cute? Adorable." Then she leaves again, saying, "I'll just let you girls talk." Frances hears a baby cry from another room, and she notices that Myrna doesn't turn her head toward the sound, ignores it, and Mrs. Samples calls, "Don't worry, Myrna . . . I'll get him," and then the baby is quiet. There's no mention of Mrs. Samples showing the baby to Daphne and Frances.

Frances doesn't know what to do or say, so she picks up a Coke from the tray and takes a sip. Daphne does the same. Myrna's goes untouched. Then Daphne turns to Frances and says, "So, Frances, tell us all about Joe Fletcher."

Frances almost chokes on her drink. Now she knows what this is all about.

She sets the Coke down on the table. How could she not have seen that coming?

"There's not much to tell," she says. "You've seen us at the Roxy."

"Oh, I bet there's more to it than the Roxy."

"No," Frances says. "That's it."

She knows she should leave, just get up and go, but she takes too long deciding and Daphne says, "Are you on the pill? You'd better be because, you know . . . or maybe you don't know. You were never that swift when it came to boys, were you? Maybe Myrna and I should fill you in, so you know what happens when you let a boy . . . well, not a boy exactly. I guess we're talking about Joe Fletcher. Tell us, Frances, what's it like to have an old man's hands under your sweater?"

As Daphne says all this, she keeps looking at Myrna, inviting her to join in, expecting praise for bringing her a gift—not the baby gift but a better one, the opportunity to be a high school girl again, to have some fun with Frances Moon.

"You know," says Frances, standing up from her chair, mad only at herself for not seeing what Daphne was up to,

"I've got some really pressing things to do this afternoon. Like wash my hair. Watch paint dry. Things like that. And high school's over, Daphne. Grow the hell up. Congratulations on the baby, Myrna. Thank your mother for the drink."

Then Myrna says, in a tired way, as though she too has had enough, "Daphne, you are such a mean fucking bitch. Get out of my house. And don't look so shocked. What did you think? That we're in a girl gang, you and me? Get out. This second, or I'll rip every hair out of your head." Then she picks up her glass from the table and throws her Coke all over Daphne.

Daphne jumps up, saying, "What the hell? You slutty whore!" and it's one of the most satisfying things Frances has ever seen: Daphne standing there sputtering, with Coke dripping from her bangs. For a minute it looks as if she might lunge across the table at Myrna and there'll be a repeat of the brawl that got them both suspended, but then Mrs. Samples comes into the room to see what's going on. Daphne pushes past Myrna's mother and heads for the door, shouting that she's going to get Myrna for that, she'll be sorry, she'd better watch her back.

"We'll see, you psycho bitch," Myrna shouts after her.

Both Frances and Myrna's mother stand speechless until Mrs. Samples finally says, "I've never liked that girl."

"Well, join the club," Myrna says. "Why'd you let her in?"

"I thought you needed the company."

"Thanks for nothing."

"I'd better go," Frances says. Then she apologizes to Mrs. Samples for the Coke all over the furniture.

"Why are you apologizing?" Myrna says. "It's not your fault." She sits down again, carefully, and then she starts to cry because her stitches hurt.

"Myrna, honey," her mother says.

"Sorry," Frances says, "but I'd really better go. I've got my mom's car and she might need it."

Myrna grabs a tissue in a way that says the box on the table is there for crying and not for ordinary runny noses, and says, "Really? Joe Fletcher? The guy who works at Borsa's? I always thought you'd be the one to get away from here."

Frances is surprised to learn that Myrna thinks anything at all about her.

"No," she says. "I don't want to go anywhere. Not really."

"You're out of your mind, then."

Frances doesn't want to hear that, not from Myrna Samples, not after her mother has finally stopped harping about university. "So anyway," she says, "good luck with the baby and all that. I'll see you around."

She practically runs out the door, and then she does run down the sidewalk, taking a roundabout way to where she left her mother's car in case Daphne is hiding somewhere, waiting to ambush her.

After she gets home, she spends the rest of the afternoon lying on a lounge chair by the house, suntanning with baby oil and iodine, trying to pretend it's still summer, picturing Daphne with Coke dripping from her hair, pleased that Myrna stood up for her (sort of), and thinking about Myrna's stitches, certain that she herself will never be tempted to have children.

She thinks about what Daphne said—*hands under your sweater.*

It's an unusually hot day for the end of September. Sweat beads up on her bare skin.

JOE HAS a sister named Martha in a town called Deer Valley, and he wants Frances to go there with him for Sunday supper. When Frances tells her mother where she's going, Alice gets a worried look on her face and says that when a man wants to introduce you to his family, he's planning something. "Marriage, Frances. For God's sake, put an end to this. You can't be hoping for a marriage proposal."

Marriage? Her mother is losing her mind. The word "married" seriously applied to her, Frances Moon, before any other girl in her graduation class, before even Myrna Samples, when she'd had only one date in her entire high school career? Her mother is certifiable, and she tells her so.

She and Joe arrive at a small, dark house on the edge of Deer Valley. The lack of privilege revealed by the house's interior is disconcerting. Frances has never been in a house like it. It has only two rooms: a combination living room and kitchen with a woodstove, and a second room with a curtain rather than a door, which Frances assumes is the bedroom. The house appears to have sunk into the ground since its construction, and the doorways are so low that Joe has to duck. Martha is wearing a dark navy dress and black stockings and oxford shoes. She looks like a nun, or maybe a Hutterite. She's older than Frances's mother and is very much a spinster lady, and also, it turns out, a religious Holy Roller with a deep suspicion of young people. It's immediately obvious the reach of her suspicion extends to Frances.

Joe and Frances sit on the small couch while Martha puts the food on the table. Every piece of furniture in the room is topped with at least one crocheted doily; you can't sit without knocking one out of its place, and Frances finds herself straightening the doilies behind her obsessively until Martha calls them to the table. Martha behaves as though they're late, as though the food has been waiting for hours, as though it must be Frances's fault that they're late (when, as far as Frances knows, they are precisely on time).

At the dinner table, Martha picks up Frances's left hand and Joe's right, and launches into a prayer. After that, the word "Lord" finds its way into almost every sentence that comes out of Martha's mouth, like she's channeling him into the conversation. Martha makes pronouncements such as "I do not approve of the young people in this new generation. They have grown away from the Lord and behave scandalously." Frances is actually afraid of her, thinks she might be a witch. In an effort to impress Martha, she says, hearing the nerves in her voice, "I don't go around with the kids in town much." Then it turns into an interview, with Martha asking the questions (presumably on behalf of the Lord) and Frances sitting primly with her hands folded in her lap, trying not to hyperventilate with fear.

"If you don't run with the other teenagers, what do you do?"

"Oh, I help out at home" (pretty much a lie), "and I read a lot" (the truth).

"You read?"

"Yes. I read all the time."

"And what do you read?"

"Novels, mostly. My mother bought me a set of classics. *Jane Eyre*, like that. I go to the library a lot."

"Novels are nothing but lies and romance. What do you think is the point of these romances you read?" (She didn't say romances.)

"No point, I suppose. Entertainment." Then, trying to show off her brains, "Maybe an exploration of, you know, the human condition."

"There is no point in reading made-up stories. Lies, that is. The only book of which I approve is the Good Book."

"Well, that too." (Frances isn't even sure there is a Bible in her house.)

"And which book of the Bible is your favorite?"

She tries to remember which book contains the story of the birth of Jesus, thinking that's bound to be an acceptable one. She can't, and ends up saying Genesis.

Martha says, "I am particularly fond of Revelation. It describes events to which I am looking forward, when all the sinners on this earth will get what's coming to them. I suspect that includes you."

Then Martha indicates that the interview is over and turns to her carrots and potatoes and roast beef, and Joe gets Frances out of there not long after their plates are clean, before Frances is forced to offer to help Martha with the dishes.

When they're on the way home, Joe says, "Don't mind her. You did fine."

Frances has the thought that she's spoken more words in response to Martha's questions than Joe has ever heard her say. She's mulling this over, thinking about the conversation and Martha's zeal for the end of the world, when Joe does in fact ask her to marry him, although his proposal is not phrased as a question. They're driving down the highway and he says, "I wonder if you might want to get married. To me, that is."

Stunned. Dumbfounded.

Her mother was right? She must not have heard correctly. She doesn't immediately say anything because she so believes this must be the case. He's never even kissed her. They've never really even *talked* about anything. It's one thing to walk around with a little voice in your head saying, *Frances Moon has a boyfriend who looks a bit like Clint Eastwood*, but marriage? That is something else altogether. And does he look anything like Clint Eastwood? She sneaks a glance. Not really.

On the other hand . . . there's an unfamiliar path ahead of her here, at this moment, and curiosity leads her to wonder where it will go next. What will he say next? How will he explain himself? What does a man do who has just asked a girl to marry him, and especially when that girl is her?

Here's what he does. Instead of driving Frances straight home, he pulls off the grid road and bumps the truck through an open pasture and up a little hill that overlooks a creek bed. The windows are down and the air is rich with the smell of fall and the sound of crickets. It's still and warm. Body temperature. The radio is on the country station, Conway Twitty and Loretta Lynn. Joe is sitting on his side of the bench seat, Frances on hers, until he slides over next to her, and she can feel that body temperature up against her thigh. Joe puts his arm around her and pulls her toward him.

"I know you're young," he says, "but I'll treat you right." Then he kisses her. It's the first time she's ever been kissed. And he *really* kisses her, like in the movies, not just a peck on the lips. She can hardly breathe, the intensity of a warm body so close, a man's body. The curiosity path stretches out, inviting her to choose, choose, and she can feel the heat of him in her mouth.

He stops, even though she doesn't want him to.

"What do you say?" he says.

"I'd better think about it," she says. (Was that her voice? It didn't sound like her. Also, it was a stupid thing to say—

"I'd better think about it." He might think it meant no.) "It's just . . . well, you know, we haven't known each other that long."

"Take your time," he says. Then he pulls her head to his shoulder. "No rush, eh." A few minutes later, when he slides back over behind the wheel and starts the truck, Frances is sorry. She wants to stay here, likes the way the truck cab has filled up with anticipation.

He says, "Your mother will be wondering where you've got to."

Her mother. Why did he have to bring her into this? Well, at least Frances can report that the marriage proposal came before any hanky-panky.

When they pull into the yard and the truck stops, she doesn't get out right away. She waits, thinking that Joe will kiss her again, wanting him to, but he doesn't, and so she opens the door.

"Tomorrow I'll drive you out to my place," he says. "You'll want to see it."

Frances nods and says, "Okay, then." (*Stupid, stupid. "Okay, then"—did she really say that?*)

Her parents are still up when she gets inside. Her mother sees something in Frances's face—*damn her*—but Frances can't bring herself to tell them about the proposal.

"His sister is off her rocker, if you ask me" is all she says.

Her father is looking at her too—well, not really looking, since he's blind, but still, he's studying her. She can't read his expression.

She goes to bed but can't sleep. She closes her eyes and pretends that Joe is in the bed with her, tries to imagine what that would be like—her head on his shoulder, his arm around her. His kiss. His tongue in her mouth. *She, Frances Moon, has had a man's tongue in her mouth!*

By morning, she's decided to say yes.

She tells her parents about the proposal at breakfast. Her mother looks sick, about as close to deathly ill as a healthy person can look.

Frances says, "We're going out to his farm this afternoon."

Her mother grabs the dishes off the breakfast table and throws them in the sink so carelessly it's a wonder they don't all break.

"He says it's picturesque where his house is."

Crash. A dish breaks in the sink. Maybe more than one.

Alice says, "God help us."

Frances thinks about what she should wear to her wedding.

6. A Marriage Bed

WHERE FRANCES'S PARENTS LIVE, the land is almost all cleared for farming, but north of town there are only pockets of cultivated land mixed with acres of bush.

"Bought the place from an old trapper," Joe says. "Used to be a log house here. I lived in it for a while, me and the mice. Then I knocked it down and put this up instead." He's referring to the square-looking bungalow that sits in a clearing ringed with poplars, their leaves beginning to turn bright yellow.

They get out of the truck and Frances follows Joe to the house. A collie-type dog appears from somewhere and tries to jump on her.

Joe kicks it away and says, "Get, you."

"It's okay," Frances says. "I like dogs. What's his name?"

"I just call him Dog," Joe says.

She calls the dog back, holding out her hand. He comes to her and she scratches him behind his ears. He wags his tail so hard it seems as though he's going to fall over. He's so excited he piddles on her shoe and she wipes it in the grass before Joe sees and chases the dog away again.

The house smells of woodsmoke. The door opens into the kitchen and Frances looks around and tries to imagine herself cooking and cleaning here. She tries to picture herself scrubbing the kitchen floor, tries to absorb domestic responsibility into the shadowy but gradually sharpening image of herself as a married woman.

The furniture in both the kitchen and the living room is sparse and old—not surprising, Frances thinks, for a bachelor. She'll get some matching blankets and make covers for the couch and the armchair. There's a TV on a wooden stand that looks homemade. At least there's a TV, and it's newer than the one her parents have.

She pokes around and discovers a small washroom, with a washstand and basin and a stainless steel tub. The tub has a drain and one tap for cold water, but there's no hot water and no toilet.

"Biffy's out back," Joe says. "You have to heat water on the stove. Maybe I should put in proper plumbing. Didn't really matter when it was just me here."

When it was just me. He's assuming she's going to say yes.

She looks in the bedrooms. There are two of them. The smaller one is being used to store an old motorcycle, which is in parts all over the floor.

"I'm trying to get that thing running," he says of the motorcycle. "So far, no luck."

A motorcycle! Frances thinks. Will she really get to ride on the back of a motorcycle?

The other bedroom is bigger. It has a double bed and two old dressers. There's a plaid wool blanket on the bed. Joe sees her looking at it and turns away, as though he's ashamed by the bed, the fact that he's shown it to Frances.

He says, "I'll make us a pot of coffee." Frances doesn't much like coffee, but she doesn't say so. She steps from the bedroom back into the living room. The view of the trees from the window reminds her of a calendar picture. She'd be like Heidi living out here, she thinks, or maybe Laura Ingalls. Laura Ingalls with a motorcycle.

"Joe," she says. It just slips out, intimate, like skin on skin.

He hears that she's said something. "What was that?" he asks, coming to stand with her in the window. He kisses the back of her neck and then drapes his arm around her shoulder, and she feels as though she's going to faint, just drop right out from under his arm the way you could slip through a Styrofoam ring in the water. She's sure she shuddered and wonders if he felt it.

"Have you got an answer for me?" he asks.

She nods.

"Is that a yes, then?"

"Yes." Her voice speaking, but it has a mind of its own, not her mind.

"We'll talk to your folks when I drive you home," Joe says.

He removes his arm from around her shoulder and then turns in such a way that his hand brushes down the front of her sweater, against her breasts. She steps back, thinking it was an awkward accident, like hands touching in a popcorn box, but then . . . *of course, he did it on purpose!* She's just told him that she's going to be his wife. He *wants* to touch her, *hands under sweaters*. The thought makes her knees shake. She's not afraid, though. Why should she be? She has something that a man wants, a real man, not an awkward boy scrubbed and polished by his mother. Who would have believed it just a few months ago, when she walked up to the stage in the school gym to collect her twenty-five-dollar award? Frances's future: marriage, looking forward to being felt up. She wants to laugh.

They take their mugs of coffee out to the yard. Joe shows her the spot he thinks would be good for a garden, points beyond the meadow to where his farmland is, tells her how many acres he seeds and how many acres of hay he leases to a neighbor with cattle. He has a trapline that he works in the winter. Sometimes he works in the bush. And at the dealership in the summer, of course, but she already knows that.

"Can't earn enough money farming this land," he says. "It's not like your father's land, not like south of town."

Frances doesn't care about seeded acres and farmland. She asks, because it's on her mind, "How come you've never been married?" She doesn't actually know that this is the case.

Joe says, "I was just waiting for you to be old enough."

"You weren't," Frances says. "That's a lie." Here's something else new, a side of Joe she has not seen before: he's teasing her. She feels a confidence growing between them. From now on, people will see them both the way they saw them in the past, but this thing that's growing will be apparent just to them. Again, she wants to laugh. She's in a secret world no one told her about.

They spend a couple of hours walking around the yard, up the trail through the bush, and by late afternoon, when Joe drives her home again, she's certain she's in love. How did it happen so quickly? she wonders. When Joe asked her to marry him yesterday, she wasn't sure. Now, when she thinks of him kissing her, she can hardly stand the thrill of it. She wonders about the term "engagement." Is she officially engaged, or do you have to make some kind of announcement?

She has no ring. Does that mean anything? She remembers Myrna Samples's diamond. Obviously, that ring didn't mean anything—not even a promise, since the wedding was off a month later. She doesn't want a ring, she decides, doesn't need one. Then she thinks, What is engagement anyway? Why don't they just get married? Right away. They both know what they want.

After Joe drives her home, he stays for supper, at Frances's insistence. When they're all seated at the table, he says, "Frances has agreed to marry me."

Frances's parents look at Joe, then at Frances.

"I said yes," Frances says, to break the silence.

She looks at her father. No expression gives away what he's thinking at this moment. He hasn't said a word about Joe Fletcher since he agreed with Alice that Joe was too old, had simply turned silent, turned a blind eye (or two), and let Alice deal with Frances.

When she looks at her mother, Frances can clearly see what she thinks. Alice says nothing more than "Please pass the salt," and for a minute Frances wonders if she might throw some over her shoulder to prevent any more bad luck. Why isn't anyone happy for her? Why isn't her mother jumping up to hug her, ask her when, find out what color bouquet she wants to carry?

Finally, after what seems like an eternity of silence, Joe says, "I'll take good care of her." Frances wishes he would say a bit more, be a little more convincing.

"See that you do," Frances's father says. Then he sighs and gets up from the table, and Frances thinks he'll go to the bedroom and close the door, but he goes to the root cellar and comes up with a bottle of his homemade chokecherry wine. It's the first time Frances has ever been allowed a glass of wine. Her mother pushes her glass away when Basie puts it on the table in front of her, and she actually says, "I hardly think this is cause for celebration."

Frances wants to kill her. *Kill* her, really, for not understanding that this is what she wants. She'd like to scream it: "This is what I *want*, Mother. Be happy for me. It's my life!" She's worried that Joe will leave in the face of all this rudeness from his future in-laws, but there he is, lifting his water glass of chokecherry wine, and now her father is asking him about a tractor part or—no, tires, that's it, and they pass the serving dishes and eat, and then Frances's mother is clearing the dishes from the table, stirring up a hurricane in the soapy water in the sink. Frances picks up a tea towel to dry, but her mother says, "Never mind. Go and sit with your *fiancé*." The way she spits out the word "fiancé," she might as well be talking about cow manure.

When Joe leaves an hour later, Frances walks out to the truck with him. Her head is light from the wine and she trips over her own feet and has to grab his arm. Before he gets in the truck, he puts his arms around her and then his hands find her breasts, and this time Frances is sure it's no accident. She begins to push him away, afraid that her parents will see because she and Joe are standing almost right under the yard light, but she feels that flush again, that tingle, and curiosity gets the better of her, and she lets him slip his hands up under her sweater, lets him fumble with her brassiere. She moves her arms to give him more room and . . . *oh my God, this is why girls let their boyfriends do things.* Why had no one told her this? She feels his hardness against her and she's curious about that too.

"Let's go somewhere in the truck," she says.

But he backs away from her and says, "The wedding. You and your mother decide."

After he leaves the yard, she struggles to hook her bra, sure her parents will know what she's been up to—that is, getting *felt up*. She straightens her hair and takes a few deep breaths. When she goes back inside, she finds that her father has gone to bed.

Her mother, though, is waiting for her in the living room. She has the brochure from the university on her lap, the one with information for first-year students. Frances had assumed it was long gone, turned to ash in the burning barrel along with the ripped-up letter.

"What should I do with this?" her mother asks.

"I'm not sure why you still have it," Frances says. Then she adds, "I won't be needing it, obviously."

"I was hoping," her mother says.

"Please stop," Frances says. "I have a future. I would think you'd be glad."

"Joe Fletcher? I should be glad that Joe Fletcher is your future? I despair that you've chosen marriage to a man like him. For God's sake, Frances, he's not even a proper farmer. He's some kind of jack-of-all-trades."

Frances bites her tongue, and then says, in place of what she wants to say, "How long does it take to arrange a wedding?"

Her mother leaves the room.

Two weeks later, when Frances's new blue velvet dress from the catalogue is hanging in the closet, Alice tries once more, one final attempt. "You're going to regret this choice, Frances," she says.

"You mean the blue dress? No, I won't. White is old-fashioned. And I look good in blue. You always say that."

"That's not what I meant. You can't just come running home. It won't be that simple."

"You mean you're kicking me out?" She's trying to lighten her mother up. Keep her from *ruining her happiness*.

"It's not funny. This is not something you can just change your mind about. You sign the papers and it's legal. You're married."

"Tell me something I don't know," Frances says.

Her mother looks as if she is about to tell her something she doesn't know, but she hesitates.

"What?" Frances presses.

"Since I can't seem to do anything about this, I have a piece of advice," her mother says. "I hope you and Joe will use . . . precautions, at least for a while."

"Well, that's a good piece of advice," Frances says. "I was wondering."

"There's a pill now. Do you know about the pill? I think we should go to the doctor and get you a prescription."

She thinks about Myrna Samples and the stitches and the crying baby, and agrees with her mother that she should get a prescription.

It's the first thing they've agreed on since Joe Fletcher came calling.

Maybe long before that.

A WEEKNIGHT. Wednesday. Late. Joe drives into the yard unexpectedly, and it's kind of exciting, the way he drops in like he can't live without seeing her, stands at the door waiting. Frances's father is already in bed. Her mother puts on

212 ~ DIANNE WARREN

her most disapproving look as Frances grabs her favorite gray kangaroo sweatshirt to wear against the cool night air. Frances and her mother have been arguing all day about the wedding, which is just a few weeks off. Her mother pulls her into the living room.

"I think I smelled liquor on his breath," she whispers.

"You did not," Frances says.

"If he's been drinking, do not leave this yard with him."

"Like I would," she says, deciding right then that she's going somewhere with Joe, no matter what state he's in.

"My mother thinks you've been drinking," she says when they're in the truck.

He doesn't deny it. "We don't have to go far," he says.

Go far for what? Frances slides over to sit close to him as they leave the yard.

Just a few miles from the farm, Joe pulls off the road onto an approach. It's not a romantic spot. There's a falling-down old farmhouse in front of them, and a line of dark trees that hides the sky and the stars. He turns the truck off but doesn't say anything. He's distracted. His arm is around her, but it feels like a dead weight, not a comfort. She begins to worry that he's changed his mind, or that he wants to wait. She can smell the alcohol on his breath. She's afraid of drinking, has never really been around drunk people, and is beginning to wish Joe hadn't come for her.

Then he says, "Martha thinks we should call off the wedding."

"What?" Frances says. "Call it off?"

"If you don't want to marry me, you can say so. I'll understand."

"What are you talking about?"

"I won't blame you if you want to change your mind," Joe says. "Martha thinks I might have pushed you into this."

Pushed her into it? He's barely spoken ten words about the wedding. She wonders if he's telling the truth about Martha, or if her father has taken him aside and said his piece.

She doesn't know how to respond, so she says, "Why would I call it off? I love you."

And the minute she says "I love you"—which she has never said before—she thinks it might not be true. How would she know? What does she know about love? Nothing. She's utterly confused by what she's done, what she is about to do, what she wants, why he is telling her to reconsider . . . and she starts to cry. She hates crying. She hated all those weepy girls at school crying over boyfriends and complications that were about as difficult as deciding what color lipstick to wear, and she can't stand whatever is making her feel this way.

She can tell that Joe doesn't know what to say to her. "Don't do that," he says, squeezing her shoulder awkwardly.

She tries to shove him away, but that isn't really what she wants. What she wants is for him to squeeze harder, swallow her up, and she finds his mouth with hers, asks for his kiss— craves it—even though she can smell the alcohol, and then his hands are all over her, under her sweatshirt, the zipper in her jeans down, his hand between her legs, and she parts her legs for him and is willing to go on, *all the way*, as she has heard the girls at school say, to hell with that grade nine public health nurse, *keep your knees together*, but she's sobbing now, sobbing like a child, and Joe pushes her away, saying, "Stop. Stop that." She doesn't know if he means the crying or the other, the way she wants him. "No," she says, her hand searching for his belt buckle, but he pushes it away, roughly, and says again, "Stop that."

She moves away from him and straightens her clothes, pulls up her zipper, dismayed by her loss of control, as though she is the one who's been drinking, ashamed of her desire, and then Joe says, "Maybe Martha's right. You're too young."

Too young for what? It's not clear.

She says, "My mother doesn't want us to get married either, but I'm not letting her make my decision for me. Do you want Martha to make yours? She wouldn't approve of any girl you wanted to marry, no matter how old."

Joe seems to be thinking about that. He takes out his tobacco and rolls a cigarette, and they sit in the darkness while he smokes it, saying nothing. Then he drives her home.

In the yard, he says, "If you haven't changed your mind, I won't mention it again." She counts to ten—tap, tap, tap, her old trick—her stomach in a knot, and she thinks, Everyone feels this way before they get married. How could you not—it's the rest of your life.

"I haven't," she says. It'll be a frosty Friday when Martha Fletcher decides what happens in her life.

That night, tap, tap, tap, her fingers unable to stop. When she gets up into the hundreds, she loses count.

A TRIP TO YELLOWHEAD. To buy Frances shoes to go with the blue dress. A doctor's appointment to acquire the "precautions," because Alice doesn't want her talking to the local doctor about such a thing. The cake decorations (even though Frances argued that a cake was not necessary). Then home again. Housecleaning. Someone to perform the ceremony, the United Church minister with the long hair, who still lives in Uncle Vince's house, and who insists on meeting with Joe and Frances before he'll agree to come to the farm and do the honors. He asks Frances if he can bring his guitar to the wedding and sing, any song she likes, but Frances says no, no music.

Food to prepare for the reception. Flowers to order. Wedding napkins. The invitation list includes a few of the Moons' neighbors, also farmers. Alice says if the wedding is going to be in her house, it's going to be a proper wedding so it can't be said that her daughter has run off behind her back, up the duff or with something else to hide. No friends of Joe's are invited—he doesn't want any friends there, just that horrible Martha on his guest list—but surprise . . . Myrna Samples is coming.

Frances has no idea why she asked Myrna to her wedding, except that she happened to run into her at the gas station and they had a laugh about what a loser Daphne was, and before Frances knew it she was telling Myrna about the wedding. *Just a small wedding, nothing fancy. I'm wearing a blue velvet dress instead of a white one, just to be different, I guess.* Then Myrna told Frances that she had been planning to wear a green tie-dyed dress when she married Buddy, only that wasn't happening now and she was going to make curtains for her bedroom out of the fabric. Frances impulsively asked her if she would come to the wedding, and Myrna said, "Might as well, since I won't be going to my own anytime soon." Then she told Frances that Buddy Hynde had been cheating on her with some girl named Pamela from another town. "There I was, pregnant," she said, "and there he was, acting like he had nothing to do with that and I was put on earth just to keep him from fulfilling his potential. As if he ever had any in the first place."

Frances can't believe how happy she is that Myrna is coming to the wedding. Maybe it isn't too late and she and Myrna can still be friends. She wonders if she should ask Myrna to be a bridesmaid, but decides that's going too far. Anyway, she doesn't want a bridesmaid. Even the word.

In the days before the wedding, Frances packs up the things that she wants to take with her to Joe's. There isn't much. Her new green suitcase and a few boxes filled with her clothes. A few books, some family pictures. Some things from England that belonged to her grandmother on Basie's side: a set of silver-plated coffee spoons, a tablecloth with embroidery at each of the corners—things that were oddities when her mother gave them to her years ago, and still are. She decides not to take any childhood treasures with her. Her dolls and stuffed animals stay in the closet in her room. She considers taking the guitar, but she hasn't learned to play it, and besides, it's a teenager's toy. Technically she still is a teenager, but she's in a different category now: about to be married.

Her mother presents her with what she calls a "trousseau present." When Frances opens the box, she finds a pretty satin nightgown with lace trim and a matching satin housecoat lined with soft flannel. She thanks her mother, but really, she can't imagine herself wearing such a thing. She doesn't know what could have possessed her mother to buy it. She thinks, *It's not like I've ever wanted to be a princess bride.*

She puts the nightgown and housecoat in her suitcase and closes it.

.   .   .

EVERYONE TALKS about how lucky Frances is that it's such a nice day for her wedding. It's November, they say. Anything could have happened. One of the neighbor women has already dropped off a plate of lemon squares, and Martha Fletcher is in the living room, having been delivered by Joe before he went home to change. Alice thought Martha might be an extra set of hands to help with the preparations, but instead she's plopped herself in Basie's armchair—her face as dark with disapproval as the witch's dress she has on—and she's now reading Bible passages aloud to herself. "Like a person who needs to be locked up," says Alice when she and Frances are alone in the kitchen. At least no one will have to make conversation with her, Frances thinks, as long as she's droning Bible verses in Basie's chair. Her mother says, "Thank God *you're* marrying him and not me. I'd kill that woman if I had to have anything to do with her after today." It's the closest thing to acceptance of the marriage that her mother has said out loud. Frances tells her she's not planning to have anything to do with Martha Fletcher, and her mother says she might not have a choice in the matter; she'll likely have to nurse Martha into purgatory, or wherever Holy Rollers go to suffer their way into heaven. Frances says that being nursed by her would likely be suffering enough, and her mother actually laughs.

The other guests begin to arrive, and Frances goes to her room so she can make a proper entrance once everyone is in the house. Joe returns for the ceremony driving a new truck—two-tone, copper and white. He's wearing a suit, the first suit he's ever owned in his life. When he arrives in the truck, still sporting its factory shine, the first thing the guests do—including the long-haired minister—is put their jackets on and go outside to admire it. Frances is already dressed in her wedding outfit and is in her bedroom, but she watches through the open window, tucked behind the curtain. Her dad shakes Joe's hand for no reason at all, as if having a new truck is as good as winning the Irish Sweepstakes.

Is it goodwill, Frances wonders, or something else?

Then her mother comes into the bedroom and pulls her away from the window because the guests and Joe are walking back toward the house—"It's bad luck if he sees you"—and she does a last-minute touch-up of Frances's hair.

Her mother says, "You're not exactly marrying a rich man. I just hope he's paid cash for that truck and hasn't borrowed money he can't pay back."

"I don't know what he's going to have to do to prove himself to you," Frances says. "Build a mansion with a swimming pool, I guess."

"Time will tell, won't it?" her mother says.

Then she gives Frances a quick hug—a gesture as unnatural as the congeniality in the yard. It's as though everyone is trying to stay in good spirits for her sake, making the best of it. Frances, the condemned.

Alice says, "Trust you to buy a blue dress for a wedding. Well, as I always said, blue looks good with your hair."

Then Frances's father knocks on the bedroom door, and the three of them walk together into the living room, where the guests are waiting. Basie immediately trips on a chair leg because the furniture is all out of place, even though Alice had walked him through the new configuration. Frances is able to keep him from pitching into Martha Fletcher's lap, and her father rights himself and safely delivers Frances to where Joe stands with the minister.

The ceremony is brief. Frances hardly hears what the minister says, but there's something about her promising to love and him promising to honor. All just a formality as far as Frances is concerned, but this is the way it's done—a few "I dos" and they're married and signing their names in the registry book. When the minister says, "You may kiss the bride," Joe does kiss her, but it's a peck kind of kiss, not the other kind.

Afterward, Myrna—wearing the tie-dyed dress that didn't become curtains after all—tells her she loves the blue velvet. Nothing about how strange it is that she married Joe Fletcher, nothing about the age difference, just ordinary talk about dresses on her wedding day. "Too bad you're an old married woman now," Myrna says. "We could have had some fun together." (*Married!* It's true.) Frances says, "We still could. I'm not moving away to Timbuktu or anything."

"You kind of are," Myrna says, "out there in the bush."

One of the neighbors pops into the conversation. "You'll get some use out of that outfit," she says. "Not like a wedding dress, which just hangs in your closet until you get sick of looking at it." Then she asks, "Why did you decide against a formal wedding dress?" And Frances says, "I didn't. This *is* a wedding dress. It's just blue."

After the neighbor is out of earshot, Myrna says, "She thinks you're knocked up. You aren't, are you?"

"Of course not," Frances says. "I'm on the pill."

Myrna says, "She probably thinks I'm knocked up too, just because I usually am."

For a brief moment, having Myrna for a friend trumps

being married. They're still laughing when Alice interrupts them to make Frances and Joe stand for pictures, which she snaps on a new Instamatic camera with a built-in flash, and then she serves a buffet lunch. After that, Frances and Joe cut the cake, which Alice made herself and placed in the middle of a card table that she's set up especially for it. It's a plain square layer cake, but she's decorated the edges with scallops of blue icing to match Frances's dress, and it's topped with the bride-and-groom ornament they bought in Yellowhead. Besides the cake, the table holds a floral arrangement and two blue candles in glass holders, even though Frances had argued against decorations—"It's not a school dance, Mother."

As they stand over the cake for pictures once again, this time holding the cake knife, Joe whispers to Frances, "You're mine now," and it's so unexpected and she thinks, *No, I'm not*, and out loud she says, "What in the world gave you that idea?" making a joke, but she doesn't like the way he'd whispered, as though the conspiracy of marriage includes ownership.

She shouldn't take any of this seriously, she thinks. They're all play-acting, she and Joe, her parents and guests. That's what a wedding is. Martha is the only one there who is behaving exactly as she does every day of her life.

When Myrna says she has to go, Frances wants to say, *Don't leave me with all these adults*, but of course she doesn't. She tries to get Myrna to stay until the gifts are opened, but Myrna says she has to get home to Morgan, and at first Frances doesn't know who Morgan is and then she remembers that's the baby's name. She realizes she's forgotten all about Myrna's baby.

Once Myrna is gone, Frances grows impatient for the whole thing to be over. What she wants now is for everyone to leave so she can move her things to Joe's house and unpack them, put her clothes in the drawers and her toothbrush in the little washroom, anticipate the moment when the sun goes down—or maybe they won't wait for that. She isn't sure how it will happen, but she knows it will, and she says to herself, *It's what I want*. She hurries things along by suggesting to her mother that now is a good time to open the gifts.

The presents are carried, one by one, to Frances and Joe, who are seated on the well-worn wagon-wheel couch—by now Joe's tie is hanging from one of his jacket pockets—and Frances's mother writes down who gave what as Frances peels away silver-and-white wrapping paper until household objects are revealed: a dinner set from her parents, a pop-up toaster from one of the neighbors, sheets from another, a crystal cream-and-sugar set, a wool Hudson's Bay blanket. Myrna's given her something called a sand candle that she found in a craft store in Yellowhead. Frances loves it. The last gift she opens is an ominous black Bible from Martha, which she accidentally drops on the floor, almost causing Martha to keel off Basie's chair.

After the gifts have been opened, Frances thinks it's done, over, time for everyone to go, but her mother serves coffee and cake again, as though she's trying to keep people there.

"When are they going to leave?" Frances whispers to her, and her mother says, "Don't be rude." Like she's still a child.

Eventually the guests do begin to leave. One of the neighbors offers to drive Martha to Deer Valley so the bride and groom don't have to. Joe and Frances's father load the gifts and boxes, as well as Frances's new suitcase, into the back of the even newer truck. Frances keeps the sand candle with her, to carry on her lap so it doesn't get chipped. When they're ready to go, Frances's mother says sadly, "I haven't seen the place. I don't even know what you're moving to."

"Now, Mother," says Frances's father, but Frances can hear the sadness in his voice, and she's annoyed with both of them for making her feel bad on her wedding day.

"Let's go," she says to Joe, getting into the truck. When she slams her door, she catches the skirt of her dress and the rubber jamb leaves a big black mark. Her mother looks at the mark, and Frances knows what she's thinking—that Frances won't have a clue how to get it out—and she's right. She closes the door again and looks away from her mother, wanting to tell Joe to hurry up, take her away, but also wanting to jump out of the truck and hug her mother and assure her that all will be fine, you can learn how to get marks out of a dress, anyone can learn that.

"Ready to go, then?" Joe asks, and she nods yes.

The highway north of Elliot is a road used by logging trucks. When Frances and Joe are halfway to his turnoff, they come across a load of logs spilled over the highway and down into the ditch, blocking traffic in both directions. The police are nowhere to be seen, and a couple of local farmers are doing their best with tractors and chains to clear a path. Several of the stranded people have got out of their vehicles so they can better see what's going on. The day is getting cooler and Frances zips up her jacket as she steps out of the truck. Joe, still wearing his suit, walks up ahead to see if there's anything he can do to help, while Frances waits with a couple who have so many kids she wonders how they all fit into their truck. One little girl notices the mark caused by the door closing on Frances's dress, and Frances says, "This is my wedding dress. I just got married."

"Are you a bride, then?" the girl asks.

"I guess I am," Frances says.

"A new bride!" the mother says. "How wonderful." People within hearing distance congratulate her, although when Joe comes (*So he's the groom?*), they fall silent.

Eventually there's a path through the log spill, and the trucker who lost his load guides a single lane of traffic through it. When they're on their way again, Joe says it's lucky that no one was hurt when the first few logs spun off at sixty miles an hour and bounced along the pavement. Most of the load cascaded off the truck after the driver managed to pull over.

It's early evening when they finally arrive in Joe's yard, where the dog is waiting for them. Joe carries Frances's boxes into the house while Frances carries her suitcase to the bedroom. Should she unpack? She doesn't know. They pass by each other awkwardly as they make trips to the bedroom with Frances's things, until finally Joe steps in front of her and blocks her path, and Frances thinks, *So this is it*. They're standing in the living room, the picture window without drapes, and there are no curtains to pull closed, but then, *It doesn't matter, does it? We're alone out here*. As her dress drops to the floor, her bra, her stockings, she stands, self-conscious, wanting to cover herself, but also simply dying of curiosity to know what will happen next. Joe picks her up and carries her to the bedroom, completely naked, her clothes strewn on the living room floor, and then she's on the bed and Joe's hands are all over her, and she thinks, *This is what people do. This is what girls do, Myrna and the others.*

Afterward, Joe pulls his pants on and leaves without saying where he's going, and Frances lies alone on the bed, under the sheet now to escape the roughness of the blanket, thinking, *I, Frances Moon—Frances Fletcher, that is—am no longer a virgin.* The thought is exciting, but at the same time there's a feeling of disappointment that is working hard to ruin things. The fun part—those moments in the living room in front of the bare window—lasted such a short time. She waits for Joe to come back, but he doesn't.

She hears a vehicle in the yard and her first thought is that her parents have come to check on her. But of course it's not her parents—they wouldn't come to call on her wedding night. Who, then? She pictures her dress on the living room floor. Even her bra is there. She quickly jumps up, covers herself with the blanket, and retrieves her clothes. She has nothing else to put on; she hasn't unpacked her suitcase yet. As she zips up the dress she feels something warm and sticky run down the insides of her thighs.

She looks out the bedroom window and sees a couple getting out of a car. Who would drop in unannounced on the evening of Joe's wedding? Unless they don't know. She checks to make sure no one is in the house and then slips into the washroom to try to clean herself up. There's no hot water. She washes in the basin with cold water, then pours the water down the bathtub drain. She tries to fix her hair with Joe's comb, which is sitting on the edge of the wash-stand. Her hairbrush is still packed in one of the boxes.

She hears the kitchen door, and a woman's loud laugh-ter. When Frances joins the visitors in the kitchen, she sees a bottle on the counter and Joe already getting glasses out of the kitchen cupboard. There's a gift on the kitchen table, wrapped in wedding paper. Joe introduces the couple to her as Saul and Ginny. Frances is baffled. Who are these people? Joe hadn't mentioned any friends when she asked him if he wanted to invite anyone to the wedding.

"Here she is," Ginny says. "Come on over here and tell us why Joe's been keeping you such a secret." She pours Frances a glass of whatever is in the bottle and holds it out.

Frances shakes her head and manages to say, "I don't drink."

"You don't drink? Well, it's time to start, girl. This is Saul's homemade. You won't find any better."

Frances says, "I don't like it." Even though she doesn't know whether she likes it or not.

"Leave her alone, Ginny," Saul says. "Not every woman drinks the way you do."

"Woman," Ginny says. "That's a bit of a stretch, don't you think? And I wonder why we didn't get an invitation to the wedding. Sorry. None of my business. Just curious."

"It was a family wedding," Frances says quickly, overlooking the insult about her age. She wonders why Joe doesn't step in, but he doesn't appear to be listening. Frances says, "We wanted to keep it small."

Ginny drains the alcohol in her glass and says, "Oh, who cares. It's party time. Frances Fletcher, nice to meet you."

There it is again. Frances Fletcher. That's her. She looks across the room at the man who is *her husband* and sees him through her mother's eyes, sees the whole thing through her mother's eyes, the fact that she has moved into this house with the man she will share a bed with forever—*forever!* What if she doesn't want to sleep in that bed forever?

Frances hears another car in the yard, and then the dog

barking. Joe finally looks at her, sheepish, and says, "Ginny and Saul arranged a little get-together, invited a few friends and neighbors over to meet you."

More people are coming over?

Ginny says, "Don't worry. Clay and Nancy are bringing food," and when Clay and Nancy come into the house, they have crackers and chips and a dip made from Philadelphia cream cheese and onion soup mix. Another wedding gift is placed on the table. Frances doesn't recognize any of these people from town. More strangers arrive—all of them much older than she is, none of whom she recognizes—and she concludes that town for them must be one of the towns on the line going north. They've all brought bottles of liquor with them, or cases of beer, and wedding presents.

Frances tries to help Nancy lay the food on the kitchen table, but in the end Nancy does it herself because she knows where things are in the kitchen and Frances doesn't. Frances hopes no one will drink too much. Several times Ginny tries to get her to take a drink, and finally Joe tells Ginny to leave Frances alone, and Ginny sulks until someone cracks wise about the age difference between the bride and groom, when she throws back her head and laughs like a mallard duck.

By now there are fifteen or so people in the kitchen. The more they drink, the louder they get. They laugh and talk at the same time, and they're crude. Saul teases Ginny about the new bike she's bought herself. He says she likes to ride a bike because it feels good on her little thing—*What little thing?* Frances wonders—and then Ginny says to him, "Maybe you should try it; maybe it would feel good on *your* little thing," and everybody laughs, and Clay even tries to pour a beer over Saul's head, but Saul pushes his hand away and for

a minute Frances is afraid he's going to hit Clay. Their behavior is like nothing she has ever seen. She's thankful when
Joe moves to stand beside her, and although he seems to be
drinking just as much as the others, he's quiet, the same as
always. If he behaved like the others, she doesn't know what
she would do. Run, she thinks. Run into the bush and hide.

She doesn't like the way Saul and Ginny keep looking at
her, studying her.

Eventually, Frances excuses herself and goes to the bedroom, telling Joe she's going to change out of her dress. She
gets as far as searching one of the boxes for her jeans, but
when she can't find them, she lies down on the bed. She
doesn't want to go back out to the party. She thinks she will
stay here until they all leave, and hopes no one will miss her
and come looking for her.

Twenty minutes later, Joe does come looking for her
because Ginny thinks it's time to open gifts. Frances reluctantly returns to the kitchen with Joe, and she opens the presents. She doesn't bother writing down who brought what, the
way her mother told her she should. She simply opens the gifts
and lines them up on the kitchen table: another toaster, a set
of three china robins in various sizes, a chip-and-dip tray, a
ceramic cookie jar in the shape and costume of a Mountie
(this one gets lots of laughs). When she's opened the last one,
Saul says, "One more, buddy, just for you," and he takes a small
gift wrapped in wedding paper from his jacket pocket and
tosses it to Joe. He opens it: a green plaid cap.

"Oh, cripes," one of the women says. "Here we go. That
goddamned cap again."

Frances thinks the cap looks used, and even if it were
new, what kind of wedding present is that?

"Don't look so confused," Ginny says to Frances. "Just a reminder that marriage isn't going to stop your hubby from having his fun with the boys. He's still in the club."

"Damn straight," Saul says, and the men all raise their drinks and everyone laughs, even the women, Ginny's duck laugh loudest of them all. Then Joe tosses the cap through the doorway to the living room and it's forgotten.

Frances looks at the gifts and cards on the table next to a big bowl of ripple chips and she doesn't know what to do, what's expected of her, so she picks up the wrapping paper that was lying on the kitchen floor and throws it in the woodstove. At least she knows how to lift the iron plate so she can shove the paper in. She doesn't light it, though, because she doesn't know how to work the flue. She endures the party for another ten minutes and then can't stand it any longer, so she slips from the kitchen, planning to hide once again, hoping no one will follow her.

As she steps into the living room, the toe of her shoe catches the green cap, which is lying on the linoleum floor. She stops to pick it up, and as she does she sees two initials written in black marker on the inside band. They're blurred with age and wear, but she can still read them: SC. She doesn't think anything of the cap or the initials. Her only thought is that an old used cap is the stupidest thing ever to give someone as a wedding present, even as a joke. She sits on the couch with the old cap in her hand and mindlessly twirls it on an index finger the way she's seen her father do—the way she saw Silas Chance do with another green cap all those years ago. A voice in the kitchen says something uproariously funny and everyone laughs. Outside, the dog barks.

SC. Silas Chance. She stops twirling the cap and stares at it, the green-and-black plaid, the blurry old initials on the worn band. It couldn't be. It couldn't be Silas's cap. But all the same, she drops it on the floor at her feet.

"Hey, Frances, where'd you go?" Ginny calls from the kitchen. "You're missing all the fun."

Frances gets up and runs for the bedroom and closes the door. It couldn't be. It's Saul's cap. S for Saul. Who knows what the story behind the cap is? Who cares?

But what if it is Silas Chance's cap? If so, there's only one way it could have got into Saul's possession: he was there when Silas died. Had he come across Silas on the side of the road, injured, maybe dead, and done nothing? Or was it worse? Had he caused the injury? Had he hit Silas on purpose? Either way, he'd taken Silas's cap, and now it was a souvenir to give to a buddy on his wedding day, like a set of antlers—only worse, because he thinks it's a joke. They all think it's a joke.

She lies on the bed and tries not to panic about where she's found herself. Everything will be okay in the morning, when these people are gone and the house is quiet, but she knows—knows now, without a doubt—that she is no more in love with Joe Fletcher than, say, with the man who picks up the milk cans from her father's dairy. If she were still in high school and Joe Fletcher were her boyfriend, she would break up with him. How many times had she listened to the girls in her class talk about breaking up with their boyfriends? They were madly in love one day and breaking up the next. She thinks about the word "engagement" and how she dismissed that step as unnecessary. Now she sees the sense in it. She lies on the rough blanket in the dark, listens to the sounds of the party coming from the kitchen, and tries to convince herself it's just her, she's just being Frances.

She wants to go home. Right this minute. Run away from this house and these coarse people, this nightmare, which now includes Joe, because whatever happened to Silas Chance, he knows. Whether he was there or not, he knows. The way Joe had tossed the cap into the living room as though it were insignificant, as though that life—the life of the man to whom the cap belonged—didn't matter.

She could do it. She could climb out the bedroom window and run. But where to? And is she making it all up, panicking for nothing? She tries to remember if there were initials in Silas's cap that day she picked it up off the floor and handed it to him. She can't remember—but how could she? She was just a child. She rolls into a ball and holds her stomach, feeling sick, trying not to throw up, and somehow she manages not to. Tap, tap, tap on the wool blanket, and somehow, in spite of the noise in the kitchen, she falls asleep.

She has no idea what time it is when she wakes up and hears noises, whispered laughter outside the bedroom door. The door opens and in the light from the living room she sees Joe being shoved into the room by a crowd of people. He's naked, except for his socks and his undershorts.

Someone pulls the door closed again, and Frances sits up in the dark. Then the whooping starts, and the banging, metal on metal, pots and pans, a pounding on the bedroom door. Outside the house, someone starts a vehicle and drives it up to the bedroom window and honks the horn, over and over again. The vehicle lights cast wild shadows through the plastic blind. Frances can feel her heart pounding, the way it does in dreams where you're being chased. She can see the shadow of Joe's near-naked body stumbling toward her.

"What are they doing?" she says to him, shouting over the noise.

Joe climbs onto the bed, searching for her. When he finds her, he pulls her to him. At first she clings to him, terrified by the noise, but when he begins to kiss her, saying her name over and over again, breathing on her with his boozy breath, she tries to pull away, becomes frightened of him too. "What are they doing?" she says again, "Why are they doing this?" She knows she sounds hysterical, and when Joe begins to pull at her dress, she becomes hysterical, thrashing under his weight, fighting like a frightened animal. She hears someone yell something like "Go at 'er, Joe," and then raucous laughter.

She bites Joe hard on the arm and claws with her fingernails at his back, but he doesn't even seem to notice. It isn't until she screams as loud as she can, right into his ear, and jams her fingernails into his cheek, raking down, that he realizes she's fighting him. He stops and sits up and slurs, "What's wrong?" She pulls away and wraps herself as tightly as she can in what she can grab of the wool blanket, and then Joe rolls over on his back and is still. Frances puts her hands over her ears to try to block the noises still coming from outside the door, the window, everywhere, until gradually they stop. She hears the kitchen door slamming as people leave, and one by one the vehicles start up and drive out of the yard.

Finally, it's quiet. Dark. Joe's breathing sounds desperate, as though he's fighting to stay alive. Do people die from drinking too much? She doesn't know whether to hope he lives or dies. She lies awake all night listening to him, and as the sun comes up and the room grows light, she can see him stretched out on his back with his socks still on, still breathing. He'd managed to get only one leg out of his undershorts, which are now wrapped around one white thigh, and his hands cup his testicles. She can smell the alcohol and stale aftershave.

He's disgusting, she thinks.

She creeps from the bed and opens her suitcase and begins pulling things out, dropping them in a pile on the floor. At first she tries to be quiet, afraid Joe will wake up, but when she realizes he isn't going to, she stops caring about the noise she makes. She goes through the suitcase and the boxes, throwing things out onto the floor until she finds what she wants—her faded jeans, clean underwear, a T-shirt, her Keds, her gray kangaroo. Once she's changed into her favorite clothes, she picks the blue dress up from the floor and takes it to the kitchen. On her way through the living room, she sees that someone has moved the cap to the coffee table and draped it on top of a beer bottle. The sand candle is on the coffee table too—the candle and Silas Chance's cap.

In the kitchen, she finds some scissors and a carving knife in a drawer, and she sits in a chair by the stove and cuts her dress to pieces. The stove is still warm from the fire someone lit the night before. It takes her an hour to cut up the dress. By the time she's done, it's a pile of velvet strips on the kitchen floor. And then she returns to the living room and snatches the cap off the beer bottle, and she takes the scissors to it too, not really seeing it—*Silas Chance's cap, it has to be*—as she struggles to cut through the tough canvas band, just a blur of green and black, not wanting to see the initials of a dead man's name. When she's done what she can with the cap, she isn't sure what to do with the pieces. She lifts the plate on the stove and sees there are still embers, so she adds kindling and gets a fire burning, and then she spends the next hour throwing scraps of fabric in, along with blocks of wood. As the fabric burns, smoke begins to build up in the kitchen because the flue isn't set right, but she doesn't care. She doesn't care if she burns the whole place down. When the last of the scraps are in the stove, she puts the plate back on and finds her jacket and goes outside and follows the trail into the bush. She sits on a rock that rises out of the dew-damp grass, shivering in the cold air, the smell of rotting poplar leaves round her. She wants to go back in time—just twenty-four hours would do—and call off the wedding, tell her mother that she was right, that Joe Fletcher is not the man for her, he's too old, too rough, and he knows horrible, crude people. Tossers. Are these the kind of people her mother ran away from in England? If so, Frances knows why. When she sees Joe's dog watching her from the edge of the meadow, she calls him and he comes to her. She feels sorry for him that he belongs to someone who named him Dog.

Hours later—judging by the sun, it must be mid-afternoon—Frances hears Joe calling her name. The dog's ears prick up and he starts to trot off in the direction of the house, but when Frances calls him back to her side he comes, and he stays with her even though he keeps looking at the house. Eventually, Frances decides she can't stay in the meadow forever.

When she opens the kitchen door she finds Joe cleaning up. He has a healthy fire going in the stove, and the smoke from her fire has mostly cleared. She isn't sure what she expected to find, but it isn't this. Maybe she thought he would be dead, lying on the bed in nothing but his socks. At the very least, she thought she would find him with his head in his hands, or maybe over a bucket. His hair is wet and it looks like he's showered, even though there is no shower. He has scratches on his cheek where she dug in her fingernails. She wonders if he remembers she did that.

"Quite a mess they made here, eh?" Joe says when he sees her in the doorway. He says it as though the party and the cap and the terrifying pot-banging circus were nothing out of the ordinary, nothing to apologize for. "They like to go hard, that crew. They don't mean any harm."

He pours hot water from a copper reservoir into the kitchen sink, carries glasses and empty bowls from the table, and drops them into the soapy water. There are several saucers on the table, all of them filled with cigarette butts, and he empties the butts into the stove and adds the saucers to the dirty dishes. He begins to collect empty beer bottles and stack them in boxes by the door.

"You'll get used to them," he says.

Did she have any desire to get used to a single person who was in the kitchen the night before? No. Not one person. Not even Joe Fletcher. She stands in the doorway and watches him as he walks from the stove to the sink, from the sink to the table, back to the sink.

"What's wrong?" he asks.

Does he really not know? Does he not remember? How they all drank themselves stupid and laughed as Joe tossed Silas Chance's cap like a toy? How he climbed on her and groped at her like an animal?

"Where did Saul get that cap?" she asks. She wants to

ask, also, *Am I married to a man who could have come forward all those years ago, when the police and Silas's sister were searching for someone—anyone—who knew what happened?*

Joe says, with his back to her and his hands still in the sink, "Close that door there, will you? You're letting in the cold air."

Frances steps inside and pulls the door shut. She wishes that she hadn't destroyed the cap so she could hold up the proof, wave it in his face. She says, "I burned the cap and threw it in the stove. It was half mine, I guess, since it was a wedding present."

He's refusing to look at her. Guilty, she thinks—guilty and relieved that the proof is now ashes. She's done him a favor. He says, placing a bowl in the drying rack, "Don't feel bad on my account. Although it beats me why you'd want to burn it. It was just a joke."

She goes to the bedroom then and lies down again on the wool blanket. She hadn't slept all night. She's exhausted, and cold from sitting outside for so long. When she hears Joe come into the bedroom half an hour later, she pretends to be asleep. He stands over her, says her name a few times, and then leaves, closing the door after himself. When she's sure she will be alone for a while, she really does fall asleep.

It's dark when she wakes up. She smells something cooking. She gets up and goes to the kitchen, where Joe has a stew ready and the table set for supper. The kitchen smells good, but when Frances sits down to eat, she finds she has no appetite. She sits at the table saying nothing, and Joe clearly doesn't know what to do. Finally he says, "That was kind of a mean trick. Don't let it bother you."

Frances doesn't understand.

Joe says, "We did that on their wedding night, years ago. Ginny and Saul's. Payback, I guess."

Frances thinks, *He's telling me this so I'll believe everything is all right.* She picks up her fork and has a bite of stew and a chunk of potato, and she thinks there is a possibility that things could be all right—that the cap is not Silas's, that she'll never see those people again, that Joe will turn back into the man who'd taken her to the movies, the one she'd wanted so badly to sleep with. But it's a slim possibility.

After supper, she goes to the bedroom again, and eventually Joe comes in and sits on the edge of the bed in the dark. He reaches out his hand to touch her, but she pulls away from him and rolls herself into a little ball in the wool blanket, still in her clothes. She remembers how she'd decided she was in love with Joe Fletcher, and then doubted herself, and then convinced herself she did love him. What was wrong with her? Now, it seems, she's decided once and for all that she doesn't love him, and it's not just because of the cap. She could convince herself that the cap belongs to Saul. It wouldn't be that difficult—much less difficult than convincing herself she can stay here. She should ask Joe what Saul's last name is, but she doesn't. She doesn't mention the cap again.

She stays in Joe Fletcher's house for eleven days. She does not let him touch her. He's patient for the first few days, and then he becomes surly. He doesn't force himself on her, but he's sarcastic when she won't undress in front of him and changes into her pajamas in the bathroom. He calls her a baby, says he thought he was marrying a woman but got Daddy's baby instead. She decides she has to leave. There's no other solution. When she tells Joe this, he doesn't argue. He carries her cardboard boxes and her suitcase out to the truck and drives her home. She takes the presents from the wedding with her, predicting that her mother will want to return them, but she leaves the presents brought by Joe's friends. She also leaves the Bible Martha gave them. He can deal with those. She carries the sand candle on her lap again. They don't speak at all on the way, not a word.

When they arrive at the dairy farm, Joe stops on the approach and unloads her suitcase and boxes. Frances can't look at him. She risks a glance when the last box is on the ground and Joe is lifting the tailgate to close it. She sees that he has something to say and she fears that he is about to beg her to reconsider.

He's not. She meets his eye and he says, "What did you think? That you could try me out, go for a test-drive and then say thanks, but no thanks? Well, go to hell, Frances. I'm glad to be rid of you. I should have listened to Martha."

For the first time she sees his side of it, and she understands that he hates her. She tries to say sorry, thinks she might even *be* sorry now that she's safe at home again, but then he leans toward her, his whiskered face just inches from hers, and says, "One more thing. Forget about that cap. Don't go spreading lies if you know what's good for you. You don't want to mess with Saul's bunch."

She steps back, alarmed. It was a threat. *You don't want to mess with Saul's bunch.* She remembers the way Saul and Ginny stared at her the night of the party. Joe Fletcher has just warned her that something terrible will happen to her if she ever mentions the cap.

All she can think is, *Stupid, stupid Frances Moon.* And then, not even that, because Moon is not her name anymore.

After Joe is gone, she sits down on one of her boxes and

waits. The sand candle is still in her lap. She sits on the box and waits until the milk truck pulls into the yard and drives slowly past her.

Shortly after that, her mother comes running.

THIS, DELIVERED by her mother as a command: "Forget it. Everything. The marriage, the wedding, Joe Fletcher. Just thank your lucky stars that you got out of there. From this day forward, it didn't happen." Frances spends the first week of her return home lying on her bed and thinking about those words, *It didn't happen.* She tries to think of them as a pardon for the mistake of the marriage. Most days, she sleeps all afternoon, and when she wakes up and smells supper cooking, she goes to the kitchen and they eat together, the Moon family, but they don't speak. It's as though they're all too fragile for conversation. Her parents are relieved—she knows it—but their relief is not joyful. The three of them are traumatized, like people who have stepped out of a bomb shelter and found themselves at a dinner table with the walls around them blown apart.

Her mother returns the wedding gifts as Frances thought she would, even the dishes. All but the candle, which Frances says she wants to keep. She thinks of it more as a friendship present than a wedding gift.

"We'll get a divorce," Alice says, but the word "divorce" is as bad as the word "marriage" to Frances, and she says, "It didn't happen, remember? That's what you said." Her mother says they should at least get her name changed back to Moon—some government department called vital statistics does that—and Frances beseeches her to stop, please stop talking about it, stop reminding her of what a disaster her life is.

Her mother says, "At some point, Frances, you are going to want a divorce. You have to face that."

"It didn't happen," she says again, and her mother lets it go for the time being.

Myrna Samples comes to see her. They should drive to Yellowhead, she says, go shopping, check out the clothes in the Sally Shoppe, the new fall shoes in the Bata store. Frances agrees to go, but she has no enthusiasm for the things Myrna holds up and suggests she try on. Wide-leg jeans. Shoes with big block heels. A red corduroy jacket with little flowers embroidered on the collar. "This would look super fabulous on you," Myrna says about the jacket, and Frances says, "I don't know. Red hair. You should try it on. It would look better on you." Myrna does try it on, and she buys it. Frances doesn't buy anything. She's such bad company. They go into a new record store that Myrna has heard also sells hash pipes, but Frances leaves right away when she sees the pipes under the counter, afraid the police will come and arrest them along with the hippie owner. It starts to snow and they decide they'd better head home before the road blows in. By the end of the day, as they approach Elliot, Frances knows they can't be friends. She can't be anyone's friend.

When they pull into the yard at the dairy farm, Myrna says, "Isn't that Joe's new truck?"

Frances looks. It is Joe's copper-and-white truck, parked in front of her father's shop. She panics. She tells Myrna to turn the car around and take her the hell out of there, which Myrna is about to do when Frances's mother comes out waving her arms for them to stop and says, "Don't worry, he's gone."

Frances gets out of the car and Myrna drives away, and Frances asks, "What's his truck doing here?"

Her mother says, "Apparently, it's your father's truck now.

I'm so mad I could spit." It turns out that Basie bought the truck for Joe without telling Alice. As a wedding present, he said, because he didn't want his only daughter running around the country in a rusty old truck. Joe had returned the truck while Frances was in Yellowhead.

Within the week, the truck is sold and gone from the yard.

And then Frances asks her mother if it's too late for her to tell the university that she'd like to attend after all, and her mother immediately looks into it, not even trying to conceal her excitement, and finds that it isn't too late. The school is on a semester system and Frances can start after Christmas.

She will put in her time, then, Frances thinks. Endure the next few months, push aside the fear she feels whenever a vehicle passes on the road. She sees her move to the city as her best option—exile, escape to the place where a lesser mistake was made years before, the simple mistake of not locking car doors against petty criminals.

She burns the sand candle in her room until the wax caves in on itself, and then she throws it out.

She tries the guitar again, figures out three chords, and is astounded by how much her fingers hurt. *This is the bed I made for myself,* she thinks, *the price of what happened not happening.*

She tries, for her mother's sake, to show some interest in her own life.

The falsehood of her compliance: that she has finally come to her senses.

7. Snow

HER PARENTS FIGHT when they think Frances isn't listening. Her mother brings up the truck over and over. How could Basie have done that, bought the truck without telling her? She keeps harping at him. Maybe, she says, that was Joe Fletcher's plan all along—to marry Frances, an only child, and end up with a profitable farm instead of that liability he owns in the bush. Basie played right into his hands, she says, by buying him that new truck. Basie listens, or doesn't listen, until he says something like "Judas Priest, give it a rest." Frances thinks that she caused this; she brought this discord into the house. She worries that her father doesn't care about her anymore. He's hardly spoken a word to her since she left Joe Fletcher.

Then finally, finally, on the morning she is to embark on her new life, he says something that expresses at least the possibility that he cares what happens to her. At the breakfast table, he says to Alice, "You're sure about this room you've rented—that it's a proper family she's moving in with?"

"I'm sure," Alice says. "I've spoken to them on the phone. Several times, in fact."

"Maybe I should be coming along," he says.

Frances wants him to come, but Alice says it's not necessary. She needs to stay overnight to get Frances sorted, and there's too much to do on the farm for them both to be away.

When Basie says, "You be careful in that city," it's clear what he's getting at.

"Phhft," Alice says, dismissing his concern, but Frances doesn't trust that *phhft*.

An hour later, after the car is packed and they're about to walk out the door, Frances turns back to her father, who is still sitting at the table, a cup of coffee in front of him, and she says, "Hey, Dad, how did the blind man meet his wife?"

He doesn't answer at first, and then he says simply, "That old joke." As though the days of jokes are over.

Once they're on the road, Frances watches her mother pretending: that she isn't worried Frances will change her mind and come running home to Elliot; that she's not afraid to be on her way back to the city where she was once car-jacked; that she doesn't care about the snow that's beginning to fall, even though it's windy and the visibility is reduced. Alice says, "What's a little drifting snow? We're used to that, are we not? Say something, Frances. Are we not used to drift-ing snow?"

"Yes," Frances says. "We are."

Everything grows white with new snow. Tammy Wynette is on the radio, singing that sad old song about the woman following her man to Utah and Texas and Alaska. The land-scape is a blur of passing fence posts, and Frances can't stop looking at them. She tries to focus on one fence post, but they're passing too quickly. The snow lets up once they're on the other side of Yellowhead. Thankfully, the wind has also died down. If it were still blowing, they wouldn't be able to see a thing.

Frances looks out at the white world, the ditches level with the roadway, hay bales and sheds and machinery obscured by mounds of white, and says, "I wonder if we'll know when we pass the place where we stopped the car when Tobias died."

"I wouldn't have a clue," her mother says. "But we're not going to ruin the day by talking about that, are we?"

Frances goes back to staring at passing fence posts. Every so often they pass one with a magpie sitting on it. She thinks about the way she left her father, sitting with his coffee at the kitchen table. She feels convinced that he's given up on her.

When they reach the city, Frances tries to pick out the strip mall where they were carjacked. As they pass a familiar-looking convenience store, Frances sees her mother looking at it, thinking the same thing she is, but Alice says, "Keep your eyes open for our turn. The third set of lights. Here's the first."

They follow the instructions they've been given and find the address they're looking for, the downtown home of a Greek family with a one-room furnished suite for rent in their third-story attic (her mother calls it a flat). After Frances's belongings and Alice's white overnight case are inside and up the stairs, Alice is desperate for a cup of tea. She pulls a little container of tea bags out of her purse, makes tea in an aluminum pot, and drinks it without milk. Then she finds the landlord and asks him to draw a map of the route from the house to the university campus, and they drive there with Frances navigating. They find the business office, and then take a walk around the campus while Alice babbles about the world that Frances is entering—what she will learn, the smart people she will meet. Frances only half listens.

After a quick stop in the cafeteria to check the prices (reasonable, Frances's mother proclaims), they drive to a grocery store and find a bank near the apartment. Once Alice has set Frances up with a checking account, they drive back to the apartment with the groceries and cook macaroni and cheese on the hot plate, and afterward Alice insists on making hot chocolate (*like they are roommates*, Frances thinks). Then they go to bed, the two of them squeezed onto the twin-size mattress. In the early morning, Alice cooks oatmeal and then packs up her nightgown and toothbrush, and says, "We'll see you at Easter. You can tell us what you've learned. I know you'll do us proud."

She leaves when the sun is barely up, so used to an early start to her day. Frances goes back to bed and falls asleep thinking about Easter. She already knows she doesn't want to go home at Easter. She may never go back to Elliot again.

Later, the Greek couple look in on her and give her a lesson on the old house's fragile plumbing system, and also how to say hello in Greek at different times of the day. That night, she wakes up in the dark and doesn't know where she is. She thinks she's on the top bunk of her bed at home and is surprised when she sits on the edge and feels the floor under her bare feet. Then she sees the outline of her suitcase across the room and remembers.

The sound of children in the house wakes her the next morning. She bundles up against the cold and walks to the university for orientation day. It takes her almost an hour to get there. Once she arrives, there's a tour of the campus, classes to choose, more forms to fill in. When she sees "legal name" as the first question on all the forms, she is sickened that her legal name is now Frances Fletcher. She writes Frances

Moon anyway, since the application was in that name, and after she's completed everything that is required of her, she finds a phone book hanging from a chain under a pay phone and pores through the government listings until she finds the vital statistics office, and she takes a taxi there. She provides identification, writes a check (the first in her life), and fills out another form that will change her name again, back to Moon. The official name change will take time, they tell her. She doesn't care. She already feels a weight lifted, the weight of Joe Fletcher's name. She walks home from the government building, and when she passes a lawyer's office—J. C. Homan, the name on the sign says—she goes inside and asks for an appointment. J. C. Homan is free that very minute. She tells him the bare bones of her story, and how she doesn't want the man she married to get her parents' farm. He says he couldn't anyway—"He didn't marry your parents, did he?"—but he tells her about de facto separations. He creates a file with her name on it and puts a statement inside. Come and see him again, he says, when she's ready for a divorce. She writes him a check. She leaves his office and stops at a corner store and buys a bag of ripple chips. There's a rough-looking man—a drug addict?—hanging around the drink cooler, and she wonders if he will follow her and try to steal her purse, but he doesn't. She gets all the way back to her apartment without anything bad happening. She locks the door after herself and sits on the side of the bed and eats the chips without even taking her coat off.

FOR THE FIRST several days of classes, Frances walks to the campus because she doesn't know how to take a city bus, is afraid she won't know how to tell the driver to stop the bus and let her off. After three days of enduring the January cold, she decides she's being ridiculous—daft as a wagon horse, her mother would say—and she stands at a bus stop and tries to look hopeful when the next university bus comes along, and it works because the bus stops and the door opens for her. There's a sign on the coin box that tells her how much change to deposit, and she doesn't have to do anything when they get to the university. The bus pulls up in front of the library and the doors open and all the students with their armloads of books spill out the doors and push their way into the building against the bitter wind. Boys with long hair. Girls wearing workboots and colorful scarves. No one she recognizes, not one person. No one from home—not even Jimmy Gulka, who has gone off to a bigger university in Alberta.

She finds herself walking next to a dark-skinned boy she thinks might be in one of her classes, and for some reason that she cannot fathom, she speaks to him. She assumes he is a foreign student from some primitive village even smaller than the place she is from.

"That was my first time on a city bus," she says.

"Really?" he says. "I thought everyone took buses in a city like this. Where there are no trains, I mean." He has perfect English, with only the slightest accent, which sounds British, if anything.

She says, "I'm from a small town," and then she looks away and hurries off down the long, crowded hallway to her lecture hall, which is the same one that the boy, Rudy Bustani, enters. He sits in an empty chair beside her.

The instructor is late, as usual. Rudy Bustani is talkative. He tells Frances that Rudy is the Western version of his given name, not the name his mother knows him by, and he is, as she'd assumed, a foreign student. His father is guest lecturing at a prestigious university in New England. The family is from London, and before that Egypt—yes, he says, where the pyramids are, and the Nile River, and the Sphinx. He's in his first year of university, like Frances, and is at this school because it's where his parents sent him. There are no extra costs for foreign students. The entrance requirements are modest, and he is not, he says, a genius like his father. He applied to go to the university where his father is, but was not accepted. His parents are separated, and his mother has gone back to her family in Egypt.

"My parents are English," Frances says. "From the north, I think, but they lived in London during the war."

"Have you been there?" he asks. "To London?"

She says that she hasn't been anywhere. She asks Rudy what he's studying, and he says, "Not much." He's pretending to be in pre-law, but he has no intention of becoming a lawyer. Law school sounds like too much work. Frances doesn't know what to say about why she is here, her choice of career. She tells him she is in first-year arts but is going to switch to science and find a cure for cancer. It's not a direction she has previously considered, but suddenly cancer research sounds like a good idea, or at least good enough.

The class they are in together is an introductory biology course that involves endless memorization of plant and animal taxonomies. Frances doesn't find it hard—memorization has never been a problem for her—but as the weeks pass, she hears the other students complaining. The course is too difficult, they say. The instructor marks unfairly. Although Frances has not spoken to Rudy since the day of her first bus ride (she now has her own student transit pass), she notes his dejected look every time one of the Friday quizzes is handed back the following Monday. When she leaves the lecture hall beside him on one of these days, she again speaks to him.

"So how bad is it?" she asks.

"Me?" he says, not sure that he's the one she's speaking to.

"I guess you're not doing so well in this one, huh?"

"Failing," he acknowledges. "You?"

"Pretty good, actually," she says.

"That makes sense for a science major."

A science major. He remembered what she'd said. Well, she isn't a science major just yet, but she doesn't point that out.

"I could maybe help you if you want," she offers. She can't believe herself, but she does believe she can help someone pass biology. They agree to meet in the cafeteria at the end of the day. Afterward, they take a bus downtown to a movie. They begin meeting every day for lunch, and before long they're sleeping together and Frances goes back on the pill. At first, they sneak up the stairs to her apartment in the attic, avoiding the Greek family because she's pretty certain she'd be kicked out if they knew Rudy was spending the night. Rudy has a similar third-floor apartment in an old house—he calls it a flat, like her mother did—but the owners don't live in the building, so they begin spending more and more nights there, and by the time spring comes and the city lawns are turning green, Frances has stopped paying the rent at her own apartment and moved her things to Rudy's, which is bigger, although still one room.

She and Rudy don't tell their parents that they're living together, or even that they're seeing each other. Frances is able to transfer the phone number she had at the Greek family's house to Rudy's apartment, and only she answers the phone when it rings. Rudy has not given his parents the new number and is careful to phone each of them weekly so they won't try to get in touch with him. Frances leases a post office box at a nearby drugstore and tells her parents that her letters were going missing at the Greeks' house. She begins to write them short weekly notes about things she sees around the university, such as the crazy French professor who talks to herself in the hallways, the flea-market clothing worn by the hippies, and the flyers posted constantly by the campus activists: "End the Oppression of the Proletariat," "Marriage Is an Institution," "Let the Ruling Classes Tremble." She hopes that her parents, especially her father, will find her anecdotes amusing, and that they will keep them from wanting to check up on her. She doesn't go home for Easter, or at the end of the semester. She tells her parents she's staying in the city for the summer term and making up for the time she missed by starting after Christmas instead of in the fall. Her mother seems pleased with that idea. She writes in a letter, *We're so happy that you've buckled down, Frances. You will never regret having a good education. But please . . . take a weekend soon and come home on the bus. Your father is eager to see you. And I am too, of course.*

Frances promises, yes, before school starts again in the fall. She worries she's once again being reckless, the old Frances, committing a major taboo by sleeping and living with a boy, but she gets over it because there's no stigma attached to cohabitation within the student community. Male and female students are living together in houses and apartments all over the city, as well as in housing co-ops and communes, with incense burners and candles on every surface and music blaring from open windows. No one looks twice when Frances and Rudy come and go together, and shop for groceries, and mingle their laundry in a single washing machine at the coin launderette. For the first time in her life, she feels as though she's doing what everyone else is.

But she can't tell her parents.

She tries to explain herself to Rudy one night when they're playing a game called five that they've made out of chart paper and pennies, half of which have white nail polish on one side. Rudy taught her this game. It's as easy as checkers.

She says, "My parents are old-fashioned. I'm here for an education, not to find a man or have a good time."

Rudy says he can't even begin to explain to Frances all the things that would be wrong with what he's doing in his parents' eyes.

"I'm not a Christian," she says, moving a white penny into line with three others.

"But you're not Muslim," Rudy says. His father might not care, because his own religious practice has lapsed, and he'd had, at least for a short time, a non-Muslim girlfriend in London, but Rudy absolutely couldn't tell his mother about Frances. She's devout, and believes all North American girls are vain, and has warned him to keep up his prayers and protect his modesty, to save himself for God and a good Muslim girl. He's told his mother that he belongs to the Muslim Students' Association on campus, and that he keeps up his prayer ritual.

"So in other words, you lie," Frances says.

Rudy shrugs, and then places a penny and wins the game.

Frances likes the fact that they are each other's secret.

. . .

THREE MORNINGS IN A ROW, she throws up. She thinks she has the flu. Then she starts to feel sick all the time. Could she be pregnant? How could she be when she's on the pill? It's true that she forgot to fill her prescription a month ago, but she hasn't missed that many days and she read in a pamphlet from the pharmacist that there's still some protection if you miss. She finds the pamphlet and reads it again, and there's a list of pregnancy symptoms. She has them all.

She tries to keep it from Rudy, hoping she will lose the baby.

She phones home to say she's not coming as planned between the summer and fall semesters; there's a music festival she wants to attend, folk music. Her mother pleads— "We haven't seen you since you left"—and Frances gambles and suggests they come to the city and see her, knowing that it's harvest and not a time when farmers are able to take a holiday.

"Maybe we can come for Thanksgiving," her mother says. "Find someone to do the milking. I suppose we could stay in a hotel."

Yes, Frances says, they could. There's one not far away.

Rudy's father asks him if he wants to come to New England for a few days before the fall semester starts, and when Rudy says he doesn't think so, he should really study, his father says he's going to fly to London, then, for ten days.

"He sounded relieved," Rudy tells Frances, "that he could go to London without me."

In September, just as classes begin again, there's a heat wave and their apartment is unbearably hot. Frances feels sick every day because of the pregnancy and spends most of the time lying on the bed. She misses the first week of school, and hopes every day that she'll wake up not pregnant anymore. In spite of the heat, she takes steaming baths that turn her skin red, because she heard somewhere that might cause a miscarriage, but the baths just make her feel sicker. She knows she has to tell Rudy what's going on, but she can't find the words. There's a narrow section of rooftop right under the window overlooking the street, and Frances takes to climbing out to sit on the asphalt shingles once the sun has moved around behind the house and the roof is in shade. There's a houseful of what she thinks must be art students across the street. They come and go from the house like ants, carrying cardboard portfolios, rolls of paper, cans of paint. They wear plaid shirts and overalls with paint splashed on them. In the evenings, they dress like gypsies. She begins using the art students as her excuse for sitting on the roof.

Rudy thinks she's acting strangely and he keeps sticking his head out the window and asking her what she's doing, why she's missing school, why she's so interested in the hippies across the street. When she throws up all over the shingles one day, she has to tell him about the baby. He hands her a plastic pail filled with water through the open window, and she splashes the water around on the roof to clean it up. He says, his head out the window, that he doesn't care what his family thinks, he will do the right thing. He will marry her.

Marry. Frances well knows that she is not in a position to marry anyone. She throws the last of the water on the shingles and watches it run down the slope of the roof and into the rusty eaves trough. A girl with long straight hair and wide-legged jeans walks by on the sidewalk below and

Frances thinks how lucky the girl is not to be pregnant. She can't stop herself—it must be the hormones—and she starts to cry because once again she's found herself where she doesn't want to be, about to make a mess of her life, and she has no one to blame but herself. The old Frances has sabotaged the new one.

When she's done crying, she hands the empty pail to Rudy and climbs in the window and tells him she doesn't want to get married. Marriage, she says, is an institution they don't have to believe in. Rudy looks concerned. He asks her if she's not worried that her reputation will be ruined.

Her reputation? It's the seventies, she says, women's lib and all that. She tells him he's not Westernized enough if he's still worried about her reputation. She tells him to get used to her independent spirit.

"I'm a feminist," she says. A word she's never before applied to herself.

Rudy seems to be thinking that over.

FOR HER NINETEENTH BIRTHDAY, she gets a card and a new sweater in the mail from her parents. Rudy buys her a flower, a rose, which they put in a glass spaghetti sauce jar on the table. She also gets her summer session marks and they're surprisingly good, better than she expected. Rudy's marks come in the mail as well and they are not good: two failing grades. But he has managed to pass his mathematics class, thanks to Frances's tutoring. Rudy gets called to the dean's office for a review of his foreign student status, and he's given one more semester to improve his grade point average or he will have to sit out for a year, which also means that he will have to leave the country.

"I can help you," Frances says. "We'll just have to work harder." But Rudy doesn't seem to be taking the warning seriously. She worries that he will lose his student status.

Lie after lie to her parents. She convinces her mother not to come for Thanksgiving.

The baby is due in April, and as Christmas approaches and Frances begins to show, she wonders in earnest what she should do. She doesn't want the baby. She doesn't say so to Rudy, but she seriously considers giving the baby up for adoption. Another poster she's seen on the walls at school: "Need Birth Control? Pregnant? Come for Counseling." The poster gives the location of the women's center and Frances takes note. If she can find a way to keep from seeing her parents until after the baby is born, she can give it up and they will never know. To cover Christmas, she invents another lie—that she's met a girl from Montreal and they've become close friends and she's been invited to Montreal to spend the holidays with the girl's family, who don't speak English. A once-in-a-lifetime invitation, a cultural experience, being in a French city. Her mother will appreciate that. Once she's had the baby, she will take the bus home for a quick visit, a weekend. Maybe the time will be right to tell them about Rudy—not everything, but that she's met a boy her own age. They will like the possibility of normal.

She doesn't get a chance to visit the women's center, or to give the baby up without her parents finding out. A few days after Frances tells her carefully worded Christmas lie, there's a knock on the door. When she opens it, still in her housecoat, there is her mother, her white overnight case in her hand. Frances instinctively draws her housecoat farther around herself, hoping her rounded belly won't give her away.

They both stare, one as shocked as the other, until Frances says, "You'd better come in before you die in all those clothes."

After Alice is seated at the small kitchen table, her winter coat on a hook by the door, she says that she knew something was wrong because of Frances's refusal to come home, all those crazy letters about hippies and oppression and God knows what else. In spite of the icy roads, she drove to the city by herself and found the Greek family's house again, and they told her Frances was no longer living there. They gave her Rudy's address, which Frances had left so they could forward any mail that came for her. "We think she might have a boyfriend," the landlord said. "We think she might have moved to his apartment."

"I was mortified," says Alice, almost in tears. "Imagine my not knowing where my own daughter lives. How could you, Frances? How could you? And who is this boyfriend? Surely you're not living here with a boy."

She looks around then. Rudy's running shoes by the door. Jeans across the foot of the bed, not Frances's. An open gym bag with a soccer ball in it. A boy's sweatshirt draped over the back of an armchair in the corner.

Frances comes clean. She says, "Mother, I am living here with a boy named Rudy. And brace yourself, I'm expecting a baby. It was an accident, obviously, but I'm doing well at school and there are services here that will help me with the adoption, because I've decided I'm not keeping it. You don't have to worry or do anything. I have it figured out. No one at home needs to know—the neighbors, I mean." She thinks she is being so mature. It's not the best situation, but it's not as bad as the one they've already been through, the mistake that was Joe Fletcher. She's relieved that she can stop trying to think up new lies. The envelope with her summer marks is in a bowl on the table, and she picks it up and holds it out to her mother and says, "Have a look. My grades are really good. I even got a call from the biology department asking me to change my major. I think I should start applying for scholarships."

Alice won't look at the envelope. Frances isn't even sure her mother is breathing.

"Say something, Mother," she says, although she's now worried about what might come out of her mother's mouth once she does decide to speak.

Rudy comes home just then. She hears him coming up the stairs two at a time, as usual, and then the door opens and he stops dead when he sees Frances's mother.

"This is my mother," Frances says. "She knows. I told her."

Rudy closes the door and takes off his coat, and then Frances introduces him to her mother as Rudy, originally from Egypt, later London, his father a professor in New England (thinking this will impress her mother), Rudy himself with a high school education from London ("They call it A Levels there, but you likely know that") and now here on a student visa. Rudy holds out his hand for Alice to shake and says, formally, in his slightly accented English, "I'm very pleased to meet you, Mrs. Moon. I understand that you too lived in London, during the war. It must have been a difficult time."

Frances's mother looks from Rudy to Frances and finally says, "So this is what 'doing me proud' means. First a man twice your age, and now a foreigner."

Frances can't believe what her mother has said. She's embarrassed with Rudy standing right there, his hand still out. Racism? The student union holds antiracism rallies on campus. Is that what this is? It never occurred to her that her mother might react this way. She hasn't said a single word about the baby, or Frances's plans.

"Mother," she says, not knowing what to do, sounding desperate, "Rudy is really nice. You'll like him."

Alice gets up from the table and grabs her coat and boots and walks out of the apartment. Just walks out without another word, forgetting her overnight case on the floor, thumping down the staircase in her stockinged feet. Frances is confused—what should she do?—then furious that she's been so humiliated in front of Rudy. She runs out the door after her mother, follows her down the stairs, shouting things without thinking, things she doesn't even mean. "You don't like the color of Rudy's skin? Is that it? I've just decided; I'm keeping this baby. Did you hear that? I'm keeping this foreigner's baby."

Alice stops in the foyer at the bottom of the stairs and shoves her arms into her coat sleeves and struggles to get her boots back on. "Don't go twisting my words," she says. "I'm disgusted because you, Frances, are the most selfish and irresponsible child ever to be raised in a good home. Can you think of any other ways to put me into an early grave?" She leaves the house, and Frances lets her go.

Later that evening, after Frances is sure her mother isn't going to return for her overnight case, she places it in the closet. She supposes her mother's toothbrush is inside, her nightgown, a pair of shoes—things she'll wish she hadn't left behind—but that was her own fault, the way she'd stormed out.

Rudy's been mostly quiet since her mother left, but now he says he's sorry.

"For what?" Frances says. "You didn't do anything wrong.

We made a mistake. We're not living in the Dark Ages any-more. She's the one who should apologize." Not really believ-ing what she says.

Rudy asks, "Who did she mean? The man twice your age?"

"No one," Frances says. "Just a boyfriend I had for a while. A very short while."

Rudy goes silent again, and then he asks, "*Are* you keep-ing the foreigner's baby? You should likely tell me what your plans are." Frances thinks she hears a bit of sarcasm in his voice.

"Don't you turn on me too," she says.

"I'm not," Rudy says. Then he says, "She *is* your mother. She's worried about how the world will see you. You need to consider that. I think we should get married."

"No," she says. "I told you."

Tell him, she thinks. *Tell him you are already married.*

But she can't, and the thought that she's still living a lie— even though her mother now knows about the baby—makes her cry again.

Nothing Rudy says is a comfort.

THE CALL COMES from a neighbor woman just days before Christmas. Frances can't absorb the news—the woman is saying that her father is dead of a massive heart attack, the result of being kicked in the chest by a cow. It can't be true. Where is her mother? Frances asks. Resting, the neighbor says; she's had a terrible shock. The neighbor has already checked the bus schedules and tells Frances what to do: come immediately, she'll pick her up in town.

Frances catches the next bus to Elliot. She doesn't wait for Rudy to come home from wherever he is—the gym, indoor soccer—but writes him a note and leaves it on the kitchen table. She dresses in a way that mostly hides her pregnancy and takes a taxi to the bus depot. Five hours later, the neighbor picks her up at the bus and delivers her to the farm. The woman says things on the way—she's so sorry, such a freak accident, her father was such a good man—but Frances barely hears her.

"Frances," her mother says when she sees her. She's lying on the couch under a blanket, the teapot on the coffee table beside her.

The neighbor woman leaves them alone.

"I was waiting for you," her mother says. "I can go to bed now. We both can, although I don't suppose we'll sleep."

Nothing is said about her missing father. Nothing about the baby.

In the days leading up to the funeral, Frances avoids giving anyone the opportunity to guess that she's pregnant. She goes to her room whenever people drop by to offer condolences and deliver food, shake their heads at a tragedy. *Terrible time of year for such a thing*, they say, *well, no time is good, but Christmas . . . makes you wonder if there's anyone looking out for decent people, doesn't it?* At the funeral—in the United Church, with the long-haired minister presiding—she sits next to her mother in a bulky sweater. There's a reception in the basement after, and Frances sits by herself, her belly hidden beneath a tabletop, and people mostly leave her alone, other than to squeeze her hand or pat her on the shoulder on their way by. All she can think about is how she disappointed her father and never got a chance to make it up.

In the days that follow, the neighbors pitch in to help

Alice with the milking and the chores until she can decide what she's going to do—attempt to carry on alone, find a hired man, sell the cows—but whatever she decides, she tells Frances, they might as well start boxing things up, because sooner or later she'll be selling the farm and moving to town. Not a single word has yet been said about the pregnancy or Frances's plans, nothing about Rudy. Nothing about Joe Fletcher, although Frances does overhear a neighbor woman telling her mother that she heard Joe Fletcher had moved to British Columbia to work in the bush.

She stays home for ten days, tortured by the thought of her father sitting at the kitchen table with his coffee cup, not wanting to believe he's gone, but knowing he is. She tries to make a start on sorting through the things stored in her closet, but she doesn't get very far. She wants to tell her mother that she doesn't have to worry—the baby is a mistake she won't make again, one that won't get in the way of her education—but her mother withdraws into deep silence, and Frances returns to the city with nothing resolved between them.

She hopes her father is watching from somewhere.

She hopes he can see inside her, and know that her intentions have never been bad.

THE SEMESTER has barely started when Rudy disappears. He simply doesn't come home one day. When he still isn't there two days later, Frances goes to the foreign students' office because she doesn't know where else to go. It's immediately clear that the woman behind the desk knows something, but she isn't about to tell Frances. She can't, she says, because Frances isn't family. Frances starts to feel faint and has to sit in a chair and put her head between her knees, and she hears herself saying to the woman, "I'm pregnant."

"Rudy Bustani is the father, then?" the woman asks, and Frances says that he is.

The woman takes pity on her. "I'm not supposed to say . . ." but then she does. She tells Frances that Rudy's father has withdrawn him from school and taken him away. She doesn't know where to, or if she does, she isn't letting that part slip.

Rudy must have told his father about Frances and the baby. New England. London. Egypt. How will she ever go about finding him? It's hopeless. He will have to find a way to return to her.

She waits to hear from him but nothing comes. No letter. No phone call. She quits going to classes. Her belly grows as she waits to hear from Rudy, certain that he will escape the clutches of his family and come back. But nothing. No contact at all. Surely he can find a way to write or call, she thinks. Finally, she has to accept that he's not coming back, that he does not want to come back to a pregnant girl who refuses to marry him, or even if he does, he is not prepared or able to defy his family. She has to accept that she is one more girl with a baby inside her and the baby's father no longer in the picture. She's been deserted.

She doesn't know what to do. She's sure she's failed all her classes by now. She decides to find the women's center at the university, but when she does, she stands for half an hour outside the door without going in. A woman leaving the office notices her and asks if she can help, and Frances says she'll come back later.

She catches the bus in front of the university and gets off at her stop and walks the last few blocks to the apartment, considering her options, no longer sure of anything. As she goes to step over a snowbank and cross the street, she loses her balance and falls over, not hard, but with both legs deep in the crusty snow and her belly weighing her down like she's got heavy stones in her coat pockets. When she tries to push herself up, her arms sink into the snow and she's stuck there. The snow has got inside her winter boots, her mitts, the sleeves of her coat. It must be the hormones again, she thinks as she feels the tears coming. She half sits, half lies in the snowbank and cries until one of the art students—a girl she recognizes—comes along, not on the sidewalk but sliding up the middle of the street as though she's ice-skating, and she sees Frances there and offers her an arm, with which Frances manages to get herself back on her feet. The girl is wearing an old fur coat and a multicolored striped knit scarf and matching mittens.

She asks Frances if she's all right.

Frances says no, she isn't all right, she's a mess, pregnant and with nowhere to go, which the girl takes to mean homeless. Frances is surprised that the girl doesn't recognize her as the one who looks down from the rooftop, but maybe she hasn't seen her there, maybe she's never looked up.

"Come with me," the girl says. She tells Frances her name is Edie, as in Edie Sedgwick. Frances doesn't know who Edie Sedgwick is.

"Was," the girl says. "She died."

"Like everyone else," Frances says, feeling more sorry for herself than she ever has.

Edie takes Frances home to the art students' house and sits her in a rickety bamboo chair at an old wooden kitchen table painted the color of Velveeta cheese. She gets her a glass of milk and makes her a peanut butter sandwich. Frances eats it. She doesn't tell her she lives across the street. Edie says there's an extra bed that no one is using at the moment if she needs a place to crash. The house, she says, is a cooperative. "Just do your share," she says. "Put money into the kitty when you can, clean the bathroom, wash the dishes—whatever you can do to help out." Frances takes all the money she has in her purse and puts it in the jar in the cupboard.

A boy with long hair in a ponytail comes into the kitchen carrying a paperback book with his finger holding his place. He tells Edie that he thinks the author and his friends were desperate to find authenticity in a world driven mad by war. They were looking for something genuine and beautiful, he says, as an antidote to greed. He waves his hands in a way that takes in everyone in the house, including Frances, and says, "Everything wrong that happens here, in this house, is about greed."

"You are so full of shit," Edie says. "If you're so into Kerouac, why don't you hit the road?"

"Who are you?" the boy says to Frances.

"Just Frances," she says.

She stays with the houseful of art students for two weeks, sleeping on a narrow cot in a hallway, like a person waiting for a bed in a hospital. During the day, she sits on the ragged couch in the living room, watching the ebb and flow of the house, people coming and going, listening to the unfamiliar music of the various occupants, and she thinks she doesn't understand any of it. One girl asks her if she is considering a home birth, because if so, she knows a midwife. Frances says she hasn't really thought about it, which is true, she has not thought at all about the moment when this baby decides to make its way into the world. She hasn't even been to a doctor.

In the evenings, a joint gets passed around, or a water pipe, hash burning between a pair of hot knives, and she says no thanks and wonders if the smoke in the room will deform the baby. She wonders what her hair would look like if she grew it long. One evening there's a new girl in the living room, one who has been away and just came back. She's wearing a long Indian skirt and she keeps looking at Frances, studying her. Eventually, she says, "I've been thinking you look familiar. Don't you live across the street? I'm sure you're the one I've seen on the roof." Edie, the girl who saved her from the snowbank, looks at her accusingly and says, "Really?" Frances doesn't know what to do, so she gets up from the couch, retrieves her coat from the closet, and leaves. She crosses the street to her own house, sure they are all watching her from the main-floor window.

The next morning, she phones her mother.

By the end of the week, she's back in Elliot.

THE BABY IS STILLBORN. In the hospital, they ask Frances if she'd noticed that the baby had stopped moving. She says no. They take that to mean the baby *was* moving, but what she really means is that she hadn't noticed one way or the other. She didn't know how much a baby was supposed to move.

Her mother takes care of everything, and within days of the baby's birth, Rudy and the pregnancy are things of the past, things that didn't happen, just like Joe Fletcher. Frances goes from the hospital in Elliot to her bedroom at the farm and stays there for a month, and then she begins to pack her possessions into boxes because her mother is planning to move into Vince's house.

When her mother thinks enough time has passed after the baby, she sits with Frances at the kitchen table and pours them each a cup of tea and says, "You're not the first girl to get herself into trouble."

Frances hates the term "in trouble." She won't use it.

Her mother says, "That boy, no matter how much you think you loved him . . . the baby . . . well, I'm just thinking of you when I say it's all for the best. You've been lucky once again. I hope you'll come to see it that way."

Not so long ago, at this same table, Alice slapped Frances for her insolence. Now it's Frances's turn. Alice holds her hand to her face, where a red mark is forming.

"You deserved that," Frances says, everything she's feeling compressed into those three words.

Her mother says, her chin trembling, "I only want the best for you."

"No, you don't. You want me to be less trouble, to go away and get good grades and be a success you can brag about."

Her mother, fighting back tears, says, "I don't understand you, Frances."

It's like a confession, and Frances realizes that she doesn't understand her mother either; they don't understand each other, and probably never will. She says, "That's the real disappointment, isn't it? You should have had more than one child."

Her mother looks at her, her hand still rubbing her cheek. "There's so much you don't know," she says. "In spite of what happened to you, a woman doesn't just snap her fingers and have another child. Don't you think your father wanted a son? All men do."

Another barb, but another confession at the same time. She'd never imagined her parents had failed at having more children.

Then her mother pushes away from the table and carries her cup to the sink. With her back to Frances she says, "And don't go thinking that means your father didn't love you enough. He loved you just as much as I did. As I do."

Frances takes this in, sees the mountain her mother has climbed to say these words.

She says, "Mom, is there anyone we can call in England? Would you like to take a trip back there? After you sell the farm? Maybe I could come with you."

Silence, and then her mother says, "There's no one. Anyway, it's too late for that."

Too late, as in too many things for the two of them to get past? Or too late for her to return to England?

Her mother clarifies: "I have no interest in going back."

A neighbor drives into the yard just then, the one who has made an offer on the farm, and Alice goes outside to speak with him.

Frances sits at the table by herself, feeling like an orphan.

WHEN SHE RETURNS to the city, she is relieved to find that the apartment she shared with Rudy has not been cleaned out and rented to someone else. She boxes up the belongings that Rudy left behind—textbooks, a few clothes, his gym bag and soccer ball—and as she's going through the drawers and closets, she finds her mother's white overnight case. She should hang on to it, she thinks, take it back to her, but it reminds her of the day when her mother came and Rudy was still here, and she moves it to the pile of things she's getting rid of. When she's finished sorting, she takes it all to the Salvation Army in a taxi. Afterward, she climbs out the bedroom window and sits on the roof. It's April, spring, but the air has not yet warmed up and she watches her own breath rise as though she's smoking a cigarette. If she had a cigarette, she thinks, she *would* smoke it. Music comes from the house across the street—Joni Mitchell. She guesses that Joni is the choice of the gypsy in the long skirt.

She returns to school for the spring session. Although she was given an incomplete grade in all her classes the previous semester, the dean allows her to continue her study of general arts and science because of extenuating circumstances. When she's asked to choose a major, she selects psychology. She doesn't know why, maybe because she suspects she's a lost cause and wants to find out the reason. She registers for two spring classes, but she begins sleeping in every morning, and by the middle of the session she's hardly going to school at all. She fails both classes, and she doesn't bother registering for the summer.

She goes back on the pill and begins going out in the evenings, to a hotel bar near the university, where students congregate. She sits by herself until some boy—there's always a willing boy—picks her up, and then she goes home and sleeps with him, never in her apartment, never staying the night, walking home afterward by herself along some dark city street. She doesn't care what the boy's name is. In fact, she tells them not to give her their real names, and she calls them all Steve McQueen, after the actor who'd dropped out of Hollywood and was traveling around the country in a motor home. He might be in Canada, who knows. She makes up different names for herself: Lulu, Maggie, Isabel. There isn't one boy who ever asks to see her again, and she likes it that way. Once, when she's sitting by herself at a table in the bar, she overhears a group of girls talking about another girl ("She gives them whatever they want"), and she realizes she's the one they're referring to. Later, when she's leaving with a new Steve McQueen, they pass the table of girls and she stops and says, "For your information, it's not what *they* want that matters." They look at her like she's crazy, and she says, "Come on, Steve. Let's go figure out what *I* want."

One boy after another. Frances is drunk every second night. A tough-looking waitress at the bar, an older woman named Josie, takes her aside and says, "Careful, honey. You're going down a bad path here." Frances says, "Thanks, but mind your own business."

Until she wakes up one day at the end of August, and she's in her own apartment, in her own bed, and there's a boy in the bed with her. He has curly blond hair. It's hot in the room and his hair is sweaty, sticking to his forehead, making him look vulnerable, like a child. Somehow, she knows that he's a nice boy, or at least nice enough, and she recoils from this knowledge, slips quickly from the bed as though she's discovered a spider under the sheets. She doesn't want to know anything more about him than what she's already sensed, doesn't want to know his name, but she sees his wallet on the floor next to his jeans, and she looks inside and sees that his name is Daniel. She remembers a conversation, laughter. The fact that Daniel plays the bagpipes. She doesn't want to know this either. She puts his wallet in his jeans pocket and then wakes him up and says, "Go home, Daniel. Right now. Don't talk. Don't say a word. Just go home and don't call me, and don't come back." Daniel slips out of her bed and quickly dresses, and when the door closes after him, she gets in the shower, and begins to feel as though she's walked through a dark and dangerous tunnel and has emerged, in spite of herself, at the other end. She strips the sheets from her bed and makes a trip to the coin laundry to wash them. When she gets home, she flushes her birth control pills down the toilet, not caring that she's in the middle of a cycle. She takes the bus to the university and registers for the fall semester—she's on probation, they tell her, because of the failed classes. She buys a new bathing suit and starts to swim every day at noon in the university pool. One day in the middle of the afternoon, Frances stops at the hotel bar where she'd met all the Steve McQueens and finds Josie there waiting tables, as she hoped she would be. She thanks her for trying to save her from herself. Josie pretends she doesn't remember, but Frances knows she does.

She stops watching the mail for a letter from Rudy. She realizes that one isn't coming and gives up hoping that he will come back, accepts that he will not be a part of her life, that she will not get a chance to tell him there is no baby. She does send a letter to him, explaining what has happened, care of Professor Bustani at the college in New England, but she has no way of knowing if Rudy ever receives it. She hopes he does because she wants to relieve him of any guilt he feels for not being able to come back.

In the fall, she changes her major.

Three years later, she graduates with an honors degree in microbiology. After working at a summer job in a city hospital lab, she is hired to a permanent position. Her mother places a notice in the Yellowhead paper: *Congratulations to Frances Moon upon her graduation with a bachelor of science degree. Frances's future: hospital laboratory technician. Way to go, Frances.*

She sends Frances the clipping and attaches a note that says, *I knew you could do it.*

Frances leaves the clipping on the table and catches the

bus to the university and goes for a swim. For that one hour in the pool, she feels content. *Remember this*, she tells herself. *This is a feeling to strive for.*

On the way home afterward, it starts to spit rain. The late-summer leaves on the trees shine, the way the sun hits them through the clouds. When she gets home, she steps out the window onto the roof with an umbrella, a cup of tea, and the newspaper clipping her mother sent. She reads the notice over several times, trying to decide if happiness and contentment are the same thing. She's not sure she knows what happiness is, or whether it matters as long as you're not *un*happy, which right now she isn't. She sips her tea and enjoys one last hour on the rooftop, and when she begins to shiver in the damp air, she tears the newspaper clipping into shreds and lets them drift over the edge of the roof. Then she climbs back in the window and calls the landlord to say she's moving out, and she starts looking in the paper for a new apartment.

A resolute Frances moving up in the world.

Stepping from the ruins of a life that didn't happen.

8. The Ballad of Dooley Sullivan

HE'D BUILT the screen porch—the summer porch, he calls it—for days just like this, warm days that you dream about all winter, that your skin longs for. On this day, he sits at the picnic table, waiting, playing checkers against himself. *Damas*, the game was called in Mexico, meaning "ladies." Whenever he plays against himself, he makes up a name for his opponent. Today, it's Lady Clara. She makes her move while Dooley thinks, not about game strategy but about penitence: step eight, back up, revisit the wreckage. Every act of penitence counts, they tell him at meetings; where there's a possibility of forgiveness, there's hope. Hope is a rumor about town that's caught his ear, one that has him on edge with expectation. He sits in the porch all day, playing checkers with Clara, drinking coffee after coffee until the caffeine—one foot twitching and his knuckles rapping the tabletop—forces him to switch to iced tea.

The next day, his opponent's name is Valentina. She chooses the red checkers, normally a disadvantage to Dooley, since he has better luck with red, but in truth, neither one of them is paying attention. Every time Dooley hears a vehicle cross the tracks, he looks for it to turn up Liberty Street. When no car does, he returns to the game. Valentina's move, or is it his own? He can't remember. Doubt goes to the lady. Later, when he gets hungry, he plucks a few cherry tomatoes from the hothouse plant he has staked in the porch, then he goes inside and makes himself a sandwich, puts it on a plate along with a pickle and the tomatoes, and eats it at the banquette for a change of scenery.

At sunset, as usual, he carries his disc player outside to thank the sun for another day, or at least he thinks that's what it's all about. Angela knew. He just followed her lead. He looks to the west, where the sun is red from the fires burning farther north, and remembers the red steel ball sinking into the Pacific. He hasn't seen that for years now and probably won't again. He puts on the music and begins to move. It would be called dancing if Angela were doing it, but he's well aware that what he does is an insult to the art form. If anyone were to ask, he would say he's trying to keep his old body in shape, but no one does ask. There's no one here to see.

Half an hour later, he's back in the house, away from the horseflies that glom on to the sweat on his skin, into the shower, and then back to the porch, where he plugs in the patio lights for the evening. Red, yellow, and green plastic globes from the dollar store in Yellowhead. Creedence and the Grateful Dead on the disc player. He puts on the headphones and stretches full out on the picnic table and thinks about that other life, the one he made for himself, fueled by drugs and tequila and a perfect climate. People who disapproved back then—the ones who didn't get the miracle of throwing away your watch and toking on a nice fat doobie—would say, "It's not real; you're fooling yourself," and he would think, *That's the point, suckers. It's not real. I've had my fill of real.* His ears tuned to the sound of the ocean. His skin in love with the comfort of the sun. Waves slapping rhythmically on the long sandy coastline, or sometimes crashing like cannon shots. A beach populated by refugees from snow and other, more bitter kinds of cold. Those were days of freedom, and he was a man released into a new life. A life that officially came to an end when Angela left, although truly it had ended much earlier, and many more years went by before he began to dream, mysteriously, of snow, and made his own exit.

Such nostalgia, he thinks, rolling over him like waves on a beach, threatening to wash him off the table and into the surf. One of the patio lights blinks on and off, the yellow one. The bulb must be loose, but he doesn't bother to get up and fix it, trapped as he is by the tide of memory.

Mañana. There's always mañana.

The picnic table (he made that himself too, when he built the summer porch) reminds him of another picnic table, in San Clemente, California, in a campground not far north of the Mexican border. His last night before he entered his new life. It was late in the year, December, too late in the season for tourists to camp in Southern California. Just he and a boy and girl, also hardy Canadians, a few years younger than he was, who thought the weather, compared to home, was warm enough for sleeping in a nylon pup tent. They had escaped from university, they said, but had decided to go back to Canada for the winter term rather than cross the border into Mexico the way he was about to do. They'd been to Disneyland that day and hadn't known that the last bus south left Anaheim at six o'clock, and they'd had to hitchhike along the Coast Highway back to the campground. They'd been picked up first by a vanload of sun-blond surfers, and then by a man who'd advised them they should be carrying a *blade*

274 ~ DIANNE WARREN

if they were going to hitchhike that highway. He'd scared the bejesus out of them because surely he was carrying one, and was he just checking to see if they would resist if he pulled it on them?

The three of them—Dooley and the Canadian couple— pondered the man's intentions. He was a Vietnam veteran, they decided, driven into paranoia by the horrors of an unjust war. Then they walked from the campground to the edge of the cliff overlooking the ocean because they'd been told you could see Richard Nixon's house from that vantage point, and sure enough, there it was. They stood high above the beach drinking beer and staring across the bay at the compound, and the girl said she felt as though she were looking at the home of someone evil. How, she wondered, could he be the sitting president of the country they were in? Dooley said he thought they were likely being watched by Secret Service agents with high-powered binoculars. They talked about the draft. They didn't understand it—how a country could force its young people into public service, any public service, but especially one that involved weapons and killing people. Dooley had grown up where there were lots of guns, so he didn't have the same aversion to guns *in principle* as the other two, but he agreed about the forced military service and killing people, other than yourself, on purpose. He didn't tell them that he himself had considered joining up as a means of escape after he'd learned there were Canadians in the U.S. forces. It was a brief, misguided moment for several reasons, not least because of his limp and the metal plate in his head. The girl said Richard Nixon and the other war presidents— who were they? Eisenhower? Lyndon Johnson?—were criminals, they had to be. Johnson was the president when My Lai happened. Dooley didn't know what that was. Kennedy was the only U.S. president he knew anything about. He knew he'd been assassinated in a convertible in Texas. They'd listened to the news coverage on the radio in school that day.

When a cold wind began to blow off the ocean, the three of them returned to the campground, sat at the picnic table near the pup tent, and smoked themselves blind on Dooley's pot. They tried to smoke all he had because he didn't want to carry drugs over the border, but they couldn't do it, and so in the morning he'd left what remained in a plastic baggie on the picnic table, along with a note wishing the couple luck, wishing himself luck, not really thinking about how pissed off they'd be when they found it there because what if the park warden had found it first? At sunup he'd packed his sleeping bag and walked away from the campground, down an access road and into San Clemente, where he waited for the bus in a little waiting room with a dozen boys with shaved heads—that's all they were, just boys, younger than he was, younger even than the couple he'd left sleeping in the tent—on their way to San Diego, next stop Vietnam. He tried not to think about them, tried not to think about the Vietnamese they would be sent to kill and the fact that he himself had considered volunteering. From the scared faces he could tell these boys thought they were doomed, and he was glad he wasn't one of them.

In San Diego, they all got off the bus, and the recruits went to a military bus that was waiting for them while Dooley found the Greyhound that would carry him to the border. He was sure he felt the eyes of the recruits on his back as he walked away from them, imagined their envy, but he didn't look back, didn't want to see his own face reflected in a military bus window. He boarded his Greyhound and placed his back-pack on the seat beside him because he wasn't going to let it out of his sight. It contained all his possessions, everything he owned, everything he wanted to own. At the Mexican border, he got off the bus and walked through customs and no one stopped him or asked him for anything—not ID, his name, a reason for his visit. Nothing. They just waved him through. He was surprised by how easy it was. No one knows I'm here, he thought when his feet hit Mexican territory. No one but the couple in the campground, whom he'd told about his plan to disappear—but they didn't know his name, Dooley Sulli-van, or where he was from, Elliot, Saskatchewan. He'd told them his name was Dewey, like Donald Duck's nephew.

As he walked across the bridge into Tijuana, he looked down along the riverbank at the cardboard-and-tin make-shift houses, the cooking fires and sewage ditches, the dogs and dark-skinned children and poverty. This wasn't what he'd expected. He'd expected . . . what? Mariachi music and cheap tequila. He wondered if he could really do this, but he told himself, *Keep going.*

He wasn't sure where to go, so he followed the tourists and he found himself walking past the stalls of trinkets and Mexican blankets and sombreros and huaraches, past the cantinas and massage parlors, the calls and shouts of "Hey, hippie gringo"—*heepee greengo*. He didn't realize at first that the catcalls were for him (he didn't think of himself as a hippie), but the taunts *were* for him, and he tried to ignore them, did ignore them, even when the vendors stood in his way. When one of them said, in heavily accented English, "Gringo, what happened to your leg? Did you get bit by a dog? I have a cure for that, special for gringos," Dooley couldn't stand it and he stopped, and there must have been something in his look, some body language the man understood, because he put up his hands and backed away. "Have a nice day, hippie gringo," he said, and was gone.

When Dooley came to a sign that said Fernando's Hideaway Cantina, he believed he had found a clue to his future. He knew what "Hernando's Hideaway" was, a song from a musical that his grandfather listened to on the record player. Dooley decided to go inside, ask for a *cerveza*—about the only word he knew in Spanish other than *si* and *amigo* and *gringo*. Spanish, he thought, as he pulled open the door to the cantina, an important step to survival. *Learn it*, he told himself, *as quickly as possible*.

Inside, he immediately spotted a group of young people sitting at a table in the corner, drinking and laughing and speaking English. They had backpacks with sleeping bags piled up beside them, a table laden with half-full glasses and bottles of beer. He locked eyes with a laughing girl with the whitest skin he had ever seen and long, dark hair, and he walked right over and sat down with her and her three friends, and they squeezed together to make room for him, no questions asked, as though he were part of the adventure they were on. He thought of the couple with the pup tent, who had made it as far as San Clemente and Disneyland before deciding to spend their student loans on university rather than a trip farther south.

Suckers, he thought.

"*Cerveza,*" he called to the man behind the bar. He wondered if his name was Fernando.

"*Por favor,*" said the girl, whose name was Angela Mazlanka. She poked him in the ribs as if she'd known him for a long time and hadn't met him just thirty seconds ago. "Didn't your mother teach you manners? Be polite."

He almost said, "I have no mother," but instead he called, "Sorry, *amigo*." He asked Angela, "How do you say that—sorry?"

"*Lo siento.*"

"*Lo siento, amigo. Cerveza. Por favor.*"

And the man—an American named Karl, not a Mexican named Fernando—brought him a beer. Angela directed Dooley to say *Gracias*, and Karl answered in Spanish—*De nada*—and Dooley added that to his vocabulary. Then he held up his beer to clink bottles, and thus began his new life. Angela and her friends didn't actually know much Spanish, so Dooley found himself at the bar talking to Karl, asking him how you say this and how you ask for that . . . How much? What time? How far? And where, Dooley asked Karl, does someone go who wants to disappear?

Karl told him about a couple of places.

The five of them—Dooley and the three girls and a guy named Dave—spent the night in a hot room above the cantina. Dooley was happy to learn that Angela was not *with* Dave, although one of the other girls apparently was, because he heard them going at it in the night. They were all sleeping (or not sleeping) on top of their sleeping bags because it was so hot. They were covered in bug bites by morning.

"Who cares? It's Mexico," said Angela, scratching her arm, her dark eyes laughing, looking at Dooley, her hair wavy from the humidity, and *right in front of him* she took off the pink tie-dyed T-shirt she'd slept in and changed into a peasant blouse she'd bought the day before. Dooley noted the small breasts, the ribs he could see when she lifted her arms.

Her skin was so remarkably white. He thought she would make a good angel in a Christmas pageant and wondered if that's why her parents had named her Angela, if she'd looked that way when she was born, small and white.

"How old are you anyway?" she asked Dooley as she adjusted her blouse, gathered in the neck and then tied the strings in a bow.

"Twenty-four," he told her. "Next up, twenty-five." Cocky, as though twenty-five made him a man.

"Huh," she said. "You're a bit of an antique."

She was nineteen. She told him that Dave's girl—Izzy was her name—was only sixteen and had run away from home. Dooley wondered why he hadn't thought of doing that when he was sixteen. The way Angela was sitting with her legs crossed, he could see she had an old scar that started above her ankle and ran up her leg. He couldn't see where it ended.

"What happened to your leg?" he asked her.

"I used to be an ice dancer," she said. "You know, figure skater. Then my partner ran over me with his skate. He didn't mean to. We were trying too hard to do something spectacular, which in a way we did. You should have seen the blood on the ice. It was like a massacre."

If she noticed his limp, she didn't say anything, at least not then.

They all went downstairs to the cantina and had *huevos rancheros* and beans and *cerveza* for breakfast, and then they said goodbye to their new friend Karl and found the bus station and a battered blue bus with "San José" written on the front window in white paint and the Virgin Mary hanging from a mirror (Our Lady of Guadalupe, he found out later). They weren't sure where San José was, but it was in the right direction. They threw their backpacks on top— not Dooley, he kept his close—and got in with the Mexicans and headed south. He and Angela were sitting together, Dooley in the window seat. She was carrying an embroidered baby blue suede jacket lined with some kind of fur, rabbit maybe. It looked expensive. Once they were on their way, Angela picked up her jacket and reached across Dooley and waved it outside the bus window, and then she let it go. The jacket was immediately grabbed by a cactus and hung there like a coat on a hook, waiting for someone to come along and pluck it off. She stayed in the window for a minute, watching her jacket disappear, stretched across Dooley's body. He put his hand on her ass. Her hair blew into his face. Then she moved away and settled back on her side of the seat.

"Won't need that where we're going, will I?" she said, about the jacket. She used the word "we." Dooley couldn't help noticing.

They got off the bus at a fishing village somewhere along the Baja peninsula. Dooley hoped it was the right place, the one Karl had told him about, where you could live on the beach without being told to move on. They walked south from the village and found a dozen concrete huts a hundred yards back from the water, a former compound of some kind, now occupied by the stream of traveling young people moving in and out of them. Dooley and Angela and her friends moved into one that was vacant, spreading out their sleeping bags on the sand floor and claiming wooden boxes and makeshift shelving for their backpacks and the few belongings they'd carried with them. Dooley hadn't stopped thinking about Angela's body draped across his on the bus, and neither, apparently, had she. They made out in a hidden spot in the sand dunes before the sun was barely down, Angela making it clear that she didn't believe in exclusivity, Dooley saying he didn't either, both of them trying to avoid the cactus that was everywhere and trying to remember what they'd been told about snakes and scorpions. Dooley thought about the word she'd used—"exclusivity"—and was happy to have met someone who seemed to think the way he did. He wondered why it had taken him so long to discover a life like this.

"I never want to go back," Angela said.

"You won't have to if you stick with me," Dooley said. "I have a nest egg."

She started to laugh.

"What?" he asked. "Why is that funny?"

"I come from a bottomless pit of money," she said. "There's nothing as modest as a nest egg in my family."

He should have known. The expensive jacket she'd thrown out the bus window as easily as if it were an empty cigarette pack.

He saw she was looking at the scar on his leg.

"I drove into a bridge," he told her.

"Don't you hate it when that happens?"

Without words being exchanged, without commitment being spoken of, they became exclusive.

DOOLEY DIDN'T HAVE much interest in the people coming and going on the beach. He'd spent most of his childhood hanging around with kids who were older than him, driving all over the countryside when he was only eleven or twelve years old. Now he was with people who were barely out of their teens, if that. Most days he ignored the band of dreamers and walked into the village and struck up conversations with the more interesting fishermen and the vendors in the market, and he kicked the soccer ball around with the Mexican kids in the plaza, not caring if they laughed at his limp, his complete lack of skill with both soccer and Spanish, his gesturing and mistakes and bad pronunciations. He learned. He could soon speak Spanish better than anyone else on the beach, even the Americans who'd studied it in school. The others began to look to him to take care of things, to talk them out of trouble when it appeared, to deal with the *policía* when they occasionally stopped for payment, some pesos or cigarettes. They began to count on Dooley to make decisions. Once he'd accepted that role, there was no arguing with him. It was Dooley who asked people to move on if they weren't pulling their weight or following the few unspoken rules that kept things copacetic.

"What the fuck?" whined one such evictee when Dooley informed him he wasn't welcome anymore because he was suspected of helping himself to the pesos in someone's wallet and he kept referring to Mexicans as *bandidos*.

"They are *bandidos*," the boy whined.

Dooley gave him a friendly pat on the shoulder and said, "*Vamos. Ahora.*"

The boy left.

Angela told Dooley he had some kind of weird power over people, the way they listened to him and didn't argue.

"You're like the king or something," she said.

It reminded Dooley of the school principal who'd tried to save him from truancy and called him cock of the walk.

After the boy left, sulking his way up the road to town

and the bus station, Dooley sat in the sand with an unopened bottle of tequila. Angela sat next to him and said, "You do have a nest egg, don't you?"

He was tempted then to tell her about his grandfather dying and Basie Moon's solution to the trouble Dooley found himself in, the look on Basie's face as he handed him the check. The look that said it was money well spent if it would get Dooley out of Elliot.

Instead he said, "I have my resources."

Angela said, "I like a man of mystery. Are you Howard Hughes? I think you might be."

He didn't know who Howard Hughes was. For the first time ever, he wondered if he'd missed something by disregarding school. When it came to facts, there seemed to be a lot he didn't know.

He opened the bottle of tequila and passed it to Angela.

THE WORST THING that happened was when one of the beach inhabitants drowned. The boy—a twenty-year-old American—hadn't been listening when he was told about the currents, and he went swimming and found himself being sucked out into the surf, and he wasn't a strong enough swimmer to last until help reached him. A fisherman with a boat tried. It was too late, but at least he was able to retrieve the boy's body. No one on the beach knew who he was, but they found his driver's license in his things and gave it to the authorities. A few weeks later his father showed up from Nebraska, grief-stricken, wanting to know about his son's life in Mexico, wanting affirmation that his life had not been wasted and that he'd been doing something useful—learning something, at least—but no one had known the boy well enough to tell him much. Angela stepped up then and asked the man, the father, if he wanted to go for a walk with her along the beach, and she pointed out the spot where his son had gone into the water and made up some things about how he—Alec?—was teaching English to poor children in the village, and in return one of the parents had given him a guitar and taught him to play Mexican folk songs and he was very talented, they all thought so. Alec spoke sometimes of his family, Angela told the man, and he was planning a trip home before too long and considering a return to school to become a teacher.

"Really?" the father said when Angela told him these good things about his son. Disbelieving but wanting to believe, choosing to do so, and then asking Angela if she knew where his son's guitar was, he would like to have it, and Angela had to think quickly and asked the man to wait while she went to find it. There were lots of guitars around, and she walked into the huts, searching, and took the first one she came to, with a plan to purchase a better one for its owner, a girl who sang mournful English ballads. She gave the girl's guitar to the man. He thanked her for spending the time with him, and then he left with the guitar to take his son's body home.

"Did you see he was crying?" Angela asked Dooley afterward. "It was incredibly sad. What was his name, anyway? The boy who drowned. I hope it was Alec."

Dooley thought it was Allen, but he didn't say so. He was flabbergasted by Angela's kindness. He had never before met anyone like her. How, he wondered, had he, Dooley Sullivan, had the good fortune to walk into Fernando's Hideaway Cantina and find Angela there waiting for him? Dooley Sullivan, who had been raised by a grandfather he couldn't seem to please and who carried with him, always, a feeling of disappointment, even though he lived in one of the nicest houses in Elliot and there was plenty of food on the table. Always a feeling that his grandfather wanted to punish him just for being there, disappointment morphing into an anger that almost killed him in a flaming wreck. As he and Angela walked along the beach after the grieving father left, he wanted to ask her about her past, why she was here, what so-called advantages she had run away from. The thing he didn't understand was how she could have grown up with all the privilege of wealth—obviously more privilege than even he had had—and be the person she was.

Instead of asking her this, he asked if her parents had had pretentious fucking international dinner parties when she was growing up.

She looked up at him, studying him, until he wished he hadn't asked. Then she said, "Exactly. How did you know?"

He had a homemade clay pipe in his pocket and he took it out and lit it, and they passed it back and forth. He felt himself seething just thinking about the dinner parties, and how he had been well aware of his grandfather's wish that Dooley be absent while the guests were in the house, pretending. Pretending to be richer than they were. Pretending to know the right people. Pretending to live somewhere other than Elliot. His grandfather hadn't wanted Dooley, the boy who seemed always to be in trouble, ruining his epicurean charade.

What no one had understood was that Dooley didn't want to be in trouble. He wanted to please people. He tried to be smart, but he wasn't, at least not in the way his grandfather wanted him to be. He was funny, he knew that, but teachers didn't appreciate funny. They told him to stop being clever, and then they turned around and told him to smarten up. When he tried to be good, he got in trouble for that too. He'd had a teacher he liked in second grade—they called her a practice teacher, and *she'd* thought he was funny and spent extra time with him on arithmetic—and he'd wanted to give her a present when she left, so he took a pair of bookends from his grandfather's house, two praying hands, and wrapped them up himself in gift paper he'd found in a drawer. It was red and green for Christmas, but he didn't think that would matter. The practice teacher's face fell when she opened the present; he saw that, recognized the look, and knew he was in trouble again.

Sure enough, someone called his grandfather, and he accused Dooley of stealing the bookends. *Stealing*, of all things, when his grandfather was always giving away books to people, books by novelists and poets—classics, he called them. He'd take them right off the shelves and say, "Take this one, please. You'll like it." Now Dooley was not only in trouble for stealing—which he didn't think he'd done, or not intentionally—but also embarrassed in front of the teacher he liked, who gave the bookends back to him. She tried to be nice and said they were too much of a gift, she couldn't accept them. "But thank you, Dooley," she said. "I appreciate the thought, that was really nice of you." And he knew she'd been told by the principal what Dooley had done, that he'd stolen them. "You're a good boy, Dooley," she said, and that was the worst, because she hadn't had to say that to anyone else, no other child in the class. Dooley wanted to hang his head, ashamed, but instead he threw a rock at the school and broke a window. That was the first time he'd had his after-school playtime taken away. Grade two and he was already grounded.

After that, Dooley didn't try very hard to be good. He didn't seem to know how, and it turned out he was better at being bad. He could make the other students laugh when he was bad, and sometimes even the teachers, who couldn't believe what he had just done. It was like he could please them—or at least give them a way to understand him—by being bad. He started smoking in grade four, as soon as he found a way to buy cigarettes from the older boys. Not long after, one of them asked Dooley if he wanted liquor to go with his cigarettes and he said sure, and he went with them in a car, out into the country, and he got drunk for the first time. Then he was stealing his grandfather's liquor—he hid his thefts by topping up the bottles with water—and he lied when his grandfather confronted him. He started skipping school, and the principal would drive around Elliot until he found him and hauled him back, calling him a truant. Once, he said to him, on the way to the school after one of Dooley's attempts to skip, "You're lucky your grandfather isn't still principal. He wasn't as lenient as I am," and Dooley thought, *You don't have to tell me that*. The principal had delivered him to his classroom and Dooley swaggered in like a hero, and the other students clapped until the teacher said, "Don't encourage him." When the principal saw him in the hallway after school that day, he said, "You're just the cock of the walk, aren't you, Dooley?"

In seventh grade, he failed five subjects. He got 13 percent in science, and when his grandfather saw that on his report card he said, "Thirteen percent . . . you've learned nothing," and Dooley said, "Technically, thirteen percent isn't nothing," and his grandfather called him disrespectful. He was held back that year. That's what they called it, "held back," like you were trying, wanting to go somewhere, even though Dooley wasn't. Dooley's grandfather called it failing. He called it a great humiliation that a Sullivan and the grandson of a former principal would fail a grade. He told Dooley about the hedge schools in Ireland and the lengths people went to in order to make sure their children were educated, even when the rich English tried to prevent it. "You're lucky," he told Dooley. "Privileged. You've had every advantage."

Every advantage. That's not how Dooley saw it. And where were his parents, he wondered, if he was so privileged? Why was he living with his grandfather, who didn't even seem to like him much? And if his grandfather thought living with a teacher was an advantage, he had that wrong.

He failed grade seven again.

By the time he finally got to grade eight he was both the tallest and dumbest boy in the class. He didn't like being the dumbest, not really, but he just couldn't seem to figure how to put any effort into school, and anyway, if he did make an effort, that would mean he cared. He skipped regularly, even though there was some enjoyment in keeping the other students on the edges of paying attention to the teacher, keeping them constantly aware of him, the way you are aware of a wild animal—a sly coyote, say—lurking, up to something. The eighth-grade teacher called him disruptive, which meant that he could make the others laugh pretty much anytime he wanted. Like the day he swung his legs out the open second-story classroom window while the teacher had her back turned to write something on the blackboard, and he silently polled the other students as he sat in the window, mimed "Should I? Should I?" and raised his hands to ask the question while the teacher wrote with chalk in her neat hand, pleased with her ability to keep the lines straight, ignorant of what was going on behind her.

Dooley wasn't really planning to jump, but he was enjoying that all the other students were nodding their heads and trying not to giggle. He milked it—*Should I? Should I?*—until he noticed one girl frowning at him, and he knew, just knew, she was about to tell. He could see her hand shooting up, hear the words "Teacher, teacher, Dooley's in the window," and so he impulsively jumped. Without really thinking how far it was to the ground. He heard the collective roar of laughter behind him as he went hurtling into space, trying to figure out how to roll when he landed, past that little girl in the window, Basie Moon's daughter, with her curly hair framing her face, and he landed all wrong and broke his ankle and a rib, and that wasn't actually funny. There was a big fuss when Elliot's only ambulance came and he gave the thumbs-up from the stretcher to all the kids sneaking peeks from the various classroom windows, even though they were now closed. The little girl with the curly hair was still there, leaning out of an open window. She waved at him and ducked back inside, and then they'd hauled him away in the ambulance. When he ventured out a few days later and hobbled around town with his taped ribs and his cast and crutches, he got lots of "Hey, Dooley, good one!" This coming from high school boys wanting to sign his cast. Girls, lots of girls, saying, "Let me sign, Dooley." Just to be a smart aleck, he asked his grandfather if he wanted to sign, but of course he didn't. Surprisingly, his teacher did. "Dooley, Dooley, Dooley," she said as she wrote her name in blue ballpoint, "what is the world going to do with you?" For some reason that question unsettled him—the way she used the word "world" instead of asking, "What are *we* going to do with you?"

When Dooley passed grade eight—barely—his grandfather bribed him to keep him from dropping out of school. A car, he said, to be confiscated if he quit. Dooley negotiated. He wanted a truck. Not a new one, but one he could work on himself. They had a shop in the high school. He could take motor mechanics and auto body and work on his own truck. His grandfather didn't want him to take shop classes. That was for boys who weren't academically inclined, he said. Dooley thought, *Are you losing your mind, old man? What have I ever done to give you even an ounce of hope?* He didn't say this out loud, but he drew a line. The truck and motor mechanics, or he was quitting. He was sixteen now, so no one could stop him. His grandfather argued, but Dooley won. He didn't think for a minute that he would stay in school long enough to get his graduation certificate, but he got his truck, a 1952 Chevy short bed with a lot of miles on it and a rusty body crying out for restoration. He pictured himself cruising around town. Red. He would paint the truck red.

That fall, he started drinking in earnest. He hung around with farm kids who'd been driving since they were twelve or thirteen, and with older town kids who had their parents' sedans or their own beaters, and every weekend they hit the roads and found new places to party—in an old barn or grain bin if it was cold, outside on nice summer nights, in a stand of trees in someone's pasture, at the gravel pit, where it was sheltered and you could have a fire and no one would notice. He'd get so drunk he would have no recollection the next day of what he'd done, but whatever it was, it must have been entertaining because wherever he went he'd hear "Hey, Dooley! Epic, man!"

There were girls at the parties, and Dooley liked them—chicklets, he called them. He liked to hang out with their little cadres and cliques and tease them and make them giggle, but he was not obliging with the girls who wanted too much of his attention, and he developed the reputation of being a *difficult catch*, which made some of the girls want to be with him all the more. He pushed them away. He'd have sex with them, yes—in a stand of trees, on the beach, in the backseat of someone's car—but only once, and if one of them got drunk and cried at the next party because he'd moved on, he'd turn his back. He didn't want to hurt anyone, but he didn't want a girlfriend. Brushing a girl off was better than breaking her heart.

In June, after he turned seventeen, he finally got to drive the truck out of the shop and park it in the driveway of his grandfather's house for all to see. Gleaming, shimmering candy-apple red, specially ordered for custom paint jobs. He was proud of the truck as he'd been proud of nothing before in his life. He managed to pass grade nine thanks to the applied arts classes he was now taking and the work he'd put into the truck. His grandfather came around and grew hopeful that there was at least some kind of graduation certificate within Dooley's reach. Dooley let his grandfather think he now cared about school. He was not unhappy about going back in the fall. He had plans to put a new motor in the truck.

Then Basie Moon went through Elliot's only stop sign and ran smack into him. When Dooley saw the other truck coming at him, felt the smack, heard the sound of steel buckling, saw all his work going for shit in a few careless seconds, he wanted to go crazy, scream, hit someone, beat the living crap out of Basie Moon right there in the street.

But then he saw the girl staring at him wide-eyed, and he remembered—the girl in the window—and he held back, although he couldn't stop himself from calling Basie Moon an idiot. He could have said a lot worse. He could have *done* a lot worse. And then the cop who showed up accused Dooley of drinking, when he hadn't had a single drop, not yet, and everyone in town knew that Basie Moon was blind as a bat and shouldn't be driving. He looked at his truck with the buckled hood and the hanging bumper—all that work for nothing, he should have known—and he felt a surge that he didn't recognize, something he'd never felt before, an all-consuming contempt for everybody, snaking from his feet up through his body.

Everybody except the girl. Frances Mary Moon, watching, sitting on the bench in front of the bank with her curly hair like Little Orphan Annie, staring at him with her eyes wide, looking at him as though she were about to speak, ask him a question, invite him to sit down beside her, and it was she who stopped him from going off completely. She sat by herself while Basie Moon inspected the vehicles, or pretended to, and when her father sat down beside her, they whispered something to each other, and she reached over and touched her father's hand, perhaps to make him feel better, comfort him, and Dooley thought, Why? Why don't I have a father instead of that impossible old man? He tried to think back to a time before his grandfather, but there was nothing there. Why did he have to get stuck with an old man who liked to hang stainless steel pots in his kitchen so everyone could see them, and have stupid dinner parties—international cooking parties, he called them—and cook egg foo yong and chop suey, pretending that he, Dooley, didn't exist whenever the house was full of teachers and the town doctor and the couple who owned the hardware store, all of them dressed up the way you don't have to dress up in a town like Elliot, and laughing and trying to eat with chopsticks? Why did he have to be the one that happened to? Dooley watched the curly-haired girl and tried to imagine what she was whispering to her father, and he couldn't. She was talking a foreign language. He'd never cried about being deserted by his mother. He wanted to cry now. He had to work harder than he'd ever worked to keep from crying, to keep Basie Moon and the girl and the cop and the others who were now standing around from seeing him—Dooley Sullivan, who had a reputation to uphold—break down in tears.

The cop told him to calm down—"Dooley," he said, "Dooley, calm down and tell me what happened or I'll have to put you in the back of the car, and you know you don't like it back there"—and he took their statements, and then Moon and the little girl drove off. The cop *let* Basie Moon drive off with his daughter, which was outrageous, criminal. If he ever had a child, Dooley thought, he would not put that child in harm's way. And then he thought that he was already putting people in harm's way because he drove as drunk as a sailor half the time, and so he resolved to quit drinking, to make something of himself so he could have a family someday, a real one.

Only he didn't quit drinking. He quit school instead. He tried to make a new start on the truck, but he was too angry. He was angry all the time now, and hating school and all the teachers, even the grade eight teacher, who still said "Dooley, Dooley, Dooley" whenever she saw him, and he understood this to be a sign of affection of some kind or another, and that just made it worse, that his former teacher was the most affectionate person in his life and all she could say to him was "Dooley, Dooley, Dooley" as she walked by, not even stopping to say it, but saying it in passing as though he were hopeless, no point in stopping.

He quit school before September was even over. He took the truck away from the shop without fixing it, just banged the dents out as best he could, and he left his grandfather's house and moved in with a couple of guys who were older than him and worked in the bush. He tried that too, working in the bush, only he wasn't very good at it. The work was too hard and the men too rough, and Dooley was tall and skinny, not muscular, and they didn't like him, and he didn't get called to work very often. So he spent what money he had on booze, and he spent the fall of that year driving the mangled red truck in a blur of inebriation until the night he'd hit a deer and sent it flying through the air like a foot-ball, and then he'd hit the bridge, drove his truck right into it, thinking he and the truck would fly together like the deer, only that hadn't happened. The truck had slammed into the bridge and stopped without flying anywhere, bursting into flames right after some Good Samaritan dragged him from the cab. The tow truck had only a burned-out shell to haul away.

He remembered almost nothing as he lay in a hospital bed, first in Yellowhead and then back in Elliot, the room in darkness because the light bothered his eyes, but he could still see the deer lit by the headlights, its four legs flying end over end and disappearing into the night, and then—*smack!*—there it was again, four legs flying, over and over, endlessly.

Until his grandfather accused him of hitting that man on the highway, the Indian who worked at the lumberyard. He didn't remember a man; he remembered the deer. He wanted to explain, tried to talk, one last chance to prevent people from believing the worst of him, but then his grandfather leaned over him in his hospital bed and said, "Don't you say a word, Dooley. Not one word about that man. It will ruin your life completely, if it's not ruined already. And I'm sick and tired of trying to bail you out of trouble. What's done is done. Not one word." And Dooley had thought, *You miserable old prick*, and he quit trying to explain.

When the police came, he said he didn't remember, which was mostly true.

He clung to the image of the flying deer being swallowed by darkness, but then one day it disappeared entirely and didn't return, and the deer was replaced by the image of a man. Struck by the bumper of his truck. A man going end over end into the snow. He began to see the man whenever he closed his eyes.

When he was well enough—"He'll never be completely well," the doctors said—they sent him back to the hospital in Elliot, and Basie Moon's daughter, the red-haired girl, delivered a get well card, the only one he received from anyone. Eventually, he limped away from the hospital with one steel plate holding his leg together and another in his head, and he moved to the city, cut off all ties with Elliot, and didn't go back until three years later, after he heard his grandfather had died. He'd been doing not all that badly in the city, working as a carpenter's helper, keeping his drinking under control—perhaps because he'd discovered cannabis, which made him feel almost normal. He didn't know why he was drawn back to Elliot after his grandfather's death, but he was, and then it all went wrong again, and he almost incinerated himself in his grandfather's house and ended up in jail, and then Basie Moon, the same one who'd run into his truck, offered him money to go away again, and he took it. He divided his money in two, left one half in a bank and tucked the other half into a false bottom that he crafted in his backpack, and he decided to really go away, first to Alberta, then to Vancouver. He tried to find work there on a fishing boat, but no one would have him because he had no experience. Eventually he went to California to see what that was all about—beaches and surfers and Hollywood—and that's when he thought about joining the Marines as a way of turning his life around, but only for about five minutes because he had no interest in getting killed in Vietnam, and anyway, the Marines wouldn't want a recruit with metal plates holding him together.

Then he heard about Mexico and how you could disappear there. That was more his style, he thought: disappearing. Deserting the country of his citizenship, the place where they had records, where he was *registered* as a person. And when he walked across the border into Mexico and no one asked him anything, not even his name, he knew he could make that happen. And then he met Angela, and they lived on the beach with an endless stream of people coming and going, and sometimes she looked at him the way Basie Moon's daughter had looked at her father that day on the bench in front of the bank, a day when Dooley had not been able to imagine that he could be so lucky. That he would ever feel so free. When he told Angela this—that she made him feel free—she laughed and told him that he had discovered his own soul.

"It's not me," she said. "You've made yourself free."

Then she said that Dooley had given her an idea. Because she had been a dancer—she and her skating partner were junior provincial ice-dance champions before the accident—she decided she and Dooley should express their gratitude for this life by dancing every day at sunset. You could hardly call what Dooley came up with dance, even Angela said that, but it didn't matter. It was a spiritual act, she said, and whatever Dooley did, as long as it was done honestly, would be good for his soul.

"Think of your soul as a newborn baby," she said. "You need to nurture it, keep it alive."

"How did you get to be so enlightened?" he asked her, and at first she thought he was being sarcastic, but he denied that, and she said, "I should have known. You, Dooley Sullivan, do not have a sarcastic bone in your body. You're an innocent. That's why I love you so much."

He shivered from the pleasure of hearing her say those words, "love" and "you," in the same breath. And the word "innocent," which had never been applied to him before.

They danced on the beach every day, Dooley in a pair of surfer shorts he bought at a market and Angela in a bright yellow bikini. Sometimes they had live music—guitars, bongo drums, a harmonica. If not, there was always someone with a battery-operated tape player. They danced to whatever music was available in someone's backpack. Everything from Three Dog Night to classical flute to Dr. John or Memphis Slim. Periodically, a group symbiosis happened and there grew a great crowd of gyrating, swaying bodies on the beach, in bare feet and bikinis and cutoff jeans, sometimes no clothing at all, first one person shedding a wraparound peasant skirt, a tank top, a pair of surfer shorts, and then the whole line of them naked, stomping and twisting, hair and limbs and hand-made jewelry flying, every person in his or her own private world of motion. Once in a while, some young man or woman with a crush on Angela misinterpreted her free spirit as a loose spirit and tried to cut in, but she danced within herself and paid no attention whatsoever while Dooley watched, amused by the futility, still hardly believing that what this hopeful intruder wanted was reserved for him.

And then the sun would suddenly drop, sink into the Pacific so quickly you could see it move, and the sky would go pink and dove gray and then blue-black, and everything would go still without anyone announcing, "That's it for today, I guess."

When Angela stopped dancing, so did Dooley.

She was the real cock of the walk, he thought, not him.

TEN MONTHS PASSED. A year. The magic of the beach began to wear thin. Dooley felt the old restlessness creeping in, irritation with the naiveté that he saw around him, the lack of connection between himself and the other expats. He was afraid to tell Angela he was ready to move on in case it gave her the chance to say she was ready to move on too. From him. But when he finally brought it up, she agreed that the squatters' beach was losing its appeal and he was relieved when she suggested that they—*they*—go farther south to where she knew of a couple who owned property, the daughter of one of her parents' friends. Angela said she didn't know this couple very well and didn't really expect to like them. "But let's check it out," she said, just for a change from communal living. A real shower. A washing machine. Probably maid service.

Maid service? Dooley thought she must be joking, but he retrieved his nest egg from its hiding place and they packed up and caught a ride from the peninsula to the mainland with an American fisherman in a fancy boat. A few people wanted to go with them, but they said no, they were traveling alone. Dooley grinned all the way across the Sea of Cortez over having Angela to himself. On the mainland, they took a series of buses south down the coast until they came to the town they were looking for, situated on a cliff overlooking the Pacific. They found the house and stood looking at the locked gate and the razor wire looped along the top of the fence, until finally they rang the bell and a maid let them in, surprised when Dooley spoke to her in such fluent Spanish.

They didn't last long at Angela's not-exactly-friends' house. The community was new, and the people who lived in it were all wealthy Canadians or Americans. They reminded Dooley of his grandfather, pretending to be people they weren't. They were shallow, Angela said, too much like her parents, and they didn't approve of Dooley, didn't approve of his drinking (even though you rarely saw one of *them* without a margarita in hand, no matter what the time of day), so Angela and Dooley made plans to leave again, but not before getting roaring drunk one day and dancing crazily on the pool deck. Dooley lost his balance on his bad leg and fell into the pool, and then Angela jumped in after him, both of them in their clothes, while the friends (by this time, decidedly *not* friends) sat in lounge chairs on the tiled deck and glowered at them over the tops of their Ray-Ban sunglasses. When Angela took off her T-shirt and threw it up on the deck, and then stripped Dooley down and threw his wet shorts out of the pool, their hosts had a hushed conversation and then went into the house. Angela said she could just imagine the report that would get back to her parents, but she didn't care. In fact, she overheard a phone conversation that night in which it sounded as though her father might be flying down, so she and Dooley quickly left without even saying thank you; they didn't even wait for the bus but rather hitchhiked to Mexico City, where Angela replenished her money supply—Dooley didn't have to replenish his because it was all in his backpack—and they found a hostel and stayed for a month, awed by the size of the city and the cultural wonders it held. When they began to crave the ocean again, they caught a bus as far south as they could go, moving from beach to beach, staying in each new place until they grew tired of it or until Angela suspected that someone hired by her father was following them. Dooley was never convinced of the truth of her suspicions, but he went along.

"Is your father in the Mafia?" he asked once, thinking it was a joke.

"Of course not," Angela said, sounding, he thought, defensive. "He's just rich. Too rich."

"If he found you, would he try to take you back?"

"I don't know. I suppose not. He would have snatched me by now if that was it."

"What about your mother?" Dooley asked, barely knowing the meaning of the word himself.

"Why are you asking so many questions?"

He didn't ask any more.

Sometimes they went inland, to the old colonial towns in the mountains, or to the cities, Guadalajara or San Miguel de Allende, where they stayed for over a year. They spent another year in Belize and Guatemala, having managed to cross the borders even though Dooley had no passport. They traveled from one end of Mexico to the other several times over until their nomadic life began to grow tiresome, although neither of them was quite ready to admit to feeling dissatisfied. They talked about settling somewhere, but then another town would beckon and they would yield to the promise of a place to which they had not yet been.

On Dooley's thirtieth birthday, in a hot hotel room overlooking the *plaza central* in a town in the Yucatán, Angela finally said, "I'm sick of being an itinerant. Are you?"

Dooley was relieved to hear it. He felt the same way, he said. It was wearing him out. Angela teased him then, said he was getting to be an old dog and needed a porch to lie on.

They settled down in the state of Quintana Roo on a beach so white Dooley thought it looked like snow. From an American who called himself Don Orlando, they rented a hut on stilts with a *palapa* roof and hammocks for beds, just the two of them. Dooley met a local fisherman named Eduardo who was happy to have a partner, and some days Dooley went with him in his boat, beyond the reef. He learned about fish. He met a *vaquero*, a cowboy, who taught him a bit about horses. He liked the way the horses watched him, quietly. He watched them back. Angela, who knew about massage from her days as an ice dancer, bought a portable table and set up on the beach every morning. She led yoga classes at sunset. They paid their rent and bought food and beer and tequila without having to use either Dooley's nest egg or Angela's bank account. They became a part of a community of mostly Canadian and American writers and artists and jewelry makers. Angela called herself a masseuse. When asked, Dooley said he was a fisherman. He was drinking a lot now, and smoking pot all day long, every day, but he told himself it was for the headaches he'd begun having again. He couldn't stand the pain without drugs and alcohol. Sometimes Eduardo worried that Dooley was going to fall out of the boat and drown, especially beyond the reef, where the sea was rough and threw the boat around. Eduardo had an old life vest that he tried to get Dooley to wear, but Dooley declined. Even had he agreed, the vest looked as though its days of saving anyone's life were long over.

The hotel that Don Orlando owned began to offer wedding packages. One night when he and Dooley were drinking together, he offered to marry Dooley and Angela for free. The more Dooley thought about it, the more it seemed like a good idea. A week later, he drank himself into a state of courage and told Angela about the offer.

"Why would we want to get married by a hustler like Don Orlando?" she asked. "It would be like getting married in Las Vegas."

"That's true," Dooley said, hiding his disappointment. "Anyway, Don Orlando was so drunk he wouldn't remember. It's not like him to do anything for free."

He tried not to sulk or act like his feelings were hurt. He never brought up marriage again, but he didn't forget either how quickly Angela had dismissed the idea.

They lived in this place for five years. Angela forgot about men hired by her father. They moved up the beach into a bigger *cabaña*, which Angela decorated: a blue glass vase by the door, a ceramic fruit bowl for the table, woven blankets used as curtains for the open windows. Most days, Dooley's head felt as if it might explode. He and Angela began to argue. She said she was concerned about his headaches and wanted him to see a doctor, but he refused, accused her of plotting to have a doctor tell him to quit drinking. Once, he snapped back at her that she looked pale, maybe *she* should be seeing a doctor. It wasn't normal for a person to be as thin as she was, he said; he could see her ribs. She turned away, and later he thought he could hear her crying.

Then one day Dooley found himself sitting on a rock with a bottle of tequila watching Angela dance on the beach at sunset instead of dancing with her, and he realized that they had stopped sleeping together. A few days later Angela told him that she was going away without him. She offered no explanation. He drank himself to sleep that night as usual and woke up alone the next morning. He stayed in his hammock all day and tried not to think about what Angela had told him when they first met—that she didn't believe in exclusivity, that sex and love were different things. Where was she? he wondered. He imagined that she'd gone inland to a city where there was more action or headed up the coast with a man she'd met on the beach—Bill from Chicago or Gunnar from Sweden. He'd been lucky, he thought, to have her to himself for as long as he had. Who was he to think he could hold on to a woman like Angela forever? He convinced himself that she wasn't coming back.

But she did, three days later, and she told him that she'd had to go away on her own to think because she was going to be thirty years old on her next birthday. She'd taken a ferry to an island and stayed at a meditation center and fasted the whole time, thinking about her future. "Thirty!" she said, as though she couldn't believe that she'd lived this long. Later, they sat on the beach with a pitcher of beer and a plate of tortilla chips on the table between them (Dooley trying to keep his drinking in check), and Angela confessed that she had decided the feud with her father had reached its statute of limitations. She had called him from a pay phone and spoken with him. He'd agreed, she said, that he couldn't force her to return home, but he had reminded her of her approaching birthday, a milestone. He said that she could no longer pretend to be a gypsy child.

"He was only saying what I had already decided myself," she said.

They sat on the beach until it was dark, the sun dropping into the mangroves behind them, and Angela said she missed watching the red ball sink over the water the way it did on the Pacific side. She thought they should consider returning to the west coast; she wanted to dance the sun into the ocean again.

We should think about it, she'd said. Still using the word "we."

The decision to leave was made for them when a tropical storm slammed into their beach. Everyone evacuated inland, but when they went back, they found all of Don Orlando's *cabañas* destroyed and the beach littered with debris. Angela's massage table was missing; Eduardo's boat was gone. All Angela and Dooley had left was what they'd carried inland in their backpacks.

They got on a bus and headed west again.

Angela said, "I'm having a pre-midlife crisis."

Dooley asked her if she wanted to go back to Canada.

No, she said, but she wanted to settle down, *really* settle down, not live in another rented hut somewhere. Dooley worried that she might be talking about a house with razor wire and a maid.

That afternoon, they got off the bus in a small city and found a hotel room with a ceiling fan trying to turn the hot air into something breathable. It was a decent hotel, better than many they'd stayed in over the years. Still, Dooley was miserable. He didn't know what Angela was thinking, where her epiphany would take them. Maybe it wouldn't take *him* anywhere, he thought, returning to his old worry that she would leave him. They bought tamales from a street vendor and he bought a bottle of tequila, and they returned to their hotel room. Dooley found two glasses and placed them on the room's small table, but Angela didn't drink from hers. A tiny gecko clung to the ceiling and Dooley wondered why it didn't give up in the heat and let go. Angela lay down on the bed with a crime novel that she'd taken from the book exchange in the hotel lobby, and Dooley left his glass on the table and lay down beside her, and he found himself talking about his headaches, even went as far as saying they were caused by the accident, when he'd crashed into the bridge, and she said, "Tell me about it, Dooley. You've never told me the whole story."

He wanted to, but he couldn't, because once he started he would tell her everything, about the deer bouncing off the truck's bumper, the deer that had probably been a man, because how else did the man end up on the side of the very road on which Dooley had been driving so drunk that the center line had become a long white snake sidewinding in the headlights?

"There's not much to tell," he said. "It's the story you read in the news every day, drunken kid crosses the center line and drives into a logging truck or some family's station wagon. If he's lucky, it's a bridge and there's no one in the vehicle but him. He thinks he's doing the world a favor, but then some well-meaning doctor puts him back together again."

Angela set down her book and picked up his hand.

"Poor Dooley," she said. What Dooley heard was that teacher—*Dooley, Dooley, Dooley*, as though he were a lost cause.

"Don't say that," he said, pulling his hand away. Surprising himself and Angela with the anger in his tone. There was a long silence before she said the thing that he knew was true, the thing she had been working up to but he dreaded to hear, especially from her, because it meant that they were not equals, that she was judging, that he was weaker than she was, and was not anymore, if he ever had been, the cock of the walk, *you're like the king or something.*

"Maybe you should try to quit drinking," she said. "Just try. I'll quit too."

Dooley stared up at the gecko and imagined its transparent toes giving up their hold, one at a time, until it fell, upside down, like a body falling into a grave.

"The headaches," she said. "It could be the drinking, and not the accident at all. Maybe the accident is an excuse."

If only she knew, Dooley thought. All the excuses, going back as far as he could remember. Too many of them ever to explain, even to himself. All banging around like steel drums inside his head. He wasn't an idiot. He knew why drunk was his preferred state of being and had been since he was a teenager.

Instead of giving himself over to Angela, coming clean, he got up from the bed and retrieved his glass from the table, and even though it made him miserable to do so, he said, "The easiest thing for you to do is tell me to leave. Just say the word."

Angela said, "I'm not looking for the easy way," and then she looked away.

She picked up her book. Dooley finished his drink. He looked at the glass he'd poured for Angela, but he left it there and lay down again on the bed.

There was a lot of street noise under their window. They tried to go to sleep but couldn't, so they turned the light back on and read in bed until the noise settled down. Dooley had taken a volume of selected Spanish poetry from the book exchange. He could read the poems—he knew the words—but the meanings were elusive. He kept reading, trying to understand the point of poetry, not getting it at all, and he was about to say so—*What is the point of poetry, anyway?*—when he came to a line that made him stop. He read it again and again until tears welled up in his eyes, and he said the line out loud, in English: "I love you without knowing how, or when, or from where."

Then Angela surprised him by laying her book carefully on the bed and straddling him. She removed her shirt the way she had the day after they'd met, bent and kissed him, slipped her hands down the front of his jeans, and they made love the way they hadn't for a long time, the way Dooley thought they might not again, and afterward she wrapped her leg around one of his and said, "Dooley, are we just sad hangers-on? Should we be doing . . . I don't know, more?"

He wasn't sure what she was asking.

The next morning he woke up when he felt Angela shaking him. She had already been out and bought coffee and pastries for breakfast, and they were on the little table waiting for him.

"I have a plan," she said. "It's a good one."

Dooley got up and bit into a pastry filled with cream and honey.

"Okay. Let's hear it."

The plan was Casa del Sol.

Proprietor: Angela Mazlanka.

Handyman and gardener: Dooley Sullivan.

THEY SCOURED THE COAST for a town they both liked, and they found one not far from the beach where they had lived originally, but on the mainland. The day Angela turned thirty, she told Dooley the details of her trust fund, which had been set up by her wealthy, since-deceased grandmother. Angela had been living on an allowance, but now that she was thirty, the whole fund was to be released to her. This was how she was going to buy a lot close to the beach and build her casa. She showed Dooley some sketches, her design ideas.

"What do you think?"

The casa contained a suite with a kitchen and bedroom and living room, and two additional rooms on the back, each with a private entrance. These rooms she would offer for rent to artists, or dancers, or writers. A dipping pool in the garden, a courtyard in front, a high wall surrounding it for privacy, but without razor wire because, she said, she trusted Mexican people, unlike the hordes of other foreign owners who were flocking to the coastal towns. Dooley was impressed that she'd designed all this herself.

The difference between his advantaged life and Angela's became evident when she was able to tackle the project so efficiently, hire an architect (Dooley barely knew what an architect was), arrange permits and work crews, order tile and fixtures and furniture that would withstand salt air and the rainy season. When he told her that he had once worked as a carpenter's helper, she recruited him to act as a foreman of sorts. It was immensely helpful, she said, to have someone who could speak Spanish as well as he did and knew something about construction. He kept an eye on the various contractors, the cement work, the plumbing and wiring, the installation of tiles and cupboards, and the painting of the casa, blue and white.

And finally, the construction of a casita, a small house within the walls of Casa del Sol, touching distance from the casa's kitchen window. The casita was Dooley's idea. He needed his privacy, he said, away from the paying guests. He couldn't see himself coaching them on Spanish phrases, or making restaurant recommendations, or pointing out whales breaching in the bay. And Angela was a businesswoman now. No hungover, pot-smoking partner at the breakfast table. He didn't want to be a liability.

When he tried to give her what was left of his money to help pay for the casita, she wouldn't take it.

"What's this?" she asked when she saw the roll of Canadian bills.

"My nest egg," Dooley replied.

"No," she said. "I'm not taking it. I told you, my grandmother is paying for this."

So Dooley bought her a gift, a huge blue glass vase to replace the one she'd had in the Yucatán *cabaña*, and he also bought ceramic tiles with the letters for Casa del Sol to embed in the wall by her gate, and the letters for El Nido, The Nest, which he hung on the casita's door. Angela put the vase in the corner in her living room and said he could make it his job to keep the vase supplied with flowers.

The guests began to arrive. Angela advertised her casa in Canadian and American arts magazines. A painter came who had just had a show at the Museum of Modern Art. A famous Canadian playwright and his boyfriend stayed at the casa and staged their own wedding by exchanging vows on the beach, just the two of them. A writer booked a room for a month and asked Angela to have a desk installed so she could work on her poetry collection. Dooley found one, and when he carried it to the writer's room, Angela introduced him as the gardener.

Sometimes Dooley watched Angela through the kitchen window, making tea for the guests at bedtime. Sometimes she stayed overnight at the casita with Dooley. They began dancing again as the sun went down. The red ball dropped into the ocean, and they claimed a spot in front of the spectacular sunset they'd both missed. They thought of it as *their* spot. Dooley did his jerky interpretation of their old beach ritual, knowing he could never emulate Angela's lithe movements. She wore a blue bikini now (a pink one with flowers had replaced the yellow one, and the blue one came after that), and she moved her thin body beautifully and fluidly, a private smile on her lips. They were happy again.

Then she left. She told Dooley she had to go home for a while, to Canada, to her parents. She'd heard her mother was sick. "Don't worry," she assured him. "I'll be back." She hired a woman named Maxine to stay in Casa del Sol and look after the guests while she was gone. When Dooley showed up at the door the day after Angela left, with flowers for the blue vase, Maxine said, "No, *gracias*," as though Dooley were any old vendor and not the gardener of Casa del Sol, even though Angela had very clearly introduced him as that before she left, and had told Maxine what she was to pay Dooley for his services.

"Just until I get back," Angela said. "It makes you official They'll take you seriously if they pay you."

A month later, Maxine left and another woman, Ardelle, moved in; she'd been hired by a vacation rental company. Yes, she knew Dooley was the gardener.

"Have you heard from Angela?" he asked her.

"Who?" she replied, which he thought was odd. He wondered if Angela's father had got her in his clutches and wouldn't let her go. He wondered if he should go to Vancouver and retrieve her, but something told him not to. Something told him that Angela would not want to see him there.

Dooley was cleaning up leaves and flower petals in the courtyard one day when a woman with a small dog walked by and asked him over the fence in English if he had the time for another gardening job. "You're an American, right?" she said. "You speak English?"

Sensing that his job at Casa del Sol might be in jeopardy, he said yes, and he ended up working for two American families who owned property in the town. They didn't seem to care that Dooley wasn't a real gardener. They wanted someone who spoke English to keep their gardens watered and patios clean, and to do a few handyman tasks for money under the table. He had learned about swimming pools from the man who took care of Casa del Sol's, and he added pool maintenance to his services. The Americans trusted him because he spoke English and he wasn't Mexican. He wondered why they hadn't just bought their winter property in Florida or Arizona.

Ardelle left Casa del Sol six months later, and then a

woman named Lola from Montreal showed up and immediately installed razor wire along the top of the wall. She
and her husband had purchased the property, she informed
Dooley. This news should have surprised him, but it didn't.
He accepted it as inevitable. He'd always believed Angela
would leave him one day, although he still held out hope
that she would return. Lola told him how much she wanted
him to pay in rent for the casita, and she warned him that
they might be tearing it down before long because they had
plans to expand the casa. They never did, though, and in
fact Lola spent very little time in the casa and it mostly
sat empty. Dooley never saw a person on the premises who
looked like he might be a husband. When no money for his
gardening services was forthcoming from Lola, he stopped
watering the garden and sweeping up the courtyard. The
money didn't matter. He was earning enough to keep himself by working for the Americans, who paid him too much,
he thought, for what he did. He quit dancing on the beach.
Without Angela there, people just looked at him as though
he was either insane or shit-faced drunk. Sometimes he was
shit-faced drunk. Once, one of the people he worked for
walked by and saw him, and he worried she might fire him
because of it, but she didn't.

Angela didn't come back. The Americans seemed happy
with his services. When they went away, he maintained
their homes and kept them secure. He drank, but never
when he was on their property. A Canadian named Roger
opened a little bar at the top of the cliff overlooking the
bay, and sometimes Dooley went there for French fries and
gravy. He thought about Angela every day, wondered why she
hadn't been in touch with him. Had she married someone in

Vancouver? He came to believe she had. After three years had gone by, he was able to picture her with a small child. He wondered if she'd gone back to school. He turned forty without her and realized that he'd done all right looking out for himself. Another few years and he almost quit thinking about her. Almost.

Then one day in a small Mexican bar on a side street, away from the water and the new *malecón* that had been developed for the growing tourist industry, he ran into someone from the old days of the beach huts on the Baja peninsula. He didn't recognize the man who had been a boy named Dave the last time he saw him, but Dave recognized Dooley.

"Is that really you?" he asked, studying Dooley's face and then holding out his hand to shake. "Have you been down here all this time? Almost twenty years, right?"

Dooley remembered him now, remembered that he was a Canadian, and that he'd had a girlfriend named . . . what? Izzy? Dave and Izzy. He was a high school teacher now, Dave told him, sliding onto the stool next to Dooley. He gestured toward his own bare arms, white skin. "Just got here. Quick vacation with the fam, good deal on an all-inclusive. But look at you. Still with the long hair and brown as a Mexican. I should have tanned before I came down, but I didn't have time. Wow. Those were the days, weren't they? Those days on the beach. A long ways from teaching social studies. I'm bored out of my mind half of the time, but it's a living. How about you? What are you up to?"

"I'm a gardener," Dooley said. "Can I get you a beer?" He motioned to the waiter to bring Dave a beer. *"Y otra para mí, por favor."*

"Ha ha," Dave said. "Same old Dooley." Then he said, sobering, "Shame about Angela, eh?"

Now Dooley remembered that Dave was from Vancouver, that he'd been one of the people with Angela that first day in Tijuana.

"What about Angela?" Dooley asked.

Dave stared at him. "You know. When she died. Too bad. Everyone liked her." Then he saw the look on Dooley's face. "You didn't know? Sorry, man. I thought you would know. You were—I don't know—you and Angela. And it was a while ago . . . six, seven years, maybe. Sorry, Dooley. I assumed that . . ." He trailed off, not knowing what to say.

Dooley looked away from Dave, looked down at the empty beer bottle with his hand wrapped around it, managed to ask what had happened. He was thinking, *Six or seven years ago. Not long after she left here, then.* That's why he'd never heard from her. Why hadn't someone told him?

"I don't know for sure what happened," Dave said. "But she had some kind of weird disease, some blood disease that she'd had in childhood, I think, only it came back and got out of hand when she was down here in Mexico. When she got home, it was too late. I don't know. That's what I heard. Maybe it's not right. Maybe she had, you know, breast cancer or something. Sorry to be the one to tell you. Are you okay?"

Dooley stood up from his stool. His bad leg gave out and he stumbled, almost falling into Dave, but he caught himself and grabbed on to the bar, only he knocked over the full bottle the waiter had just placed there and spilled beer all over the counter. He fumbled in his pocket for money to pay, and he could tell Dave was embarrassed for him.

"Hey, I've got it, Dooley," he said. "Don't worry about it."

So Dooley just left without even saying goodbye to Dave, and he knew he was weaving as he walked out of the bar but he didn't care, didn't care what Dave thought. So what if Dave thought he was a hopeless drunk? He tripped on the cobblestones and almost went face-first into the street, but a Mexican man in a neat white shirt grabbed his arm—*"Estás bien, señor?"*

"Lo siento, gracias," Dooley said, and he found his legs and was able to walk back to the casita, which Lola and her absent husband seemed to have deserted.

Could it be true, what Dave had told him? He knew it was.

That night, he broke into the casa and slept in the master suite, in Angela's bed. He dreamed about her. He hadn't dreamed about her in a couple of years, but there she was in her yellow bikini, standing in . . . what was that? White sand? No, it was snow. She was standing in her bikini, her skin whiter than he had ever seen it, bare feet in the white snow. Snow began to fall all around her. She didn't look cold. She looked bewildered. When Dooley woke up, he was covered in sweat. He went to the kitchen and almost expected to see her there, making herself a pot of tea. But the casa was in darkness and she wasn't there, hadn't been there for a long time. Hadn't been anywhere for a long time, as it turned out. He went back to the casita.

He began to dream about snow almost every night. Snow falling, sometimes gently down like confetti, sometimes whipped into a whiteout, or a blizzard. Other times the snow drifted up against his casita until it was completely covered and he'd wake up feeling smothered, as if he'd been caught like a backcountry skier in an avalanche. He began to think about snow during the day when he was sweeping up bougainvillea petals, imagining himself with a shovel instead of a broom, wearing snowpack boots instead of huaraches. He began to wonder what he was still doing there.

When a wealthy-looking Mexican in a suit knocked on his door to tell him he had just bought the property—Angela's casa and the casita—and was planning to tear it down and build a twenty-two-unit condo complex with a swimming pool on the roof, Dooley packed his things, including the El Nido tiles, and left. He walked away carrying the same backpack he'd come with. There was a rooster on the road in front of the casa, right in his path. It was hunkered down as though it were night instead of the middle of the morning. Something was wrong with it, Dooley saw; it couldn't seem to move. Any other time, he would have stopped to see what was wrong. Maybe it had been hit by a car. He might have picked it up and taken it, squawking, to his little courtyard, or maybe placed it in someone else's courtyard to keep the dogs from getting it.

But on this day, he didn't stop. He stepped aside to avoid the rooster, and he kept on walking. For some reason, perhaps because of where he was going, the thought occurred to him that he had not driven a vehicle since the day he crashed his truck into the bridge. They'd taken away his driver's license then and he'd never applied for another. The country to which he was returning was a country where you had to drive to get anywhere.

Four days later, he got off a bus in a frozen town just south of the Canadian border, and he bought a pair of rubber boots with felt liners, wrapped his body in a Mexican blanket, and set off walking. He walked for hours through pasture hills and across snow-crusted fields of stubble, until he came to a paved road with a highway sign telling him the

American crossing was to the south, and he knew he was in Canada. He stood on the shoulder and waited, numb with cold. He'd slipped across two borders to get here, the way illegals did. He didn't have a single piece of ID—no health card, not even a library card—but incredibly, after living in Mexico for twenty years and smoking a football field's worth of pot and drinking a tequila distillery dry, he still had a good chunk of his nest egg hidden in his backpack.

He wondered if the rest of his money was still waiting for him in the bank where he'd left it. He also wondered if, having made it all this way, he was going to die here on the side of the road. The air was so cold he could hardly breathe it in. He thought of giving up and lying down in the ditch, but then he saw a pickup truck coming toward him out of the blowing snow. He stuck out his thumb, thinking that if the driver stopped, he would live, and if not, he would freeze to death by the side of the road.

The truck stopped. Oldies country music was playing on the radio, so loud that Dooley could hear the familiar tune—"Mammas, Don't Let Your Babies Grow Up to Be Cowboys"—before the door was even opened for him. The driver turned down the radio and told Dooley he was going as far north as Yellowhead. He told him this as though Dooley might choose not to get in if the destination was not to his liking. Dooley knew there was no choice if he wanted to survive. He was half dead already. The boots he'd bought had not kept his feet warm and he wondered if his toes were too far gone to be saved.

He got in the warm vehicle. They were barely back up to speed on the highway before he began to shake so violently that the young farmer looked alarmed, as if fearing that

Dooley might die on him. He had a sleeping bag behind the seat and he reached back and pulled it out for Dooley, apologizing because it was covered in dog hair. Dooley took it and wrapped himself in it. His feet burned as they began to thaw. He let the young farmer believe the shaking was only because of the cold, but in truth, he hadn't had a drink since he'd left Mexico. When they got to Yellowhead, he asked if there was a detox center in town, and that's where the man let him out. Dooley tried to give him all the Mexican money he had in his pocket, but the man sped away like someone making a lucky escape.

Dooley stood in the snow and looked at an old two-story house with a Salvation Army sign by the front door. He felt as though he was making one more live-or-die decision, but no, he thought, that decision had been made when the farmer stopped and picked him up.

He took a deep breath—several, felt his chest rising and falling, saw the steamy evidence of his own life in the cold air—and he walked up to the door and knocked. Then he felt all the strength leave him, his legs buckling, himself sinking, so that when the door opened, he was on his knees.

"What have we here?" a man said. "A pilgrim on his knees for Christ?"

Dooley struggled to keep himself from falling across the threshold.

"Y usted es probablemente un idiota para Cristo," he said. "But as you say, I am on my knees. I need help. Have I come to the right place?"

The man took Dooley's arm and helped him to his feet.

Led him inside to thaw.

9. The Car Hank Died In

Sustenance

1. *Get busy. Begin immediately. DO NOT PROCRASTINATE.*
2. *Take everything to the church rummage or the dump. DO NOT get hung up on the fact that the good people in Elliot will end up with the family fortune (ha ha).*
3. *Ask Mavis to sell the house and then GET THE HELL OUT OF TOWN.*

I STUDIED THE PLAN I'd written for myself twenty-four hours earlier and then stuck to the fridge door with a flower magnet. It wasn't bad advice, although "Get busy" and "Begin immediately" were perhaps not explicit enough. I'd spent the previous day gazing at the horses across the road, and had not done a single useful thing.

I took the pie plate containing the last two blueberry muffins from the fridge and went outside to eat one of them on the step . . . where I discovered a jar of homemade orange marmalade in a recycled store-bought jam jar. It gleamed like amber, with the morning sun shining on it. I reached down and picked it up, and the glass felt warm in my hand, like the marmalade had been freshly spooned inside. It was such an intense color, my mouth watered just looking at it. I carried it into the house, thankful that there was no need to return either the pie plate or the jar, since they were both disposable, although I didn't know how I would do that even if I wanted to because of Mavis's odd denial of responsibility. I called her again right away. It had to be her. Again she said it was not.

"Really?" I said. "Because nothing else makes sense."

"You must have an old friend in town," she said.

"I don't."

"Not even one?"

"I never did, so how could I now?"

"It couldn't be the trailer guy, could it?"

"What old bachelor makes marmalade?" I said. "Can't be him."

I ended the call and thought about the possibility that it *was* my neighbor. Do those old campers even have proper stoves? I wondered. This thought made me thankful there were a couple of lots between Vince's house and the trailer. I pictured the trailer blowing up in a spectacular propane explosion, not from something as nefarious as a crystal meth lab—which, when I thought of it, did not seem completely unlikely—but from a home-canning accident.

It had to be Mavis, and the denial was just some strange form of humility. I ate the last muffin with a big dollop of orange marmalade on the side, and then put the jar in the fridge and decided I had to go for groceries, like it or not, because I was still hungry and couldn't get through the day on marmalade.

I got in my car and drove across the tracks and up Main

Street, straight to where the little Co-op grocery store should have been but wasn't. There was an empty lot surrounded by a board fence plastered with flyers and graffiti. I parked anyway and got out of my car and looked up and down the street, trying to see something that resembled a grocery store, wondering what I was going to do for food, and if I would have to drive all the way to Yellowhead for supplies. Just then a woman with an expensive three-wheeled baby stroller came jogging up the street and said, I thought, *"Hola."* She stopped, barely puffing, and asked if I needed help, and I said I was looking for someplace to get a few groceries. While her toddler stared at me, she directed me to the new Co-op superstore on the highway west of town, and then she jogged on up the street.

I drove to the road I had come in on from St. Agnes and soon found a monstrous new building with metal siding and a bright orange roof and gas pumps, a grocery store, a feed supply, and a lumberyard. I parked near the entrance to the grocery and went inside, wondering how I had missed it. The young clerk at the till gave me a quick once-over, but then went back to texting when she realized she didn't know me.

I grabbed a cart and quickly threw in a few things: bread, milk, peanut butter, fruit, sandwich meat, canned soup, a bag of Cheetos, coffee, dish soap, toilet paper, and at the last minute, a canvas lawn chair in a bag. When the clerk routinely asked, "Co-op number?" as though it were unthinkable that I wouldn't have one, my parents' number came immediately to mind—371—and I almost said it out loud before I could stop myself. The clerk's hand hovered over the till keys as though it were not possible for her to sell groceries to a customer without a number.

"Sorry," I said. "No number."

She rang up my groceries and bagged them, and I carried them to my car and left. I stopped at the hotel on the way home and bought a case of beer.

When I got back to the house, I could see a dish on the porch next to the geranium before I even got out of the car. I looked more closely and found homemade macaroni and cheese with a bread crumb topping. My first thought was that this was a new development, because the dish would have to be returned. I carried my groceries and the beer inside, leaving the chair and the casserole on the porch, and called Mavis.

"This has to be you. Because you're truly the only person who knows I'm here." I was staring at the trailer as I spoke, wondering if I was being watched.

"Sorry to disappoint you, not I," Mavis said. "Anyway, it's a small town. I imagine someone has noticed you." She sounded chipper, which was more frustrating than if she'd spoken the words with sarcasm. Then she again denied that she'd left anything on the step. She was a vegan, she said, and didn't eat cheese. The only casserole she ever made—and it wasn't really a casserole, more of a stew—had mushrooms and lentils in it.

I tried to reconcile yoga and lentils with real estate. I wondered, Who in the world—the guy in the trailer or anyone else—would leave me these gifts of food? It was not as though there'd been a death.

"Have you changed your mind about meeting in person?" Mavis asked. "Tomorrow's a yoga-class day."

"Let's wait a few days," I said. "I'm still not organized here."

I put the groceries away and then looked at the casserole

through the screen door and thought of a stray dog lying on the step—a golden Lab, perhaps—and then I thought that I couldn't just leave it there, so I went back out and picked it up and carried it into the house. I set the casserole down on the kitchen counter. It was still warm.

I stared at it through the glass lid, slightly steamy. It looked so good, the top perfectly browned. I lifted the lid and smelled warm, melted cheddar cheese. Why waste it? One taste on the tip of a spoon and then I was devouring it right from its Pyrex container.

After the empty casserole dish was soaking in the sink, I went to the west-facing bathroom and studied the trailer through the window. I saw no movement or indication that anyone was inside, although the truck was there. That night after dark, I looked out the bathroom window again and saw a string of patio lanterns glowing.

The next morning there was no food delivery, and by noon I'd still heard no car on the road, no footsteps on the porch. Good, I thought, maybe cordiality had run its course. I spent the afternoon wandering aimlessly through the house, looking into kitchen drawers and mostly empty closets, and finally I plopped myself down on the couch and stared at my mother's old record rack, which automatically shuffled through the LPs as though they were a deck of cards (another vintage item that Mavis had retrieved from the basement). I pictured myself at the garbage dump, winging records out the car window onto an enormous pile of unrecycled small-town trash, and with that thought, I got up off the couch again and unlatched the door to the basement, which I knew I'd been avoiding. I flicked on the light and descended into the clutter of my family's possessions.

Cardboard boxes stacked on wooden pallets, the wagon-wheel armchair with garbage bags full of old clothing piled on it (I recalled that we'd thrown out the couch), a hideous chrome pole lamp, two mismatched coffee tables that I barely remembered, a wood-veneer bookcase complete with old books and glass doors that didn't properly close, my old twenty-five-dollar guitar with the neck warped absurdly, a metal clothing rack full of barn coats mingled with town coats, including my mother's three-quarter-length muskrat, which was what women bought when they couldn't afford mink. I shuddered, imagining it full of moths or sow bugs or whatever it was that got into old animal fur.

I didn't want to touch the coat. I didn't want to touch any of this.

I went back upstairs, turned out the basement light, and closed the door again.

By suppertime, I was regretting that I'd eaten all of the casserole, since I would now have to cook for myself. I decided on mushroom soup from a can, but it reminded me of salty, flour-thickened gravy. I ate only half the bowl before I threw the rest out and washed the pot, and then I ate most of the bag of Cheetos. I couldn't help thinking of Ian as I looked at my orange-stained fingers. He hated Cheetos and didn't see how anyone could think of them as food. I wondered if he had considered calling me. Probably not.

Before I went to bed, I stepped out onto the porch to catch the night air, and there at my feet was a plate of cookies. Two kinds, chocolate chip and oatmeal, on an old-fashioned blue-and-white china dinner plate and protected from insects by a serious triple wrap of plastic. I picked up the plate and carried it inside.

Whoever had wrapped the cookies had done it so thoroughly I needed a knife to get at them. Once I had the plastic off, I was torn between the anticipation of pleasure and the uneasy thought that something was wanted of me. No one could be that persistently welcoming, not without wanting payment in return. I studied the cookies for a long time before I bit into one, and then I closed my eyes and savored. I couldn't decide whether I liked the oatmeal or the chocolate chip better. I wondered why the cookies had come on a china plate when the muffins had been delivered on a disposable pie plate. It seemed like an escalation.

The next morning, an aluminum pot was waiting on the porch. When I removed the lid, I found a good-sized serving of freshly made paella, the top sprinkled with peas and chopped egg. I looked around. All was quiet. No signs of traffic on the street, no dust in either direction, no sound of a vehicle in the distance. I looked toward the trailer. It was appearing more and more likely, I had to admit, that my neighbor was responsible. I considered throwing the paella out, just tossing it over the side of the porch in hopes that the cook was watching and got the message.

What message, though? So far, I'd eaten everything that had been sent my way, so would that not be like the restaurant customer who sends back a meal after eating three-quarters of it? And who throws out a pot of homemade paella? Even with the lid back on the pot, I could smell the onions and garlic and seafood, and when I removed the lid to look at it once again, I couldn't help myself. I got a big spoon from the kitchen, and even though it was still morning and toast would have been more appropriate, I sat down on the step and ate it right out of the pot, one spoonful after another, as though I hadn't seen food in weeks. I could hardly believe it when the pot was empty. I went inside and washed it, then I realized I was still licking my lips and wishing there was more.

I stood in the kitchen and contemplated the empty food containers. I felt an invisible cloak folding and unfolding around me, like slowly beating wings, and thought I must be going mad.

I phoned Mavis and asked her whether I should be calling the police about the food deliveries, hoping that she would fess up to being the Welcome Wagon. She assumed I was joking. "Wouldn't that be funny," she said, "if you called 911 about a plate of cookies?"

Yes, hilarious.

The next morning, there was nothing. That afternoon, after spraying myself with repellent from a can that I found in the bathroom, I went for a walk up Liberty Street, avoiding even a glance at the trailer as I passed by. When I reached the end of the street, I turned away from town and walked down the grid road into the country, farther than I had intended to walk, seduced by the smell of cut hay. When vehicles passed on the road, I put my head down. When one driver slowed alongside me to make, I presumed, the inevitable offer of help, I waved him on. Best not to speak, I thought, and give the inhabitants of Elliot a story to pass around like a chain letter.

When I got back to the house, I found an old Coca-Cola tray with the rusty image of Santa Claus waiting for me on the top step. An appetizer—three shrimp carefully arranged and swimming in butter and garlic. A bowl of gorgeous-looking pasta with what appeared to be a marinara sauce. A side salad with cherry tomatoes and cheese slices and fresh basil leaves.

There was also a small plate containing a serving of cake with chocolate shavings on top. Tiramisu? Really? Each dish was carefully wrapped in plastic.

I carried the tin tray inside and put it on the kitchen table, and then sat down and thought about what I should do. In spite of the aroma escaping the plastic, I decided to take a chance and return the meal to the trailer—it had to have come from there—but then I hesitated, and that moment of hesitation was just long enough for my willpower to reduce itself to nothing, and then I couldn't stop. I was at the plastic with a knife, and I ate every bite.

When I was carrying the dishes to the sink I dropped the dessert plate, which broke perfectly in two with a sharp crack as it hit the tabletop, and this crack seemed to tell me it was time to put an end to the anonymous deliveries. They had to have come from my neighbor. I washed the dishes and stacked them all—everything that had arrived over the past few days, including the broken halves of the dessert plate—on the Coca-Cola tray. There was still a half jar of marmalade in the fridge, so I emptied it into the garbage can, washed the jar, and put that on the tray too. Then I carried it all through the grass to my neighbor's.

Once I was there, the trailer a few feet in front of me, I wasn't sure how to proceed. The trailer's screen porch was decorated with the patio lights I had seen glowing in the darkness. On the screen door was a ceramic tile sign with bright blue letters spelling *El Nido*. Spanish, I thought. Tourist kitsch from Mexico. I could see a picnic table inside with a checkerboard on it. I would have to enter the porch and squeeze by the picnic table to knock on the main trailer door. I didn't want to. My arms were getting tired and I considered leaving the tray on the ground where I stood. Then I realized that the truck was not there, which meant that my neighbor wasn't there either.

I opened the screen door and entered the porch, setting the tray down on the picnic table. There wasn't much of note in the porch. A few plant pots with fresh basil in them (there had been basil in the salad). A huge tomato plant already loaded with cherry tomatoes. Without thinking, I picked one and popped it in my mouth, then was horrified with myself for doing such a thing. I left the tray on the picnic table and cut across the vacant lots again. When I got home, I realized I hadn't left a note saying thank you. I thought of quickly writing one and returning to tuck it among the dishes on the tray, but it was too late; I heard the truck coming up the road. I hurried to the bathroom window, thinking that I could get a look at the neighbor, perhaps see his reaction to the tray. But the truck blocked my view, and I saw only the driver's head with a hat on it as he left the cab and slipped inside.

What, I wondered, could this man possibly want?

There was no need for supper that evening. At seven o'clock, I made myself a fresh pot of coffee, and I was just about to carry a cup outside when I heard a buzzing sound coming from somewhere inside the house. I went looking for the source, coffee cup in hand, and found a wasp trapped in the dusty bathroom window, banging itself against the glass in its attempts to get out. I was wondering whether I could open the window and release the screen without getting stung when I saw my neighbor step into full view, carrying a portable disc player. He was tall and thin with a long gray ponytail, and he was wearing nothing but multi-colored long-legged shorts. I watched as he parked himself in what might be called his front yard and faced the sun that was now in the western sky. He balanced with one leg in the air and positioned his arms like wings, frozen open. Then he began to move, slowly at first, with jerks and flaps followed by seconds of stillness, building eventually to a convulsive and continuous full-body workout. He looked like a spastic old crane, I thought, his string-bean body twitching itself into a concoction of movements, the purpose of which was hard to imagine. I couldn't take my eyes off him.

Half an hour later, he stopped abruptly, as if a timer had gone off in his head, or perhaps the music had ended. He saluted the sun in the west with a polite bow, his back still turned to my bathroom window, and after his salutation, he touched his toes a few times, then hiked up his shorts, picked up his disc player, and went back inside the trailer.

My coffee was cold and the wasp was still buzzing in the window. I poured the coffee in the sink, grabbed a home-decorating magazine from a basket left by Mavis, and slipped my cup over the wasp. I let the curtain fall closed again, and I carried the wasp, held in the cup by the magazine, to the door and released it.

The air outside felt still and peaceful in spite of the mosquitoes. Instead of pouring myself another cup of coffee, I got a beer from the fridge and settled on the porch in my new canvas lawn chair, and watched the horses across the road as they stood along the fence slapping their tails obsessively. As the sun began to turn red in the west, I noticed my neighbor emerge again from the trailer, now wearing baggy, faded jeans, a T-shirt, and sandals. He was carrying something in his hand—a plastic bottle, it looked like—and he crossed the road without noticing me, climbed through the fence, and proceeded to wipe down the horses with what I assumed was some kind of insect repellent. When he was done, he happened to glance my way and I saw his arm rising in what was likely to become a friendly wave, so I quickly looked away and stood to withdraw into the house. As I did so, one of the chair's aluminum legs slipped into a hollow spot between the spruce boards on the porch, and the chair tipped to one side and I had to grab the porch rail to stop myself from going sideways with it. I saw myself the way he saw me: with an empty beer bottle in hand, stumbling out of my chair and onto my feet. I quickly righted the chair and went into the house without looking to see what he'd made of my performance. I felt twinges of guilt at my rudeness—returning the dishes without a thank you, the way I'd ignored his neighborly wave—but at the same time I was glad to put to bed any chance that we would become friendly.

Later, when it was fully dark outside, I put on my nylon hiking shoes, the ones I'd bought for the trip to Ireland, and went for another walk. As I passed the trailer I saw that the patio lights were on in the porch, but no sounds came from the trailer's direction, no music or television. As I walked, I realized the horses were following me along the fence line. Although I was not much of an animal lover, I walked over to the fence to look at them. When I reached out my hand to run it up the face of one of the horses—a black-and-white-spotted one (a pinto, I believed it was called)—it spun away and ran, and the others followed, their hooves thudding on the dry ground. I continued along to the end of the road and then went back the other way, and I walked back and forth in the darkness until the insect repellent wore off and the mosquitoes sent me into the house, where I sat on the couch and wondered what Ian was doing, and whether he missed me or was just glad to be rid of me. I wondered whether anyone from work had called my home phone, because no one had called my cell number. Then I wondered whether anyone at all was curious about what had become of me.

Self-pity, it was called. I went to bed. When I got up the next morning, I discovered that my phone had been disabled. Someone had finally noticed I was gone.

Luck

IT CAME IN THE FORM of a rusty nail. Luck, that is. I was in my bare feet, spraying the dust off the outside of the windows of Uncle Vince's house with the garden hose, when I stepped on a spike (was it big enough to be called a spike?) that was sticking straight up out of an old scrap of lumber hidden in the overgrown quack grass. It took me a minute to come up with a hypothesis, put the pieces of information together: the board I was standing on, the incredible searing pain in my foot (a wasp?), the fact that my foot now appeared to be attached to the board. Not a wasp, then. A nail.

At that moment, just the moment when I was realizing what had happened, my trailer-dwelling neighbor chanced to look out his east window—the tiny window above what he calls his couch (just one of the many details of his existence that I have since learned), which is really the dining banquette with the removable tabletop put away—and he saw me standing oddly, looking down as though there was something peculiar on the ground in front of me, or at least this is how he described it. In my hand was a yellow garden hose from which water was flowing liberally into the grass around me. I was wearing shorts and a yellow tank top, roughly the same color as the hose. From where he was looking, I might have been much younger than he knew me to be—a teenager, perhaps, sent out to water the lawn and then getting lost in a daydream about what she really wanted to be doing with her summer day. He was seeing me from a distance, the sun shining on my blond hair. He remembered my hair, he told me later. It should have been red, but then no hair color was natural these days except his.

Dyed hair aside, why, he wondered, was I standing there in a daze with the water running around me? He saw me take a step, or try to. I appeared to be unable to walk. Had I had a stroke? he wondered. Or was it possible that I was mocking him and his dancing—he'd seen me watching—the exaggerated way I was trying to lift my foot with my arms out for balance. Then I was motionless again, staring down at my feet, the hose running like a waterfall, until I lifted one foot high enough above the grass that he could see that something came along with it, as though I was wearing snowshoes. Then he realized that the snowshoe was an old board, and it was stuck to my bare foot, and the reason had to be a nail, still embedded. He figured it out much the same way I did, only a few seconds behind me. He watched as I tried to shake the board loose, but it didn't come and the act was obviously a painful one. He thought I was shouting. He imagined a vocal conga line of *ow, ow, ow, ow*—it was actually quite a bit more colorful than that—as I kept my weight on the good foot, then tried to hold my balance while deciding what to do and how to free my other foot from where it was impaled.

He wasn't sure what he should do. Should he try to help? He thought I had made it clear that I didn't want anything to do with him, but still, he couldn't just leave me stranded there. There was no one else. If anyone was going to help me, it would have to be him. He grabbed his straw hat from where it hung by the door and set out, through his summer porch, then through the weeds in the two lots that separated our properties, to help me out of my predicament.

"Hola," he said as he approached me.

In the time it had taken him to get there, I had managed to free my foot from the board and I was now trying to stand on one leg and hose the wound. Even though the act of doing that without falling over took concentration, the word *hola* registered. This seemed to have become the greeting of choice in Elliot, no doubt because half the town now went to Mexico or Cuba on all-inclusive vacations to escape winter. But why would they swap their usual hello for a Spanish greeting? You didn't hear people in the city saying *hola* to each other. It was a conceit, irritating.

"Holy is right," I said. "Holy crap, that hurts."

He was studying me, I could feel it. I might have studied him back had my foot not been burning as though it was skewered on a fireplace poker.

"How can I help?" he asked.

"Just stand there while I do this." I reached out and put my hand on his arm so I could balance while I hosed the bottom of my foot. "In case I fall over and land somewhere life-threatening on that goddamned monstrous nail. You would not believe how this hurts. I thought I'd stepped on a wasp nest."

The hose was splashing water and we were both getting

wet. My neighbor looked at the board in the grass, nail side up. It was a four-inch construction nail. Rusty.

"When did you last have a tetanus shot?" he asked.

I accidentally sprayed his legs with the hose. Rusty nail . . . tetanus. Of course, why didn't I think of that?

"Well, not for about a hundred years," I said. I stopped hosing my foot and turned the nozzle off. The water slowed to a drizzle. "I guess I know what I'm doing, then," I said, dropping the hose in the grass. "I suppose I can get a tetanus shot at the hospital."

"I would think so. Maybe I should drive you?"

The fire in my foot was such that I wasn't really thinking about the man whose arm I was holding—my neighbor, the one who had sent me the excess of food gifts.

"It's okay. I can drive myself," I said. Then I added, "Sorry, I've sprayed water all over your jeans."

"No problem. It'll evaporate in the heat. Look. Already happening."

He shook his pant leg at me.

He helped me around the house and up the steps so I could retrieve my purse and car keys. He waited in the kitchen as I limped into the house's interior, and when I hobbled back into the kitchen with my purse, I saw that he was reading the note I'd affixed to the fridge door with the flower magnet.

"Are you sure you don't want me to drive?" he asked. "I don't mind. I wasn't planning to go into the office today." He paused. "A joke. The office."

"Oh," I said. "Well, me neither. Thanks, but I can drive myself." I stuck out my hand. "My name is Frances Moon." I immediately wished that I'd thought to say Bonder, Ian's name, keeping my identity from coffee row, if that's where my neighbor liked to spend his time.

He looked confused. I wasn't sure why, but of course he'd assumed there'd be no need for introductions.

"Thanks for coming to my rescue," I said.

He took my hand and shook it and said, because it appeared to be necessary, "Dooley Sullivan. Nice to meet you."

It was my turn to be confused. Dooley Sullivan? Dooley Sullivan was dead, long dead, a victim of drug-related violence or some form of addiction, maybe more than one. Explanations tried to form themselves in my head—two Dooley Sullivans, a son who looked older than he was—until something had to be said, and what came out was "You can't be Dooley Sullivan."

"Frances Mary Moon," he said.

Then he understood that I really had not known. "Sorry to be such a shock," he said.

"I thought you were dead," I said.

"I get that a lot. Or at least I used to. Not so much anymore." Then he said, "Seriously, who but me would claim to be Dooley Sullivan?" and the tension was broken and I wanted to laugh, almost did, but then my foot reminded me that I had other pressing business, and I said, "I'd better go."

Dooley went out through the door first, and I followed.

He asked me if I needed help with the stairs, and when I said no, he went down the steps ahead of me ("Well, see you, then. Hope your foot is okay. And the tetanus thing, probably not, but better to be safe") and started back across the lots to the trailer, his wet pants flapping against his long, thin legs.

I hopped to my car and got in, and then sat watching

my neighbor walk away from me, having difficulty believing what I had just heard, that he was Dooley Sullivan. He walked hesitantly, a few good strides and then a slow step, as though he might turn around and offer his help once more, insist on driving me to the hospital, and then I realized that he too was limping, and I remembered the school window and the broken ankle, and then the accident, when he had driven into a bridge and broken his body into a marionette of parts, and who knows what had happened to him after that. The whole town had been grateful for my father's orchestration of his banishment. In the years that followed, my mother would regularly come home with new stories: dealing drugs, addicted to heroin, living on the streets. A rumor of his death, and then people quit talking about him. But here he was, back in Elliot, a cat with his nine lives.

Once he was inside the trailer, I returned to the possibility of tetanus and started the car. I drove up Liberty Street and crossed the tracks and took myself to the hospital, which had been rebuilt since my time in Elliot but was still small, a main entrance with a wing on either side. It was remarkable, I thought, that the town had kept any hospital at all. I hobbled inside, my foot throbbing, and found a nurse on duty. Her name was Kelly. She was wearing purple scrubs and looked too young to be a real nurse, but she was, in fact, a nurse-practitioner, trained to do some of the things a doctor did because there's only one doctor, she said, and there's not enough of him to go around. She cleaned my foot and wrapped it, and told me I was lucky the nail hadn't hit anything important, like a tendon. Then she gave me a tetanus shot and told me I had seventy-two hours to get the shot, so I should be fine, but to come back if I noticed any signs of infection.

"You mean if I wake up one morning and my jaw is locked?" I asked.

"Not expecting that to happen," she said. Then she explained to me what sepsis was, and provided a further explanation of how antibodies develop after a tetanus shot, and how really I should have kept my shots up-to-date, especially tetanus—case in point—and of course hepatitis, especially if I did any out-of-the-country travel. Kelly was a talker, it seemed. I wondered if she was paying enough attention to what she was doing.

"Do you?" she asked me. "Travel?"

"Not much," I said. "Ireland recently."

"I'd like to go to India," she said. "And I'll be getting every shot known to man if I ever do get the chance. Lots of people here go to Mexico or Jamaica in the winter, and they don't all get their shots. They'll be sorry when they start turning yellow or get dengue fever."

I resisted the temptation to correct, or perhaps refine, her explanation of sepsis and antibodies—to tell her that I was a microbiologist responsible for safe drinking water in the city, or at least I had been until recently. I tried to imagine how old I must look to young Kelly. There was a mirror on the wall behind us and I noticed the lines around my eyes, the dyed blond hair in need of a good styling.

After she took my health card information ("Moon, that's an interesting name"), she left me alone at the admitting desk while she went into a storage room to get me a handful of antiseptic wipes so I could clean the wound at home. I happened to glance at an open binder that appeared to have the names of the hospital's patients and the rooms to which they were assigned, and I mindlessly read the names upside down, just to see if I recognized anyone. I didn't, until I saw the name Joe Fletcher.

Seeing that name should have been less of a shock than meeting Dooley Sullivan. I should have known there was a chance Joe Fletcher was alive. But reading his name on the hospital log was truly like being told that a dead person had come back to life. Impossible, I thought.

But there it was. Joe Fletcher, room 18.

Then Kelly emerged from the storeroom with a plastic bag in one hand, pushing an empty wheelchair in the other, and I wondered if she was planning to wheel me to the door, which would be a bit unnecessary, I thought. I looked well away from the binder, not wanting to be caught snooping.

"Here you go," Kelly said, handing me the bag. "Just keep it clean and come back if you're not sure. Sorry, gotta run." Then she was off down the wing to my right with the wheelchair.

I looked at the list again. Joe Fletcher, room 18. I hadn't imagined it.

But Joe Fletcher was a common name, much more common than Dooley Sullivan, so this was not necessarily the same man. I considered following Kelly and asking, but then I looked up the hallway where she had gone and saw that it was dead quiet. I looked at the directions posted on the walls; room 18 was the other way, to my left.

Finding out what had happened to Joe Fletcher—if it was in fact him—had not been among the things I'd expected to accomplish that day, but how could I not take this opportunity? I remembered what I'd heard many years ago, perhaps around the time of my father's death, that he'd moved to the interior of BC. It was possible he'd returned, also many years ago.

Could I just walk by the door and peek inside and see for myself that the patient was, or was not, Joe Fletcher? If it turned out to be, he wouldn't recognize me, not in a million years. I would likely not recognize him, but the age would be a clue, one way or the other, and if there was a chance, then I could ask my new friend Kelly whether it was the same man.

I couldn't resist the possibility of knowing, couldn't stop myself from hobbling down that hallway, even with my foot wrapped, even though it hurt like hell now and what I really wanted to do was go home and lie down with my leg elevated, as Kelly had suggested I do. I left the admitting desk and, with a quick glance in the other direction to make sure Kelly wasn't watching, limped down the hallway that housed room 18 and someone with the name Joe Fletcher.

And just like that, there was the room. I was so taken by surprise that I didn't have a chance to feign an innocent walk by the door, peeking inside as I passed. I found myself staring full into the room, with an old man staring right back at me, saying, "Help me, help me." I looked into his eyes and tried to recognize the man I had known, but he wasn't there. It wasn't him. Then I realized the room had two beds in it, both occupied by old men, and my gaze shifted to the far bed, and there he was, most certainly the same Joe Fletcher. I wanted there to be doubt—how could I be sure, after all these years?—but there was none. Absolutely none, even though the man in the bed was old and thin and gray-looking and possibly comatose, or was he just sleeping?

I couldn't look away. The first man's voice kept saying, "Help me, help me," but it faded into the distance and nothing existed in the room but the man in the far bed, Joe Fletcher, the man I had married, the man to whom I was still married. It was not like stepping into my past, not like facing the dairy farm or the graveyard or the things stored in the basement—things I knew I *could* do but just hadn't. Seeing Joe Fletcher was different, because for so many years I had lived as if he hadn't happened, didn't exist. I was tempted to walk over to the bed and get a better look, poke him the way you might poke a prostrate dog to see if it's dead. On the other hand, I regretted that I had ever stepped into the hallway. I thought of his sister, Martha, could almost see her waving her Bible at me. And I thought too of Silas Chance for the first time in years. What I knew, or maybe knew, about what had happened to him.

Then the man in the bed near the door grew louder, more demanding, and I saw that he was reaching out to me and trying to disengage himself from the tight wrap of the bed linens, as though he were desperate to escape. It appeared that he thought I was someone else, a person he knew, someone who could save him from whatever hell he was in.

I looked away from the man, not knowing what to do, and I backed away from the doorway, desperate now to leave, and when I saw an exit sign at the far end of the hallway, I limped toward it. I wanted only to escape, get out of the hospital as quickly as possible, run back to Uncle Vince's house, where I could hide.

I made it to the exit and pushed on the door without seeing the sign that said Fire Exit Only.

The alarm went off.

"Fuck," I said, looking at the outside through the open door, wanting to run, to hell with my foot.

But I didn't. I did the responsible thing and went back inside and let the exit door swing closed again, and when I saw Kelly coming, I said, "Sorry, that was me. I didn't see the sign." She headed back the other way to turn off the alarm, and when she passed room 18, I heard her say, "Mr. Weins, you get in that bed right now, you hear me." I was forced to hobble down the hall toward the front entrance, and by now there were several visitors and patients standing in doorways to see what the ruckus was about.

"Sorry," I said all the way down the hall, to no one in particular. The people in the doorways stared at me when I walked by.

They knew. They all knew who I was and exactly when I'd arrived, that I'd been staying in the Liberty Street house and keeping to myself. They all knew I was Frances Moon, who'd married Joe Fletcher and then left him immediately after. Joe Fletcher, who was in room 18, the one I was now walking by without giving a glance inside—only I did glance, and I saw that Joe had not moved a muscle and Mr. Weins was sitting on the edge of his bed looking lost. I limped by on my bandaged foot, and just as I reached the admitting area again, the alarm stopped ringing.

Kelly was there waiting for me.

"Okay," I said. "There's no use my trying to ignore what the whole town probably knows. I was married to that man, Joe Fletcher. I haven't seen him for forty years. What's wrong with him?"

"He's dying," Kelly said simply. "Congestive heart failure. Some kind of cancer, but we can't find it. He'll pass soon."

"How soon?"

"Soon. A few weeks at most."

"Does he have any family?" I asked. "His sister?"

"No one," Kelly said. "If he had a sister, she must be gone."

"Does he talk, or is he in a coma?"

"He drifts in and out. Sometimes he mumbles a few things. I wouldn't say he talks. I doubt that you could have a conversation with him, if that's what you mean."

"It's not," I said, "but thank you. Sorry about the alarm. And thank you for . . . well, you know, the foot."

I turned to walk—hobble—toward the door, and Kelly said something else.

"He hasn't had a single visitor since he's been here. You feel bad for them, but I don't have time to sit and hold a person's hand. We're not Florence Nightingales anymore. Think about it, if you've got time."

Time for what? I wondered. Surely she wasn't suggesting that I, now that I'd admitted to being married to him, should visit?

I pushed my way through the entrance door without responding and drove home and lay down on the couch. I didn't feel well. Maybe it was the tetanus shot. Maybe it was the heat of the day and the antiseptic smells of the hospital, the fact that Joe Fletcher was still in this world, although barely. I missed Ian. I missed having another person around. I missed being able to pretend that a big lamentable chunk of my life hadn't happened. I closed my eyes and fell asleep.

I woke up at midnight to the boom of thunder and the flashing light of an electrical storm. My foot hurt like crazy and the storm was so loud and violent that I couldn't go back to sleep, so I made myself a pot of tea. I got a jar of peanut butter from the fridge and a box of crackers from the cupboard, and I sat on the couch with a knife and the jar, and drank tea and ate crackers and watched the storm. With each bolt of lightning the world outside the window was illuminated, and when the hail began to rattle on the roof, I wondered what it sounded like to someone in a trailer—hail on a tin roof.

The power went out. I got up and looked out the window, and when lightning flashed, I saw that the ground was white with hail. There was a terrible wind. I saw things tumbling across the lots, but I couldn't tell what, or from where. Something blew against my living room window, but by some miracle the glass didn't break. I found myself worrying about Dooley Sullivan in the flimsy trailer, could picture the roof flying off, the trailer being blown apart. When the wind died down and the worst of the storm had passed, I put on my rain jacket and went outside and waded in my flip-flops through the mounds of hail in the lots between Uncle Vince's house and Dooley's trailer, my feet freezing, the bandage on my foot soaked through.

The trailer was still there and not blown into a hundred pieces, as I had imagined it might have been. I opened the door to the screened porch, and just then there was a flash of lightning and I saw that Dooley was sitting at the picnic table. The checkerboard was on the table in front of him and I assumed he'd been playing against himself before the power went out.

"Sorry," I said. "I didn't mean to scare you."

"I saw you coming. *Hola*."

"Is everything okay?" I asked. "I was worried you might have blown away."

"Still here. How's the foot?"

"I'll live," I said.

He invited me to sit down and I did. Then his long, tall shadow slid itself out from the bench he was sitting on.

"Don't go away," he said, and he went inside.

The trailer wasn't much more than an aluminum box and I could hear him rummaging around. While I waited, I wondered if he'd had things to settle when he made his way back to Elliot. Perhaps, I thought, the means to one of them was now sitting at his picnic table, the only person left with even a dubious connection to his grandfather, and Esme Bigalow's will. Did I have an explanation for the gifts left on my porch? He'd been paid to leave town, but had that been a legal settlement? I had no idea how much of Esme's money my father had given him. Maybe it wasn't enough. Maybe Dooley's inheritance had funded my education.

He returned a few minutes later with a couple of gaudy crocheted afghans and an old-style coal oil lamp. My parents had had a similar lamp, and we'd used it whenever the power went out. Dooley lit the lamp's wick and placed the glass chimney over the flame, then set it down next to the checkerboard. He handed me one of the afghans. I realized I was shivering as I took off my wet jacket and draped the throw over my shoulders. Dooley set up the checkerboard for a new game and said, "Your move, Señora Luna."

Luna. Moon. I moved a checker forward, a black one.

"I apologize for not recognizing you," I said. "I do remember you. Not because of the house fire. Before that. We danced together at an anniversary party when I was a little girl. You were a teenager with your leg in a cast from jumping out the school window."

He made his move on the board and said, "As I recall, it was a long way down. I obviously didn't think that through."

We played checkers until we both had queens on the board, but the game seemed like a prelude to something else, and it was as though we were both waiting for whatever that was to begin. The hail was melting now, and ice-cold water ran into the porch and pooled under our feet. I lifted my injured foot out of the water and rested it on the bench. A sudden gust of wind blew a new sheet of water through the porch screen and across the table. We both jumped up and moved out of its way, and stood pressed up against the trailer's exterior. Dooley retrieved the checkerboard and set it on the little step leading into the trailer. The lamp blew out.

"I should probably go," I said. "I just came to see if you were all right. And to say thanks for the food gifts, which I should have done sooner. It was all delicious, much appreciated. You're quite the cook."

Dooley said, "Come inside. You don't want to walk back in this rain."

I thought of him doing his crazy chicken dance, but I went inside with him anyway. I was not afraid of Dooley Sullivan. I never had been. He offered me a La-Z-Boy recliner that he'd somehow squeezed into the small trailer, and he placed the lamp on his kitchen table and relit it. The small flame cast a surprising amount of light now that we were inside. On a shelf under the little kitchen window, I saw a neat row of well-worn cookbooks, and I could even read some of the titles: *The Spanish Kitchen*, *Flavors of Italy*, *French Cuisine*. Dooley put the kettle on the propane stove, and he saw me looking at the cookbooks.

"The rummage sale in the church basement," he said. "They belonged to my grandfather. I recognized them as soon as I saw them stacked up on a table. Who knows how many hands they went through, how many times they were bought and then given away again. They're the only things of his that I own. I'm not sure why I brought them home. At first I thought I could smell smoke on them from the fire. Maybe that was it. They're my version of a hair shirt."

I knew what he meant.

When the kettle boiled, he made tea and handed me a cup, and then he sat down at the banquette and set his own tea on the table in front of him.

"I'm not sure what I was hoping to accomplish," he said. "The food, I mean. But when you didn't respond, when you left the tray while I was out, I thought the hard feelings must have been passed on from your father. Or maybe you were afraid of me. I never thought of the possibility that you had no idea who I was, which says more about me than it does you." He paused and took a sip of his tea, and I did the same. In the lamplight, I could see traces of the old Dooley. Not the angry one who had paced around his battered red truck, more the Dooley who had come to me in dreams after the other fiery accident on the bridge. The boy I'd wanted to save.

"When I saw you coming through the rain," he said, "I knew that no matter what you thought of me, I was going to have a chance to speak to a Moon." Then he cleared his throat and said, as if he were reciting wedding vows, carefully rehearsed, "I didn't mean to set my grandfather's house on fire. I was drunk. I didn't mean to hurt anyone, especially not his wife, none of my problems were her fault. I'm relieved to finally get the chance to say that to you, the only person I can think of who might appreciate an apology." Then he laughed, perhaps to defuse the awkwardness, and said, "You're never done with penitence."

I wasn't sure how to respond. I wished my father could

have heard him, as well as Esme and all those other people who'd never believed Dooley Sullivan would come to anything good. But it was down to me. I said, "Okay, then. Apology accepted."

Then he said, "Your dad drove a hard bargain. But he was fair."

I didn't leave. Dooley handed me a dry blanket, which I wrapped around myself, and we sipped our tea and topped it up when it cooled down. And he told me a story, a long one that took all night to tell. It began with him waiting for my rumored return to Elliot (the source of the rumor was a participant in Mavis's yoga class), and then he slipped into memories that rolled over one another like waves on a beach. He told me things that he had never told anyone, not even in the anonymity of AA meetings. When he got to the part about the red truck and the last time he'd seen its remains in the Texaco parking lot, I wanted to cry for him. When he got to the part about the deer turning into a man—the vision that still haunted him—I knew I had to tell him another version of that night, my version. And for the first time, I told my story—the wedding night, the green cap, my flight from Elliot, and the disasters that followed before I reinvented myself, before Ian.

All night the rain was a soundtrack on the trailer roof, until the man turned back into a deer and both of our stories ended on the same mostly deserted street in Elliot.

It was almost morning when I fell asleep in the chair. Dooley slept too, awkwardly, slumped into a corner of the banquette. Once, I was awakened when I thought I heard him talking. "Now I lay me down to sleep," he said, but then again, it might have been a dream.

The power was still off when we woke up, but the rain had stopped. The sun was out and mist was rising eerily from the low spots across the street. Before I left, I asked Dooley about Tobias's estate, whether he felt like he'd been cheated. He said no. He'd taken the money my father had offered and run like a bandit, knowing it was more than he deserved. I was relieved to hear it.

I went up the steps and into my house and sank into the brown couch, my foot aching again. I wished that I had solid proof of my version of the story so that Dooley could truly be relieved of guilt for the worst thing he'd done, or thought he'd done, in his messed-up younger life. He was sixty-eight years old. If he could live his old age without that burden, I thought, he would be a freer man than he'd ever been living on a beach in Mexico. He said that he'd once gone to the RCMP detachment with a plan to make a confession, but then he'd turned around and gone home again, losing his nerve, clinging to the smallest particle of doubt.

The smell of dampness made me get up off the couch and look for its source, although I knew it was going to be the basement. When I opened the door and flicked on the light, I was greeted by the sight of water halfway up the staircase. Debris was everywhere. The bookcase floated on its back, empty of books, the guitar bumping up against it like flotsam. The fur coat resembled a moose with its head underwater. The pole lamp poked its own bent head up in an elegant way, a bit like a swan. An old steamer trunk was lodged under the staircase, bulging with wet linens, and soggy cardboard boxes had spilled their contents into the water. It appeared that nothing stored in the basement had escaped.

The house's breaker box was on the wall beside me. I

switched off all breakers and closed the basement door, not believing my good fortune—the need to sort judiciously through possessions now gone—although I did not yet realize the extent of the new problem I'd have to deal with.

That evening, I sat on the porch and watched Dooley Sullivan do his bird dance in the water pooling in front of his trailer. Deeper water lay in the lots between us, and I imagined my house rocking the way it might if it were floating on the ocean. I thought about Joe Fletcher dying in the hospital, an opportunity flickering like a candle burning out, and I saw Dooley's dance in a new way—not just because of the water, but because now I knew about his life since Elliot had lost track of him. Nineteen years he'd been sober. Three times in detox, but the last time it took. Now he went to meetings and took medicinal marijuana for the pains in his body, caused by injuries he'd inflicted on himself, he said, by driving drunk into a bridge. He didn't blame anyone, he said, not his grandfather, not my parents or Esme for packing him off with a check and a bus ticket, not the teachers for missing his cries for help.

When he finished his ritual, I went inside and opened the fridge a crack, trying to keep the cold air in, to see what I might have that could be turned into a meal not requiring electricity. I made myself a sandwich, and then I sat on the porch and watched the horses across the road as they grazed their way down the fence line and out of sight. They belonged to Dooley. They were rescues from an animal cruelty seizure not too far away and had been fending for themselves in a bare pasture without food or water. Dooley knew a bit about caring for horses from his time in Mexico, so he took them because no one else would and they were destined for the slaughterhouse. He'd been rescued, he said, many times. Everything deserved to be rescued. The town had been happy to lease him the empty lots across the street.

I wondered if Mary, the supposed mother of all rescue, was still on her hill. I scrambled through the barbed-wire fence and made for the shrine. When I got there, I found only the stone grotto and what looked like the remains of an old fire. Someone, it appeared, had burned up the holy mother.

The mosquitoes found me, and then I heard the horses galloping toward me, and it was terrifying, but they stopped before they ran me over and left as quickly as they'd come when they saw I had nothing for them. I hobbled back through the wet grass and crawled through the fence again. I heard a car crossing the tracks and thought it might turn up Liberty Street, but it passed the turn and the sound receded. No one ever came up Liberty Street.

I went into the house and went to bed, thinking I could hear the sound of water lapping. I lay there and contemplated what to do about Joe Fletcher.

THE NEXT DAY, I phoned Mavis from a pay phone in town and reported that my basement was full of water.

"Oh, dear," she said. "Well, I hear half the basements in Elliot are flooded, so it's not surprising. Main Street is under water, or at least it was. Did you know that?"

I told her yes, there were pumps going everywhere in town. She asked me if the water in my basement was receding. I said I'd closed the basement door and hadn't checked since. There was silence on her end of the line, as though she couldn't believe what she'd heard.

"I have no electricity," I said. "I'm pretty much camping. I don't really know who to call."

Mavis said she would try to find someone to pump out the basement and check the electrical.

Later, Dooley knocked on my door. "I was wondering," he said, "if you might like to go to the hall with me tomorrow night. Apparently, someone is throwing together a benefit to raise money for flood victims, people with house damage and no insurance. There's a good local band. They have a young girl who plays the fiddle, and she's kind of famous around here. She almost won one of those TV talent shows. A lot of people got the Internet just so they could vote for her." Then he said, "Just to be clear, it's not a date or anything like that. I don't complicate things by having relationships. Sobriety is my mistress. Just thought, two people, not much going on with either of us that I can see. Might as well go together. You think?"

I found myself nodding and saying, "Okay. What do people wear to these things?"

"Anything you want," he said. "It's Elliot."

I wore jeans and a T-shirt with a flower-shaped pattern of cheap crystals. I didn't have proper shoes with me and likely couldn't have worn them anyway because of my foot, so I wore flip-flops. When Dooley came to pick me up, he was wearing jeans and boots and a silver belt buckle. There was still a touch of swagger in Dooley Sullivan, I thought, which amused me quite a bit.

The parking lot at the hall was under water and the puddles glistened. Cars and trucks were parked all up and down the street. The hall itself had been spared any damage—the same hall where all those years ago I had hidden underneath a table and then danced with Dooley Sullivan when his foot was in a cast. I asked him if he remembered that night and he said no. I said, "You crawled under a banquet table where I was hiding and pulled me out to dance with you, much to the annoyance of the ladies who were following you around like you were a rock star."

"It's been a long time since any ladies followed me around," he said.

There was a donation box at the door and we both dropped bills inside before we found chairs against the wall at the back of the room. Lots of people said, "*Hola*, Dooley," to which he answered, "*Hola* yourself." In a way, the lack of attention paid to me made it seem as if I had lived in Elliot all my life, because that's the way it had been when I did live there.

It was a long night. It was hot and humid in the hall, even with the doors open. I didn't much like the band, and the girl with the fiddle—wearing a light cotton dress and red cowboy boots and looking too young to be onstage in a place where they served alcohol—wasn't doing anything particularly impressive. Dooley kept telling me to wait, assuring me that a solo set was coming. By the time the girl finally stepped up to the mike and the other musicians put their instruments down, I was falling asleep in my chair and dying to go home. I watched her settle her fiddle on her shoulder, pluck the strings, tune, slide her bow back and forth a few times, and then launch into something I recognized. Everyone recognized the song—was it "Orange Blossom Special"?—and before I knew it, I was being pulled up to dance a circle around the hall with Dooley and everyone else, sore foot and all. Then someone was cutting in and I was dancing with a strange man, and then another, and then Dooley cut in again. Everyone in the hall was dancing, and when the girl stopped playing, the room erupted. Someone took the mike and told the story of how much fun the whole town had had voting for her, and she should have won—she was robbed, wasn't she?—and everyone clapped and stomped again, until the girl began to play another tune and the hall thundered with the sound of dancing feet.

When her set was done, the band took a break and the crowd spilled outside to cool off and smoke cigarettes, and the hall went more or less quiet. Dooley went out too and I sat on my chair against the wall, resting my foot on another chair and trying to think what proof I could offer Dooley to keep uncertainty from creeping back in. I was almost the only person left in the hall. A woman with a cane and wearing white oxford shoes walked by and said, "Hello, Frances. How are you tonight?"

"Fine," I said, "thanks. And you?"

"Oh, I'm all right for an old lady. Shame about this rain, though. Once in a hundred years, they're saying."

Then she walked toward the bathrooms, tap-tapping her cane on the linoleum floor. I had no idea who she was.

I got up and stepped outside and found Dooley talking to someone, and I said I was ready to go home, but I could walk if he wanted to stay. He insisted on driving me, because of my foot.

On the way, I said, "You mentioned that you'd worked for a while in the bush north of here, right?"

He nodded and said that he had.

"The night of my wedding, there was a man—the one who brought the cap. Saul Something-or-other. He was older than you by quite a few years. I remember that he worked in the bush and was married to an awful woman named Ginny. She sounded like a duck when she laughed."

Dooley thought for a minute. "There was a guy named Saul and he might have worked in the bush, but I knew him because he sold homemade liquor and didn't care how old you were. I think his last name was Danko, or Demko. That was it, Demko. Why do you ask?"

I was picturing the bottle of homemade booze that Ginny had carried into the house on my wedding night. I was picturing the initials SC.

"The initials," I said. "On the cap. SC. That cap definitely didn't belong to Saul Demko."

"Oh," Dooley said. "No, I suppose not."

He sounded hopeful.

No HANDYMAN SHOWED UP at my door. I assumed they were all too busy for me and my basement. Many homes in Elliot had suffered the same fate as mine—almost six inches of rain overnight, a freak storm. I tried to buy a pump at the Co-op, but they were all sold out. When I explained my predicament to Dooley, he managed to borrow a pump, and he pumped the water out a basement window and then checked the electricity and said he thought I could turn the breakers to the upstairs back on. He suggested I buy a dehumidifier, and I got the last one in town. There was no point in even attempting to salvage the ruin in the basement, which I saw as a liberating gift. Dooley helped me out once again by offering to haul everything to the dump for me in his truck. I wouldn't let him do the work of carrying the Moons' waterlogged belongings up the stairs, and as a result it took me days to get everything out and piled in a molding heap in front of the house. Together, we carried up the few pieces of furniture that were heavy or awkward, and then we loaded up the truck.

The only keepsake I salvaged was my mother's mahogany tea caddy from England. It had floated to the surface of the floodwaters and washed up on the dry land of a stair tread. After Dooley left for the dump, I sat on the couch with the tea box and lifted the lid. There were still tea bags inside, although when I touched one the paper fell apart and loose tea spilled out into the bottom of the box like dust. The thought did not escape me that it had once survived a bombing in London and had now survived the disaster of a hopelessly flooded basement. It was the one thing I would take with me when I left, I decided. How could I leave it behind after what it had been through?

I held it in my hand and thought it was a lovely thing.

No Song Like a Country Song

I SCRUBBED DOWN the basement walls and floor with bleach.

I bought a new smartphone and a data plan at a wireless outlet in town, and then booked a plumber to come and tell me if I needed a new furnace.

I went to visit Joe Fletcher.

"Is he in pain?" I asked, and the nurses said no. They came in periodically to make sure he was comfortable. They were amazed that he was still alive. I waited, hoping he would open his eyes, perhaps speak, but he didn't. I thought of Esme Bigalow and how her eyes had popped open long enough for her to say the words "We are all such mysteries to one another."

Perhaps Joe Fletcher would do something similar: "I want to come clean."

While I was there, a priest came to visit. I told him I didn't think Joe Fletcher was Catholic and the priest said it didn't matter, he visited everyone. He stopped to see Mr. Weins in the next bed, but Mr. Weins wouldn't say a word to him and pulled the covers right up to his chin. When I asked the nurse afterward why Mr. Weins didn't say, "Help me, help me," to the priest, she said he spoke only to women, and seemed to be afraid of men. Did he really believe he needed help? I asked. She said no, it was just something he liked to say, a way of communicating. He was waiting for a room in a nursing home, one with a dementia ward. His wife was being difficult and kept rejecting placements because they were too far away, she said, and she would not be able to visit him. The nurse said the wife couldn't visit him anyway because she was almost bedridden herself with arthritis. She kept threatening to take him home.

I followed the priest out to the parking lot after his visit with Joe. "Has he said anything to you?" I asked him. "You know, confessed any big sins on his deathbed?"

"No," the priest said. "Although you know I wouldn't tell you if he did. Surely you know that."

"I wonder if he could be pretending," I said.

"To die?" the priest asked, incredulous.

"No," I said, "that's not what I meant." But I didn't explain further and left it at that.

I went back again the next day and sat by Joe's bed with my new phone, searching for information about comas and deathbed confessions. I tried to find out if it was possible that he could hear people talking to him. I tried to find cases of people snapping awake from comas to say final words to their families, confess sins, make up for lost time in their last hours. I found a story about a woman in Ontario who had gone public on behalf of her father, claiming that just before he died he'd admitted to killing the man who'd been having an affair with his wife, the woman's mother. I wondered if he really had confessed, or if she was confessing for him, having known that he was guilty all along. I tried to remember the name of Silas Chance's sister so I could find out if she was still alive. I didn't know enough about social media to use its resources, so I googled, entering words indicative of what I remembered—Silas's name, the year, Elliot, hit-and-run. Nothing useful came up. I wasn't sure why I was doing this. I didn't know what I would tell Silas's sister even if I could find her. Which version of his death was the correct one, if either? I knew which version I wanted to believe, but how could I be certain?

An explanation of how Facebook worked came from a young nurse-in-training doing a practicum, to whom I happened to say, "I'm trying to find someone. Does Facebook do that?" She returned when she got a break and set me up, saying, "My grandma's on Facebook. She doesn't really get it, but anyway." She took a picture of me with my phone, and this became the profile picture for an account under the name Frances Moon. In the course of learning how to find friends—"Go ahead," the student nurse said, "enter the name of someone you used to know"—I discovered that Ian was on Facebook. That came as a surprise.

"Look at that," she said. "You found someone already. Now send him a friend request."

"Later," I said. "Thanks for showing me."

She went back to work, but not before sending me a

358 ~ DIANNE WARREN

friend request and then accepting it for me, and showing me how to send someone a message—too much information for one lesson, but I took notes.

After she left, I tried to scroll through Ian's posts, but I couldn't. I saw who his friends were, though. He had eleven. His brother. His nephews. A couple of people whose names I recognized from his office. A woman named Meika.

Meika? I didn't know anyone by that name.

I looked up from my phone to see that Mr. Weins was considering going somewhere. "Help me," he said, swinging his legs over the side of the bed. I wasn't sure what to do.

"Be careful you don't fall," I said to him, alarmed, but he ignored me.

He managed to rid himself of the bedcovers and stand on both feet, but he looked like he didn't know what to do next. He stood by the bed saying, "Help me, someone . . . help me," and I felt terrible ignoring him but there was nothing I could do, or wanted to do, so I pushed the call button by Joe's bed.

Mr. Weins stood on his skinny, shaky legs then and looked right at me and said, "Get away from that man, you hussy." He stood with one hand on the bed, swaying as though he might collapse, and said it over and over, getting more and more agitated, until finally a nurse arrived—Kelly this time—and told me that he likely thought I was his wife and couldn't figure out what I was doing sitting by the wrong bed. Kelly talked Mr. Weins back into bed and tucked him tightly in the sheets and he calmed down. He stared at me the whole time, his eyelids fluttering, until finally he closed them and nodded off.

Joe Fletcher's eyes remained closed. He gave no sign that he was aware of my presence, even though I'd said, several times, "Joe, it's me, Frances." He appeared to be un-conscious, inching toward the inevitable, but the nurses told me that just that morning he had opened his eyes, and they thought he understood what they were saying to him. Once I got the idea in my head that he could understand what people said to him, I couldn't get it out. I felt stupid talking to him, but I did anyway. I knew time was running out. I tried to be hon-est. "I was too young. My mother was right. I was too young and you were too old for me, and your friends terrified me." It seemed I was trying on memories, getting my tongue around things that I'd never before spoken of. Once, I said, "I was so frightened, I thought I would die. I thought someone was going to kill me. Not you, I didn't think that. But it all felt so out of control. And then the cap. Silas Chance's cap, or at least that's what I believed." I thought I saw him twitch. When the student nurse came into the room, I pretended that I'd been singing to him so she wouldn't know what I was really saying. "Crazy," the Patsy Cline song, a few scattered lines, since I couldn't remember the words. I tried not to think what a young nurse with no life experience might make of that.

As I talked, I studied Joe's eyelids, the rise and fall of his chest, his breathing, which was not erratic the way I thought a dying man's should be. He can hear me, I kept thinking. He's listening. I began easing my way into what I wanted from him. If anything good was going to come of me step-ping on a rusty nail, it had to be this. "Joe," I said, "is there something you want to get off your chest before you go? Silas Chance and that whole business with the cap. How it ended up in Saul's hands, and yours. It will help so many people if you tell me—more than you know."

On the one hand, I thought it was possible. Joe Fletcher

would open his eyes and tell me the whole story as I imagined it happening, a drunken accident, the way Dooley thought it had happened but with a different vehicle, different people.

On the other hand, I knew what I was hoping for was far-fetched, and worse, I was being hugely self-important, because I was speaking as though I thought I was special, a person who meant something to this dying man, or some saint, able to conjure a miracle. St. Frances of Elliot. Hardly.

But I believed I saw the slightest movement of an eyelid.

"Just lift a hand," I said. "Anything to let me know you understand what I'm saying. There's an opportunity. You should take it."

Nothing.

I leaned back in my chair and studied Joe Fletcher, the man in the bed, the one I had married. It was the same man, but it was hard to imagine this man ever having had the strength for bush work in the dead of winter, and it was hard to imagine I'd ever convinced myself that he was as attractive as a movie star, or that I was in love with him. This dying old man was the first man I'd ever slept with, disastrously. As repulsed and frightened by him as I had once been, he now made me sad. He was dying alone. I knew I couldn't take the blame for that, but I felt guilty anyway.

The intercom crackled and a voice announced that visiting hours were over, and I left. As I passed Mr. Weins in the other bed on my way out, he opened his eyes and asked me if Joe was my son.

"No relation," I said. "A friend of my father's."

That seemed to satisfy him.

"Well, then," he said, "you must be a good daughter."

"No," I said. "I am not a very good daughter."

"Good for you," he said.

Dooley made chicken and dumplings for supper that night, which we ate at his picnic table.

The next day, Joe Fletcher slipped into the final hours before his death. I was in the room with him when Kelly told me that it wouldn't be long. I didn't want to be there when he died. I didn't believe it was important for him to have someone there, especially not me, and it was clear that he was beyond making any kind of confession. Still, I leaned over him in the bed, leaned over his chest with its barely perceptible rise and fall, and said, "I accept that the disaster that was us was my fault. I was selfish, a silly teenager, Daddy's baby, as you said. But the fact is, you had his cap. You must have been there. And it was wrong to keep that secret. It was just wrong."

I thought I saw an eyelid flutter. More distinct than the movement I thought I'd seen the day before.

I straightened up, stared at the body on the bed. His hand lifted ever so slightly off the bedsheet where it lay. Was that it? A confession? I leaned over him again, watching, confused, wondering whether I was about to witness the saintly miracle, something that couldn't be explained—when the same hand came up from the top of the sheet again, came up completely unexpectedly, and caught me off guard. The hand hit me in the chest, not hard—how could it, coming from a man so close to death?—but nonetheless I stepped backwards, and I lost my balance and fell, and my shoulder landed on one of the hard wooden arms of a chair, and then I fell sideways and hit my head on the radiator and landed on the floor.

I lay there with my eyes closed for a minute or so, seeing something like stars, and I could hear Mr. Weins saying, "Help me, help me," over and over. Then I opened my eyes and pushed myself onto my knees and tried to get up, but it seemed my legs wouldn't hold me. I thought that I might vomit, so I lay down again, my cheek on the cold floor. I felt my forehead. There was blood. "Help me, help me," droned Mr. Weins, and I felt trapped by his voice. I listened to him until I couldn't stand to hear his plaintive cry one more time, and once the nausea had passed, I struggled to my feet and walked over to his bed and pushed the call button.

"Shushh," I said. "Someone is coming to help you. It's just not me."

A drop of blood fell from my forehead onto his white cotton bedcover. I thought it might frighten him, but he was smirking.

Kelly in her purple scrubs came into the room. "What happened to you?" she asked when she saw the blood on my forehead.

"I think Joe Fletcher pushed me," I said. "I could swear it. I was standing over him and he pushed me and I fell. Honest to God."

She took my arm and led me from the room and down the hall to a treatment room, the same one where she'd patched my foot. "Not possible," she said. "You must have tripped. You might have a concussion."

I said, "He was trying to tell me something."

She said, "He wasn't. He's past that."

She sat me down in a chair and took my blood pressure to make sure I wasn't going into shock.

"I'm fine," I said.

At that moment, the nurse doing her practicum—my Facebook friend—came to the door and told us that Joe Fletcher had died. "Mr. Fletcher has expired," she said. It must have been her use of the word "expired," the formality of her announcement. It seemed hysterically funny. I started to laugh and Kelly had to ask the girl to leave us alone. She wondered if I needed a sedative, but I waved her away and told her I was going home.

I returned to room 18 to collect my purse, and I saw that a curtain had been pulled between the two beds to conceal Joe's body. I grabbed my purse from the floor without looking at him, and as I left the room, crazy old Mr. Weins said to me, "He's mad at you, lady, isn't he?"

I stopped. "What did you see?" I asked him. "Did you see that man push me?"

He didn't answer. He started with his "Help me" mantra and wouldn't stop until Kelly came and restrained him by tucking the sheets around him so tightly that he couldn't move.

Once I was home, I stood in front of the bathroom mirror and tried to see if there was a bump growing on my head. I filled the bathtub, and as I lay in the hot water, I thought about what I should do, whether it was possible that Joe Fletcher had made a deathbed confession of sorts, or whether it was what I believed miracles to be—that is, wishful thinking followed by happenstance.

And then the name of Silas's sister popped into my head. Darlene. Darlene Chance. No, Darlene Cyr. I got out of the tub and found my phone and searched for Darlene Cyr on Facebook. Nothing came up, so I tried the name Cyr combined with Yellowhead. There was a Lynette Cyr who listed Yellowhead Comprehensive as her high school. I found my Facebook teacher's instructions and sent Lynette Cyr a message along with my e-mail address. A reply came quickly: *My mom had a brother named Silas.*

An hour later, this e-mail: *Who are you and what do you want?*

It was from Darlene Cyr.

That night, lying awake in the darkness, I couldn't stop thinking, *I am no longer married*, but I was surprised by how little that now meant. I also thought about the flyers Darlene Cyr had posted around Elliot: *Someone knows*. What exactly did I know? It was enough, I thought, to relieve Dooley of the guilt he'd lived with for so long, but was it enough to relieve an old lady, to end the story of what had happened to her brother? There was no evidence, no green cap, and no real confession that I could truthfully put forward.

I went over and over what had happened in the hospital room, and I had no answer.

And all night, I went over and over the year I turned eighteen and married Joe Fletcher, and I thought about the mistake I'd made, and the ones that followed, the many mistakes, and there had to have been reasons aside from the obvious, but I didn't know what they were. I thought about the time of the Steve McQueens, which had been one of the lowest points in my life, and I thought of Daniel, the last Steve McQueen, and I wished I could say to him, "I wasn't really all that tough, I was just pretending." Which is likely the truth with all bad girls, something the barmaid who'd taken me aside had known, and I wished I could thank her again for trying.

I wished too that I could say to Ian, "I don't know why I wasn't able to tell you everything. It doesn't seem that bad now that I've told someone else."

And at that moment, life after Elliot began to seem possible.

. . .

THE FIRST CONSEQUENCE of being no longer married—a widow, that is—came unexpectedly when I was asked to decide, in the absence of anyone else, about a funeral. A funeral director from Yellowhead, a man named Gregory Dern, called me, having got my phone number from someone at the hospital. He said, "Ms. Moon, Frances . . . may I call you Frances? I understand you are Mr. Fletcher's widow, although separated. There doesn't seem to be anyone for us to contact. Might you provide us with some direction? Will there, for example, be a funeral? Or a memorial service, perhaps? A celebration of life?"

When I got over my dismay that Gregory Dern would ask me these questions, I said that funerals were for families and Joe Fletcher had none. If he wanted to be buried in a family plot, I said, he would have left instructions. I told Gregory Dern to choose the least expensive coffin and cremate the body; I would pay for it. There were forms, he said then; signatures were required. I told him to e-mail me the forms and I would find a way to get them back. When he asked if I wanted the ashes—a ceramic urn, perhaps—I was beyond dumbfounded.

"Gregory," I said, "may I call you that? Seriously, an urn? So I can keep his ashes on the fireplace mantel? We've been separated for forty years. You have to be joking."

In an overly solicitous voice, he said, "All right, then, Frances. I understand."

I let that go. He clearly didn't understand much.

The second consequence of being Joe Fletcher's widow came when I learned that because there was no will and no one else to claim his house in the bush, I was to become its owner. When I found this out, I called Mavis and told her she could sell the property and give the proceeds to the Elliot flood relief fund when all the legal work was completed.

After that, I did stage a sort of memorial, for the Moon family, of which I was the only surviving member. I visited the dairy farm.

The gravel road from town was so familiar I didn't think a single thing had changed, but when I parked near the approach to my old home, I saw that the big wooden barn was gone and there were grain bins everywhere, including the spot where my mother used to have her garden. The sun shone on the farm machinery lined up neatly in the yard—tractors and seed drills and sprayers of a staggering size, four times as big as anything my father had owned. There were no animals to be seen—black-and-white cows or otherwise—and what used to be the pasture was now a field of canola coming into bloom.

But the house itself was the biggest shock. When I inched my car forward until I could see it through the trees, I thought for a minute that I had the wrong place, not because the house had completely changed shape thanks to a huge addition that included a double garage, but because the whole monstrosity was painted a hideous lemon yellow with bright pink trim. Even the trim on the original log house was painted pink. I laughed out loud when I saw the colors through the trees. Lemon yellow was the last color my mother would have chosen, and I imagined her cursing the fools who'd made her house look like an angel food cake. My own response to the paint job was a desire to thank the current owners for saving me from nostalgia. When I saw a vehicle coming up the road I started the car and drove on so I wouldn't be reported to the new owners and accused of spying, or worse yet, invited in for coffee.

After that, I went to the graveyard and spent half an hour at my parents' graves, and the stillborn baby's grave, which was next to theirs. The small headstone on the baby's grave said, simply, *Baby Moon*. I had not gone to the graveyard at the time of the burial. I did not know if anyone had. I'd let my mother make all the arrangements and had seen the little headstone only once before, when my mother died. As I looked down at the grave, it was as though the baby belonged to someone else and had been placed there, next to my parents, by mistake. There was an unused plot on the other side of my parents and I wondered if it was meant for me. I walked around the cemetery until I found Uncle Vince and thought it was too bad that he wasn't in that empty space in the family plot. Maybe I could get him moved, since I had no intention of spending eternity there.

That evening, I wrote Darlene Cyr an old-fashioned, handwritten letter telling her what I believed had happened to her brother, and the next day I scanned it at the post office and sent her an e-mail with my letter attached. I did this because I thought she deserved to know at least as much as I knew.

I waited for a reply, but none came.

Then, a week later, I received a Facebook friend request from Lynette Cyr, and not long afterward a story appeared on my News Feed, along with a picture of her uncle, Silas Chance. It was a story about his life, his boyhood, residential school, the Korean War, the extended, loving family that made sure he was remembered. When I looked at the picture of him, I recalled his face as clearly as if I had seen him yesterday. The story didn't mention how he had died, or Joe Fletcher's confession—the one I had relayed—but it ended with "Rest in peace, Uncle."

I thought I understood, but probably I didn't. What do I know about big, loving families? The only blood relations I had ever known took up four plots in the Elliot graveyard. "There's no one," I remembered my mother saying when I had offered to go to England with her. I remembered being relieved that I didn't have to follow up on my offer, and perhaps that is the real fallout of my parents' emigration, whatever it was they ran away from.

IN THE EVENINGS—they will be my very last in Elliot—I sit on the porch in my canvas chair and watch the horses grazing across the road, their tails slapping, first in one direction, then the other. Sometimes I hear the faint sound of what I know is Dooley's dance music, and when I do, I turn to watch his ritual tribute to Angela's memory. He's told me he's now lighter on his feet when he dances, although honestly he still looks to me as much as ever like a crane with a broken leg. He says he is as content, most of the time, as his rescued horses. He claims he is not sorry for his childhood or his years of exile. He'd bet dollars to donuts that he has had a better life than many.

I've sent Ian my new phone number. Since then, I've spent possibly too much time thinking about how a call might go.

I believe I have finally come to my senses.

IT'S SATURDAY, a yoga day. Mavis is coming before her class to sink a For Sale in the grass in front of the house. For some reason, this is bothering me. I don't like to think of the house being sold after all it's been through. The house is a survivor, a bit like the tea caddy, although it hasn't exactly been through a war. Half an hour before Mavis is to arrive, it comes to me: I'm not selling it. I'm giving it to Dooley Sullivan. I phone Mavis and tell her I've changed my mind.

At first, Dooley won't accept.

"Why not?" I ask. "You moved into the casita when Angela built it for you. I know this is not the same, but I want you to have it. It would make me happy if you accepted the house as a gift. The house has never had a proper owner. It deserves one."

He thinks about it and comes back to me with a counter-offer. The house in exchange for the Mason jar of Mexican bills and coins he's kept on a shelf in the trailer since his return to Elliot. He would buy me a blue glass vase, he says, if he knew where to get one. I tell him that if I ever go to Mexico again, I will buy one with the pesos in the jar. We make a deal.

He calls me Señora Luna when I hand him the keys.

Señora Lunatic is more like it, I say.

MY LAST NIGHT in Elliot. The car is filled with gas. My bag is packed. Nothing from the house is coming with me except the tea caddy, which is now on the kitchen counter next to the jar of Mexican bills and coins. One family memento is enough, more than I thought I'd want.

Dooley makes me a Mexican meal complete with home-made tortillas cooked on the barbecue. As we sit together at the old chrome kitchen suite, the smell of barbecue coals coming in though the screen door, I tell him about Kentucky Fried Chicken, how at one time I'd thought it was the best food ever invented, and how later, I would pick up two snack packs when I visited my mother in the care home in Yellowhead before she died, and we both thought it was funny, that I had become so educated—I had a master's degree by this time—that I could buy KFC whenever I wanted. It was a relief, I told Dooley, that my mother and I could finally laugh together again, share a joke about her obsession with my education, and agree that it had paid off. Not exactly *we two girls*, but close enough. We loved each other. We both knew it.

After supper, Dooley and I settle on the couch and spend the night listening to my mother's records. Skeeter Davis, Patsy Cline, Kitty Wells, Tammy Wynette—the women of country.

I tell Dooley that I was named after Skeeter Davis, but then I wonder if that is even true. "I once thought my mother went to Nashville to become a singer," I say. "That was definitely not true."

We throw Hank Williams and Buck Owens into the mix. Bobby Bare, the album I won at the drugstore.

Sometime before dawn, I fall asleep and tip over sideways onto the arm of the couch. When I wake up in the early morning, the record player is silent and Dooley has gone to bed. I peek in the door at him—stretched out, sound asleep, still in his clothes as if he's not completely sure he's in the right house—and decide to leave before he gets up, no goodbye. I collect the tea caddy and the jar of pesos from the countertop, and make my exit.

I'm just about to step into the car when, in the distance, I hear the rumble of a train approaching. A sudden memory of

Uncle Vince and the flattened penny comes to me. Could I possibly execute the old trick without losing a hand? I set the tea caddy on the front passenger seat and fish a few Mexican coins out of the glass jar before carefully tucking it into the folds of a sweater in the backseat. I walk behind the house and toward the tracks, dodging puddles that teem with mosquito larvae, trying to beat the train.

The tall grass has been leveled in large patches by the hailstorm, and a rusty shape I had not before noticed is now visible—an abandoned vehicle, a car, halfway between the house and the tracks. I stop, not quite believing that it could be my mother's. Forgetting about the coins, I make my way through the grass and patches of scrubby bush to look more closely at the car, and it is indeed a 1956 Ford Fairlane. My mother's old pride and joy, although the body is so rusty you can barely tell that this was once the most stylish set of wheels in the countryside. The whitewalls are gone, the windows smashed out, and the passenger door is missing. The hood is popped up, left that way by looters salvaging parts. The front bench seat is still there, the springs showing through a deflated covering of ripped and cracked leather. I look into the backseat, grass poking up through rust-ragged holes in the floor, and remember Tobias Sullivan lying there, never to wake up again, just like Hank Williams.

I lower myself into the front passenger seat, hoping my weight won't send it, and me, through the floorboard, and it holds. A horsefly the size of a bat persistently buzzes around my head and some kind of striped fuzzy caterpillar makes its way across the hood. I try to picture my mother beside me with a scarf in her hair, her sunglasses on, enjoying that car as much as anything else in her life, but I can't. Too much time has passed; it's all too far gone. The train draws near and I hear its familiar mournful whistle.

The car radio is still in its nook in the dashboard, although minus its turquoise on/off knob. I reach over and attempt to turn the stem, as though I might be able to switch the radio on, turn up the volume on a Hank Williams song, a staticky rendition of "I'm So Lonesome I Could Cry" or—because I'm not lonesome and don't feel like crying—"Hey, Good Lookin'." Ha ha. But of course the stem is corroded, impossible to move one way or the other.

The train rumbles louder and louder, and then passes by, blowing a cloud of diesel and noise behind it, sucking Hank's words, the sad and the happy, along the steel rails. When it's gone, the morning is mostly quiet again. I sit for a long time in the peaceful remains of my mother's car, not yet able to will myself away from this place. The grass hums with the buzzing of insects. I can almost feel it, a fine and soothing vibration in the air around me.

Soothing, that is, until I am discovered by a swarm of mosquitoes. I lift myself out of the seat, waving my arms like a dancer, and make my way, feeling strangely satisfied, back through the lot, past the house and the sleeping Dooley Sullivan.

Toward my own car with an old mahogany box on the passenger seat.

An urn sheltering tea dust.

The car waiting to take me somewhere.

Acknowledgments

I WOULD LIKE TO THANK the following people for reading drafts or answering questions: Malcolm Aldred, Pat Aldred, Ramses Calderon, Connie Gault, Lynda Oliver, Jordyn Warnez, and Marlis Wesseler. Thanks to my agent, Dean Cooke, and my editors, Jennifer Lambert and Marian Wood. Thanks also to Janice Weaver, Sarah Wight, and Alexis Sattler. The poem quoted by Dooley in that hotel room in Yucatán is from "Love Sonnet XVII" by Pablo Neruda, as translated by Stephen Tapscott. The title of the last chapter, "The Car Hank Died In," is taken from a song written by Mike Licht and performed by the Austin Lounge Lizards; it is used with permission.

The Playlist

HERE ARE THE TITLES of the songs referred to in *Liberty Street*, along with the names of the songwriters: "Cold, Cold Heart," Hank Williams; "Kaw-Liga," Hank Williams and Fred Rose; "It Wasn't God Who Made Honky Tonk Angels," J. D. Miller; "Heartaches by the Number," Harlan Howard; "The Times They Are a-Changin'," Bob Dylan; "In the Ghetto," Mac Davis; "Do You Know the Way to San Jose," Burt Bacharach and Hal David; "My Elusive Dreams," Billy Sherrill and Curly Putnam; "He Called Me Baby," Harlan Howard; "Hernando's Hideaway," Jerry Ross and Richard Adler; "Mammas, Don't Let Your Babies Grow Up to Be Cowboys," Ed Bruce and Patsy Bruce; "The Car Hank Died In," Mike Licht; "Orange Blossom Special," Ervin T. Rouse; "Crazy," Willie Nelson; "I'm So Lonesome I Could Cry," Hank Williams; "Hey, Good Lookin'," Hank Williams.

WITHDRAWN
From Arundel Co. Public Library